Tricked

A Novel

By

Cynthia A. Minor

ROSEAPPLE PUBLISHING LTD.

Nashville   Chicago

RoseApple Publishing, Ltd.
702 Wedgewood Park, Ste. 306
Nashville, TN 37203, U.S.A.

1524 W. Monroe
Chicago, IL 60607

Requests for permission to make copies of any part of this
work should be mailed to:
Permissions Department, RoseApple Publishing, Ltd., Suite C
702 Wedgewood Park, Ste. 306, Nashville, TN 37203
RoseApple Publishing.com
1 (800) 887-5857
Library of Congress-In-Publication Data

Minor, Cynthia A.
Tricked/ Cynthia A. Minor
p.   cm.
ISBN 978-0-9746019-2-2
LCCN 2003097016

Jacket Art by Paige Summers
Jacket Design, Cooley Video Productions, Inc.
Printed in the United States of America · First Edition

Copyright © 2009

To Dock and Dallin

Who inspire me

ACKNOWLEDGMENTS

Too many lives have touched mine in ways yet to be examined in spaces too small to contain. Each is owed my unfailing gratitude for this or that. My anemic attempt to recognize you falls short of my intent to keep your contributions to my life alive forever in words.

My grandmother's glorious gift of story telling still rings in my imagination. Funny aunts and uncles turned the colors of my world from shades of gray, brilliant in the sunshine of their laughter. Steadfast parents provided the platform for success. My prayer partner Dawn's devotion over a lifetime of consistent encouragement and belief. Sharon and Desi kept me laughing and believing. Stigler kept me digital. Gail kept me sane. And Ms. Anna Conner, whose single joy seemed to be throwing me out of her library, while inspiring me daily to write with passion, read the great works, steward the incredible power of words and learn the undying wonder of literature, your significance cannot be calibrated. Thank you.

Finally, how does one thank love? Neither measurable nor quantifiable, it flows unending from sources known and unknown, seen and unseen. God. Husband. Daughter. Family. Friends. Teachers. Loves. Life.

PROLOGUE

To Whom It May Concern:

Grief and greed take many forms in their quest for relief. Satisfaction. Peace. Closure. Either, if denied, converts ordinary behavior into extraordinary compromise. Whether turned inward, vanquishing your soul; or outward, corrupting the souls of others, when they have finished their tattered collaboration, what is left? Pain. Regret. Anger. Sadness. Danger. Death.

Charles Roberts and Edward Jacobs are the only living founders of Roberts Jacobs & Pellman International, the richest securities and brokerage firm in America. With prime seats on the New York Stock Exchange and a network of offices from New York to Tokyo, RJP leads the world in, among other things, forecasting financial trends, coordinating corporate takeovers, setting the economic pace of the nation, and influencing the market with such vigor, only the very elite qualify as employees or clients. I work in the Dallas office. It houses the office of corporate counsel where all international securities transactions for RJP's wealthiest clients are evaluated. Joshua Pellman is my boss. He is dead.

Prior to his death, he was asked to give the most potentially lucrative speech of his career. He'd share revolutionary theories for protecting global economies from what he believed were new forms of economic chicanery. The most knowledgeable financial leaders, brokers, traders and economists of our day salivated for invitations to the event. Not so coincidentally, he'd also roll out a new wireless digital security system, with customized protection and detection devices, to guard against the implementation of those very theories.

The device provides indispensable assistance to securities watchdog agencies protecting the market from international criminal activity. Pellman owned all intellectual rights and with RJP as the exclusive distributor, and a point or two thrown in for me, there would be too much money for us to count.

Internal security was high. Corporate spies hovered, willing to kill to get their hands on it. Everything was hush hush. Even I didn't know every integral component, which was odd since lately I'd become Pellman's intellectual confidant. He seldom kept anything from me. Yet, I knew it would send the economic world and financial markets spinning. Our market value would skyrocket. What a ride it will be!

The night before he left for a brief but tragic vacation, Pellman dropped by my home. He handed me a folder containing a series of notebooks, disks, and a large envelope marked 'CONFIDENTIAL.' "I cannot emphasize the degree of discretion you must use to protect this. Under no circumstances are you to let this information out of your sight or possession. Do not open these packages until or unless you hear from me. Matters of national and international importance are inside. I trust you completely. Please keep them safe until I see you again."

"OK. Have a great trip," I said in an assuring manner, determined to read everything when I got back from a date I made earlier that day. "I'll call you later," he said as he drove away. He never did.

At his sad but brief memorial service, I noticed his wife Darla exiting one of the many limousines lined up in front of the church. Clay Sims, the new President-Elect was at her side. She saw me and began waiving, motioning me to come near. I'd avoided her since learning of Pellman's death. Grief and anger gave me particular trouble drawing back debilitating veils of pain and loss. I was destroyed. Joshua Pellman recruited, hired, trained and mentored me.

My loss eclipsed anything she or anyone else could have possibly felt that day. We shared no sick or scandalous closeness. A basic understanding of numbers provided us a binding commonality. Unambiguous respect. Fervent esteem. Fierce competition. Zeal to be the best. He understood my mind. I understood his. Now suddenly I was point person in charge of his looming legacy. Alone.

RJP was suddenly chaotic, since Pellman was key to luring and retaining our most lucrative clients. All eyes focused on me. My leadership. Knowledge. Ability. Had I learned enough? Could I replace the irreplaceable? I was confused. Lonely. But at the same time, I was determined. Confident. Prepared. Undeterred.

As I reached Mrs. Pellman, she pushed past Clay Sims, who'd won the presidency in a squeaker two weeks ago. RJP was a major fundraiser for his campaign and Pellman was his economic advisor. Key RJP staff played major roles in his election. There was talk that he'd name Pellman to a cabinet post, but I knew he wouldn't take it. Not enough money.

Sims was Pellman's roommate at Harvard. They were closer than brothers and kept each other's secrets. He often reminded me, "There are no real secrets, just truths waiting to be revealed."

As Sims' lead economic adviser during the campaign, Pellman outlined the hotly debated Sims' economic policies and provided great answers to key economic issues facing the nation. Pellman wrote it. I humanized it. Sims memorized and parroted it. Masterfully. We were all excited because the win promised to translate into huge numbers and greater influence for RJP.

Out of the corner of my eye I noticed RJP's VP of PR. During the campaign he took a leave of absence to work as Sims' media advisor. He was pegged to be press secretary. He and Sims worked together for years prior to his association with RJP. As mastermind of Sims' blistering media attacks, his scorching advertising campaign struck with deadly precision. Laden with fear mongering and half truths, they were cruel. Indefensible. Dirty. Destructive. They worked.

Mrs. Pellman grabbed my hands as she pressed a small key into my palm. Her reddened green eyes spoke sadness. Desperation. Fear. Danger. She obviously didn't want anyone to notice the exchange, so I slid into her trembling arms, pushing the key deep into my pocket. "It opens something in Joshua's Washington office. He said that if there's information you need and if you can't find answers anywhere else, you'll probably find the answer there...in time," she whispered. Then with a pleading stare, "He told me to tell you if anything ever happened to him, you must use this. He said trust no one...but your own instincts. He always said you were very special. To him. To both of us. Brilliant is how he described you. Until today, I was jealous of those words. I no longer have room in my heart for hating you." Why should she hate me? "You need to be as smart as Joshua always said you are. My hope is that you'll forgive me one day. That...you'll...forgive...us all...remember...for all our sakes, remember everything. Above all else, remember Joshua loved you. You were the daughter he...we never had." She held me tightly. "Be careful darling." Then she kissed my cheek.

Tears broke my vigil of indifference. Before I could begin asking the thousand questions bombarding my intellect, the press of mourners, reporters and secret service agents surrounded us, lifting and carrying her into the chapel and pushing me aside. Clay Sims looked deeply into my eyes as if searching for something. He took Mrs. Pellman's arm and whisked her away. She glanced back, as I silently acknowledged her instructions.

Touched that Joshua would leave me anything, confused about the mysterious message, stunned that he cared so deeply and sadder than most, I joined the others inside the church.

CHAPTER ONE

FIVE YEARS EARLIER

The train to New York was stuck just outside Philadelphia. There was no sense panicking, so I closed my eyes and let my mind wander to my finals. My future. The luncheon. The prize. Pellman. I had every intention of meeting him today.

I'd read everything he'd ever published. Reviewed every commentary he'd ever given and researched all databases containing references to his work. No one ever knew that while I was a TA at Wharton, I cleaned out a file cabinet that belonged to legendary 'Professor Emeritus" Leonard Jackson, who'd won the Nobel Prize for economics 40 years earlier. He taught Pellman international finance at Harvard. Everyone was eager to take his class and his sudden death and disappearance shocked our academic community. Dreadful and mysterious.

His estate requested his papers. Dr. Stovall, head of the department, asked me to do the job. To my delight, inside a dusty box at the bottom of a cabinet was a paper Pellman wrote years ago. He received a 'D'. The professor's comments were brutal. I surmised the only reason he hadn't received an 'F' was because the paper was written with exemplary style and clarity. I had to read it. I did.

Keeping a watchful eye on the door, I sat on the floor behind the large desk inhaling the essay. I cruised through about twenty pages before I decided to make a copy. Somehow the paper slid into my backpack. Completely distracted by my discovery, I managed to get back to the boxes just as an instructor peeked her head into the room. "Anything interesting in there?" she asked. "Nope. I'm not defiling, I'm boxing," I smiled.

I'd take the paper. Copy it. Return it. No one would know. It would be back among the mountain of other papers, notes and books before anyone would miss it. But after I finished reading it, I decided no one in Jackson's estate knew it was there. He left no heirs and everything would probably go to some dusty archive. That would be tragic. After all, this wasn't his paper. It was Pellman's. It should belong to someone who appreciated Pellman's analytical talents. It should belong to me.

Finding this treasure was and the greatest thrill of my Wharton experience. It was what finding 'Lucy' must have been to the archeology students who discovered her remains in Africa. A rare dig. Significant find. Historic moment. Evidence of his innate genius. It was mine. It wasn't stealing. Not really.

Later in my room I deliberated the essay's possibilities, pondering what financial and legal impact Pellman's hypothesis would have on global economics. The young lawyer in me delighted in the number of federal and international laws his hypothesis violated. Its fatal simplicities made me smile. The applications were elementary and highly improbable. Still, I couldn't help being impressed with Pellman's seamless greed. Brilliant design. Flawed execution. Legal disregard. Numerical excellence. The flaws made the paper important. I spent the remainder of my stay at Wharton resolving them.

When the train finally chugged forward, I looked at my watch. I'd still get to the Plaza in plenty of time. RJP International sponsors an annual essay competition for MBA students. Candidates are selected from the top business schools in the country. Essays are submitted from a choice of three topics having the same general theme. Winners of the local contests are entered into regional competitions. Regional winners are automatically entered into the national contest. RJP brings all regional finalists to New York City for its annual charity luncheon. That's where the winner is introduced to a hungry financial industry. The winning student receives a certificate; a plaque; $85,000.00 cash and the certainty of employment. I was a regional finalist.

Penn station was packed with morning commuters. I raced from the train, jumping into the first empty cab. "Take me to the Plaza!" I ordered, looking through my resumes and checking for writing samples and letters of recommendation. The taxi stopped abruptly. "What happened?"

"President's in town."

"Is there another route we can take?"

"This ain't no helicopter lady. When he moves, we move."

The cabbie pulled out a newspaper and began reading. I took a deep breath settling into the backseat. Time ticked slowly as the morning crowd marched by. Just as I was about to tell the driver that I would walk to the hotel, traffic moved and the cab jerked forward. We arrived at the Plaza without further incident.

"Good morning. I'm Ms. Pichon from RJP's public relations department. We've been anticipating your arrival and welcome to the Plaza. The other candidates arrived last night. Your suite is on the 6th floor. Room 610. Will you need assistance with your bags?"

"No. Thank you." She handed me a folder and a key.

"The luncheon will be held in the Grand Ballroom. You are to meet your party over there," she said pointing. "The elevators are to your left. Have a pleasant stay and if you need assistance during your visit, we are at your service. You should be downstairs in 30 minutes. Don't be late. Again, the elevators are to your left," she said pointing.

"Thank you."

"My pleasure."

I hurried into the room. Changed clothes. Looked in the honor bar. Freshened my makeup and I called Iris. No answer. We planned to see each other later that evening. I grabbed my resumes, pushed my hair around and rushed downstairs. The other students were instantly recognizable. While introducing ourselves, a perky lady who I suspected of having had too much caffeine approached rapidly. She rattled off names, instructions and information, while handing each of us nametags. She took off toward the ballrooms at a sprinters pace. We followed. "Do not approach head table guests. If someone approaches you, that's OK. This year the winner will make a one or two minute speech. Not one second more. Any questions? Good. Remember two minutes only. You may order one bottle of wine for the table. Any additional alcohol is not covered. Everyone here is over 21, right? Good. You may hand out resumes when the luncheon is over, not before. Any questions? Good. Please pin the nametags on your left lapel. Those of you with family here today, they will be seated at tables 80 and 81. You will be seated at table 2. Any questions? Good. Remain with the group until the luncheon is over. Your seats are pre-assigned. You will find cards on the table. The cards have your name. The card will be in front of your plate. Do not change seats before the luncheon is over. Any questions? Good. Are you having trouble with your pin?" She asked heading straight for me, ripping the pin from my hand. "I'll help you with that."

I gently grabbed her hand as she lifted my lapel. "If you wouldn't mind, I'd prefer a lanyard or a badge clip. Is that possible?" I smiled. I wasn't putting a hole in my new silk suit.

"Not a problem. I'll be right back." She turned and walked past a series of tables, barking orders to people who quickly dispatched themselves to do her bidding. We watched in bemused amazement. "She must be important," one of the students whispered. We joined in commenting and laughing about her rapid-fire instructions. She returned, securing the necklace around my neck. "Good luck," she whispered to each of us, with winks of approval as we entered the room.

As we made our way to the table, I studied the crowd. They studied us. Over 800 people filled the bustling room. Standing. Laughing. Talking. Hugging. Smiling. Where were the black faces? I knew they were there. Somewhere. Silent. Supportive. Influential. They were my family for the afternoon.

We were seated in the most splendid ballroom imaginable. Iris would love this. Everything was golden. Huge, colorful, fragrant flower arrangements decorated the tables. Sparkling

Tricked

chandeliers and long tapered candles made everything and everyone glisten. Porcelain. Linen. Crystal. Real silver. A golden chord held the napkins in place. Even the trim on the luncheon programs were gilded and tasseled. The programs included a picture and bio of each contestant. A list of head table guests. Corporate sponsors. Menu. Mission. Short excerpts from our essays.

Today Florida A & M takes its rightful place among schools recognized for cranking out top level economic graduates. I was the only African American raised by a single parent. HBCU grad. Female and fabulous. I felt tremendous. Pride added two inches to my stature. I sat up straight, silently thanking God for this invitation to the campy club where talent and education dance with opportunity and success.

Glancing around the table, I realized these boys were very smart. Intense. Ambitious. The newness of their suits whined as we engaged in small talk about our papers. Our futures. Our lives. The winner would land a prime position with any firm on Wall Street. Which in our young minds was about one block away from Easy Street.

Bits and pieces of conversation about their papers whetted my inquisitive appetite and sparked my interest. Our commonality transcended our papers. Schools. Prestige. Race. Sex. Politics. Status. Each paper contained creative concepts premised on precise economic theorems. Even so, my chances of winning seemed to diminish with each revelation. Not because my paper lacked precision, but because its themes were primarily centered around a theory of using quantum mathematical manipulations of economic sequential formulae to secretly purchase and sell international science and technology securities, undetected. I named the process, "Distributive Loss."

Since every dimension of modern life involves aspects of science, technology or chemical based products, the owners of those companies are critically influential. With uses too numerous to list and too vast to conceive, they ultimately decide who benefits from their use or misuse. Fundamentally deciding who lives and who dies. Who wins. Who loses. What if a small group cornered the market on biological, genetic and chemical technology, with a few pharmaceutical stocks thrown in for good measure? What if no one could discover their locations or identify their motives? What if it became impossible to trace them at all? What might they do with such power? Monitoring exists, but what about the co-signs? Suppliers. Haulers. Distributors.

Although my essay wasn't fact-based, I explored in vivid detail how manipulating these securities could be used as the ultimate weapon. Loss. Simply put, by denying access to beneficial chemical and technological products while manipulating them at will could be devastating. Everything we use is touched by chemicals and technology. The basic nature of man, greed. Power. Fear. And the redistribution of international wealth makes the impossible seem at least relevant.

Winning the regional contest vindicated me, especially after the tremendous fight I had with my economics professor, who reviewed all RJP Essay submissions from Wharton. His comments included Outlandish. Impossible. Garbage. He ordered me to a meeting. He huffed. I puffed. An impasse. I assured him that not one word would be changed. He assured me he wouldn't submit it as written. "I'll submit it without your endorsement." He believed me. "You wouldn't dare," he snarled. "I'll submit your preposterous paper under protest but I also plan to write a letter to the Dean and the Chairman of the department reflecting your insubordination and insolence."

Too smart for his bluff, I understood his need to maintain at least the aura of control. I left the meeting without saying another word. When Dr. Stovall passed me in the hall two weeks ago, he asked me to step into his office. "You won the regional competition." As a craggy smile broke across his stony face, he said, "We haven't had a winner in a long time. I'd like to discuss your theories in more detail before the end of the semester. Congratulations. You'll probably receive the letter in two or three days. They inform the schools first. I just thought you'd like to know." He offered his hand. I shook it. "You're my best student."

"Thank you. I appreciate this. No hard feelings?"

"None. You stood your ground and you were right. That takes guts."

"Thanks Dr. Stovall. You taught me to fight for my position and that's what I did."

"I taught you well."

"You did indeed," I smiled too.

That was as close to an apology as I could expect. Professor Stovall was an erstwhile adversary. World known for his encyclopedic knowledge of economic impacts on financial systems. He taught Pellman at Harvard and spoke highly of him during many lectures. There was no need to gloat. As worthy a foe as he'd been, he'd become an invaluable friend. I never mentioned our fight to anyone. He'd be here today. Wharton bought two tables.

My delight swelled as I scanned the dais. There he was. Joshua Pellman. He looked more like a movie star than an economist. Tall. Tanned. Lean. Important. His face was strong. Charismatic. Confident. Rich. Cool. Everybody was trying to see him. Touch him. Know him.

Turning my attention back to my tablemates, I noticed Ross Bennett from Stanford. He'd already made millions developing new technologies in sound automation for music recording studios. A studio was not considered state of the art unless it had a Bennett system. He was in the process of designing a device he claimed would revolutionize music distribution, but wouldn't give further details. "You see, I really don't care anything about winning this award. I just like meeting new people…like you." He was flirting. "And I never miss an opportunity to network with rich people who trifle in the money game," he whispered, showing a perfect smile and suave demeanor. I detected a slight accent.

He was cute and must have thought the same about me since he asked for my telephone number back in Pennsylvania.

Uncharacteristically, I gave him mine and I got his. Networking starts right now.

Wine was ordered and everyone was excited. Happy. Anxious. We all enjoyed the program and delicious lunch. Halfway through a slice of the most stupendous chocolate mousse cake with strawberries and whipped cream ever made, the Master of Ceremonies took the microphone. Not one of us paid the least bit of attention to the speeches or remarks. Then like thunder, "The winner of this year's RJP Essay Competition is from the Wharton School of Business at the University of Pennsylvania and Florida A&M, Ms. McClain Summers! Come up here Ms. Summers! Dr. Stovall where are you? I know you're out there somewhere? Give her a hand everyone!"

What?!! No way! I won? The boys at the table leapt from their chairs. Cheering. Clapping. Smiling. Ross pulled me from my seat, pushing me toward the stage. A bright light lit the way. I licked what was left of the whipped cream from my lips, hoping some lipstick was still in tact as I drifted through a gauntlet of praise and applause. People were standing. Clapping. Yelling.

Unlike my tablemates, I hadn't prepared a speech. I hadn't looked through the New York classifieds to find an apartment and I didn't want to be a broker or blow an artery as a financial banker. I wanted to work where the action was. I wanted to combine law and money in a way no one else ever had. I wanted to be a player. Where my decisions would make markets soar like fireworks or tumble like dominoes. People who made those decisions on a daily basis were in this room cheering for me.

Flash bulbs nearly blinded me as my hero rushed toward me, raving about my paper and my potential. "You're fantastic. You're brilliant," he smiled, handing me the check. The plaque. The certificate. Joshua Pellman was hugging me and shaking my hand. He pulled me closer as we posed for a variety of photographers. I was standing in the grip of the man I knew only from books. Papers. Magazines. Television. Reputation. I was so excited about being near him, I became instantly stupid. Tongue-tied. Impotent. He was beaming as though he'd known me my entire life and all I could manage to whimper was an anemic "Thank you."

He pushed me toward the microphone where words spilled from my mouth that came from somewhere other than my head. I can't remember one word of it but I must have been eloquent because the room erupted in applause again when I'd finished. Some luncheon guests wiped their eyes, but I couldn't tell whether their emotional outburst was from hysterical laughter or if they were actually touched by something I said.

I descended the platform into the waiting arms of financiers and elite brokerage house representatives. Investment bankers. Recruiters. Managers. They cornered me with offers. Barely able to make it back to the table, I stuffed cards and congratulations into my pockets along the way.

Expensive champagne arrived. We had our own celebration. Ross bought it. He had style. My fellow contestants hovered around me like gracious losers at a beauty pageant. Reading the certificate. The plaque. The check. Some nice. Some pissed. All surprised. Then without missing a beat, they scattered working the room like seasoned politicians. Compelled and certain to find their bright futures and lucrative destinies in this golden room.

When the luncheon was over, I was surrounded again. People wanted my resume. Room number. Telephone number. Address. Interviews. Dinner. Drinks. Either. Both. Me. I took pictures with people I didn't know. I spoke with presidents and CEO's of major trading houses about great opportunities. My favorite math instructor from FamU surprised me and came to represent the university. Dr. Stovall and many other instructors smiled and nodded from across the room. Today they were all beautiful.

Winning the RJP award was equivalent to winning the Hiesman. The Lombardi. National championship. I was the number one pick in the first round of the draft. The key difference, the work was a lot harder and salary cap a lot lower. My credentials were excellent. My essay would be published in the

Wharton Business Review and I was a double threat, having earned both an MBA and JD. This win confirmed my analytical and writing skills, and I was a diversity director's dream. Black. Female. Smart. Confident. Competent. Ambitious.

My mother said, "Beauty can be a curse. It's never enough. You've got to be smart. The best. The brightest. Give the brightest light with the lowest heat. They may forget your smile, but they'll never forget your ability to think." I always remembered her words. She said them every chance she got.

Two RJP representatives approached as the waiter offered me another piece of cake. They'd be my escorts for the rest of the afternoon. "I'll have it delivered to your room and congratulations Miss," the waiter offered as the duo rushed me into a large black limousine. Then we headed into the tangle that is New York City traffic.

Travis Dixon, the CEO and director of the New York Stock Exchange met us at the doors and gave me a personal tour of its impressive offices. Later, I walked through RJP-New York, a marvel of technology and wealth. They'd keep me overnight. The team interview process would begin the next day.

After meeting the New York brass, a limo took me back to the hotel. I called Iris again. No answer. Where was she? I called Ross to tell him that I couldn't join him for dinner. Just as his telephone rang, someone knocked at my door. "These are for you." The bellman bowed presenting me with a glorious bouquet of four dozen perfect white roses, decorated with fabulous white hydrangea. The card read, "Congratulations! I had to leave. Ring me when you think of me. You're beautiful. I think I've fallen in 'like' with you. Enjoy the day. Ross." I rushed back to the telephone to call my mother. She was thrilled. I told her about my wonderful day while eating the most wonderful chocolate mousse cake with strawberries and whipped cream ever created.

Three different RJP executives took me to dinner and a Broadway play that night. I did everything right. I dressed right. I laughed at the right times. I ate with the right cutlery. I stayed away from discussions of politics. Religion. Sex. I reiterated my good points and sold myself. One omission of protocol involved batting my eyes at a fine brother looking at the marquee outside the Helen Hayes Theatre. I don't think they noticed. Neither did he.

After lunch the next day, I had the customary job offer. No decisions would be made until after graduation. So I thanked them for everything and left for Pennsylvania.

Bright daylight collapsed into a damp misty afternoon as the train slipped the grasp of Manhattan. Thoughts of how instructors complimented my ability to quickly understand complex economic theories saturated the moment. They encouraged my incessant inquiries, rewarding my work with high marks. High hopes.

Exceptional professors at FamU, took exceptional interest in my goals and aptitude. They shared today's joy. Dr. Leo Kennedy, head of the science department convinced me to study finance or math. "You have a head for numbers. Your only interest in science centers in the mathematical components. If you really want to excel, focus on numbers. They'll never fail you." I appreciated his advice and my love for analytical theory became all consuming. Math instructors respected my ability to grasp and grow. I was diligent. Driven. Focused. A hard worker. I constantly pushed my intellectual limits. And theirs.

Considering the dynamic effect this award posed for my postgraduate career, I leaned the seat back pulling my coat over my legs. Thoughts bounced around in my brain as my head bounced gently against the window.

Pellman and I spoke briefly after the luncheon. He read my paper and said "I like the way your mind works. It reminds me of someone." I worried that he noticed similarities my paper had with his. Interestingly, by the time I returned to the hotel last night, he'd delivered a note offering me a position at RJP Dallas.

My ambition and ego could tolerate nothing less than the best. He was the best. His ideas and slashing style were thrilling. I like thrills. Although routinely recognized for his brilliance, he had equal repute for being utterly impossible to work with. I could take that. By the time the train lurched before arriving at the Philly station, I'd decided to begin my career at RJP Dallas. Under his tutelage and leadership I'd be a strategist. Financial wizard. Player. Superstar. Gambler. That meant RJP. That meant Dallas. I'd never been to Dallas and the only thing I knew about the central Texas town was that it was where President Kennedy was assassinated.

Walking through the station, I plotted my future with each excited step. If I applied the same work ethic in Dallas as I had in school, I'd do well.

Sharon pulled to the curb. I dashed from the protection of the covered doorway and into the warm car. My incredible day was as exciting to her as it was to me. The sign of a great friend. In 90 days, I'd be a Texan. YeeHiii!!!

CHAPTER TWO

RJP's executive training course began exactly 90 days after graduation. I notified RJP New York and others that I'd accepted a position with Joshua Pellman. Needless to say, they understood.

Having learned to never take the first offer, I negotiated an additional $25,000.00 to the generous six-figure salary he offered. Additionally RJP would pay off my student loans. First six months rent. All moving expenses. Vest my retirement in five years and I'd share in the profit structure of my department if we out performed other RJP divisions proportionately. He agreed. You can negotiate anything. My mother taught me that.

I finished my finals, graduated with honors and attended Dr. Stovall's retirement dinner. After taking both the Pennsylvania and New York bar exams, I left Philadelphia for the last time.

Papers. Books. Maps and brochures arrived at my mother's house in Milwaukee. Included in the mélange of literature, was a textbook and syllabi outlining the first five chapters I had to read before the first class.

With $45,000.00 to put into Ross Bennett's IPO, I'd invest the rest in high yield bonds and a savings account. Mother gave me her four-year-old Volvo, deciding it was time for a SUV. She surprised me with four extremely expensive outfits and a new brief case. She drove all the way over to White Fish Bay because she believed they sold better things than the stores downtown. She was determined I would start my career dressed for success.

Boxes, holding precious bits and pieces of my life were neatly packed into the car. I kissed my mother in an awkward goodbye and got into the car. She showed no signs of despair at my leaving, and went back into the house before I drove away.

As I reached the O'Hare tollbooth, I thought how funny it was that my life fit so well on the backseat of a car. Clanking coins hit the metal counter, lifting the gate to my new life in the world of international finance. I followed the signs toward Little Rock.

The next four and a half years rushed by quickly. Flourishing under Pellman's tutelage, I played the corporate game of musical chairs with precision and daring. I spent less time than any junior executive in required areas of RJP protocol, mastering each financial and legal endeavor with such haste that supervisors grew intimidated by my proficiencies. They passed me from position to position so quickly that within eighteen months I was working directly with Pellman as his Assistant Director of International Financial Development.

This was novel. Revolutionary. Unheard of. They even canned my predecessor so that I could fill his position. Pellman put me in charge of monitoring the activities of our senior NASDAQ analysts and key international scientific forecast managers too. Six months later, he promoted me to Manager of International Scientific Equities Worldwide.

My quick instincts and focused ability to do in depth research became highly respected by our New York and European staffs. We traded no less than $27,000,000,000.00 on a bad day. My staff forecasted all research and development science related chemical, pharmaceutical, and technology securities, IPOs, and secondary offerings. I also sat in on critical high yield structured leveraged buy-outs. Pellman required my input on cross border trading problems and, he gave me additional responsibility for monitoring our Western European markets. Office drums banged out that I'd soon be monitoring the Asian markets too. I eagerly anticipated the challenge.

About two years later, Josh, (he recently told me to call him that) told me to bring all concerns or problems I encountered directly to him. He was fatherly and frank. His critiques useful and instructive. Proud of each accomplishment, he never took credit for anything. He admired my work ethic. I admired his. "You're just like me with better legs," he mused. He was wrong. I was more than that. My mind was a sponge thirsty for knowledge. His. My ego was eager for approval. My ambition primed for success.

No mistakes were permitted. Those who worked under my supervision were held to the same standard. Consequently, my division became the most productive component of RJP and we received sizeable bonuses after quarterly reviews. It wasn't long before applications for openings in my department tripled.

Headhunters with ridiculously lucrative offers from revered finance houses consistently raided my department. It was a standing joke around the office. Their tempting recruiting tactics provided constant water cooler banter but my loyal staff typically rebuffed their inducements, eager to learn. Earn. Grow.

Friends in New York approached me with ideas of starting a small boutique type firm, specializing in research stocks. It sounded like a good idea, but I was happy at RJP. My salary paid me more than I ever thought possible. I was rich. My bonuses made industry history and the benefits package was among the best in the business. That spring my retirement vested and absolutely nothing could pull me away from Joshua Pellman. Not yet.

My friendship with Ross was solid. He was invaluable for digging up useful information with extremely interesting details on people's financial, personal and private interests. We were good friends. Nothing more. I was happy to keep it that way.

At precisely 10:45 a.m. Josh called me into his office. Gushing with praise and albeit politically incorrect, I gave him a tremendous hug for being selected to present a speech at the World Economic Symposium in London. Additionally, it was a prime opportunity for RJP to articulate plans and specs for his new market security device.

Being asked to deliver this address was perhaps the highest single honor an economist could receive, other than the Nobel Prize. He already had that. Josh thanked me, and immediately began discussing work he needed me to do.

I sank into the red leather club chair in front of his desk, retrieving the pen I kept tucked in my hair. I took notes. Pellman leaned back rattling on about how his partners were initially against hiring me. There was a message in this diversion.

"Eddie and Charles threw serious road blocks up against hiring you. But I knew you were the woman for the job and probably the smartest person here, besides me of course," he smiled walking toward the windows where he surveyed the Dallas skyline.

"You've shown them what you're made of, and I'm proud of you. Much to their surprise, they've found your work superb. They tried everything in the book, fair and unfair to trip you up." I knew it. "Your aptitude is unchallengeable." He returned to his desk, perching himself on the arm of the huge leather chair he called 'mission control.' "They brag that you're one of kind. RJP is fortunate to have you.

Anyway, we all know how excited you are about this London presentation. Unfortunately, after a protracted and heated fight with my partners, we've agreed that Todd Winston will travel with me instead of you." He sat in the chair, spinning from side to side. "You've been there for me with every important speech since coming aboard. I've depended on your insight. Intellect. Analysis. Research. Skills. But they believe…we believe someone else should have a chance to work on important RJP presentations."

He walked toward his private bar area. "Would you like some water?" I shook my head no. "You'll need to double check Winston's work. Teach him how I like presentations made." He sat again. "This may lead to another Nobel," he laughed.

Racist was my first thought. I saw his mouth moving, but anger struck me stone deaf. I was crushed. Winston goes. I stay. Now I'm responsible for teaching this bimbo. Teach him what Pellman likes and show how to make presentations. Am I supposed to feel good because they think I'm one of a kind? Is that a compliment? Who came up that that?

Residual sensibilities I'd done everything to repress snapped into full alert. They dusted off their weapons and prepared for battle. I wanted to tear that office up. Tear him up. The first sign of rage burst in. Sweat formed on my nose. I quickly slid my hand across the bridge. Never let them know you're angry.

All the money I'd made them. The loyalty. Dedication. Sacrifice. The only negative thing anyone ever put on my reviews was that I worked too hard. I planned to fix that as soon as Pellman shut up. Winston would be on his own. I wasn't going to show him diddly.

My hearing returned when Pellman inquired about the independent research I started. I hadn't told anyone about it. How did he know?

The research centered on inconsistencies I noticed in the foreign banking patterns of four major clients. They had important global chemical holdings, but I was unable to identify them. Curiosity caused me to speculate how they had such lucrative holdings when no one knew who they were.

"I want you to stop the research you've been doing and concentrate on the new files I put on my desk this morning." The second signs of this apocalypse stood straight up. Shock turned to anger. Anger became fury. Fury was about to get him hit. Just as I opened my mouth to declare war, he said, "Thanks McClain...I'll talk to you later," then spun around and began speaking into his dictation machine.

Oh no he didn't just dismiss me. Still fighting against the riot that was just about to break out in these plush surroundings, I rose from the chair and turned toward the door.

Not going to London would be a major blow. Everyone knew I was supposed to make the trip. Failing to join Pellman would be a signal the corporate piranha would interpret as permission to attack.

With each step I sunk deeper into the plush carpet, fighting back tears of red hot anger. "Suck it up. Suck it up," I commanded myself. Not one tear would stain my new yellow suit. The headhunters were on my speed dial. Today was their lucky day.

Then Josh said, "I'm leaving tonight. I've always wanted to

ride the rapids. I'll be back in one week and I'm depending on you to take care of everything while I'm gone...Like you *always* do."

Typical. I never turned around. "Oh...by the way, did I mention we're promoting you to Vice President and General Counsel of International Markets & Scientific Technologies?"

"What?!" I shrieked, spinning around. His eyes twinkled.

"Gottcha!" he laughed. "You've got to loosen up McClain! You have absolutely no sense of humor, and you work much too hard," he laughed. After all, you'll be starting your new position....,"looking at his watch, "Immediately..... like right now...pack your glad rags Ms. Summers, you're going to London. I couldn't make such an important presentation without my number one man. I had you going with Winston didn't I?" he laughed, wiping tears from his eyes and walking from behind the desk. "That was pretty good," he howled. "You should have seen your face," he laughed falling into a chair, trying to gain his composure. "You'll need to cover the Evans merger next week in San Francisco. Donahue was supposed to do it, but his wife is having a baby. I'll be on a raft in Colorado freezing and getting wet! So its up to you. Details on the London speech are on your PC. Clean it up. Do the outlined research and when I get back, we'll make the final changes. I couldn't be more proud of you, even if you were my own...."

I didn't hear the rest of his sentence. Tears of disappointment had quickly turned to joy. I fell into his arms and gave him another hug. He hugged back. Today I was his partner. His equal.

"Did you tell her yet?" RJP partners who'd flown in from around the world peered from behind the adjoining conference room doors.

"I did," Pellman smiled, leading me into the conference room where the partners had convened to welcome me to their status.

Champagne corks flew just as loudly as the congratulations that filled the room. "You earned this McClain. You really did. I'd like to take credit for your success here, but I can't. You have a great mind and you're not afraid to use it. You're a winner and I'm very proud of you."

"Here! Here!" the partners agreed.

Pellman sat on the edge of the conference room table applauding me. The other partners joined in. Unlike the first time we met, I was now standing next to a peer. A peer who knew me. My ambitions. My goals. My curiosities. He steered me in the right directions. Backed my decisions. Respected my instincts and demanded respect from those who questioned my talents or my place. "I hand picked her. She's my protégé."

This promotion had additional significance. It was redemption from the barbs of peer managers who thought I didn't have the "right attitude" for the power that came with my status. They complained behind my back that I blurred the lines between support, housekeeping and executive staffs. That's white-folks 'code language' for the workplace caste system they cherish. It keeps the boundaries of socio-economic and educational bigotry alive. Those brave enough to comment out loud asked, "Why do you associate with employees who are not your peers? What could you possibly have in common with them?"

Incapable of understanding that my interest in the doorman was just as intense as my interested in Reynolds, Jacobs or Pellman was inconceivable. Such closeness shouldn't be shared with porters. Valets. Clerks. Deliverymen. Janitors. Runners. I insisted on lunching with them at least once a month and I couldn't wait to tell Gerald and Jack about my new position.

With unlimited access to everyone's office, Gerald was the most important man in the RJP building. He moved virtually unnoticed from office to office. When we discussed complicated economic theories, he understood their complexities better than any UT and Ivy League executive trainee. I often wondered why he never went to college. He never told me. I never asked. He was a friend and the inner office mailman, who hung out with the maintenance people.

Amazing things wind up in the trash. They watched my back and kept me current with internal office politics. I helped get their kids scholarship money and jobs with friends around the country. They also kept me grounded with arms full of home grown wisdom. Tomatoes. Greens. Peas. Humility. Acceptance.

Gerald and I met when circumstances warranted, usually at the Donut Shoppe on Lovers Lane at 5:30 a.m. If he had special information to share, he'd place an empty donut bag in my garbage can. It was our signal that he had something good to share. After reviewing the information, I'd go into meetings with brilliant initiatives, plans, and answers to problems, issues and questions yet to be made public, as though I was a fly on the wall. Too fast to swat.

Jack was my best friend. He never needed an excuse to celebrate, and today was no exception. He cancelled his afternoon appointments and made lunch reservations.

The promotion was also a reward for the many days I felt isolated on 'Black Island', where my presence was tokenized; my proficiency seen as a series of fortunate flukes; and my abilities constantly questioned. Of course there were those who thought and will always believe that I was 'doing' Pellman which accounted for my place on the fast track. Sheer envy motivated their whispered attacks. It was implausible to them that Pellman and I had mutual respect for the slippery slopes of international law and finance. We also had an unqualified respect for each other.

Adept at recognizing and deciphering economic trends, we loved riding the cutting edge of financial forecasting, wanting to be the first with vital new information and mind splitting market analysis. We worked late into the night, many holidays, and most weekends preparing reports and projections that made the firm rich and our clients richer.

Some believed I was merely a sell out. The 'white man's plaything.' They had no idea that my ultimate goal was to learn as much as I could and execute my plans. Those plans included a vested and insured retirement. Capital. Contacts. Clout. There was no better education than the one I was taking advantage of at RJP while establishing credibility. Expertise. Knowledge. Reputation.

Early in my career I understood that before you make waves, make a very big boat. Those who upset the waters while sailing turbulent seas in rafts, inner tubes or canoes usually sink. Alone.

Others thought I was too young. Too inexperienced. Too green and too Black. They said I was "too personal with the minority junior executives" and that made other 'JE's' feel that they wouldn't receive similar attention from me. Further, my reviews tended to show bias. Ain't that a blip?

Always the consummate professional, I was thorough and available. Sacrificing any semblance of a personal life, I attended firm functions. Entertained clients. Amused partners. Nothing and no one interfered with my goals. My work.

Honorary mention goes to RJP's obvious racists who didn't believe anyone of my hue no matter how proficient, should have her hands on anything other than a mop, a rag, or a white man's dick.

CHAPTER THREE

Raul recognized me instantly. I was late. He waived me to the front of the long lunch line. "Beautiful day Ms. Summers. Your party has arrived. Henry will direct you to your table."

"Hi Raul. Have I told you that you're the best Maitre' D in Dallas?"

"Every time you come in."

"It's true."

"Thank you and thank you so much for getting my son that scholarship to UT."

"He got the scholarship. I just gave someone his name."

"Whatever you did, I want you to know that my wife and I appreciate it very much, and we'll never forget your help."

"Just tell your son to make the best of this opportunity and pass his good fortune along."

"I will. Have a fantastic lunch."

"I always do."

I looked around as the waiter led me through the crowded eatery. He was there. I hoped I'd see him again. He saw me too. I paused briefly at the dessert cart, looking down at my left calf, cocking my head to the side. My hair fell gently over my eye. When I slowly raised my eyes, he quickly diverted his glance. "Um-hmm," I thought. "Made ya look."

Jack waved from our favorite table near the windows. I waved back, quickening my pace. Rapid conversation harmonized effortlessly with melodic tunes the piano player looped gleefully on the grand piano near the bar.

Tricked

Cheyenne's was like a cattle baron's convention. Lawyers. Bankers. Politicians. Business people. Corporate ranchers. Financial wizards and moguls cut mind boggling deals here. Politicians emphatically argued right and left wing platforms. Dilettante socialites laden with status bags from upscale boutiques commiserated about their loveless marriages, cosmetic surgeries and designer gowns. Rich old men with beautiful young women bred for pampering dotted the landscape. Then there were those like Jack and I, ambitious misfits nudging our way into this zoo of excess.

Jack leapt from his chair and kissed my cheeks when I reached the table. "Girl, I'm so happy for you," he gushed.

Draping myself elegantly across the chair, I crossed my legs striking a mean pose. A stream of sunlight bounced across the fresh cut flowers and white table linens, providing the perfect up lighting for my bright yellow suit. "What you doing? Where is he?" Jack whispered, easing back into his chair.

Jack and I came here to celebrate high points. The high points were coming more frequently. Today was no exception. "I was introduced to my new suite of offices by the company's interior decorator. There's a huge decorating budget. Ordinarily she'd get the job, but I explained that no one could decorate my suites but you."

"You got that right Miss Thing. That's my girl!" he laughed, rushing around the table to kiss me again.

"Champagne! Let's have the best they have. Give me that wine menu. You got your credit card?" he laughed.

"Is he looking Jack?" I whispered.

"Where? Who? Is who looking?" Jack whispered, craning his neck, turning around.

"Don't look!" I snapped.

"If I don't look, then how do I know if he's looking? Who's he?" he asked.

"Just don't be so obvious."

Jack surveyed the room like a lighthouse in the fog. He knew my taste. "I hope you're talking about that beautiful man over there in the charcoal silk and cashmere suit, he hasn't stopped looking. As a matter of fact I think he's looking at me," he cackled that ridiculously infectious laugh and began waiving at the beautiful stranger, mouthing a kiss.

"Stop Jack. Are you crazy?! What's wrong with you? Let's go!"

"Go? What you mean go!? Go where? I'm *go* get me something to eat. I'm hungry. You might as well calm your little narrow behind down and eat too. You gettin skinny and you work too much. Don't nothin but a dog want a bone. Eat some fat. Get some fried chicken, some dumplins, French fries or something. That man ain't leaving. He got here right before you did. I saw him when he came in and he *is* cute. Probably gay."

Jack picked up the menu just as the waiter arrived giving the luncheon spill about today's specials. While Jack paid close attention, I peered over my shoulder. His face was 40ish. Two other distinguished looking men were at his table. They stood when a fabulously well-dressed, beautifully altered older woman approached the table. She kissed one of them and sat. When he sat, his napkin dropped onto the floor. When he reached for it, our eyes momentarily met. Never breaking my pose, I spun around and perused the menu.

Jack ordered the most expensive champagne in Cheyenne's inventory. We babbled about my new corner office in the executive suites my staff would occupy. That's when I noticed a bruise on Jack's left cheek. "What happened to your face?

"I was looking for something at the store. I reached up on a shelf and some boxes tumbled down. One hit me in the face." I rubbed my hand across the bruise.

"Do you realize that you've been tripping over things and falling off stuff a lot lately. You need to see one of those inner ear people. Maybe your equilibrium is off. I'll make you an appointment with my doctor and I'm going to buy you one of those step ladders from that catalog you love so much too."

"You go buy me more than that!" he howled. "You ain't getting off that cheap. I've got a list baby! By the way…where were you last night? I called you about three times. I started to come up there, but I was too tired and my face hurt too bad."

"None of your business." I usually told Jack everything, but kept some of my business to myself. The waiter returned with our salads.

"None of my business? Pay attention to me...he's still looking and pass me the salt. What you mean ain't none of my business? You musta forgot who you were talking to. I want to know where you were." Jack asked defiantly.

"I was out. Stop eating all of that salt. You're gonna get high blood pressure. Do I have to tell you everything? You're worse than a boyfriend Jack. Why do you always have to be in my business? Just eat and leave me alone."

"What would you know about a boyfriend?" Jack laughed out loud. "Why don't you go over there and introduce yourself to the man?"

"I can't do that?"

"Why not?" Jack looked at me inquisitively, cutting into the steamy loaf of crusty bread. "I thought you women were suppose to be liberated. Waiting to exhale and all that kind of sh...stuff.... pass me the butter...y'all go hold your breath til you drop dead that's what's go happen." Jack laughed so loudly that the people at the next table turned around wanting in on the joke.

"Jack, you know I'm not waiting to do anything. Stop putting all of that butter on that bread and stop being so country! That's not the problem." "Then what's the problem?" He smeared more butter on his bread taking a big bite.

"I wouldn't characterize it as a problem. It's a mystery. The more I have, the more I want. That includes men. It's like pantyhose."

"Pantyhose?" Jack almost choked. "What the hell are you talking about?" Jack poured spicy Italian dressing over his salad and began munching vigorously while I tried to explain.

"I've had better, so now I want better. That's how I feel about men too. Does that make sense to you?"

"Hell no," he said sucking the salad greens from his teeth.

"Jack...you know what I mean. There are lots of men out there. Good men. But for some reason good isn't good enough. I don't want drug store stockings when I can have...what's the best brand? My point *is* that although the cheaper brands serve the same purpose, they just don't have the same allure. Same fit."

"Is that how you determine whether a man is right for you? If he fits like an expensive pair of stockings? Girl, gimme that liquor. Don't you drink one more sip of that champagne. You drunk and talkin crazy." Jack laughed heartily, moving the champagne flute out of my reach. I laughed too.

"I'm not drunk Jack and I'm also not explaining myself very well. I don't want to eliminate men over esoteric qualities, but before I get a chance to evaluate them, they eliminate themselves. I'm too independent. Aggressive. Smart. Ambitious. Not available enough. Not helpless enough. Not stupid enough. Not desperate enough.

I just can't seem to find one who......"
"Doesn't sag at the knees?" Jack was cracking up.

"Whose man enough to be comfortable with all the women who live inside me."

"Now you're talking. I know what you mean girl. Do you think Mr. Thing over there can deal with the Cybil in you?"
"I ain't Cybil, but I sure do like the package."

"I heard that! I like the package too and I bet he's just my size. You better ask somebody."

Jack and I laughed joyously. Perhaps I was a little tipsy. Our waiter returned with our entrees. After eating enough for an army, Jack summoned the waiter for our check. "Hey good looking. We'd like our check please. Give it to her. I need my money."

"Can I interest you in dessert?" the waiter pulled the dessert cart to the table. "Only if you can fit on one of those little plates," Jack flirted. The waiter smiled.

"No thank you," I interrupted. Champagne always made Jack whorish. "May we have the check please?"

Tricked

"Your bill has been taken care of."

"By whom? Raul?"

"No, the gentleman over there paid the check with his compliments to the lady," he said pointing. Jack and I looked at each other. We were deliciously shocked.

"He's got class girl. Obviously he's been watching you too. Maybe he thinks you fit like a good pair of draws," Jack giggled, leaning back in the chair. "Work it right baby. Remember what Uncle Jack taught you. Reel that big fish in," he whispered.

He was consumed in conversation at his table. I pulled a note pad from my handbag, wrote a quick note thanking him for the offer to pay for our lunch. The waiter delivered it to our benefactor. With racehorse like speed I fixed my lipstick and dusted my nose. Just as I returned the gear to my bag, a warm hand touched my shoulder.

Steel gray blue eyes that sparkled like sunlight on snow stared down at me. "Hello." His face was amazingly young and much better looking up close. An engaging aristocracy filled our space. His casually intense carriage signified nobility.

Impeccably groomed. Perfectly dressed. British. Tan. Wealthy. He was out of place, but I was glad he was here today.

"Please...sit," I offered.

"Thank you." He sounded the way you'd expect a British gentleman would.

"Thank you for offering to pay our bill, but I can't let you do that," I said in my best professional voice.

"She can't, but I can," Jack interrupted. "My name is Jack Prescott. I like men." Jack offered his hand and the stranger shook it. "Jack! Please excuse him Mr..."

"My name is Ian Lawford, and you are..."

"I'm McClain Summers." He took my hand and allowed his lips to brush my knuckles.

"I'm very pleased to meet you. I was wondering, and I know it's terribly forward of me to inquire, but would you consider joining me for supper this evening?"

31

"Supper?"

"Yes supper," Jack piped in. "That meal uncouth people like you call dinner. The meal you don't eat between lunch and breakfast." I kicked Jack under the table. "Ouch," he squirmed.

"Mr. Lawford, I don't typically go out with men I meet under such circumstances. I don't know you and I'm completely capable of paying my own bill. My friend and I…"

"Ms. Summers, please allow me this great pleasure. I assure that I am completely harmless and paying your luncheon bill is the first of many meals I'd like to share with you. I must insist that you join me…please."

"Insist?"

"Yes…I'll be awfully disappointed if you say no."

"I've already made plans for tonight."

"Break them."

"Break them?"

"I won't take no for an answer Ms. Summers. I never do."

"You never do?"

"Will you stop repeating everything the man says?" Jack interrupted. "He said break the date. Go to dinner. He insists. Don't say no. What's the problem? He think you skinny too. That's why he wants to feed you," Jack translated. I glared at him.

Ian's magnetism ricocheted throughout the room. People stopped eating and watched this spectacle. My curiosity couldn't resist his invitation. "Will this dinner be worth my while Mr. Lawford?"

"I certainly hope so and Mr. Prescott, I hate to contradict you but I think Ms. Summers looks perfectly lovely as she is."

"I'm intrigued," I cooed.

"No. What you are is very very beautiful and you must call me Ian."

"Thank you …Ian."

We agreed he'd pick me up. He repeated the hand kissing stuff. Jack and I stood.

"Ian…. what……?"

"7 sharp. Until tonight."

Tricked

Jack and I made our way to the elevators. Ian and half the restaurant watched our departure. When the elevator doors slid shut. Jack screamed, "Jack Pot!!"

"Who is he? I'm not going."

"What you mean you not going?"

"There's something spooky about him."

"Spooky? I don't know who he is, but I thought he was charming, all that hand kissing and take charge stuff. You the spooky one...talking bout men like pantyhose. Now that's scary! Don't tell nobody else that OK? You smart Cheeks, but sometimes you can say some wild sh...stuff. You want to wear the expensive brand. Why wear the drug store kind? Good gracious! They all run! You a trip. Now what you go do? Miss Don't Want To Wear No Cheap Stockings? Boom! There he is! If I thought he rode both sides of the pony, you wouldn't have to worry about Mr. Ian Lawford. I wouldn't be trippin. You work with money...but I know money!"

"You do?"

"Yeah baby! He's money!"

We laughed. Jack tipped the valet, pointed his Porsche toward my office and sped down San Jacinto Street. I considered Jack's convoluted points as he fired up his cell phone, dialing frantically. He was right. I wanted this kind of man and now that he's shown up, I'm scared.

"Hey Cliff. How you doing? Did you get that stuff I sent you? No problem man. I was glad to do it. Look, this hag has a date tonight with James freakin Bond. He's rich, British and reeks of class and money. I need the most elegant little black dress you have, shoes, jewels, everything...uh huh...8 narrow. The look has to scream 'what you see is under no circumstances what you get...at least not before you pay a whole lot of money for it," he cackled. "Can you pull something together? Yeah, she's still caught between a 4 and a 6...she said 6, but the cow wears a 4. OK. OK! Pull some things out for me and I'll come by in about a half an hour. Thank you darling."

Jack whipped out his notepad and began writing, driving with his knees. It was one of his many personality quirks. He documented everything. "Hello Romeo? Oh...Hi Kevin, is Romeo there? No...no...just ask him if he can squeeze the diva in this afternoon...He can?...About two thirty? Tell him hair. Manicure. Pedicure. Waxing. All of it. We'll see him then...huh?...OK. Yeah, he knows how Miss Thang is. Soft. Classy. Sexy. No Kevin. Kevin I ain't coming to your party. I don't know. I don't care. Kevin...I'm hanging up. I'm hanging up."

"Why do you treat him like that? Isn't it obvious that he likes you?"

"Chile please..."

"Jack, don't you like Kevin a little? He's always so kind and charming. He's cute too."

"I didn't say that I didn't like him and he's cute. I just don't want him to like me."

"So how do you let him know that you don't like him back?"

"Easy. I tell you to fuck off!"

"Jack!"

"I'm sorry baby. Excuse me. I know you hate cussing, but Kevin makes me sick with all that switching and shh...stuff. Gets on my nerves. Now shut up and let me make this last call. Hey Butch, yeah this is Jack. Please run a Ian Lawford. You go have to look international. He's taking out my baby and if he don't start nothin won't be nothin. OK, get back to me fast. All I know is that he's loaded. Yeah man, thanks."

Jack pulled in front of my building. He wrote out the afternoon's itinerary, we kissed and he yelled through the window, "I'll pick you up in an hour. Have one of your minions drop off your car. Don't be late. See ya!!"

"OK Jack. I love you!"

"I love you too baby. Just think, you could marry James Bond and y'all can put me up in the manner to which I aspire to become accustomed. He's got lots of rich friends over there in

Tricked

England who need their castles and flats redecorated. Baby I know money!" We both laughed and Jack sped down Elm.

CHAPTER FOUR

After Romeo and his exquisite staff finished with me, Jack and I hurried to my place. Romeo left my hair in rollers with specific instructions on how it should be styled. Jack ran his mouth and three red lights getting home. He'd only been driving for three years.

We parked and rushed upstairs. I was anxious to see the outfit he'd selected for my date. Jack's crew dressed women better than anyone. My taste is long. Theirs short. Real short. We argued 10 minutes about my seeing the dress before I conceded defeat.

Jack thought I should do the necessary cleaning before he unveiled the black confection. As perfumed oil and bubbles filled the tub, the doorman called.

"Yes," Jack spoke into the intercom.

"Is Ms. Summers available?"

"Who is it Jack?" I yelled from the bathroom.

"Pellman's downstairs. He needs to see you."

"Tell him I'll be right down."

"She'll be right down. Why can't that man leave you alone for one night?"

Jack scurried around the apartment making things beautiful and cursing. As I rode down, I thought about the day Jack and I became friends.

After three weeks in Dallas, and having not made any new friends, I read about one of those warehouses that sell high end designer clothes on Saturdays. We reached for the same orange silk scarf. We tugged and began laughing at each other. Neither of us bought the scarf, agreeing to have lunch instead at a nearby

Tricked

McDonalds. We became instant friends and inseparable from that day.

Our apartments were within walking distance. He cooked. I didn't. Jack had been a very talented up and coming interior decorator in New York City before coming to Dallas. He left New York after his lover died from complications due to AIDS. Unable to bare the pain of memories and loss, he came to Dallas with a portfolio of wonderful projects and dramatic references.

Finally finding acceptance in the very closed decorators market put Jack on the fast track. At least that's what the Dallas newspaper said in a profile it ran on him last year. "Prescott's talents are impressive. Original. Stylish. Creative. Innovative. Fresh." It wasn't long before he landed lucrative jobs in the most prestigious homes, stores and offices.

We'd celebrated at Cheyenne's about six months ago when one of Dallas' premier custom builders selected him to decorate all of his upscale model homes. With the retainer, Jack rented space for a new store in the elite decorator's district near downtown.

Pellman gave me a disk. A notebook. A large envelop. But he was adamant about my not allowing anyone access to the information. "I'll guard it with my life," I chuckled.

"It's not funny McClain," he said seriously.

Detecting his soberness, "Even I won't look unless you tell me." His mood changed. "It looks like you're getting ready to go somewhere special. Have a great time tonight. You deserve great times. Lots of them." There was a lingering pause. "There's something I must say. McClain, live your life with passion. No matter what the circumstances, maintain your integrity, and be extremely careful. Very careful. I'll miss you."

"Have a great vacation partner," I smiled, trying to assure him against whatever he feared. "I'll see you when you get back. Don't worry about anything."

"I'll call you," he smiled.

"OK"

Then he grabbed me, hugging me tightly. That surprised me. His car pulled down the street and out of view. My hiding place behind the fire extinguisher in the parking garage was empty so I put the information there. I'd get it when Jack left.

Jack was livid when I got back upstairs. "That man can't even go on vacation without bothering you. What did he want?"

"Just business," I yelled, walking back into the bathroom. "Will you let me see the dress?" I shouted.

"No," Jack pulled the dress from the garment bag, hanging it on my closet door.

"I don't have to ask you to let me see my own stuff. I'm coming out of there and ..."

"Here it is Miss Thang! Don't have a fit."

"Oooooh Jack ...I loooove this dress."

"Me too! We've got good taste don't we? I'm go wear it next week, so don't get it funky tonight," Jack laughed.

"Cliff's wonderful. Should I try it on?"

"Cliff hell. I picked out this dress and you owe me $2,500.00. I charged it. You might need to try the shoes though." Jack took the dress and laid it on the bed. I pulled the shoes from two felt bags.

"Ooooooh Jack. I loooooove these shoes."

"I didn't see them. Cliff chose those. Let me see! Let me see! Oh yeah. They look good on your feet too. You have the prettiest feet. How can you be so pretty all over? Do you have any flaws?"

"Yep...make sure you tell Cliff I want to buy these. How much are they?"

"Wait a minute......let me see......$998.65. They were on sale."

"998 dollars?! On sale!"

"Yeah dollars! What you think? You work with money all day, asking me if the shoes cost 998 dollars. Cliff don't work at PayLittle Shoe Source! The Shoe Circus! Pick A Shoe! You making big money. Buy the shoes and stop being so cheap. You'd think you grew up poor. Y'all had money and you making crazy money now. Stop crying about how much the shoes cost."

"Yeah but $998.65 for shoes? But they are perfect for that dress aren't they?"

"Lord have mercy," Jack sighed, walking back into the living room.

It was 5:45 when I stepped into a tub of bubbly hot water. Jack ran in and out of the bathroom cursing and asking about jewelry, perfume, makeup and a black beaded shawl I wore to his New Year's Eve party. The water's gentle caress relaxed me, plunging me into thoughts about my life. Family. Work. Promotion. Responsibilities. Opportunities. Ian.

My first days at RJP were excruciating. Not knowing anyone in Dallas or Texas for that matter, I believed that I'd become friends with the other members in my executive training course. Yet somehow they always forgot to invite me to the dinners. Study sessions. Drinks. Get togethers.

Being the first African American to work as a RJP executive, I was prepared for resistance but total exclusion surprised me. I was on my own.

Committed to success, I wouldn't fail. I couldn't. If the trainer said read 10 pages, I read 50. If the trainer gave us 50 problems, I did 150. If we got 5 statistical issues to research, I researched 20. I had to be the first. The best. Flawless.

My proficiencies and tenacity delighted Pellman and attracted the interest of one of the firm's wealthiest clients, Bate Shoemaker. He was founder, president and CEO of a prominent multinational investment conglomerate with massive chemical and technology holdings. Impressed with work I'd done trampling his chief competitor; he asked Pellman if I could do a training session for his New York City investment group. I did.

It didn't take long to show his stiff staff I knew my stuff. Realizing that, they eagerly participated, lingering afterwards to congratulate me for making their training fun and informative. RJP received glowing reports. I received an all expense paid trip to Fiji.

Later that same year I saw Mr. Shoemaker at our office Christmas party. "Merry Christmas McClain. Why don't you join me for a drink?" He already seemed a little drunk as we nudged our way through the crowded party. We found two empty chairs and before I was comfortably settled, he asked me for sex. I was so surprised I almost spit pineapple juice all over him. I promptly found a reason to be somewhere else. "Wow!"

Shoemaker approached me again the following year, offering me a job running one of his pharmaceutical companies. He promised to double my salary, provide a huge block of stocks, finance the home of my choice, and every perk imaginable. He wasn't drunk this time. "Is sex a component of this generous offer?" "Of course. You're exquisite."

"Rest assured Mr. Shoemaker, if you ever approach me in this manner again, my singular ambition will be your complete personal and financial obliteration. It is a threat I am perfectly capable of implementing. Do *not* play with me. Neither should you underestimate my tenacity or my ingenuity. The results of your ruin will be unimaginable. You should fear me. Deeply." He smiled and walked away.

Pellman was furious when I told him about the conversation. Later that night I saw them on the balcony having stern words. Shoemaker apologized with flowers. I still made a number of trips to his offices in New York and Pellman urged me to keep the incident to myself. "It gives you an advantage."

CHAPTER FIVE

"Hey! You go stay in there all night? It's almost 6:30. You don't want to be a prune do ya!" Jack yelled from the kitchen.

"Give me a couple more minutes Jack."

"You don't have a couple mo minutes. Get out that tub! You can take all the baths you want when we get to the castle! Come on girl! I still got to do your face. You got to get dressed and do your hair. You know I can't stand frantic. Now get out!" Jack threw a large towel at me and left the bathroom cursing.

I sat on the edge of the tub, turning the swan shaped brass water fixtures to get the rest of the bubbles out. Jack insisted that I buy them. Aside from the great view, Jack's keen decorating sense increased the value of my home substantially.

Jack kept everything rich, but light. He used wonderful creams and pastels with bright flashes of color to create the ambiance I enjoyed everyday.

One of the best views of the Dallas skyline could be viewed from my balcony. Jack transformed it into a wonderfully luscious Mediterranean garden. My bedroom was soft and elegantly feminine, without being a shrine to flowery prints. "A woman's bedroom should be like a web. Delicate. Intricate. Deadly."

Dallas Life Magazine featured him and my home in a featured pictorial. People from the office tripped over their lips as their jaws dropped upon seeing the sheer splendor he created. They were stunned and jealous. I explained, "Jack is a creative visionary. Talented. Gifted." Resultantly, he received numerous beneficial referrals. My resale value doubled.

Success gave Jack access to the good life. He moved into the building two years ago after negotiating an outstanding deal that included his decorating the previous owner's hunting lodge. He lived on 4. I lived on 20. We were neighbors again and constantly in each other's business.

"You're 28 years old and on the ugly side of finding any kind of husband. You go wind up having one of those squirt babies if you don't get chosen. You work too much and I'll never become an uncle." Jack was determined to get me married and was frustrated that I wasn't frustrated too.

He believed I had limited or no male companionship. Not being a man junky, or feeling something was missing from my life because I wasn't in a steady relationship, I always told Jack I was completely satisfied. "You lying," he'd snarl.

Cigarette smoke kept me out of clubs, so I typically met men through people at work or friends. Someone always had a crazy brother or scary friend coming to town for the weekend and we always had "So much in common."

Very interesting men were currently in my life. They wanted more than I could give. I wanted more than they had. My work always came first and I saw them on my terms, or not at all.

CHAPTER SIX

RICK was every mother's dream for their daughter. Totally committed to his family. Gentle. Kind. Warm. Funny. Respectful and responsible. Every Sunday he had dinner at his parent's home in Oak Cliff and he called his mother daily. She was extremely nice, but perpetually distant. A trait I've found in southern women not generally shared by their northern sisters. Having never passed inspection, she was cautious about my involvement with her favorite child.

Meeting his father was all the evidence I needed to conclude that Rick's genuine kindness was inherited. Mr. Collins was a big man with a grand piano for a smile. His commanding voice dominated every space. His laugher was like fireworks. Loud. Thunderous. Bright. Brilliant. He never met a stranger. People liked him. His family. His home.

Mr. Collins was that father who yelled loudest from the stands whether his children won or lost. "I yell because they tried. Failure is in having no courage. I taught my kids that no matter what they do, they must face the choices they make with the courage to accept the consequences."

Mrs. Collins never worked outside the home. This was odd to me. As a child, everyone's mother worked. Somewhere. They were teachers. Postal workers. Nurses. Counselors. Beauticians. Clerks. Something. The only children whose mothers didn't work were on television or welfare.

Sundays were like being in the middle of the Black Waltons. Clevers. Adams. Munsters. I told Jack all about them. He always said, "Mrs. Collins is probably doing the next-door neighbor and Mr. Collins is probably gay." Jack thought everybody was a little gay.

My parents divorced when I was two. They married while still in college. From the pictures my mother hid under her bed, they seemed very much in love. He was a mechanical engineer. She was an accountant. The judge decided she should keep me and we moved to Milwaukee from Pittsburgh for a fresh start. I never saw my father again.

They hated each other for unexplained reasons, but he always paid child support. Having never missed a payment, we lived a very nice lifestyle. "Middle-class" is how my mother described it. I cherished each plain envelope containing the money orders as though they were the most fascinating correspondences ever mailed. They meant everything to me since I heard so many stories about men who didn't support their children. I grew up knowing mine supported me. This was his way of proving it.

I secretly mailed him every report card. School day photo. Certificates. Letters. Father's day cards. Birthday and holiday cards. Being a very busy man, he didn't have time to reply, but he never missed sending those checks. It was all the proof I needed.

Apparently, my father filed for divorce. This devastated my mother. Childhood whispers suggested a misunderstanding led to the break up. There were even rumors that I wasn't his child. His family acted as though I didn't exist, and mother never answered one curious question. Our house was large and quiet. She lived only to protect herself from further hurt. From me.

Periodically, I heard her sobbing late into the night. I'd sit outside her locked bedroom door crying for her. With her. She must have loved him deeply. Me too.

Unfortunately for me, behind the same emotional doors she barricaded to protect herself, lives the unconditional treasure of a mother's love. Where acceptance abounds, defining a child's essence and validating its being.

Hardened from hurt of lost love, miserable from family rejection and passionless for life, she was incapable of demonstrating the least bit of unsolicited affection towards me. I understood. I think.

Over the years she appeared increasingly bitter. She never dated, although still very beautiful. "Beauty is a trap." She hated when men looked at her. Me. Us.

Rick felt awful. "Something about her must be wonderful, she raised you." He hugged me saying, "You'll meet your father one day. I'm sure of it. You never know, maybe he's looking for you right now."

He was a professional trainer who exercised the best and wealthiest bodies in Dallas. With the financial backing of several rich clients, Rick was opening a gym in North Dallas. It would be a certain success.

We met at a detail shop on East Grand near White Rock Lake, where I admired his vintage `57 Mercedes coupe. He introduced me to camping. Fishing. High air ballooning. But I refused to go out on his boat. I never go on boats. He loved to talk. Laugh. Joke. Exercise.

Standing six feet three inches tall and 5% body fat, he had the prettiest legs I'd ever seen on a man. Bright brown eyes smoldered behind long dark eyelashes. They were his most attractive feature. Every morning at precisely 5:00 a.m. he'd call to remind me to do at least 30 crunches. "OK." Then I'd usually turn over and go back to sleep for another 30 minutes.

Sex was not an issue. Yet. "The most important thing to me in a relationship is the relationship. Sex clouds issues and keeps people from really discovering each other. The fun for me is developing the friendship. I want to know who you are McClain. I want you to know me. If it happens, it happens. It's not why I'm interested in you." I liked that too. Our intimacy was restricted to loving kisses. Long talks. Intimate hugs.

Last fall Rick planned a romantic weekend, roughing it in Colorado. When he told me his entire family wouldn't be coming too, I relaxed. He explained that he wanted to spend quiet time alone with me.

We were on the interstate by 4:30 a.m. He reached into the backseat pulling out a brightly wrapped box, tossing it onto my lap. Inside was a pair of hiking boots. We laughed. Everyone knows how much I hate walking. We were off to Colorado for a long four-day weekend.

Although we were having a great time, the 10-hour drive had taken its toll on me. Sometimes it harder being the passenger than the driver. Rick refused to let me drive. "I want you to relax and enjoy the scenery."

The sun had almost set behind the mountains by the time we reached the cabin. It was cold and dark. Before we left, Rick told me telephones and televisions were not allowed. Of course I packed my cell phone. Laptop and three movies. "Does this cabin have a bathroom?" I asked.

He laughed, pointing up and to the right. He gave me a flashlight and said, "Be careful."

I felt my way back downstairs and sat on the couch. Rick brought supplies from the car. I felt bad not helping, but I was tired. He made three trips and a fourth to bring in cords of wood for the fireplace. As the fire crackled, I dozed off.

When Rick woke me, the cabin was transformed. It was absolutely gorgeous. Lights shone brightly. He'd turned on the generator. Regular electricity would kick on in the morning. His descriptions failed to adequately describe this perfection. Rustic and elegant at the same time.

A magnificent two story stone fireplace was the centerpiece of the main living area. Overstuffed furniture combined with rugged leather upholstered pieces, complimented rare Navaho rugs and Native American pottery that lined the overhangs. The walls and ceiling were natural pine with exposed log beams. The floors were pine too, covered with magnificent rugs. Western artwork and wonderful collectables filled cases and tables.

Ultra modern is the best way to describe the kitchen and an elegant chandelier made of antlers complimented the dining room. There were no blinds. No curtains. "The bedrooms are upstairs," Rick offered.

Tricked

"It's really easy to see why this place means so much to you. It's perfect."

"It means a lot to me and I wanted to share it with you."

"Is something cooking?"

"Yeah. I thought you might be hungry," he said going back to the kitchen.

"I am."

"It'll be ready in a little while."

Cooking was not my thing. So while he cooked, I took a bath. He'd cleaned it. It smelled fresh. Clean. Lemony. A true outdoorsman, I laughed to myself.

Hot water cascaded into the claw foot tub and I submerged myself into hot oily water. I don't know how long it was before Rick knocked on the door. "Come in."

Careful to divert his eyes, he asked, "Did you find everything?"

"Yes."

"Dinner will be ready in about 10 minutes."

"Smells good."

"So do you."

We ate the tasty meal as Rick explained our itinerary for the weekend. He insisted on cleaning the kitchen and we sat in front of the fire. I eased into Rick's arms and closed my eyes. He knew that I wasn't asleep as he smelled my hair. Kissed my head. He read Keats softly. Quietly. Thoughtfully. This was perfection. I clung to him. He liked that. Although it was only about 9:30, I fell soundly asleep, again.

When I woke, I was in bed and Rick was gone. It was 7:15 a.m. Where was he? I wrapped myself in a quilt and jogged downstairs. Rick's cabin sat about 100 yards from the tranquil splendor of a marvelously mirrored lake. Towering trees engaged in a colorful competition for best dressed at the autumn dance. Chirping birds orchestrated the music while acrobatic squirrels practiced their high wire act in the treetops.

Acorns tapped the top of the Jeep calling the meeting to order. I'd imposed on something majestic. Peaceful. Serene. It looked like one of those pictures on the insurance man's calendar my mother hung on the back of the bathroom door.

Rick sat at the end of the dock, staring out across the lake at the mountains. A misty fog hovered near the surface, enveloping him. He was home. Why hadn't I allowed myself to become intimate with this lovely man? No matter how wonderful he seemed, there was something about him. Something holding me back. Something hidden. Something that compelled me to proceed with caution. I was being ridiculous, but I always trust my instincts. I walked back into the cabin leaving him with his thoughts. Peace. Calm.

We planned a private celebration tonight. His grand opening is tomorrow. Disappointed, he said, "You'll have to make this up to me in the morning."

"How?"

"Fishing," he smiled.

"Will there be enough time?"

"There's always time to fish. I'll pick you up at 7."

"7:30 and I'll cook breakfast."

"7:15 and I'll bring breakfast. Call me when you get home."

"If its not too late. Bye."

CHAPTER SEVEN

KEITH attended RJP functions with me. He is well groomed. Articulate. Stiff. Self-centered. Boring. Newly hired as executive vice president of research and development at Ross Industries, he stepped on everyone in his path to get there. No condemnation from me. Just not my style.

Keith was the current president of the Dallas Association of Black Republicans. He passionately argued that the Republican Party articulated the only valid solutions to economic problems facing Black Americans specifically, and other minorities in general. "No one ever discriminated against me. I worked for everything I have. Excellence made me successful. Not handouts. Whether you're black, white or other, you need to get up off your lazy behind, find some morality, stop having babies and get a job. Stop looking for handouts. No one's listening. There is no great society."

I never considered his positions particularly republican. I grew up with the notion that if you don't work, you don't eat. Characterizing everyone who suggests the racist threads woven throughout the fiber of our nation's consciousness might account for at least part of the plight of many less fortunate people, as whiners looking to blame others for their misery, was illogical. Specious. Unscientific.

There was no place in his erudite world of "Arrival" for me. Standing on the shoulders of ebony soldiers and working with the super rich gave me priceless access to an eagle's eye view of their world. Mindset. Expectations. Every man for himself was not the credo of the uber-rich. They knew how to keep the money among themselves and helped everyone in their circle gain access to it. As a people, we hadn't learned that. They knew it and proselytized the concept of the self made man to the masses.

One night he tried to impress me with an invitation to dinner at one of Dallas' premier restaurants. He didn't tell me that that little bald-headed black midget with the radio talk show was joining us. You've seen him. He's the one Republicans like to strut out as proof of their commitment to including African Americans in their 'big tent.' Every circus needs a clown.

Anti-republicanism never seized my thoughts. I wasn't liberal. I was logical. Realistic. Practical. Pragmatic. I understood numbers and how well they're manipulated to prove a point or gain an edge. There's money in poverty. Inequality yields big profits. Always did. Always will. If there was no economic benefit to racism or poverty, it wouldn't exist.

Recruiting as many Black and other minority kids into the International Finance Analyst Program I created was a goal. If I didn't do it, it wouldn't be done. Over the past two years my program became the best and most diverse in the world.

The in-house program was a war zone. I took no prisoners. It challenged. Critiqued. Convinced. Pushed. Pressed. Pulled. Student's tried to out think me. Out create me. Out manage me. They left the course with revved up intellects, more excited about the game than the money. It was OK to imagine. Dream. Work.

Executives, who successfully completed the class, found that their marketability increased dynamically. Many wrote their own ticket to better positions. Most stayed. Some perished.

Ultimate approval of executives who qualified for the course was exclusively mine. Pellman evaluated all middle and upper management scores. Incidentally, it was an unwritten rule that no one walked the corridors of RJP upper management if they failed the course.

Such power must be handled carefully. But I knew I didn't do this alone. Generations lifted me. Believing my efforts would blaze trails for others, I withstood RJP's madness. Those following

Tricked

in my footsteps might not have to prove themselves with the same difficulties and scrutiny I faced. But I withstood Keith's stupidity and listened as he regurgitated this nonsense at RJP events. My bosses perceived him as centered and intelligent. It's always about perception in corporate America. Isn't it?

As executive vice president at Ross Industries, Keith shot RJP the lucrative long-range financial planning and securities development business. Pellman attributed my presence at the firm to this great deal. We promised to make the huge pharmaceutical company larger.

Years prior Pellman played a key role in organizing Ross Industries for Sims Chemical. Ross manufactured revolutionary breakthrough drugs for heart disease and diabetes management. Ross Industries merged with Sims Chemicals five years ago. The Ross deal led me to the discrepancies I'd been researching. It appeared that several major shareholders with huge holdings in Sims' company were virtually unidentifiable. I asked Keith if he could get me some information about the merger. He said he'd give me the info when he picked me up for dinner about a month later.

When I came downstairs, two people sat in the backseat of his car. Before I could ask, he explained, "My parents are in town and I hope you don't mind them joining us for dinner. Do you?" I did and I was furious. They'd arrived in Dallas on their way to a convention in San Francisco.

His mother was a walking advertisement for the exclusive boutique set. She did the elevator dance with smiling eyes. His father said, "So you're the young lady who's been turning our boys head. He's told us a lot of good things about you. I hope they're true. You live in a beautiful building, just like he said. He has good taste. Just like his father."

"I love your outfit. Donna Karan?" his mother asked.

"No." I smiled, turning around in the front seat, fuming. This was an ambush.

Keith babbled about a special project he'd recently been put in charge of. I tuned out the entire discussion as the radio played my favorite song. "Keith, will you turn the music down?" his father asked. He turned it off. I cringed.

We sped down Turtle Creek toward Keith's favorite restaurant as they chattered endlessly about people I didn't know or care about.

Keith's parents remarked about his new house and my building. His mother said, "We're certainly glad to see that the struggles of our generation endured, allowing your generation to achieve such blinding success." That blew my mind. Keith was such a staunch "I Did It All By My Selfer." His mother explained that his grandfather made millions in the penny insurance business, ripping off poor black folks throughout the south. I added that part.

His parents didn't participate in any civil rights activities of the 60's until it was trendy for Atlanta's upper black middle class to be involved. It was a poor people's movement. They weren't poor.

"Do you think we can come up later and take a look at your home? Keith tells us it's just fabulous," his mother cooed, as we walked into the restaurant. Before I could answer, "Yeah! It makes my place look like a dump," Keith laughed, grabbing my shoulder pulling me to him as if he'd paid for it.

I made every excuse why they couldn't. Shouldn't. But it was crystal clear they were determined to check me out. After being seated, I excused myself to the ladies room to call Jack. "Where the hell have you been? I've been calling you forever," I snapped.

"What's the matter with you? I *do* work you know," he said with a tired voice.

"I'm out with Keith and his parents. They want to come by and see my place after dinner."

"So what?"

"Jack, they're looking at me, like I'm some kind of spavined horse. I'm expecting his father to ask me to open my mouth any minute so he can check my teeth. They're interviewing me to see if I'm good enough for their stupid son. I'm furious! Come get me!" I insisted.

Tricked

"Wait a minute Cheeks. Let me think. Let me think. Calm down. Did I hear you say the "H" word? This *is* serious if they got you cussin," he chuckled. "And what the hell is a spavined horse? Haven't I told you to stop using words don't nobody know but you? Jack will take care of everything. Go back in there and eat your dinner and bring them back here when you finish," he laughed.

"What are you gonna do?"

"I'm go do what I do. Now go back in there and eat some macaroni and cheese. Sweet potato pie. Pound cake. Mashed potatoes. Bread. Ham hocks. Something," he yawned.

"Thanks Jack," I laughed. "I knew I could depend on you."

"Yeah. Yeah. Yeah. I always have to do your dirty work," he yawned. "Ain't no rest for the weary. Where'd I put your key?"

I hung up and rejoined my party with a new attitude. I was utterly charming. Exuberant. Vivacious. We ate, using our best table etiquette and polite conversation. I charmingly complimented his mother's handbag and haircut. She was thrilled. I told his father how much I respected Keith's mind. He was impressed. Everyone was happy.

While the waiter served lobster bisque, Keith served tidbits of my resume. I wondered what 'Ms. Thing and Mr. Just Like My Wife' would think if they knew what Jack was cooking up. I wondered what he was cooking up too.

Keith was ready to find a wife to top the tree of his success. She had to be educated. Beautiful. She had to be as impressed with him as he was with himself. Women were overwhelmed by his charm. Pens. Suits. Shoes. Cars. Home. Plane. Status. Spontaneity. Personality. Florist account. He swept them off their feet and primed them for his bidding. Smart girls became dumb in their efforts to win his heart. So what could he possibly want with me?

I kept Keith around because I liked his mind and he freely provided information about Ross Industries. He was only too happy to tell me about pending research. I never considered it insider information since he was careful not to be specific. I was just smart enough to connect the dots.

When we arrived back at my building, I implored Keith's family not to come up, or at least allow me to invite them over for dinner on their next trip to Dallas. Keith gently patted my hand assuring me that everything was fine. "They just left my place. Everything was a mess. Your place always looks fabulous. I told them the view from your terrace is among the most breathtaking in the Metroplex." I managed a smile because I knew Jack was creating something just as eye popping inside.

"I'll only be here for a little while Mike," Keith said, as the doorman opened the door for his parents.

"OK sir, I'll pull it right over there if you don't mind. Good evening Ms. Summers."

"No problem." Keith pressed $20 into Mike's hand.

His parents hunched each other upon entering the impressive lobby. Surrounded by the confines of the sumptuous elevator we sped upward. Upon reaching my double doors, I warned them about the condition of my place again, and asked them to allow me to go in first. "You're being much too sensitive. We're more interested in seeing the views Keith keeps raving about than anything else." When we stepped inside, I was thrilled.

Dimmed lights greeted us. Five eight inch ball shaped gardenia and jasmine scented candles gave the room a sensual glow and luxurious aroma. Soft music wafted through the room and a bottle of champagne I gave Jack for his birthday, nestled itself inside a splendid crystal ice bucket. Two unbelievably beautiful art deco champagne flutes lingered on the cocktail table, while a sparkling fire crackled in the fireplace.

A sterling silver tray embraced mounds of scrumptious strawberries along with three small cruets holding honey, whipped cream and chocolate syrup atop a luscious white fur rug.

They were stunned. I briskly walked around turning on lights and the turning the C.D player off. Keith was stricken. Acting embarrassed, I rushed into the kitchen with the champagne bucket, yelling, "Would anyone like coffee?"

"Black," his father answered in a disapproving voice.

Tricked

I came back to the living room with a tray of dessert cookies. I grabbed the tray of strawberries and cruets and walked away. Mrs. Lewis said, "What's going on Keith?"

"I don't know."

"What was all of that?"

"I told you I don't know."

"I know." It was Mr. Lewis. "We walked in on something we weren't supposed to see. She didn't know we were going to dinner with you tonight did she?"

"No."

"Umm Hmmm. I guess she had some other kind of dessert planned....I"

"Hush Andy...she might hear you."

"I don't care. Keith we tried to teach you about common women. Common don't mean you don't have money. It means you don't have morals. You weren't raised like this. You should only associate with young women of the highest breeding. I'll admit your Ms. Summers is very beautiful. Alluring. But son, any young woman who'd create this kind of scene without being married, well...this just ain't Christian."

"Look at the stuff in this place. How much did it cost?" his mother whispered, "Are you sure what she does is legal?"

"Mother!" Keith said sternly. "I told you she has a terrific job. She makes more money than me. She's loaded. Good breeding? What does that mean? This isn't the 50s. Momma you're one generation off the farm, and daddy you know you married momma because you got her pregnant while she was at Spelman. If you want to talk about proper, how proper is it for you to ask how much a person's house costs if you're not going to pay the note?"

"Keith!" his father snapped.

"Be quiet," Mrs. Lewis whispered. "She'll hear you."

"That was a long time ago and you will not speak to us like that," his father commanded.

"Look. I'm grown. She's grown. This has never happened before and I've already explained told you that her best friend is an interior decorator. He decorated it for a spread one of those Dallas

55

magazines. He probably got most of this stuff at cost," Keith explained.

"Umph...How close is she to him? What kind of freak show is she running out of here?" his father asked.

"She's not running a freak show dad. I'm as surprised as you are. As for the homo, they're really close, like family."

"You'll need to get rid of him. Do you think we can see the rest of it?" his mother insisted.

"Keith, if your mother would like to see the rest of my place, please show her," I bellowed from the kitchen.

Mrs. Lewis eagerly bounced from the couch as Keith directed her down the hallway toward the master bedroom. I returned to the living room with a pot of coffee. Sugar. Cream. Cups. Saucers. Napkins. "I really think we should leave," his father said.

"No....no sir...it's certainly no intrusion," I stuttered. "I forgot spoons. I'll be right back."

"May I help?" Keith yelled.

"No, show your mother around."

When I supposed Keith and his mother were about to reach my bedroom, I darted from the kitchen across the living room toward the bedroom. Keith's father jumped as I jetted past him.

As they stepped inside, I laughed. Jack was crazy. He'd sprinkled the bed with pink and red rose petals. The room smelled of my expensive tuber rose sachet. A video camera sat on a tripod at the end of the bed. A half full box of prophylactics (extra-large) and an almost empty tube of K-Y jelly were on the nightstand, with a huge silver vibrator and handcuffs. A deep rose silk mesh teddy (the nasty kind) lay on the bed. "What was Jack doing with that?"

Keith's mother was horrified. She grabbed her chest and backed out of the room as though they'd seen a dead body. I thought she'd croak right there. Then I proceeded to give the best performance of an actress in a leading role in a drama or mini series. "I hope this doesn't give you the wrong impression of me," I whimpered softly.

Tricked

"No dear...uh...I...uh....," she murmured walking back to the living room.

"I'm sorry Keith. I tried to tell you. I've never been so humiliated in my life. It's just that we've been seeing each other for about six months now and when you called about dinner, I thought..." It was all that I could do not to laugh.

Keith gently tilted my face upward. "It's been two years baby and I don't hate you, quite the contrary." he said softly. "My parents will be fine. I just wish they hadn't come today. Why didn't you tell me?"

"I wanted you to be surprised."

"I am!" he laughed. "Let me take them to my place, then I'll come right back."

"No. That would be rude and I'm too embarrassed to do anything now."

"You don't have anything to be embarrassed about. I might know a few things that would surprise you. I want this to happen. I need this to happen. Maybe not the vibrator part, but McClain please baby...please let me come back?" He was begging.

"Do you think your mother saw the vibrator?"

"Hell yeah she saw it. Where did you get that?"

I convinced him that the mood was broken. We promised to talk later. He kissed my cheek and we walked into the living room like a couple of kids who'd just been caught with their hands in the nookie jar. Before I could apologize, Mrs. Lewis spoke. "We really love your home McClain. It's as beautiful as Keith said."

"Thank you Mrs. Lewis...I'd like to explain..."

"We need to go," his father said standing, interrupting me in mid explanation. "Maybe next time it'll be under different circumstances." He gently helped his wife from the couch.

"Yes sir...but...all I was trying to say..."

"Everything's perfectly clear. It's getting late and we have an early flight tomorrow. Keith," he said sternly.

"I'll call you later OK?" Keith whispered, kissing my cheek.

"Thanks for dinner."

Cynthia A. Minor

They never saw the view from my terrace. Mr. Lewis' pen was on the couch. I didn't want Keith to have any excuse to come back. So I grabbed it and ran down the hallway shouting, "Rev. Lewis!!! You forgot your pen."

As soon as the elevator doors closed, I called Jack. He rushed upstairs while I waited for him by the door. We fell inside laughing hysterically. Jack made me give him the rubbers, bottle of champagne, teddy, strawberries, vibrator and K-Y Jelly. He took his camera, cruets and fur rug too. The handcuffs were mine.

"You a freak! I knew it all along. You one of them bondage freaks ain't ya? UmmmmHum," Jack laughed. He wanted every detail. He hollered. He screamed. He rolled around on the floor holding his sides, turning red. I laughed just as insanely. In the middle of it all, the telephone rang. It was Keith. We froze. The answering machine picked up.

Keith said, "McClain, let me come back. Baby are you asleep? McClain! Call me when you get this message. I don't care what time it is. Call me." Jack and I looked at each other, looked at the vibrator and we both fell out laughing again.

CHAPTER EIGHT

MATTHEW was a paralegal at Conley & Mason. Crucial clues regarding Sims' former company had to be stored in their vast legal diaries. I had to find them.

Three years ago I noticed discrepancies in raw data associated with an international conglomerate, RossCorp, one of Shoemaker's most lucrative holdings. Conflicting information, Shoemaker's amoral behavior and the dead ends led me to explore other deals he made years earlier.

RossCorp apparently bought Sims Chemicals right around the time Pellman graduated from Harvard. Sims Chemical merged with Ross Chemicals, a subsidiary of Ross Industries and major military contractor.

Millions of dollars were traded, but no one in LA, Dallas, New York or Chicago had any historical data reflecting who owned the stocks or where the trades occurred. Tracking the patterns contained in RJP databases looked suspiciously like my Wharton hypothesis. It was inconceivable that anyone would actually attempt to use this theory in a practical environment, but the similarities were striking. I dismissed my hunch and looked for answers elsewhere.

Internal investigators sent multiple reports to my office indicating that my discoveries were no more than electronic anomalies. The information systems manager agreed, indicating they would delete the glitches from our mainframes. I didn't believe that, so I pumped Keith for information about the chemical giant.

Keith said Ross Chemicals was nervous about the RossCorp takeover rumors. Billions were at stake. I asked him whether anything came up that caught his attention. "How would a takeover affect the value of your company?"

"You must be referring to the offshore hedge accounts our investigators found."

"What offshore accounts?"

"We heard rumors that old man Sims developed some offshore accounts in the 60's. He failed to disclose some important information during Shoemaker's acquisition of Sims Chemicals. That kind of stuff wouldn't fly today, but somehow Shoemaker worked some magic with the SEC and they approved the deal."

"What were the feds looking for?"

"Something about wealthy investors manipulating or hiding stocks. We checked it out and found nothing. Crazy idea. If I remember correctly, someone who worked for Sims was involved in a lawsuit about valuations. The case was settled, dismissed or something. Conley & Mason defended the suit. They should have the file. There are rumors right now that we're about to be sold to a multinational group. Our investors are nervous. Do you know anything about that?"

"No. Who filed the lawsuit?"

"Hmmm. I think the man's name was Calhoun. Yeah, Calhoun."

Calhoun was a major piece of the puzzle. We had no records identifying anyone by his name. A brief search proved another dead end. Calhoun was dead. All records about his claims were sealed and no other information about the case was known or documented. "Why were the records sealed?" I asked.

"I don't know."

"Who would?"

"Conley & Mason?"

Barry Fisher was a partner at C & M. We met at a seminar on ethics. Discovering neither of us had any, we became good friends. We met every Thursday for lunch, trading information and watching each other's professional backs. Barry is one of those brother's who a lot of women thought were cute in the 80's. Somehow in the 90's they went out of style. He was bright (That's the way my mother described light skinned black people) with thick wavy hair. He was as good looking as a man can be without being a woman. We went out a couple of times as friends, no romance. I have a personal preference for browner brothers. They look better wet.

He charged me with being color struck, so to repent my prejudiced ways, I introduced him to beautiful women, including my friend Lita Boudreaux. Barry appreciated my selections and tried on many occasions to reciprocate. Barry and Lita had a sizzling relationship that went up in smoke about three months ago. Lita wanted marriage. Barry wanted to play. Consequently, I never introduced him to anyone I wanted to keep as a friend.

"Hey Barry. McClain. Have you found that file I asked you about?"

"Yeah. I had to go to east hell to find it. There must be some dynamite in there. What do you want with it? The file has an internal memo attached that says no one is supposed to see the file except Conley & Mason themselves. Anyone who even asks about the file is to be reported to Mr. Mason himself."

"So how did you get it?"

"I'm Barry baby! Plus I promised the file room clerk that I'd let her cook me something hot for dinner. The things I do for friends," he chuckled.

"Well I owe you. When can I pick it up?"

"You owe me, but you can't pick it up."

"Why not?"

"Can't risk it. I'll send it over with one of our paralegals. He remains with the file McClain, no matter what. I trust him and he's my boy! He can stay as long as you need the file. As long as you don't need it after today. I've got to get it back, or my ......"

"Yeah I know. Have you read any of it?"

"Hell no! Don't have time. Not interested. I'm preparing for a trial next week. I have to work for my money. The paralegal's name is Matthew Pierce. He's a good guy. Used to be a cop.

Don't try to steam roll him about this file, and don't give him no shit either."

"Would I do that?" We agreed I would.

"By the way, one of my frats is coming to town in a few months. He's a doctor on the east coast. Clarence Whitaker. I'm throwing a brisket and a turkey on the smoker and inviting some people over. Bring your pretty little brown self over. One of your friends too. I told him all about you. Y'all have lots in common. Will you be in town?"

"I'll let you know Barry. You know how it is."

"Yep. If you're in town, show up."

"I'll try. What time shall I expect Matthew?"

"He's on his way."

"Thanks Barry."

"No problem."

I instructed my secretary to hold all my calls and cancel any appointments "I'll be doing research late into the evening and unless it's an emergency, let Donohue handle whatever comes up."

"Do you want me to order lunch for you?" Sandy asked.

"Nope, thanks. Why don't you go while things are calm? The weather could change any moment."

"You're right," she giggled. "Are you sure you don't want anything?"

"I'm sure."

"See you in an hour."

"Take your time." I retrieved my USB and put it into my laptop and listened to my e-mail. Dr. Stovall called. Why hadn't Sandy told me? I needed to return his call. His housekeeper answered. "He's out at the cottage this week. He said if you called, please call him right away. It's urgent. He didn't leave a number, but said he sent you a letter. You should have received it today."

"Hold on." I looked through the stack of letters on Sandy's desk. It was there. "I have it. Thank you very much."

"He sounded funny Ms. Summers. Don't forget to call him."

"I'll try right now."

"Excellent. Good bye."

"Good bye."

"Is this my favorite professor?"

"Are you on a secured phone?" he asked.

"No. I'm at the office." I was happy to hear his voice.

"Can you get to a secured telephone?"

"What's wrong?"

"I'll explain everything when you call back. Be careful my dear."

"Careful about what?"

"We'll speak later."

"I'll call you tonight."

"Until tonight."

"OK."

With only one day to read the file, I had to work fast. Dr. Stovall was always quirky, so I dismissed his mysterious warning and shoved the letter into my backpack.

Sandy's box was full of letters, needing answers. I dictated responses to clear my desk before Mr. Pierce arrived with the file.

Sandy returned in about 40 minutes. She peeked in the door saying, "I saw this and thought you'd like it." She handed me a carrot muffin and a green apple.

"Thanks Sandy. I told you..."

"I know what you told me, but I know how you get when you start researching. You forget about everything, including eating. I'm going to warm this in the microwave and bring you some tea and you're going to eat!"

"Excuse me, are you Ms. Summers? I didn't see your secretary and the receptionist told me I could come back. My name is Matthew Pierce. Barry Fisher sent me from Conley & Mason."

"Oh yes. Come in. I'm McClain Summers." I extended my hand. He shook it gently. Can I get you something? Coffee? Coke?"

"No...no thank you," he said, looking around. "You have a lovely office."

"Thanks. I like it. The file?"

"Of course. I didn't mean to…" He rolled the large case to the side of my desk. I think I embarrassed him.

"Thank you. It's huge. If you'd like, you may sit in the lobby or I can have one of our couriers bring it to your firm when I've finished. I don't know how long this will take."

"Barry told me to stay with the file. Please don't be offended, but I'm with the file. Actually, if it's OK with you, I'll sit over there at the table by the windows. I brought some work with me."

"Of course. Make yourself comfortable. If you need anything, just yell," I smiled.

"Thank you Ms. Summers," he said as he walked to the table.

"Call me McClain," I said, spinning back toward the computer.

"OK. McClain."

Sandy returned with the warm muffin and hot tea. "Here ya go," she gushed, as she stormed the room. Surprised to see Mr. Pierce, she exclaimed, "Leapin Lizards!"

"What?" I asked.

"He scared me." Looking in Matthew's direction. "That's Mr. Pierce," I explained. He looked startled too.

"Mr. Pierce, meet my assistant Sandy Abrams." He stood and walked toward her, extending his hand.

"I'm sorry Mr. Pierce. I didn't expect to see anyone. Do you need anything?"

"I already asked him," I interrupted. "Thanks for lunch."

"You're welcomed. Is there anything I can help you guys with? "

"Nope. Everything's under control. Those letters on your desk need to go out today. You should have enough to keep you busy until quitting time. Call FamU and tell the Chancellor I'd be delighted to speak at the Award's banquet. Tell him I'm personally coming to recruit there this spring. Make sure you put the dates on my calendar."

Tricked

"OK...Uh...Mr. Pierce isn't on your appointment schedule today. What are you guys working on?"

"Excuse me?" I said staring into her hazel eyes.

"I mean...I don't know what I mean," she smiled. "Buzz me if you need anything. Nice seeing you Mr. Pierce."

"Likewise."

Calhoun's file was filled with complicated notes. Data. Charts. Certificates. I was completely engrossed. Taking notes. Comparing numbers. Evaluating data. Running tapes. Reading statements. Analyzing Reports. Depositions. Letters. Numerical sequences. Nothing, until I decided to see if the numbers matched letters in the alphabet. They did. This was code. St. Lisa. What's that? I looked at every piece of paper in Calhoun file, searching for references to St. Lisa. None.

RJP's confidential database yielded nothing. Maybe the office archives would identify St. Lisa. Microfiche. Old files. New files. International files. Closed files. Archived Files. Nothing. Dead ends.

Hours ticked by before I decided to go to the company library. Scary Stella, the librarian, never questioned my access to information so when I pulled Reynolds and Jacobs' personal files, she didn't flinch. I entered St. Lisa into the computer. Nothing. Then I entered St. Lisa's. Instantly, the name Bennett appeared. Who's Bennett? No Data. I combined St. Lisa's and Bennett in every imaginable combination. Nothing. Stella gave me the hairy eyeball and began walking toward me, so I quickly exited Mr. Reynolds's files and entered my own. Gerald gave me everyone's private computer codes months ago. I never used them, until now.

Calhoun's notes led me nowhere. What was the connection between St. Lisa's? Calhoun. Bennett. It was 6:15 p.m. before I looked up again. "Is there anything you need before I leave?" Sandy asked.

"Nope."

"I signed your name to the general correspondence. Other letters are in tonight's file for your signature. There are no emergencies. Thank God. Letters to the Chancellor are in the red folder, along with a letter to Texas Southern. The reports for tomorrow's meetings are in the yellow folder. Pellman's speaking points for your conversations with Europe are on top. If there's nothing else, I'll see you tomorrow."

"Sounds great Sandy. Thank you. Have a great evening."

"You too. Good night Mr. Pierce." He stood. "Good night."

By the end of the day, I was frustrated and tired. Pacing as usual, I was oblivious to Matthew's presence. I forgot he was even there. Matthew had been there at least 8 hours.

He sat across the room, holding his head with one hand and a torts book in the other. He'd removed his jacket and put on glasses. That's when I noticed something fine lurking beneath his clothes.

In my excitement about the Calhoun file, I hadn't noticed how handsome Matthew was. Athletic. Sexy. Powerful. He was wonderfully groomed but wore more cologne than I like.

"Learning anything?" I asked.

"Sorry?" He was startled. I'd interrupted his reading.

"Are you learning anything? The torts book?"

"Oh...yeah...I'm taking law classes part time over at SMU."

"That's great. You hungry?"

"Excuse me."

"Are you hungry?"

"Starving actually," he answered with a trace of exhaustion in his voice.

"You wanna go get something to eat? With me?"

"Are you finished with the file?"

"I think so. But do you really have to take it back tonight?"

"Barry was very specific."

"Did you walk or drive?"

"I walked."

"To work?"

"No...I thought you meant...I caught the bus to work and I walked here from our office. I think I've missed the last bus home."

Tricked

"I'll take you to your office. We'll get something to eat and I'll drop you off at home."

"Are you sure? I don't want to impose and I can't let you buy my dinner."

"Why not?"

"I'm used to paying when I go out with a young lady."

"Yeah, but I asked you and we're not going out. This is business. It's the least I can do and it's RJP's money," I smiled. He passed the first test. A gentleman.

"Well?"

"Are you hungry or not?"

"I'm very hungry."

"Good. Let me get my briefcase and sign these letters Sandy left. Why don't you get the elevator and I'll be right with you."

"Sounds like a plan." He reached for his jacket and packed his things. I rushed out just as the elevator doors opened.

We rode down 36 floors in complete silence. I intentionally allowed the split in my skirt to reveal a substantial amount of thigh. I wasn't flirting. Just playing. "Dallas is beautiful at night. Don't you agree?" I asked breaking the silence.

"The nights here can be very beautiful. Tonight is certainly one of them," he said, looking directly at my leg. "I've always admired the skies here." He was flirting, passing the second test. Not gay.

"Where do you live?"

"The Village. But I just bought the worst house in the best neighborhood in town, just off Swiss Ave. I'll be moving this weekend."

"That's a wonderful neighborhood. Historic. Idyllic. It sounds very exciting...Congratulations. Where do you want to go?"

"You choose. I'm not picky about restaurants. I like eating at home."

"Do you cook?"

"Yeah. I'm a very good cook. That's what people tell me. Can you cook?"

"No. Do you like seafood?"

"I love it. You really can't cook?"

"No. I know a good place. Tell me about your new house."

"I'm very excited about finding it. It's not huge, but it's nice and it's mine. I paid cash because I didn't want a mortgage. It has a huge backyard and plenty of room for my dog. My garden. It's peaceful and happy. It needs a lot of work, but I look forward to remodeling. I love working with my hands. Do you eat out every night?"

"No."

We found a spot in front of one of my favorite casual restaurants. Which was highly unusual since the restaurant was usually crowded with young singles trying to make a love connection. The hostess sat us in the bar area while we waited for a table. A live band played there every night. Matthew hadn't heard of it and confessed his love of jazz. He ordered a beer and made shy conversation about his new home. Garden. School. Work. Dog.

As he spoke, something inside popped. Natural urges bottled up for years sprang to life in the presence of this extremely attractive man. Several female patrons noticed him too. They were literally panting. One even sent him a drink, which he courteously declined. Slut.

Our table was ready and we were seated near the band. A blonde slipped her business card into Matthew's hand as she passed. I said nothing. After all, this wasn't a date.

Neither of us knew that six weeks later he'd make the stresses and disappointments of my days vanish in waves of passion. His touch turned off the perpetual motion machine of my life long enough to enjoy hours of ecstasy in his arms. At first, he controlled our torrid encounters. I liked that. Surrendering to him made me someone else in his arms. Sensuous. Erotic. Uninhibited.

Relenting, he transported me. Never wanting to return from the places his body took me, I was hooked. I loved everything about him. His shoulders. Neck. Arms. Back. Chest. Stomach. Thighs. Voice. Sweat.

Tricked

It was soon apparent that our togetherness had become love for him. Allowing myself to love Matthew was not an option. I was convinced that I just loved the way he made me feel. He was making me feel this way more and more.

He couldn't play any other role in my life. Undisputedly bright, he seemed more interested in nature than commerce. This man loved roses and renovating that old house. My friends made him uncomfortable and I didn't particularly like his. His forte? Pleasure. No one was more proficient. Capable. Skillful. If there were an award for outstanding achievement in this area, he would win lifetime recognition.

He was jealous when he saw me with other men. He saw other women too. I didn't care. Confident that he belonged to me, I invited him to take out other women. It gave him no particular stature in my life. It's merely how I wanted it. I even told him if he saw me coming down the street, he didn't even have to acknowledge me. "That's ridiculous. Why would I ignore you? I love you. I'm always happy to see you." Nevertheless, it was understood that when I called he delivered. He always did.

Brazen, I'd appear at this house unannounced with arrogant expectations regarding his time. His talents. He obliged me. If he showed the least bit of reluctance, correctly or incorrectly interpreted by me, I acted like a spoiled child punishing him with distance. Ambivalence. Silence.

I wasn't jealous in the ordinary sense. I just wanted what I wanted when I wanted it. Needed it. Craved it. Those were the rules. No negotiations.

Matthew's primary assignment was taking care of me when I was bored. Lonely. Frustrated. Stressed. In return he received unbridled and uninhibited passion. But he wanted and deserved so much more. Dates. Dinners. Discussions. Movies. Six Flags. Respect. I couldn't. I wouldn't.

When he disputed the boundaries, I had answers. "You knew this was a dangerous job when you took it. I'm giving you all I have and if it isn't enough, let's just be friends."

"I love you McClain. Realize it's the only reason I tolerate your mess. You're afraid of what you can't control and if I'm going to love you, I have to accept this flaw. I'm going to love you right out of that fear. You're afraid of being loved, more than you are of being hurt. You know hurt, but I don't think you've ever really known love. Plus I'm not ready to give up on you...not yet."

"Why?"

"I haven't accomplished my goals."

"What goals?"

"To convince you of how wonderful you really are. Not how smart. Not how pretty. Not how capable. Not how ambitious. I want you to realize how remarkably wonderful you are and one day all that love will explode, and I want it to explode all over me. That's my plan."

"Sounds messy."

One night about two months ago, I showed up at Matt's house around 10:30 p.m. A strange car was in his driveway. I knocked on the door carrying a garment bag, a 4-gallon climbing rose bush and my backpack.

Amazement sprang across Matthew's face when he opened the door. I'd interrupted something. A woman was there. I could care less. We hadn't spoken for about a month prior to my unexpected visit. He made the mistake of telling me that he had to take a test and couldn't come by when I wanted him. I was only angry for a day or two. I was busy the rest of the time.

A young lady sat on the couch with a glass of wine in her hand. I bought those wine glasses as a housewarming gift. She tried to maintain, as I pushed the heavy plant into Matthew's arms. She was shook, sipping wine and shooting daggers at me from beautiful brown eyes.

I walked to the bedroom, tossing off my jacket and washing the dirt from my hands. Thirsty and nosey, I went into the kitchen searching for something to drink. Music played softly and the lights were turned down low. "Is it dark in here to y'all? I can barely see anything!" I smiled at the stunned duo, popping on the light switch. They looked at me as though I were insane.

Tricked

"Where's Pitiful?" He was scratching on the laundry room door. "Never mind." The dog rushed out wagging his tail, jumping up and down. "Hi boy." I tore a drumstick off a chicken sitting in the fridge and grabbed a bottle of apple juice. Chomping on the chicken leg and watching the stunned duo, I finalized my plans.

There was a basket of freshly washed towels sitting on the dryer. I grabbed one of them. Pitiful and I went back into the living room. He ran to the startled young lady expecting a rub. Instead, she shrunk back on the couch emitting a loud squeal and wasting the wine. Matthew shooed the frisky dog away. I called Pitiful who stood defiantly at my side. "Well…I think I'll take a shower. I'm exhausted. Excuse me for being so rude Miss? I'm McClain. You are?"

"Denise," she said, folding her arms across her chest. How could Matthew pick a girl who didn't like dogs? I ought to sic him on her.

Matthew stood in the middle of the floor. Speechless. He watched us as though looking at a ping-pong game, still holding the bush. "Are you afraid of Pitiful? He won't hurt you Denise. He's a good boy. I'm happy to have met you. You're very beautiful, but I'm sorry I can't join your conversation tonight. I'm tired and I'm going to bed. By the way, your haircut is simply fabulous. Come on Pitiful. Matthew, don't just stand there. Put that plant outside. It's dripping." He looked down and rushed toward the kitchen.

Hot water messaged away today's tension. After brushing my teeth, I wrapped myself in a towel, pulling my wet hair into a ponytail. One of Matthews shirts was on the chair, so I slid into it. I jumped into bed and began reading a report.

The front door closed and I heard voices in the driveway. A car started outside and drove away. Matthew came into the room and leaned against the door jam. He didn't say anything. He just stared. He was angry. Ticked. I'd never seen him angry before.

Before coming to Dallas, Matthew had been a homicide detective. Burnt out after seeing too many children dead in the street, he was determined to make a difference. One day he'd

71

dedicate his life to saving them. He cared too much. Now he was in love with a woman who took advantage of him. Manipulated him. Tortured him.

"What?!" I asked.

"What's the matter with you? You are really something," he said, shaking his head.

"What am I?" I asked, slipping from beneath the sheets, joining him at the door. I leaned against his chest. We kissed and I placed both arms around his strong neck, staring directly into his magnetic eyes.

"I can't believe you. You've got to be the most frustrating, obstinate, selfish, crazy, spoiled rotten woman I've ever known. They could do a whole hour about you…on one of those dreadful talk shows."

"You can do a whole hour on me right now," I whispered, biting his bottom lip. "You're irresistible," I purred, kissing him.

"You should've at least called," he whispered, kissing my neck. Inhaling me.

"Why?" I asked, closing my eyes and enjoying each sensation.

"What was I suppose to think? You haven't returned one call I've made to you in the last three weeks. Tonight you just show up. Unannounced. You just insulted my company and disrespected my house. You walk in proclaiming that you're taking a shower and going to my bed, with absolute disregard of the impression you've given Denise about me. I ought to throw you out of here."

"I thought you liked spontaneity," I mused, unbuttoning his shirt. "I said I liked her hair and I brought you a flower. Wasn't that nice? Are we fighting? Let's make up."

His shirt fell from his shoulders. "Did she leave?" I said slyly. "I've never noticed how sexy you look when you're pissed. I like that. Let's play jail." I grabbed his face and brushed my lips across his.

"You're incorrigible. Absolutely incorrigible." He wanted to laugh. "Of course she left. How would you feel if the same thing happened to you?"

"It wouldn't happen to me." I kissed his Adam's apple. "If she was important, you would've thrown me out," I whispered as I ran my hand across his crouch. "She'd be in your arms tonight. Not me." I gave him a long sensuous kiss. "Do you really want me to leave?" I whispered. He closed his eyes. "Do you? Because I'll do whatever you want." His undershirt fell to the floor.

"McClain...you've got to show me some respect baby. I could have been..." I bit his shoulder. He moaned.

"You could have been what?" I kissed him again. "It's supposed to rain tonight. Thunder. Lightening. Wind."

Matthew lifted me from the floor. We were eye to eye. "You know what rain does to me. I thought we'd make love tonight. All night." I wrapped my legs around him. "Tomorrow night." He kissed me hard, gently placing me back on the floor. I ran my hand through the smooth hair of his stomach and down into his pants. "The next night," I said softly, unbuckling his pants. He took the barrette from my wet hair and it tumbled past my shoulders.

"Denise will probably never speak to me again," he whispered, bracing himself against the doorway as I lowered myself and his pants. "She'll call," I said allowing my lips to touch him. He shook. "Where are those hand-cuffs?" I smiled slyly. He smiled as a quiet explosion sucked the air from the room. He lifted me from the floor and tossed me onto the bed, laughing.

Matt stared deeply into my eyes. His love covered me as he kissed my navel. I held my breath. Something clanked against the brass bedposts. "What am I going to do with you?" he whispered, turning me onto my stomach and taking my wrists into his hands, slowly kissing them.

"What you do best," I moaned.

"Get off the bed Pitiful."

We spent the entire next weekend together. Spending a weekend together was rare. Ordinarily, my weekends were dedicated to the office or hanging out with Jack. This was repentance for the previous Wednesday night. I was rude and I had disrespected his house. His guest. But no Miss America want-to-be was going to interfere with my desires. Jack was out of town buying furniture. Pellman was in France. There were no deadlines, so I decided to spend two days with Mat.

He lay across the bed reading a magazine, looking delicious. I brought him a snack from the kitchen. He suggested watching college football games, a cooking lesson and maybe a movie. I didn't care; I just wanted to be with him.

"Hey Matt, what movie do you want to see? I hadn't been to a movie theater in a long time. Jack kept me up to date on the latest releases or rented the hottest videos. What's good?" I asked.

"I don't know. Look in the paper."

As I flipped through the paper, a little light blue box tumbled onto the bed. Matthew acted like he hadn't noticed and continued flipping from channel to channel. "What's this?"

Matthew slid across the bed toward me. "I don't know. Do you love me?" he asked.

"What?" I asked, looking for ways to tear into the gift.

"Do you love me McClain?" he asked, turning the television off.

"You know how I feel about you silly," I whispered, neatly disassembling the bright white ribbon. I took his face into my hands and kissed him gently. This was his routine about every 90 days.

"Say you love me?"

"I love you," I answered, trying to find the tape.

"Say it like you mean it," he took the box from me.

"I love you Matthew Pierce. Very much. Gimme." Something heavy was coming.

"McClain...we've been seeing each other for a long time. I'm not seeing anyone else. You won't let me. I don't want to. I want to have a real relationship with you. I want to know everything about you. Share our lives. Feel like I'm special to you."

Tricked

"You are special. Very special."

He took my face, pushing my hair behind my ears. "I'm thirty-six years old and I've never felt this way about anyone. I've never loved anyone the way I love you. You mean everything to me. You invade every thought. You're not responsible for my feelings, but I'm starting to feel like a booty call."

"A booty call? You are many things Matthew Pierce, but a booty call is certainly not one of them. Be nice." I touched his face. He grabbed my hand and said, "Then stop treating me like one. I need more. I need you. I *love* you."

"Every three months we go through this."

Matthew walked to the chair holding our clothes. He began dressing.

"Matthew, every three months you do this. Don't get mad. You said you wanted to spend more time together. You said let's spend the weekend together. You said let's do this and let's do that. I'm here. I'm trying."

"I don't want to be work for you. Another job."

"Why would you say that? You're not. I love being with you. I even planted the peppers. Remember?"

"They weren't peppers. They were green beans. I've done everything I know how to make you feel safe. Loved. Cared for. You have to know by now that I won't abandon you. Leave you. Disappoint you. But nothing works. Somehow I thought this weekend would change something for you. Somehow I thought if I loved you enough..." Matthew wiped a tear from his eye. He was hurt. "I love you. I really do. But this hurts. Love isn't supposed to hurt so much." He sat, holding his head in one hand.

Comforting him came naturally to me. His head rested against my stomach. I didn't know what to do. What to say. I didn't know how to comfort him. Soothe him. Console him. I didn't know a lot of things, but I knew hurting him was never my intention.

"You said you weren't ready to give up on me. You had goals. What did that mean?" I asked.

"I have to protect *my* heart and I'm sad to think that means I have to leave you alone, without reaching my goals." He gently moved away.

I can handle this. "You know I'm not trying to hurt you."

"I know."

"So it's over? Just like that?" I asked, watching him dress.

"Yeah."

"Does it have to be over right now?"

"Why?"

"I still want to go to the movies and I haven't opened my gift, and you haven't taught me how to cook," I whimpered.

"I'm not laughing McClain. This isn't funny."

"I'll buy popcorn. Junior Mints. Hot Tamales. Lemonheads."

"I'm serious. Put on your clothes. I'll take you home."

"Do what makes you happy Matt. But don't think for one moment I don't respect you. I've always respected you. Very much." My voice cracked.

Matthew joined me on the side of the bed. He felt sorry for me. I saw pity. "Baby I want you in my life. Not just my bed. I imagine a life of love and happiness with you. I dreamed a vision of togetherness like no one has ever shared. The kind that poems are written about. But I'll still teach you how to cook and I'll still love you." We both smiled.

He reached for me and I slid into his strong arms. "Let me be good to you," he whispered. "You are." I whispered too.

"Let me fill your life with joy. Peace. Happiness. Laughter. Let me give you new reasons to fall in love with me every day. You'll never be bored and I'll support everything you do. You can count on that and you can always count on me."

"How?" I knelt on the floor in front of him holding his hands. He leaned back looking at the ceiling, exasperated. I sat on his lap. "I want those things Matt. I want you in my life. But I don't know how to give you what you need. I don't want to hurt you. I promise I don't." I kissed his nose and hugged him. "I'm so sorry. I'm selfish and a brat. I've been awful and you've been wonderful. Will you forgive me? It's not that I don't trust you with my feelings, I just don't trust myself with yours."

"Stop building walls around your heart," he sighed gently. "We can help each other. I'm scared too, but I'm willing to try. Learn. We can take it one day at a time...We..."

"Shhhhh..." I said, putting my finger across his lips. I kissed him warmly, whispering, "What do you want from me?"

"I want you to stop being so afraid."

"Afraid?"

"Stop being afraid of love. Stop being afraid of me."

I was tired of this lecture and if it was really over, I was determined to make our ending as memorable as our beginning. Before he could say another word I took charge, initiating my consensual assault until we were became shivering. Convulsing. Orgasmic masses. We missed the football games. The movie. The cooking lesson.

Sheer exhaustion pushed Matthew into a deep sleep. I went into the bathroom. I needed to wash this man off of me. I dressed and leaned over him to say goodbye. The tiny blue box was still on the floor. "I forgot all about you."

Inside was a heart shaped 18k gold locket. The inscription read:

Mc Clain
My Wish Come True
Matthew

He couldn't afford this. I was so profoundly touched that he bought me this lovely gift that I was suddenly ashamed to be in his presence. "I'm sorry," I whispered, fighting back tears and realizing that this was really the end of our relationship. A relationship like Matthew described wouldn't work. I couldn't risk it. I'd already played this game and I was already in too deep.

"For what?" he whispered.

"I thought you were asleep."

"Why are you sorry baby?" he asked, touching my leg.

"For hurting you."

The sports caster's voice filled the room with highlights of the games we missed. "You don't have to be sorry. Not after that," he smiled, never opening his eyes.

"I'm going to run out and get us something to eat."

"Come back to bed. We'll eat later. Who won the game?" he whispered, drifting back to sleep.

"You did."

CHAPTER NINE

BO was the only man I ever truly loved. Beside my father. Matt was wrong. I hadn't been hurt. I'd been devastated. Crushed. Destroyed. Tricked. We met during my last year at Wharton. Friends took me to a local dance club to celebrate a successful internship that summer. We couldn't help noticing him on the dance floor. He moved like a panther. Smooth. Sexy. Confident. They bet he was a male model, except he was more masculine and more muscular. I blushed at his ability to make the music follow him. "He's probably here with a white woman." "Got to be," they agreed. "Too fine to be with a sister on this campus." I just watched him. He was easy to watch.

From our vantage I could see he had one dimple. He smiled a lot. Too old to be an undergrad, maybe he was a law student, or even working on his doctorate. My pineapple juice arrived and I leaned against the bar watching the dancers and the lights. Bar flies swarmed us. I pushed pass their buzz attacks to see what moves he'd make next.

The music slowed as he edged his way through the tattooed breasts of eager undergrads vying for his attention. He stared directly at me while ordering a drink. "Would you like to dance?" his baritone voice melted like sweet caramel. Who was he talking to? I looked around. He tapped my arm. "Would *you* like to dance?"

"I don't dance."

"You don't dance? He was amused. "Is there a religious reason?"

"No. I can't dance. Never learned."

"Everybody can dance," he insisted, amused.

"Everybody but me."

"I don't believe you," he said tugging me toward the dance floor.

"No...no...stop," I yelled over the music. "I just come here to watch everybody else. I can't dance and I'm not embarrassing myself tonight."

"Are you sure?"

"Positive." He loosened his grip and I returned to my position at the bar.

Finding an eager dance partner was no problem. He grabbed a girl who deliriously bounced around the floor with him through four songs. My friends thought I was crazy for letting him get away. "He'll be back," I said confidently. They looked at me like I was nuts. After his last dance he came back to the bar. To me.

A table became available and our conversation continued comfortably until last call for alcohol. At last, I'd found my intellectual equal. He was absolutely fascinating. He was friendly, making me laugh with bright quips and wonderful stories of his childhood. "Tell me about your voice. It's mesmerizing."

"People say I sound just like my mother." We laughed as he explained that his grandfather was a great baritone who sang with one of the famous gospel quartets in the 50's. He was adamant about teaching me how to dance.

"May I take you ladies to breakfast?" He offered after the club closed. We declined but he walked us to our car. He gave me his telephone number. I promised to call him the next day. I did.

Bo Richards was a doctorial student fulfilling his residency requirement. His father died when he was 5. His mother married a military man who promptly adopted him. Naturally he attended the military academy at West Point and became an Army Ranger. Later he worked for Special Forces. When his military stint was over he went to work for the government. "I've never married and I don't have any children that I know of." He would return to his job and life in D.C. after spring semester.

Tricked

We began spending lots of time together. On and off campus. Talking. Movies. Plays. Lectures. Concerts. Antique shows. Art fairs. Walks. Starry nights. We had passionate discussions about politics. Religion. Race. Crime. Sex. Music. Everything. He was interesting and interested in everything. Me.

Bo was my first boyfriend. I never wanted one. Lots of boys and men showed interest, but not like this. None like this. Maintaining my perfect grade point average; graduating with honors; and increasing my computer proficiencies motivated me. It was the central focus of my life. Until Bo.

He opened new worlds of color. Light. Texture. Sight. Sound. Every event in our lives, subject to memorial recognition. First meeting. First date. First kiss. First everything. I became strangely sentimental, buying those insipid greeting cards. Teddy bears. Hearts. All of which ultimately winds up in the trash. How did he endure?

Time was no longer my friend. Incessantly, he seeped into my thoughts. During class. In labs. At work. I watched the clock in eager anticipation knowing he was waiting outside. When I rushed out, he was there. Dependable. Loving. Wonderful. "Hi baby. How was class? I love you."

Exercise was important to him. We jogged every morning and he took me for pineapple smoothies at a place he found downtown. I learned how to drive his Harley, and how to dance. Such a fantastic feeling of falling while standing straight up tagged me at all times. It was the most amazing sensation I'd ever known.

"McClain, I love the way you smell." It was the lightly scented sesame seed oil I used after showering, but he didn't need to know everything.

Pictures of trees and me decorated his apartment walls. Every day he said, "If I could harness the brilliance of your smile in the mornings, the sun could rest." Or something like that.

We studied in the library. Student union. My room. His apartment. My bed. His. We took long quiet walks, where blizzards of yellow leaves welcomed us. I was mesmerized, distracted and never happier.

Thanksgiving break approached quickly. We spent it together in his apartment. My mother was pissed. She got over it. His parents celebrated at his sister's home in Baltimore. He cooked the meal. I made Kool-Aid.

Four magical days to love and learn were a gift to us. Bo was romantic and remarkable. We explored each other's inner most thoughts and dreams. I was more mature than I realized. Centered. Secure. He could have any eligible woman on campus. The city. The country. He wanted me. "I can't imagine my life without you," he said as he kissed my fingertips. "By the way, are your hands clean?"

Two weeks before finals, we decided to stay away from each other. I needed time to study. Regroup. Focus. Concentrate. It was agonizingly painful not to pick up the telephone, but I didn't. I missed our warm weeknights. Weekends. Chocolate Chip Cookies. Rented movies. Nature channel.

Our old routine plagued me. I took showers because baths were reserved for us. Bo read Carter G. Woodson's 'Miseducation of The Negro' while we soaked. When he brushed my hair, he hummed. His poetry woke me every day. "My love cried out to sympathetic ears of angels. God answered with you. You arrived on angels wings. Adored and perfect." I believed him.

William Barrett Browning's prose lulled me to sleep at night and when the time was right, I wondered how he knew I was a virgin. I never told him, but he knew. He was generous and patient. Loving. Gentle. It was the most sweetly intimate moment of my life. Our lives. Something perfect passed between us. Something that only happens in songs and dreams. "I love you. Don't ever leave me," he cried. "I won't."

Whatever I was doing to him couldn't feel as good as the things he did to me. Secretly, I rented and studied adult films. That's what perfectionists do. Genuinely surprised, he rewarded my initiatives with unparalleled pleasure. I was eager to learn. He was eager to teach. Please. Satisfy. His love was safe. Warm. Natural. I never wanted to loose it. Him. Ever.

Tricked

Our Christmas plans included Bo spending the holidays with me in Milwaukee. Everyone was going to meet this man who loved me. Fiercely. Joyfully. Totally. Completely. Unconditionally. Transcendentally. Then they'd realize I was worthy of love. Attention. Happiness.

Bo took care of making reservations for the most exciting New Years Eve in Times Square. We'd have dinner at his favorite restaurant. Iris was sending a sexy dress. "Who is this man girl? I know he's fine. When am I going to meet him?" "Soon." Bo called after my last final. Elation. "Hi."

"I missed you so much," I purred.

"How much?"

"Come get me." I was like an anxious child wiggling in my seat.

"Have you been good?"

"Yes, but I'll be better when you come get me," I smiled.

"I wanted to call you so many times."

"You did? Come get me."

"Yeah."

I chatted about the torture of tests and he told me his committee approved his dissertation topic while I grabbed things to take with me. "That's wonderful. I'm so happy for you. I'll help you research."

"Guess what?"

"What?"

"I've been thinking about things."

"So why are we talking on the telephone? Come get me!" I happily yelled into the receiver. Bo acknowledged my exuberance, but needed to explain something first. He wanted to take our relationship to another level. "Our relationship lacks definition."

I laughed, grabbing my toothbrush. "Bo baby, what are you talking about?" I smiled. "Come get me. Why are we still on the phone?" Then he defined it.

"I adore you McClain. But I don't think we should let this relationship get too serious."

I didn't know what to say. He stopped me dead in my tracks. Maybe I heard him wrong.

"Baby... are you there?" he asked.

"Yeah...I'm here. I just don't think I heard what you said." Then he clarified.

"Our campus romance won't last. You know that too, don't you? They never do. I didn't come here expecting to fall head over hills in love with you. Neither of us did. You're very young. Impressionable. This relationship can't distract you. Hurt you. Divert you. We need to be realistic."

"Realistic?"

"Wisdom must triumph over our emotions."

"Triumph?"

"I'll be back in D.C. at the end of next semester. You'll be in New York or Chicago or maybe even Europe. Long distance relationships don't work. You'll probably meet someone and forget all about me."

"What are you talking about? Are you serious?"

"God, you're so beautiful. Is it inconceivable that you'll meet someone else? Someone younger? Or maybe I'll meet someone when I go back to D.C." My mind shut down. I was surfacing too fast. "Are you there McClain?"

"Are you breaking up with me? Are you saying you don't trust me? Or did you say I shouldn't trust you?" I closed my eyes waiting for the answer that would break my heart.

"Do you love me?" he asked.

"Of course. You're not coming to get me are you?"

Bo's arrow hit the mark. Tears rolled down my cheeks as the safe feeling of his love flew from my heart like freed doves circling a stadium when released at the start of an international sporting event. "You make me feel good McClain. Alive. I love being with you. Making you laugh. Loving you. Holding you. Touching you. Teaching you. Talking to you. Arguing with you. Watching you drink those dreadful pineapple things. But I'm consumed by my feelings. Suffocating. Drowning. I'm attracted to your beauty, but repelled by your ambition."

Tricked

"My ambition?" The lump forming in my throat strangled me. I grabbed my neck trying to swallow.

"Baby, I know how rejection feels. Being adopted myself, it's easy to mismanage feelings, especially a first love. I've assessed that you're self sufficient. Self assured. Self reliant. I don't believe you need anyone. Not even me."

"How can you say that?" I whispered.

"I'm not sure you can share yourself completely with anyone."

"I can. I will. I have."

"You're damaged. You've submerged yourself so deeply into the cold comfort of world economics. Business. Numbers. Theorems. International law. Finance. Logic. Nobody can reach you without drowning themselves."

"You reached me," I whispered.

"You'd never be happy with me. My life."

"I am happy. I love you. I love you. Your books. Poetry. How you bat your eyes when you eat something too cold. How your forehead sweats when you eat something too hot. How you cock your head to the right when you're thinking and to the left when you're worried. The way you smile when you're asleep. Your laugh. Your motorcycle. You."

"Maybe the truth is, I don't think I'd be happy with you."

The bubble burst. I was flattened. Lost. Weak. Dazed. Stunned. I felt like I was having a heart attack. "It seems you've given this a lot of thought." I was crying against my will. "While you were assessing my inability to love or be loved, did you ask yourself whether I could be hurt?"

"I know you can be hurt baby," he whispered. "But sometimes the truth hurts."

"Whose truth is this?" I asked impatiently.

"It's our truth. We..." I interrupted him.

"We? How's this we? Why are you telling me this tonight? On the phone?"

"Because if I saw the least bit of hurt in your eyes, I couldn't say it. I couldn't stand it. I don't want to lead you on. I'm sorry. I should have said something a long time ago," he whispered.

"I'm so stupid. I'm so stupid. I really thought you cared about me," I cried. "Why did you let me think you loved me? How could I have been so dumb? I should have known. I should have known," I cried.

"Don't do that. Don't do that. We said we'd be honest. I'm being honest."

"No, you're being mean. I want... (Sniff)...no, I need to talk about this face to face... (Sniff) you owe me that (sniff)."

"I don't think that's a good idea. Not tonight. As a matter of fact, maybe we should wait until we get back from Christmas break to talk. Let's give this some time to sink in."

"My mother has planned for you to come. She even invited our dysfunctional relatives to dinner. We never have anyone for dinner. They're expecting us. You."

"It's not a good idea. I have to go baby. I'll talk to you later." "Bo don't."

Panic and courage sang separate songs in my fainting heart and shrinking soul. Panic's solo was first. I didn't like the new definition of our relationship. But the prospect of not seeing him at all suddenly terrified me.

"Don't what?" he asked gently.

Through a torrent of impending tears, courage tuned up. "Don't hang up. I love you. How can you just throw us away with both hands? "Remember the poem you wrote me? You said 'Your love is as real and true as trees and clouds. Mingling in the heavens with the whisper of angels, who speak to places barren in winter, but not dead. Holding sheer beauty in their hands until you smile and the sun made me new, causing my loneliness to melt in the warmth of your eyes." You meant that.

It's not your responsibility to protect me. I'm not a child who's shallow or neurotic. Gullible or tragic. Only you can control what happens when you get back to Washington. Yes, you could meet someone there. You can meet someone here. Maybe you already have. Distance doesn't kill relationships. Forgetting to hold on to the essence of the one you love, does. Some how, every day you need to know you're the most important person in the world to each other. You're the most important person in the world to me Bo.

Self doubt cleared its pitiful voice, but confidence overpowered it. "You said I'm damaged. Did you say that to justify your feelings? You can't think I accept your belief just because you said it. You don't get to define me. I won't apologize for having goals. Plans. Interests. Talents. Dreams. You used to be one of them. You don't know what I've had to live through to get where I am. And since you had absolutely nothing to do with it, I reject your knee jerk analysis. Furthermore, it seems you've taken exceptional care examining what's wrong with me. Why haven't you told me what's wrong with you?

"I'll talk to you later," he said.

"But…"

"Goodbye McClain." Then he hung up.

The telephone stayed on my lap while it made that annoying beeping noise. I couldn't move. I was paralyzed. Psychotic. Comatose. What felt so wonderful this morning was killing me now. The man who'd lifted me higher than I ever thought possible just dusted me from his head and heart in less than fifteen minutes. I couldn't believe it. Is it that easy?

Daylight snuck through the blinds as sanity returned. I hadn't moved from that spot all night. The receiver was still on my lap. Had I lost my mind? Had I slept? Probably not, since my eyes stung with each blink. My skin hurt as the sun's purifying rays washed across me. Pain that vampires fear.

Suddenly uncomfortable with myself, I felt the entire campus overheard our conversation. I was completely humiliated. Dangerously confused. Embarrassingly stupid and desperately alone. Although my heart was convinced that Bo loved me. My brain convinced me that I loved myself more, refusing to let me act like a fool. His position was perfectly clear. He didn't want me. It was over.

Iris wasn't home when I tried to call her with evidence of my stupidity. I promised myself that I'd never feel this way again. I'd never give myself to anyone this way again. I'd never let another man hurt me like this again. I'd never allow anyone to define me again. My brain would take charge of all future matters of the heart.

As my father sped away that day, he took my mother's light. Bo couldn't take mine. To hell with him. I flew to Milwaukee for Christmas, three days early. Alone.

Mother never asked questions and I never offered explanations. Bo left so many messages that my mother complained, "Why don't you tell that boy you don't want to talk to him? I'm tired of telling him that you're not here."

"I never asked you to say that."

"Then what should I do?"

"Nothing."

We exchanged gifts and distant relatives from Chicago came for dinner. Mother bragged about my Grades. Papers. Scholarship. Internships. Her cousins asked about my love life. Men. School. Money.

"Girl come in here and get some of this sweet potato pie. It's delicious. You need to eat some. Ain't she skinny? Viv you better make this girl eat. How you go get a man looking like that? Men like meat." My fat aunt.

"I know you got somebody down there at that school. Wasn't you supposed to bring somebody home for Christmas? Baby ain't that what Viv said? She sho is fine to me. She just need to smile more. Pass me some more of that dressing." My skinny uncle.

"Those boys and teachers down there got to be all over that. Where you attend school? I have some friends in Pittsburgh who would…." My uncle's drunk friend, licking his lips.

Tricked

"Shut up Skillet. She ain't skinny. She fine...Reeeaaal fine. She look good to me," My uncle's stepdaughter pursing her lips and shaking her head from side to side.

That next semester Bo called almost every day. Unplugging the phone didn't deter him. He learned my schedule and stopped by my room with letters and notes which were instantly trashed. My friends refused to help him. Seeing him destroyed me.

I returned to my studies with renewed dedication. Diligence confined me to the computer lab. Study carrels. Library. Seminar rooms. My room became a respite where I slept. Changed. Showered. Ate.

Bo convinced a friend to set up a surprise meeting. A better friend warned me. Toward the end of the semester, I died a little when I saw him kissing an undergrad from Syracuse. I guess he loved the way she made him feel too.

CHAPTER TEN

The bathroom door swung open. "Look here Ms. Thang, get your little narrow chips up off that tub and into those clothes. It's 6:30. Are you *that* dirty?" Jack snapped.

"I'll be right out."

Large pink rollers tumbled onto the vanity. Jack peeked in while I brushed my teeth and gargled. He tapped his foot and sighed. "Your face is more relaxed and easier to work with when you lay down," he ordered. He pulled paints and creams over to the bed and positioned himself on a stool. "Not too much Jack."

"I know what I'm doing. Close your eyes and shut up. I do makeup right. Kevin got this stuff from one of those famous makeup artists in California. He just came out with a new line, so I borrowed it. It's all new. Never been used. Brushes and everything. There're some great colors in here. Did I tell you I used to do makeup for queens when I lived in New York? I know I did.

Cheeks, get yourself in the mood baby. This is not a test. Open your mouth a little. Your look must scream elegance. Drama. Beauty. Do you know how to smolder? Don't talk. It was a rhetorical question. I ain't go let you blow this opportunity for me. Close.

This Englishman is our entrée into the life of the rich and famous. Café society. His woman has to look a certain way. Sophisticated. Rich. Elegant. You'll be happy counting his money. I'll be happy spending it. That's after we get it. Don't smile, you'll mess up the lip liner.

Marry him and have three kids quick. That way we'll get lots of child support. Then make him buy you one of those big castles they have over there in England. Blot. He probably already has two or three, but that ain't community property. We need our own castle. Don't laugh.

I'll have to replace everything and y'all neighbors from the castle next door will come over and ask who decorated. And snap! I'm doing interior decorating for the landed gentry. Look up.

I should have been a woman. Y'all don't know shit, excuse my French. Got that Cinderella Complex. Well baby...Prince Charming has arrived and I'm your fairy godfather. This man is strictly class. Regal. Old money. I had my friend check him out. He' loaded. I mean really loaded. Wait a minute, I'm shaking. Whew! I'm back.

He's not married and his grandfather was a Lord. A Duke. An Earl. Or something. He doesn't have a criminal record and owns a home in London. A castle in Scotland. Penthouse in Manhattan. Mansion on Connecticut. Villa in Italy. So on and so on. Baby, I'll be decorating for the rest of my life. Look down.

You ain't no joke Cheeks. Don't get me wrong. You can pull it off. I'll give you that. But that pantyhose theory is straight *crazy*. Don't say that tonight please. Boyfriend is pure silk. Where the tweezers?"

"I haven't had one date with this man and you've already got me married with three kids, living in a castle, wearing silk stockings. And if you think I'll still eat my collard greens and cornbread with my fingers...You're right."

"Oh my God. You can take the gangsta out of the hood, but you can't take the hood out of the gangsta?" Jack laughed.

"Why should you? It takes a little gangsta to survive out here."

"Damn right! Cinderella is in the house and low riding. This ain't no dream. I'm going to the bookstore tomorrow. I'm getting every book on England I can carry. We've got to research this thang. I'm not go let you blow this. If you do I'll take it very personally. We go land this whale. Find out if he has any gay friends. Rich ones. I'm finished."

"Let's? Who is Let's? I'm the one going out with Ian Lawford."

"What you talking about? We all going out with Ian Lawford. You just the one wearing the dress...tonight. Now put that thing on and comb your little nappy hair."

Jack walked to the head of the bed and began fluffing pillows. "Jack, do you think I'm betraying brothers by going out with this guy?"

"What?!" Jack shrieked, falling forward across the bed, looking at me as though I'd gone suddenly bizerk.

"I've never dated a white man before. That's not exactly true, but I've never dated one I liked. The others were just something to do. Having fun."

"What the hell are you talking about? Have you been sniffing glue? Smoking Crack? Are you drunk? Tell me. Just tell me. I'll get you help. I'll call Betty. *Betty*!!! *Betty*!!!" Jack screamed.

"Jack...I'm serious."

"You have finally lost your mind. Those numbers have finally driven you crazy. I *knew* this was go happen. Now I'm go cuss and you go listen. I didn't see no white man. I saw a green man. Do you think them rich brothers give a second thought or tinker's damn about sisters when they taken them white women out? Do you think they sit around asking, "Am I betraying the race?" Hellllll no! They take them women out, spend big bucks on 'em, marry 'em and do whatever the hell they want to do with 'em, and they ain't thought about a sister yet.

That rich white man wants to take you out because you're beautiful in any color. You're smart. Great career. Pretty legs. Feet. Hands. Face. Rich. Generous. Firm body. Big ta tas. Freaky. But he don't know that yet. Plus you're a wonderful person and I love you. But I digress.

When we were at Cheyenne's, he wasn't trying to be undercover and creep with a sister, like most of these rich white boys in Texas.

Tricked

Everybody at the restaurant saw how that man was looking at you. Kissin. Bowin. Hell he probably would've sucked my dick if it meant he could be with you tonight."

"Jack!"

"Jack nothing. Baby it's time to be real and that shit today was real. You better go out with that pretty rich man and enjoy yourself. You don't have to be alone, throwing yourself on the funeral fire for trifling brothers who don't want you because they prefer white women.

Them same brothers you worried about would knock you down getting to one of those bleached blonde - Billy Bob's Secretarial College Graduate - Flat butt - Silicone Titty - Trailer Trash - Nose job - Freak of the Week – Waitresses. They would give her the world and cuss you out for being in his way.

You on the other hand have to have three or four degrees. House. Car. Money. Real hair. Please! Then they got the colossal nerve to get on TV and say the reason they want white women is because Black women ain't this. Black women ain't that. Black women didn't like them when they didn't have nothing. Black women didn't pay them no attention when they were broke... thought they was ugly. Hello! You still ugly, with your missing link looking ass.

They actually believe those white women would give them the time of day if their gruesome asses didn't make a trillion dollars playing ball, singing or whatever the hell they do.

I decorate their houses and see it every day. Them simple brothers stand there like fools telling me she so nice. Hell, she supposed to be nice. She go stay just long enough to have two babies, divorce they stupid ass, get the house I just decorated, put him out and make him pay for it. Happens all the time. That pisses me off and I ain't even a sister. Well...I'm kind of a sister..." Jack cackled. "You go give me heart trouble. Where's that whiskey Barry left here? Lord I need a drink!" Jack walked toward the kitchen still cursing.

The dress floated over my body. It was delicious. Romeo instructed me how to put my hair up. He loaned me a beautiful diamond encrusted comb to keep it in place. It was the only jewelry I'd wear for the evening. The mirror reflected a surprise. I barely recognized myself. I never looked better.

Jack swore he couldn't find my handbag. It was exactly where I told him it was be. Keith gave it to me for Christmas. It was a tiny bejeweled bird on a black satin cord. I threw in my driver's license. Credit card. Money. Lipstick. Powder. Pepper spray (just in case). Perfume. Lotion. Breath mints. House keys.

My briefcase sat near the door. I hadn't put it there. Maybe Jack moved it. I'd already removed the hard drive from my laptop, stuffing it along with my research disks into a box of Kotex Light Days. I never wore them, but my mother hid her money and important papers in one of those big old purple Kotex boxes. "It's the last place a thief would look."

My building was safe. But growing up on the fringes of the ghetto kept me looking over my shoulder. I grabbed my shawl and took one last look at myself before walking into the living room. Jack's eyes popped.

"You look fantastic. Perfect. You're the most beautiful woman I've ever seen. Ian will fall in love tonight. Be ready." Jack proclaimed whirling me around. "Did you remember to put on deodorant?"

"Yeah Jack!" I laughed.

"I don't want nothin stankin. You smell good," he said sniffing all around me. "Stop Jack," I yelled, laughing.

"Romeo and Cliff have to see this. Let me take a picture. You got a camera around here?"

"I have a camera in my office." Jack ran to my office, returning and snapping photos.

"Don't use up all my film," I said, kissing him on the cheek as he flashed a picture of both of us.

"Don't mess up my makeup job with all that kissin. That damn Rick got you so touchy feely. Did you give that man some yet? How long has it been since you've had some? You go explode girl. Face go break out and everything," Jack laughed. He didn't know about Matthew.

"Don't be nervous. Don't say nothin stupid. Don't bore him with that international global finance stuff. Don't nobody understand it no way. One suggestion."

"What?" I asked admiring myself in the mirror.

"Don't give him none tonight, but if you can't help it, here's some condoms."

"Jack!"

"Jack hell! There's AIDS out there. Just cause he rich don't mean he clean. No balloon. No party."

I took a condom and put it into the zippered portion of the handbag. "Now remember every detail. Take notes. I want to know everything. Have lots of fun. I'll clean up just in case you bring him back. I don't want him to think you're nasty. Call me the second you get back or I'll never forgive you." The lobby buzzer rang. We held our breath. Jack answered. "Yes? Ms. Summer's residence, may I help you?"

"Yes sir. Mr. Lawford's car is here for Ms. Summers."

"His car?"

"Yes sir."

"Thanks she'll be right down."

CHAPTER ELEVEN

All cities look better from the backseat of a stretch limousine. The driver smiled approvingly as he steered the velvety midnight blue car through Dallas' sleek city streets. Thoughts of Ian swirled in my head like champagne bubbles from earlier that afternoon. I was excited. Anxious. Nervous. Where were we going?

We turned onto the Toll Road. My anticipation grew as we exited at Mockingbird Lane toward Love Field. The mild fall day turned sharply chilly. A brisk Dallas wind whipped the flags into full mast. My poor hair. The driver pulled into the private jet area and I wrapped myself in the shawl, preparing for the gusty assault.

"Is Mr. Lawford meeting me here?" I asked.

"Oh no Miss. That jet will take you to Mr. Lawford."

"Jet?"

"Yes," he answered, pointing in the direction of a sparkling jet waiting on the tarmac.

The driver ushered me through the lobby and toward the waiting aircraft. He handed me off to the pilot then trotted back across toward the terminal. "Have a wonderful flight," he smiled.

"Good evening Ms. Summers. Mr. Lawford is waiting for you at the restaurant," the pilot said as I stepped aboard. Another pilot was checking equipment. It was a custom jet. I sat on a creamy leather sofa with seat belts. RJP's company jets were posh, but nothing like this.

This was as plush as it gets. A high tech living room with wings. Everything about it was more fabulous than the last. "Good evening Ms. Summers. I'm your pilot George Morgan. Kenny

Tricked

Hosfstetler is the copilot." He waved. "We have charted a course to New York. We'll depart in a few moments. Our approximate flight time is one hour and thirty minutes. Mr. Lawford left explicit instructions to make you as comfortable as possible. Mark is your flight attendant tonight and he'll assist you with anything you need." Mark waived from the galley. "Mr. Lawford left a package in the rear cabin for you. You are to open it when we arrive in New York. If you need anything, please push that button," he said pointing.

"There's champagne on ice, caviar and other goodies you might enjoy. There are a variety of drinks or perhaps you'd like to see a movie. Feel free to move about the cabin once we're airborne. I'll turn off the fasten seatbelt sign when it's safe to do so. Mark will give you further safety instructions, but for now, please sit back and enjoy the flight." He stood.

"Thank your Captain."

"My pleasure," he smiled, disappearing into the cockpit.

"Would you like to watch a movie Ms. Summers," Mark smiled.

"No thank you. I think I'll read one of these magazines."

"May I serve you something? We have a lovely cabernet tonight."

"No thank you Mark. I'm fine."

"My pleasure."

I picked up a magazine and read the entire way to New York. The familiar Manhattan skyline came into view. I closed my eyes. They burned. I hope they weren't red. "Would you like some eye drops Ms. Summers?" Mark asked.

"I would. Thank you."

A longer limousine waited on this tarmac. The captain slowed the plane and turned off the engines. When he emerged, I unbuckled my seatbelt.

"Ms. Summers don't forget about the box. I hope you don't think me forward, but you look very beautiful tonight," Mark offered.

"Thank you Mark. And Captain, thank you for the smooth flight."

"My pleasure." He opened the hatch.

"Are you taking me back to Dallas tonight?"

"We are at your complete disposal. Mr. Lawford has assigned us to you permanently," he smiled, handing me a card. "Have a lovely evening and when you're ready to leave, just call."

Assigned them to me permanently? What did he mean? New York was freezing. The driver quickly closed the door as I rushed inside. Shivering. "Would you like me turn up the heat Ms. Summers?" "Yes please." Warm air swirled around me. "Don't forget this." The driver placed the large red box next to me on the seat.

Inside was a full-length black sable coat. I tried to act casual, not wanting the driver to see my jaw drop. I called Jack. No answer. He would flip. The lining was red silk with my initials embroidered inside the front panel. I lay the coat over me like a blanket caressing its softness and calculating its worth.

"I'd put that on if I were you Ms. Summers. It's kinda nippy tonight," the driver suggested as I stepped from the car.

He helped me into the coat which fit as though it had be custom tailored for me. A wonderful pair of leather gloves hid inside. The driver nodded his approval. "Mr. Lawford is inside."

"Will you keep an eye on my box?" I asked.

"I will."

"Thank you so much."

"My pleasure Ms. Summers. Have a wonderful evening."

"I will."

A gushing Maitre `D with a fake French accent ran toward me, waving his hands and clicking his heels. "Good evening mademoiselle. Welcome to Brie. You must be Ms. Summers. You *are* her aren't you? I could tell from the description Mr. Lawford gave us. You are magnificent. Are you a super model? Of course you are. I'd know you anywhere. Mr. Lawford is sitting right this way. He's been waiting for you. He's such a marvelous gentlemen. Please follow me. May I add that you look absolutely stunning this evening. The coat and the hair comb are magnificent. I am Hubert. Here we are. Mr. Lawford, mademoiselle has arrived." Ian stood. Hubert clapped his hands twice and another man appeared. "Take mademoiselle's coat," he ordered.

A man stripped the coat off me and scurried across the restaurant. "Please be seated Ms. Summers," he instructed as another man draped a large linen napkin across my lap. "Champagne! Champagne!" The Maitre `D clapped again. "Enjoy your evening. The fish is excellent tonight. Very fresh. I'll serve you myself. If you need me to explain anything from the menu ....I...."

"That will be all Hubert." Ian stood behind my chair, moving it forward. Hubert bowed respectfully and trotted back toward the front of the restaurant, clapping his hands and barking orders.

"You're a vision. Spectacular," Ian said kissing my left cheek. He slid into his chair. Chic. Stylish. "It was audacious of me to move our dinner without speaking with you first, but it really couldn't be helped. Something unexpected occurred that required my personal attention. I took a chance and here we are. Simply marvelous."

"I don't mind at all Ian. I'm glad I'm here."

"Splendid. Fantastic. I simply can't get over how radiant you are. You were stunning this afternoon, but tonight you're absolutely amazing. You found the wrap I put on the plane for you. I didn't want you to freeze. I hope you like it. I took a chance that you aren't one of those dreadful anti fur people who eat everything that flies. Crawls. Walks. Swims or slithers."

"It's lovely. You're very thoughtful. Thank you for lending it to me. Please call me McClain or I'll feel like I'm at a business dinner," I smiled.

"How dreadful. McClain darling, the coat is yours of course. You don't already have a sable coat do you?" he asked sincerely.

"No...I don't. But I can't accept such an extravagant gift. I don't even know you," I smiled touching the back of his hand.

99

"You must keep it." He grabbed my hand. "You must. My feelings are at stake. How long should you know me before accepting a gift is appropriate?" The waiter returned with the champagne.

Changing the subject momentarily, I said, "Ian, you look wonderful tonight. So elegant. Gallant. Handsome. Charming. You're an extremely attractive man and this restaurant is fabulous. Is the food wonderful? Do you come here often?"

"I assure you that the food here is outstanding and I see you're very adept at changing the subject. I'll be tremendously insulted if you don't keep it."

"I don't want to insult you Ian, but....."

"I insist."

"Oh no…not that I insist stuff again," I laughed.

He laughed too. "McClain darling...you must understand that I'm a very generous man. I couldn't possibly be the first man who's given a gift. I like you. I like you very much. It's just a coat.

"Thank you Ian. I'll keep the coat."

"Tremendous," he smiled

"For tonight." I was determined not to open my closet to new skeletons.

He laughed again. A strong laugh. A hearty laugh. A laugh that let me know laughter came easily to this very polished man. I found him surprisingly funny. Articulate. Provocative. Witty. Thrilling. Impulsive. An intriguing chemistry brewed between us. I sensed danger. I liked it.

We matched wits, sparring over hot button issues ranging from international finance to saving the spotted owl. Ian was masterful. Well read. Smart. Deep. I held my own and the predator in him liked that.

Our conversation suffered no gaps. We chatted about our childhoods. His in London, mine in Milwaukee. I can't remember what either of us had for dinner because the delectable freedom of our intellectual discourse satiated me completely.

After the waiters cleared the table, Ian excused himself to the kitchen. A secret dessert was being prepared. He hadn't told

Tricked

me that, I just seemed to be his style. Perfect. Everything about this evening was. Did Iris know about this place? She would have mentioned it. She knew all of the great places in New York.

The restaurant was small. Quaint. Intimate. Freesias and roses in opulent crystal vases decorated each table. Muted walls held antique sconces with real gaslights. Dimly lit crystal chandeliers sparkled above us. Wonderful candles melted slowly through the evening. The harpist played magically. Mystically. Hypnotically.

Large wingback chairs, richly upholstered with soft pastel tapestries welcomed us to linger at intimate linen swathed tables. Magnificent murals soared high above us. I kept detailed mental notes. Jack would love this place. Iris too.

"Did you miss me darling?" Ian returned.

"Terribly. Ian this restaurant is breathtaking. I love it."

"It is isn't it? It opened about a six years ago. I like it very much. I come here as often as I can. You know it's nearly impossible to get reservations."

A second bottle of champagne arrived. I'd reached my two glass limit for the day. Ian also declined. He never stopped talking as he dismissed the waiter, playing with my fingers and watching my mouth as though each word was a scrumptious morsel of something wonderful to eat.

We were having a delightful time. Ian's special dessert arrived. He fed me. I fed him. People at adjoining tables smiled at us. We sparkled. After Ian ate the last bite of a chocolate mouse tower with strawberry syrup, I excused myself to the ladies room. Where was Jack? I called him again. No answer. I left a message.

Then Ian had a splendid idea. "McClain, I have a splendid idea. I recently bought a boat. Let's take it out tonight for it's maiden voyage. When was the last time you've seen the Manhattan skyline from Hudson Bay?"

I must have been drunk. I agreed to go. No one had ever convinced me to go aboard a boat. Ever. Now I was about to get on a boat, at night, wearing a sable coat with a rich white man I met today. Drunk.

Cynthia A. Minor

The waiter returned with my newly acquired sable and we stepped out into the cold night air. "Take us to the boat Carlos." Ian never let go of my hand. He kissed and stroked it the entire way, staring deeply into my eyes as we continued our joyous banter.

At the pier, Ian pointed toward a vessel that looked like a luxury cruise liner. "The helipad won't be operational until next week," he apologized. Before we boarded he bashed a bottle of bubbly against it saying, "Tradition darling. You must name a boat before its first voyage. I christen you 'Revelations' the best vessel in this man's fleet." The crew clapped and we sailed into the night.

Chilly breezes stung my face, sobering me. A cozy place along the rail was perfect for admiring the Statute of Liberty. I'd never been this close. She was breathtaking. Ian stood behind me wrapping his arms around my waist. "She's magnificent isn't she?" I nestled against him. "She is." He kissed my right temple. My eyes closed instinctively. He was warm. Firm. "You mustn't fall asleep now darling. We haven't finished our date," he whispered.

"I'm not asleep."

"But your eyes are closed."

"All things aren't seen with open eyes."

"How thrilling. A philosopher."

"You're making fun of me."

"Never darling. Will you tell me about the scent you're wearing? You smell positively luscious. Intoxicating. What is it?"

"It's the wine," I smiled.

"I assure you it's not the wine my dearest McClain. Are you having a good time?" he laughed.

"I am."

"I'm committed to making this the beginning of many wonderful adventures we'll have."

"Adventures?"

"Darling, we'll go places you've never even dreamed of."

"My dreams?" I smiled, turning toward him. The night air made me tipsy.

Tricked

"It must be extraordinarily difficult to be both brilliant and beautiful. It's not an enviable peculiarity. The combination is potentially disastrous because one typically triumphs over the other. Your colossal dreams coupled with the power of your intellect both fascinates and repels. Consequently, your mind and heart lock in battle over whether to love or to think." I nestled closer, listening to his heart. "You are unquestionably the most intriguing woman I've ever met. I want to know you deeply. Sincerely. Passionately."

"You said you know my dreams."

"You long for commitment, that doesn't confine. Honesty, that inspires. Openness, that supports. Peace of mind and spirit. Constructive advice. Not criticism. Acceptance. Understanding. Challenge. Fantasy. Ecstasy. Intellectual vitality. Creative stimulation. Nuance. You want love to come as naturally as light from heaven. You want to share yourself, your life with someone completely. Confidently. Unabashedly. Unconditionally. Un-prejudicially. Passionately. Fiercely. Freely.

You're hesitant to allow yourself to explore the capacities of a relationship. Surprisingly, you're a coward in that regard. It's inconsistent with your other exceptionally fearless traits. I suspect some insufferable dote broke your heart, and you've carried the pain of your negligent selection like a faulty pacemaker. It's time for you to trust again. Love again."

He was right. I was trapped on this boat and he'd summed me up in less than 30 seconds. I always thought I was deeper than that. It's precisely what I couldn't explain to Jack this afternoon. What Matthew tried to articulate.

The boat jerked. I needed to turn away. Run away. Get away. Clarify. Justify. Ian was too smooth and I was too drunk. "Don't let my boldness upset you darling. Your dreams are merely a mirrored reflection of my own. I've been looking for you my entire life." Those words landed like fiery darts on emotions once thought permanently extinguished. I had to change the subject. Again.

"Ian lets not think about anything tonight. Let's have fun. I want to have fun with you." I threw my arms around his neck. He held me, pressing his face against my forehead.

"You can't run forever McClain. How long will it take me to win your heart?" he whispered.

"About another hour and fifteen minutes," I smiled. Ian laughed, grabbing my hand and racing to the Manhattan side of the boat. "I believe I can wait that long. Look at the city McClain! It's glorious! See how it shines! It shines like you. For you. There's no other city on earth like it! I love New York! I'll give it to you on a platter for one kiss!" He was shouting, proclaiming his romantic intentions.

His noisy proclamations grabbed the attention of a yacht loaded with partiers about 25 feet from us. "What are you doing?" I shouted as Ian climbed onto the railings. Holding an upright, he yelled, "I'll jump if you don't kiss me!"

"Ian, come down. That's dangerous! Stop! Are you drunk?" I screamed.

"I'm drunk with thoughts of you. I'll not come down until you to kiss me," his eyes twinkled.

"Ian please come down," I pleaded, grabbing for his legs.

"Say you'll kiss me." He swerved away, taking one hand from the upright causing him to wobble. I closed my eyes.

"Kiss him already," a partier shouted.

"Give him a kiss honey," another passenger.

"We don't need anymore garbage in Hudson Bay," another partier yelled.

"I'll kiss you. I'll kiss you. Come down, you're crazy!" I shouted, laughing. Ian jumped from the rail and lifted me from the deck. He was lovely. "I'll kiss you," I whispered. I felt safe in this sudden romance. Someone shouted, "Only in New York," as Ian and I walked inside.

Music filled the salon as we danced. "Let's go. I want to show you something," he smiled.

"What?"

"You'll see."

Tricked

We left the boat giggling like teenagers as we got into the back of the car. Ian raised the privacy window and we kissed. Locked up emotions engineered their breakout. The telephone rang. "Everything's alright darling. Its just Carlos," he soothed me.

"Yes Carlos. No! I want to go to the house. Call Stinson and make the arrangements." He hung up and turned toward me.

"What time is it?" I asked.

"It doesn't matter. I'll fly you anywhere on earth where it's precisely the time you want it to be," Ian whispered as his lips gently brushed my ear.

"What time do you want it to be McClain? Will you stay until we find it?"

"No."

"Please."

"I can't."

"You won't."

"I have to go home."

"Now?"

"Later."

"Then would you like to see my home?"

"Yes."

The car stopped in front of a towering building where I assumed Ian lived. He shoved a key into the elevator panel. When the doors opened brilliant lights illuminated a helicopter. A man stood nearby.

"You live in a helicopter?" I smiled.

"A philosopher and a comedian. I keep one at my disposal when I'm in the city. They're bloody convenient. I live in a little place up the river."

"Sing Sing?" I cracked myself up. The champagne was kicking back in.

"Ha. Ha."

The helicopter jetted into the night sky with Ian holding me. I fell fast asleep. "Wake up darling. We're here," he whispered into my ear. When I opened my eyes, we'd arrived at another heliport. A car waited with no driver. I snapped into full alert. Ian still could be some kind of nut.

He explained we were on the grounds of his Connecticut estate. After about a 5-minute drive, we pulled in front of a huge mansion. It looked like a castle or one of those homes in the back of the New York Times Sunday Magazine.

"Do you like it?"

"It's magnificent. Do you live here alone?"

"I have a staff, but it could stand a woman's touch."

"Hire Jack," I smiled.

"Capital idea. Perhaps I'll do that," he smiled, opening my door.

"Good evening sir." A very proper British butler met us out front.

"Good evening Stinson. This is Ms. McClain Summers of Dallas, Texas. We'll have brandy in the study."

"Very good sir. Good evening Miss Summers, welcome to Heaven's Gate," he bowed.

"Thank you. Good evening."

"Let's get in out of the cold darling," Ian said. Stinson grabbed our coats.

"Ian your home is incredible. How many rooms do you have?" I asked. Why did I say that? Country! Country!

"I don't know darling. I've never counted them. Let's go this way," he said. I was embarrassed.

"Would you like to count them tonight? Together?" he asked naughtily, rubbing his hand across my shoulders.

"No," I smiled.

We walked through the huge carved doors into a massive study. This was a man's room. Masculine. Brawny. Powerful. It smelled of leather, pipe tobacco and burled oak. A bright fire crackled in the fireplace. Riding trophies. Proclamations. Autographed boat oars. Leather bound books. Block paneling. Portraits of horses and a family crest dominated the space. It looked like one of those exclusive restricted clubs where men go to smoke cigars and scratch. "Would you like a brandy darling?" he asked, pouring the liquor into a lavish crystal snifter.

"No...thank you, I've had enough. But go ahead if you'd like. Ian, this room is spectacular." I sat on one of the massive couches facing the noisy fire, admiring a collection of swords in a nearby display case. "You have so many books. It would take a lifetime to read them all."

He loosened his tie. "Forgive me McClain, do you mind if I...." "Certainly not. Make yourself comfortable."

"Thank you darling. This is my favorite room. It is perfect place to sit and read. The light and view of the river here is exceptionally peaceful. Relaxing. You'd adore it."

He walked over to the desk where he removed his tie and jacket. Then he unbuttoned the top button of his shirt. He looked great. When he came back to the couch he said, "I want to look at you." Sitting close enough to sense a trace of vulnerability, I sat back, leaning my head against the back of the couch. He began touching my hair. My face. My neck. Shoulders. Hands. Admiring me. He removed the pins from my upswept hair, causing the loose curls to dangle softly around my shoulders. I shook my head, making sure to put Romeo's comb in my purse. "I like your hair down," he said running his hand through my curls. I liked the way he looked at me.

"You know...McClain...when I saw you today at the restaurant, I realized it might be the last chance I had to meet you. I noticed you there before, but I thought you and Jack were...well...I asked Raul if he knew you. When he told me Jack was merely your friend...well, I'm glad I bought your lunch today." "Me too."

"Does it bother you at all that I'm British and some years older than you?"

"No. Should it?"

"Of course not."

"Good."

He sat his brandy snifter on the table and looked directly into my eyes. "McClain, it's been a number of years since I've pursued anyone. I confess that I'm rusty and I must apologize if my technique is awkward, but under no circumstances should you doubt my sincerity. This may be sudden and a trifle direct, but you'll find that I'm an extremely direct person. I'm used to getting what I want, and I want you. If you're the least bit interested in forming a relationship with me, please tell me. I adore you. Can I trust you?"

"Yes."

Wow! Had I just agreed to be this man's woman or had I merely said that I trusted him? Ian rubbed my hair and kissed my head. I rubbed his back, placing my head against his neck, still looking into the fire.

"I think this would be a rather good time for my other little surprise. I have something I want to give you. I was going to send it to you next week, but I can't wait." Ian rose from the couch and walked behind a large desk at the other end of the room. I watched him over the back of the couch. "I really hope you like it. I picked it out the first time I saw you at RJP. You just seemed to be the type of lady who could appreciate something like this."

At that precise moment, one of his servants entered the room. "Pardon me sir, Mr. Styles is on the telephone." I turned around and straightened my dress. "I told Stinson that I didn't want to be disturbed!" Ian snapped. "It's a very important call sir. If I may be so bold, I think you should take it. Excuse me Miss."

"Excuse me darling. Sit there, I'll be right back. This won't take a moment."

"I'll be fine. Go ahead. Take your call."

"Are you sure?"

"Positive." Ian kissed my hand and left the room.

Funny, he said the first time he saw me at RJP. I never saw him there. I don't see every wealthy client, but someone would have told me about this pretty man. When did he see me? The room held clues to who Ian was. I was determined to find out.

Massive bookcases held first edition reading materials. Each book was a work of literary perfection. A credenza behind his desk was cluttered with beautifully framed pictures of two boys. I

108

recognized Ian. The other boy was just as handsome, but appeared younger. The most endearing was taken on a beach. They were hugging. Laughing. Shimmering.

"May I bring you something Miss?" I jumped and grabbed my chest.

"I'm sorry Ms. Summers did I startle you?" Stinson asked.

"You did, but I'm fine."

"I'm terribly sorry Miss. May I fetch you something from the kitchen or the bar?"

"If it's not too much trouble, I'd love some hot tea."

"It would be my pleasure. Earl Grey?"

"Do you have Green Tea?"

"Yes Miss. "Honey or sugar?"

"Sugar."

"Lemon?"

"No thank you. Mr. Stinson, who's the boy in the photograph with Ian?"

"I'm sure Mr. Lawford will be happy to share with you the name of the boy in the photographs. Charming photo. It's always been one of my favorites."

He left and I continued my forage through Ian's things. Stinson re-entered the room, carrying a silver tray. He placed it on a small table nearby. "Shall I pour Miss?

"No Stinson. I'll take care of that. Thank you," Ian reappeared. "How do you like it darling?"

"Hot." I flirted.

"Wonderful." He smiled, acknowledging my flirtation handing me a napkin. "Devine!" Ian went to the desk, sitting on the edge and beckoning me with his fore finger.

What possibly made him think I was the type you beckon? I hate when men do that. Ignoring him, I turned around sipping the warm tea. "I'm sorry darling. I meant nothing by it." Ian knew better. He came around and positioned himself on the cocktail table. Ian shouted, "Open it! Open it!" shoving a brightly colored box at me. Inside was a lovely velvet case. "I'll hold that," he snatched the teacup from me.

"Thank you Ian. This is beautiful," I whispered.

"That's not it silly. Open that one too!" Inside was another box wrapped in gold paper. He smiled, with the whitest teeth I'd ever seen. "Hurry!"

I lifted the lid and gasped, "Ian! I can't accept this. It must have cost a fortune. I can't. I'm sorry." Genuine disappointment extinguished the fire in his eyes as I sat the box on the table next to him.

"A small fortune," he smiled taking my hand, fastening the clasp of a glittering diamond and emerald bracelet. There must have been at least 20 karats of diamonds. "I wanted you to have a special piece for your collection. One that would remind you of our first date." He kissed my palm. "And you shouldn't wear such a bracelet without matching earrings." Ian pulled equally astounding earrings from his pocket. "Try these on. Do they suit you?"

"Ian," I whispered. Taking my earrings off.

"They're yours. If you don't take them, I'll throw them into the ocean."

"You're not serious."

"Tonight."

"Ian, you don't have to give me gifts to like you. I liked you the first time I saw you too. You need to know, no matter how wonderful the gifts or the man bearing them, I'm not for sale. I'm not even for lease. You're going to take these things back...and the coat too? I'm uncomfortable taking these things from you."

"Nonsense. Were I a poor man and brought you flowers would you hurl them back at me? That's the real arrogance. I'm fortunate to be very wealthy. It allows me certain freedom to do as I want. There's really nothing I can't afford and giving gifts provides me great pleasure. You fear that I expect a sort of quid pro quo. How provincial of you. You astonish me. There are no more strings attached to these baubles than if I'd handed you a bunch of flowers. Consider them very expensive flowers. That way you can accept them graciously, even if they are from me." I'd insulted him and he just called me country. Jack would be furious. I had to save the moment.

Tricked

I reached up and took his saddened face into my hands. It was smooth and soft. "May I kiss you Ian?" I whispered.

"Please," he whispered back.

I kissed him for a long time. A different kind of kiss. Passionate. Fierce. It had fire. He held me as I admired the bracelet over his shoulder. "Are you sure I can keep them?" I whispered.

"As long as you'd like darling. I promise," he chuckled, kissing my ear.

"Thanks."

"No.... thank you McClain."

"For what?"

"For…tonight...everything." We continued our embrace, neither wanting to be the first to let go.

"Ian?"

"Yes darling," he whispered softly.

"I have to pee."

He erupted in laughter, pointing toward a door that led to the powder room. I grabbed my handbag and walked down the fabulous hallway. Before a massive mirror I admired the earrings and bracelet. The champagne had me reeling. It was time to go home. I repaired my lipstick, freshened my breath and dabbed perfume here and there. As I walked into the study, Ian was on the telephone. He hung it up as soon as he noticed me.

"Ian, I should go home."

"Please stay? I promise I'll be on my best behavior."

"It's not your behavior I'm worried about. I need to leave while I still have the strength to say no," pulling him from the couch.

"I hate that word. Are you certain?"

"Absolutely."

"What if I…?"

"No."

"This is positively disastrous. If you're absolutely sure, Carlos will take you to the airport. A car will be waiting for you in Dallas and I'll call you after you've been safely delivered to your door. I'll call you the next day… and the next…and the next."

"I can't wait." He kissed both my hands. "So when do we begin this courting ritual you Americans seem so fond of?"

"I'll let you know," I smiled.

"Let me know soon. I've written my numbers here on this card. My staff will have explicit instructions to direct your calls to me no matter the circumstances, day or night. This is my personal line. I'm the only person who answers it. I plan to see you very soon and very often." I rubbed my hand across his cheek.

We walked down the hall into the immense foyer with his arm around my shoulder. Stinson appeared with my newly acquired coat as the limo pulled in front of the house. Ian walked me to the car and climbed inside. "Are you going to the airport with me?"

"No. I couldn't bear to see you leave. Must our date end? Please stay. You can't leave me now."

"I have to go home."

"If I insisted, would you still leave?"

"Yes," I smiled.

"This is positively tragic." We kissed gently and he stepped out of the car. I rolled the window down and blew him a kiss. He pretended to catch it and placed it to his heart.

"Thank you for everything Ian."

"I feel glorious having something...someone...you to look forward to. Have a marvelous flight darling and I'll speak with you later." "Good night Ian."

The driver pulled away and I continued waving until Ian was completely out of sight. I slept all the way to the airport wrapped in the luxury of the coat and in the fantasy of this fascinating man.

It was the best date I ever had. Not because of the gifts; the plane ride; the boat or the restaurant. Ian welcomed my intellect without judgment or intimidation. He was completely comfortable with me. I was comfortable with him too. I didn't feel I had to explain. Compensate. Capitulate. Control. Settle.

Somehow he'd insinuated himself into my feelings with ease and simplicity. It really didn't hurt that his personal wealth exceeded the economies of most nations. He knew what I needed. Wanted. Dreamed. Sought. There was one thing. Ian wasn't Black.

CHAPTER TWELVE

A flurry of police cars, ambulances and on-lookers crowded the posh driveway. "We have a jumper at the Palladium Condominiums on Turtle Creek. Copy? Lights and sirens." The police scanner screeched.

"We copy. Are units there?"

"10-4. Three squads at the scene. One Engine Company and ambulances."

"Instruct units to secure the area and wait for further instructions."

"4"

"Do we have a positive on the jumper?"

"Not yet."

"Who's the senior officer at the scene?"

"That would be Sgt. Jason Brown, Oaklawn division."

"4 we're out."

"Morgan, this is Boykins. Do you copy?"

"Yes sir."

"Robbery Homicide will take over. Cordon the area. Allow residents and emergency personnel only. No media."

"Yes sir."

"Is that jumper still alive?"

"Medics are working on him now. Seems he took a 4 story leap."

"Whew!"

"Our ETA is 3 minutes. We're out."

I dialed her number making sure that my signal was scrambled. The answering machine picked up. Where was she? Prescott lived on the 4th floor. No gender information about the jumper was stated on the police scanner. So I wandered toward the building for more information. A guy who'd just been interviewed by a local news outlet stood there with his cap in his hand. "What happened?" I asked.

Visibly shaken, he said, "Some guy just fell over the balcony up there. I was sitting in my truck at the stop light over there, looking up at the moon, and this guy comes tumbling over down. At first I thought it was one of those dummies or something, but when the light changed and I pulled over and saw this guy. I dialed 911 on my cell phone and started yelling for the doorman guy. I told him that some guy just fell off one of those balconies up there. He ran back inside and called security or something. Then we jumped over that fence to see if we could help the guy."

"Was he dead?"

"Nope. Kept trying to say something. I couldn't understand him. I never saw nothing like it in my life. He was bleeding and making noises. I'll never forget how he looked. Are you a reporter too?"

"Yes, I happened to hear about this on my scanner and thought I'd better check it out. Let me get my pad and make sure that I spell your name right."

"Well it's just like I told the other guy, I was at the light...by the way the name is Harold Beasely. That's B-E-A-S-E-L-Y.....and I see this guy tumbling over the rail up there."

"When you say tumbling over the rails Harold, did it look like he jumped?"

"Well sir....It's hard to say.....but if you ask me it looked more like he fell."

"How could you tell the difference?"

"Well sir...It just looked like to me he was trying to catch something on his way down. You know, like he was trying to break the fall. Fighting with the air. I would have been struggling against the wind too. That's what he seemed to be doing. He was screaming the whole way. I guess he could have jumped and changed his mind on the way down, but that's a hell of a time to get wishy-washy. When will this be in the newspaper? You know my wife will get a real kick out of this. She's pregnant and craving Mexican food tonight. You got kids? It's our first and she gets these cravings. Hell, I've gained 20 pounds myself since she's been pregnant. So I'm out all night driving around trying to find this place where she ate burritos last week. I'm driving and I'm thinkin maybe it was Rosita's on Lemmon. So I took a shortcut through here and that's when all of this happened. Will this be in the Saturday or Sunday paper?"

"Probably Saturday. I'll try to get a good story out of this Mr. Beasely. If I need more information, where can I reach you?"

"My home number is 234-0679. Remember that's Harold Beasely."

"I got it."

"Nothing else for me to do here. I already gave my statement to the cops. I'd better get home. Wait until my wife hears this. She says nothing exciting ever happens. It doesn't get much more exciting than this. I just wish I had my video camera. I bought for the baby. I could've sold it to one of those 'Caught on Film' deals. Good night."

"Oh Mr. Beasely...did you see anyone come out of the building after the guy fell?"

"Yeah...now that you mention it. Two guys come out the back over there. I don't know why they caught my attention. Probably cause one of them was wearing sunglasses. I figured they must be some kind of celebrities or something, wearing sun glasses in the dark. Anyway they got into this dark car and sped off. Did you tell the police?"

"No sir. I guess I should have."

"Don't worry about it. I'll let them know."

"That's mighty nice of you..Mr...."

"Lyle. Henry Lyle."

"Thank you Mr. Lyle. Good night."

"Thank you Mr. Beasely. Best regards to your wife. I hope you find that Mexican food."

"Me too."

Tricked

Harold pulled his pants up over his twenty pounds of stomach and trudged back to his pick-up truck. I jotted down this tag numbers just in case I needed him in the future. I went back to the car and called in.

"It's me."

"Someone just took a swan dive from his balcony."

"Where's she?"

"I don't know. She's not home, so maybe he's on it."

"OK, we'll find her. Find whatever information you can and get back here tonight. There's a meeting in the morning. We have lots of work to do."

"Yes sir." I dialed her number again.

"Hello?"

"Who the hell is this?" I asked, trying to sound territorial.

"This is detective Boykins, Dallas Police. Who are you?"

"The police? Is McClain there?

"She's not home. Who's this?"

"Why are police in her house? Is something wrong with McClain?"

"I can't go into detail right now sir. What is your name?"

117

CHAPTER THIRTEEN

Emergency vehicles whizzed past us. Police cars were everywhere. News trucks blocked half the street, with huge satellite disks poking out on top. At first I thought that one of my elderly celebrity neighbors had a heart attack. Many well known people owned property in the building. Something must have happened to one of them. A fire engine zoomed by. Oh my God! A fire. My new suits. My disks. Pellman's information. The only photograph I had of my father. Not necessarily in that order.

I looked out the front window of the car, trying to see what was happening. As we turned toward the building a uniformed police officer stopped the car. "Sorry cowboy, we're not allowing anyone through except residents. You'll have to turn around over there and take another street."

"I'm a resident officer," I yelled from the backseat. The officer approached the back and I lowered the window. "I'm McClain Summers. I live in the building." I showed the officer my driver's license.

"Alright, park over there and you can come through." The officer waved his arms allowing us to pass. "Wow!" I said to the driver. "I wonder what happened?" The driver ran to my side of the vehicle and opened the door. "Ms. Summers?"

"Yes?"

"Have a good evening. I mean day. I hope everything is alright."

"Thank you. I hope so too."

I couldn't wait to get upstairs and take off these hurting shoes. Jack would be waiting for a full report. He'd faint when he saw the coat. The jewels. I was too tired to notice the inquisitive stares and questioning looks from neighbors. A hot shower awaited me. It was after 3:30 and Rick would be knocking on my door at exactly 7:59 in the morning. For the story I had to tell, Jack could wait a few more minutes.

Four other residents shared my floor. They were standing in the hallway when I got off the elevator. Their attention was focused on my place. Quickening my pace, I pushed past them and pasty men in cheap suits. When I reached my doors, one of them grabbed me.

"I'm sorry, you can't go in there," an officer blocked my way.

"What do you mean I can't come in? Are you crazy? This is my home," I protested, straining against him.

"What's going on?" Another man asked.

"Are you McClain Summers?" a tall Hispanic man looked up from my desk where he rambled through my appointment book.

"Who are you? Give me that!" I snatched my book and put it beneath my arm.

"I'm detective Jesse Garcia with the Dallas Police Department. I work the robbery homicide division and we're in your home investigating an apparent burglary."

"Burglary...? What are you talking about?" I looked around, trying to unscramble my thoughts when I said, "Will you tell that man to take his boots off my silk rug."

"Do you know Jack Prescott?" he asked flipping a note pad. "Walker, get your boots off the rug. Everybody, no boots on the silk rugs," he barked smugly.

"Jack? Of course."

"Jack Prescott jumped off his balcony approximately two hours ago. Do you know any reason why he would have done that?"

"What!!!!! Jack.....jumped????!!!!" Disbelief spun the room. I was losing my balance. An officer caught me before I hit the floor. He helped me to the couch where another officer broke a capsule of ammonia beneath my nose. "Stop!" I whimpered, regaining my composure.

"Charlie, bring me a glass of water," Detective Garcia said.

"Ms. Summers are you alright? Would you like me to call you a doctor?"

"No....I....I...I...did you say Jack? It's impossible....not Jack.....I mean....Jack would never....he'd never do anything like that. Jump?...No...No Way!!! Are you sure it was Jack...Jack Prescott?" I whispered, wanting this to be a fatal misunderstanding.

"Yes we are."

"You said attempted. Is he?"

"He's not dead."

That's when I noticed everything was in my home was in complete disarray. It looked like someone had turned it upside down and shaken it. "What happened in here?"

"Your neighbor, a Mr. Greene, reported a possible burglary. Mr. Greene said that he heard Mr. Prescott arguing with someone. When he looked out of his peephole, he saw Mr. Prescott and the other man enter the elevator. Security let us in. Your entire condo looks like this. It appears you've been robbed."

"Does this have anything to do with Jack?"

"That's what we hope you'll tell us. We understand you two are good friends."

"Best friends," I whispered.

"We need you to look around to see if anything's missing. Then we'd like you to come downtown and answer a few questions. Do you know whether Mr. Prescott was using drugs or had any enemies? Do you think someone was looking for you?"

Before I could answer his questions another man approached us. "Is this Ms. Summers?" the man asked.

"Yes sir," Garcia said, standing.

"Hello Ms. Summers. I'm detective Boykins." He extended his hand. I shook it.

"I'm the ranking detective with the robbery homicide division. I'm in charge of this investigation. I'm sure this is quite a shock for you. The other residents tell us that you and Mr. Prescott were quite close. After you answer some of our questions, I'll have an officer take you to the hospital. The truth of the matter is Mr. Prescott is in grave condition and the doctors don't expect him to survive. He's having emergency surgery later this morning, and that's all we know right now." The tears began. "Do you know of any reason whatsoever why Mr. Prescott would try to commit suicide?"

"No…no."

"Did he take drugs or participate in any activities that would have made him delusional? Like drugs?"

"No....of course not. He drank a little wine, but other than that he was a complete health nut."

"Can you tell me why he would have been in your home tonight?"

"He was waiting for me to get home from a date. He knew tonight was very special to me...he...he was supposed to wait for me…he wanted to know all of the details....and....I was suppose to give him all of the details..." I choked.

Detective Garcia handed me his handkerchief. I wiped my nose. My head pounded.

"Did Jack have any enemies?"

"No. Everybody loved Jack."

"I need you to look around...try to identify anything that might be missing. I'm sorry to have to ask you this, but do you take drugs? Are there any drugs or weapons in you home?"

"No. I've never done drugs in my life. There are no guns in my home and I have no idea what happened. I was in Manhattan this evening. I just returned."

"I'm sorry. I hope you understand I had to ask. I'm very sorry about your friend. If we have further questions may we contact you?"

"Yes."

Dazed, I took off the coat. The officers scrambled over my ransacked house like ants. All I could think of was Jack. The thought of losing him was impossible to endure. My jewelry. My clothes. My books. My computer. My disks? I peaked into the

Light Days box. Everything was still there. Pellman's information was in the garage. Detective Boykins walked into the bedroom.

"Has anything been taken?"

I jumped. "Everything seems to be here. When may I leave? I want to get to Jack before…" More tears.

"As soon as you'd like. You might want to change first."

"Oh yeah…Detective?"

"Yes?"

"Jack would never jump off a balcony. He's much too vain. He would have taken pills or something that wouldn't hurt. He would've left a long detailed note. Maybe even a video. He would've called people. Everyone would have known about it in advance. It would have been very dramatic. I'd bet my life on it."

The officer smiled and walked out of my bedroom. As I quickly changed clothes, the telephone rang. It was Ian.

"Hello Ian."

"Hello darling. I wanted to make sure you arrived safely. Without question you'll be in my dreams tonight. Did you have a good flight?"

"I did."

"Splendid. Are you alright McClain? You sound...well you sound strange darling. Has something happened?"

"I'm just tired."

"Are you sure? I'll be out of the country for the next few days and I'll miss you terribly. Maybe you can fly over and join me for dinner in Paris. I can..........."

"Ian, I have to go."

"OK.....OK...You're right. You're right. Good night darling. Sleep well. I'll ring you in the morning before I leave. Sweet dreams."

There was something more happening here. What I couldn't understand is why the detectives were in my home and why they seemed more interested in me, than what they said had happened to Jack. Ian didn't matter right now and he wouldn't be in my dreams.

"Goodnight."

Tricked

Detective Boykins hung up my telephone at the same time. "Run a background on her Garcia. I've got that funny feeling." Garcia chuckled to himself and walked out onto the balcony.

Through a threatening storm of tears and anguish I dressed, pulling on black jeans, white cotton shirt and the black snakeskin cowboy boots Jack bought them on one of his frenetic shopping frenzies. I pulled my hair into a ponytail with one of the many 'fashionable but classy' barrettes Jack gave me. "You've got regal bones girl, show them!" he insisted. Having resisted his prodding in the past, tonight I felt a tug to concede. After washing off tear stained make-up, I applied moisturizer. Brushed my teeth and gargled. I smoothed tinted gloss onto my lips and tossed my wallet, tissue, cell phone, organizer, extra strength Tylenol and the box of Light Days into my backpack.

When I reached for my leather jacket I remembered to remove the sparkling earrings. I threw them into the bag, but I kept the bracelet on. If Jack saw it, he'd feel better.

The officers and detectives were packing their equipment when I returned to the living room. I deplored them. "We'll lock up things when we leave."

"No, security can take care of that if you don't mind. I'd prefer you leave now."

"OK guys let's go. Ms. Summers will you let us know if Mr. Prescott says anything useful?" the detective asked. "Of course."

Mr. Peal was standing in Mr. Greene's doorway when we walked into the hall. He approached with a smile and hug, "I'm sorry about Mr. Prescott. Such a nice young man. Give him our best. Such a horrible thing."

"Will you see to my apartment Mr. Greene? I need security to..."

"Of course my darling. I heard such shouting. Breaking. Such a noise. I called the police. They came right away. What on earth happened?"

"I don't know. They said something happened to Jack. I just don't know what. He's in the hospital. Intensive care."

"Mr. Peal told me about Mr. Prescott. Such a tragedy. I really liked him," he said holding his face.

"He liked you too. Thank you Mr. Greene. I have to leave now."

"Give Mr. Prescott my best."

"I will. Goodnight."

"We'll take care of everything. Security will get everything locked up. Now go. Go."

A moist nauseating smell permeated the police cruiser. My stomach refused to settle itself. The officer lowered the window. "Are you going to be alright?" he asked. My head pounded. Dry heaves strained my stomach muscles. Teardrops pooled on the front of my jacket. Crumpled tissues formed no barrier against the tears that exploded from my soul. What was Jack thinking? What happened? Did he get drunk and fall? Did he trip? I needed answers. Explanations. Jack.

Dallas Hospital was a vast medical abyss buzzing with activity, even at this hour. We must have walked a mile before stopping in front of some elevators that took us to the Trauma ICU. I trailed the policeman like a zombie. Half drunk. Completely exhausted. Thoroughly stunned. Literally shocked.

Delirium showed up first. Concern came next. Fear made a grand entrance when the elevator doors opened. Oblivious to whether the elevator was headed up or down, I stepped forward. The officer caught my shoulder pulling me back. "It's going down."

Certainly if Jack intended to kill himself, I would have seen some sign. Black folks don't commit suicide. Do they? Anyway, things were going great for Jack. We just celebrated his big new account. New store. He was dating a mystery man, who was still in the closet. Things were good.

Selfishness prevented my accepting anyone sharing Jack's life. One night after a complete day of shopping, Jack ordered Chinese food and we drank two whole bottles of wine. I spent the night at his place because I'd had too much wine to safely walk home. Jack was too drunk to drive me. It was the first of our many slumber parties.

"Nobody loves me for my mind Jack," I lamented. "Nobody thinks I have mind McClain."

We laughed and told stories late into the night. Jack was gorgeous. Too bad he didn't like women. As the night progressed, Jack found a bottle of rum and decided to make pineapple daiquiris. Never being able to say no to pineapples, it wasn't long before we were buttered. I never drank that much before or since. I'd never been drunk or even had a buzz. I felt sick.

"Can I take a shower Jack?" Before he answered, I ripped off my clothes and stepped into the shower. Jack joined me. It was all very bizarre. So I left the shower and began lathering myself with lotion from Jack's dresser.

He walked into the bedroom stark naked and sat beside me.

"Pass me the Coco Butter." I handed it to him. "I need to put some on my feet," he said. "My feet are my best feature because they are as soft as a baby's bottom."

"A baby what?" I laughed.

"Shut up. You're just jealous."

"Of what? I have pretty feet."

"What color nail polish is that?" We both stared at my feet, neither of us able to distinguish pink from peach.

"Jack where's the deodorant?"

"It's in the bathroom in the medicine cabinet."

"Do you have an extra toothbrush?"

"Yeah. Look under the sink." I stumbled toward the bathroom with the towel still around me. There were two packages of toothbrushes. Blow dryer. Toilet tissue and one of those old-fashioned hot water bottles. Industrial size. I raised my eyebrows and decided not to touch it. I didn't even want to know what he used it for. After brushing my teeth, I plugged the drier into the socket and began a vain attempt at drying my hair.

Jack appeared in the doorway holding two glasses. He was still naked. "Put some clothes on boy!"

"Look…there's a corner left. We might as well kill it," he said, struggling to put on his robe while holding the glasses at the same time. After about five minutes of this slapstick, Jack sat the glasses on the vanity and tied the robe around his waist. "Lord, give me that dryer girl, you just burning your little nappy hair out. It's a wonder you ain't completely bald headed."

"Move Jack! I know how to dry my hair!" I protested. "Give me that drier girl!" He snatched it from me.

I was too drunk to fight. Jack let the hot air blow through the masses of curly tangles. My hair was dry in half the time it usually took me to dry it. It was straight too. No piles of hair cluttered the floor or sink.

"How'd you do that?" I asked.

"You're pitiful…really…just pitiful," Jack laughed as he stumbled back into the bedroom.

I put all the items away and walked back into the bedroom. Jack was already in bed. He looked sexy against the pastel blue sheets. He wasn't in the closet. He wasn't flamboyant. Feminine. Flashy. You'd never know Jack was gay unless he told you.

My towel fell to the floor and Jack leaned up on one elbow. "You have a great body Cheeks." He called me that because he thought I had great cheekbones. "There I was about to nominate you for president of the Itty Bitty Titty Committee, and you got ta tas. Girl you'd better show what you got to get what you want," he cackled.

After turning off the lights, I slid beneath the sheets and lay against him. He was warm and wrapped his arms around me. Surprised at his erection, Jack kissed the top of my head. We never spoke. Soft sweet kisses between friends quickly became the passionate prelude to a reckless interlude.

"Wait." Jack reached into his nightstand for a condom. He couldn't find them in the dark and turned on the lamp. When he reached up to turn the light off, I whispered, "Leave it on."

Jack turned around and we began laughing hysterically. We'd never kissed like lovers. We'd never rubbed ourselves together, and we'd certainly never seen each other with our hair standing straight up on our heads. What were we doing? This was ridiculous. We were ridiculous. Drunk. We laughed until our sides hurt. Tears streamed from our eyes. Our throats ached. Our stomach muscles seized. When Jack composed himself, I cracked up. When I composed myself, he cracked up. We fought for the sheets to cover our nakedness. Jack jumped from the bed and put on pajama bottoms. He threw an entire pair of pajamas at me. We laughed all night.

To this day, I don't know what we found so funny. It had to be the alcohol. We were both happy and relieved nothing happened. We became closer than ever after that night.

Jack introduced me to his 'friends', as his sister. Something was always wrong with them. Bad hair. Bad breath. No character. No class. No future. Low life. No life. Whatever. I didn't, I wouldn't allow anyone to interfere with our friendship. Our family.

"You are *so* jealous," he'd complain. I argued the point, but he was right. I'm jealous right now that death might be the final interloper against whom I have no influence.

Guilt nudged me. Third Floor. If only you'd stayed home. Fourth Floor. If only you'd gone out with Rick as planned. Fifth Floor. You could have seen Ian next weekend. Sixth Floor. Why were you so eager? Bo was right. Ambition overrides everything. Everyone. You've broken your own rules. Make the man wait. Then make the wait worth it.

Tonight the corporate games, strategies and schemes meant nothing. I didn't care about Keith, Rick, Matthew or Bo. I didn't care about Pellman, RJP International or Ian. Jack was everything. Everything.

Time to start my bilateral talks with God began when we reached the Trauma ICU. Negotiations with heaven must be heavy on this floor. I only hoped the prayer pipeline was strong enough for my prayers to hitch a ride on the coat tails of the righteous. My voice would be foreign to the Father. The Son and the Holy Ghost. At least worth a try, doubtful and hopeful, that God would feel inclined to help me now, I prayed for Jack. We hadn't spent a lot of time together and I wouldn't blame him if he sat this one out.

Cynthia A. Minor

I didn't pray. Not real prayers. Not the ones like deacons pray. I'd read the bible and liked its premise. Jack convinced me God would forgive our sins. He's the "God of a Second Chance." At least that's what the preacher at Concordia Street Baptist Church said the Sundays Jack drug me there. I just wasn't sure saving Jack was the second chance the deacon spoke of.

Jack was a regular member of Believers Rest, but he went to Concordia because he really liked a deacon who really liked him back. "That's him," Jack said pointing. "Isn't he fantastic?"

"Isn't he married?" I whispered.

"Party Pooper!" Jack sniped.

CHAPTER FOURTEEN

The antiseptic smell in the hallway turned my stomach to Jell- O. I teetered. The officer caught me. "Are you alright? Take a deep breath."

"I'm OK," I said, steadying myself.

We passed unidentifiable people hooked to a variety of medical technology. Beeps, buzzes and blips filled the corridor. In the middle of this technological jumble of medical miracles and misery lay Jack. I barely recognized him. He was obscured by bandages. Gauze. Pipes. Bags. Cords. Machines. Tanks. IVs. Before I could identify myself, a doctor asked, "Are you McClain?"

"Yes," I replied, tears coming. How did she know me?

"That's the only thing he's said since they scraped him from the pavement," she said matter of factly. "He's in a drug induced coma and his chances are bleak. He's beyond critical. He has massive internal injuries and a portion of his liver was lacerated. He has two broken legs and a broken shoulder. His pelvis was pulverized as was his sternum. His heart is bruised and he has a collapsed lung. It appears that his neck is broken at C-2 and we cannot discern at this time whether he'll be a quadruped. Our immediate concern is the very serious skull fracture he sustained. Surgery will be performed this morning to remove the pressure on his brain.

Such inter-cranial injuries are usually fatal. If the internal injuries don't kill him, the surgeries probably will. If by some miracle he survives, he'll probably live out the rest of his life in a persistent irreversible vegetative state. Do you know if he has insurance?

There's a temporary shunt in his head now. One of our social workers will speak to you about his organs, but I don't believe there are any organs left that are worth harvesting. It's procedure," she said pulling one of Jack's eyelids open and shining a light into it. "Do you know if he wanted to donate? Oh yes, if he has other relatives, you should get them here pronto. Now about the insur..."

Jack's medical prognosis trapped me in a science fiction moment. Standing there with his eyeball in her hand, this woman talked to me like I was a chump. No compassion. Empathy. Sympathy. Nothing. My Jack lay there connected to noisy contraptions with tubes, bags and wires sticking out of his head and every other part of his body and this thing in a white coat has the temerity to talk about donating Jack's organs.

It was apparent Jack hadn't a body part left that wasn't either broken off or busted up. Justifiably irritated, I became an attack dog interrupting her in mid-sentence. "Exactly who are you? Is there a resuscitation order? Who'll make that call? What's the team plan? Are you on the team? Who's in charge of neurology? Who's on the operating team? What time will the surgery take place? Did you make the assessments on your own or were those assessments made by others? And exactly what is your specialty Miss?" I used my most dismissive 'in charge' voice.

Insulted, she shot back, "I prefer to be called Doctor Hayes. I'm not certain I can answer all of your questions, you wouldn't understand most of them anyway."

That was it. I was just about to clock her when one of the machines keeping Jack alive started buzzing. Jack heard me. This was his way of telling me to knock this bitch out. I dropped my backpack on the floor and unzipped my coat. The police officer tapped me on the shoulder. I'd forgotten he was in the room.

"I don't think she can tell you what you need to know," he whispered, defusing the situation.

I composed myself, but steam rose from my pores. "Well who can? Are you the treating physician?"

"No, I'm a second year resident."

Tricked

"A student? A student? Why are you even talking to me? Since you can't answer my questions, get out my face and direct me to someone who can." I never speak to people in this manner, but the issue of Jack's life was at stake.

"I...I..." she stuttered.

"Step off lady! I don't want to hear anything you've got to say."

With my last statement the self- important little twit angrily walked away. She stopped at the nurse's station, pointing in my direction. Two nurses leaned over the desk looking at me. I put my hands on my hips, giving them the meanest glare I could muster.

A nurse came around the desk. The police officer stepped behind me. "I've got your back," he whispered.

"Hello, I'm Linda Covington. I'm the ICU nursing supervisor. Mr. Prescott is my patient. Are you family?"

"I'm the person who's gonna sue this hospital if that second year quack comes close to this room again. If Mr. Prescott doesn't receive the best medical care possible, you have no idea the trouble I can cause! I guarantee that!" I snapped.

"Rest assured Mr. Prescott will receive the best care. Drs. Lydia Freeman and Frank Jackson head the team. Brenda Jordan is the general surgeon. John Burnett is the orthopedic surgeon. Craig Brown is the neuro surgeon. Blake Goldman is the pulmonary thoracic surgeon. Donovan Theodopolus is the vascular surgeon. Henry Glasser is the plastic surgeon. There is an automatic resuscitation order until the family says otherwise.

Due to the hour, most of the doctors have left the hospital.

Drs. Brown, Goldman and Theodopolus will be here shortly to perform additional surgery. If you have any questions regarding anything, please feel free to ask me. I'll answer them as best I can, or at least attempt to get you the answers you seek. Don't be too angry with Dr. Hayes. She's new and she'll make a good doctor one day."

"She's deficient in people skills and she needs to go back to doctor's charm school," I snapped. The nurse smiled.

"Would you like to spend the night with Mr. Prescott?"

"Yes...oh yes... may I?"

"Of course. I'll see that a cot is brought into the room for you. If he has any trauma during the night, you'll be asked to leave. It gets a little noisy around here, but if that doesn't bother you, you're welcomed to stay. Follow me and I'll show you where we hide the restrooms," she said kindly.

"Thank you Mrs. Covington. This is all came as such a shock and ...well...she just pissed me off. I wanted to smack her."

"Umm Humm. If there's someone you think needs notification, now's the time. It'll be a miracle if he lives, but miracle happen everyday on this floor. The telephones are around the corner."

"I have my own. Is he in any pain? I don't want him to be in pain."

"No he's not in any pain. He's in a coma. I'm sorry, but you can't use your phone on this floor. Please use the pay phones over there. Or you'll have to go outside."

"Oh. OK. Thank you so much."

"Ms. Summer. I'll be leaving now. I hope your friend gets better," the officer smiled at me.

"Thank you officer. I don't even know your name."

"Brian Miller."

"Thank you Brian Miller." I touched his hand.

"Will you be able to get home later?" he asked.

"I'm not leaving."

"I mean later...later."

"Yeah. I'll call someone or catch a cab."

"I get off at 7. If you need a ride call me."

"Thanks."

Officer Miller stared at me shyly, as though he had more questions. "Is there anything else Officer Miller?"

"May I speak with you for a moment?"

"Sure...excuse me Ms. Covington." We stood near the elevators. "Yes?"

"I know that this isn't the right time and I'm out of order, but I was wondering, once all of this is over... whether we could go out for coffee or something." He had to be kidding. A date?

"Sure...why not?"

He gave me his card and wrote his home number on back. I gave him one of my business cards and walked away.

"Ms. Summers, after you've finished with your calls, we'll have the bed all set up for you. By the way, that's a magnificent bracelet you're wearing."

"Thank you. It was a gift."

"Some gift. That's a mighty special Santa Clause you have." She turned and headed back to the nurses station.

"Mrs. Covington?" I said quietly.

"Yes dear."

"Thank you."

"You're welcome," she smiled, winked and walked away.

A leatherette chair sat next to the phone bank in the ICU lobby. Jack's mother's number was under "M" for mothers. I took a deep breath and dialed. The telephone rang six times before someone answered. A man's voice.

"Who da hell is it!?" The gruff voice thundered on the other end.

"Hello. I'm trying to reach the Prescott residence. Yjean Prescott." I stammered. "Do I have the right number?"

I could hear the same angry voice speaking to someone in the room. "Wake up. It's for you. Sound like some white lady. I guess they don't have no clocks where ever she is!"

"Hello?" I heard a timid high pitched voice whisper.

"Hello, Ms. Prescott......Yjean Prescott?"

"Yes this Yjean, who is this?"

"Ms. Prescott, I'm McClain, Jack's friend in Dallas. I've spoken to you..."

"Oh yeah.....uh huh....yeah....Jack talk about you all the time. Say you and him big friends. He's been saying he wants me to come down there and see how good he been doing. But why you calling me this early in the morning?"

"Ms. Prescott, tears finally coming. Jack's had a terrible accident. More tears. Sniffing too. I'm calling you from the hospital. Intensive Care. Choking up. The doctors told me to contact his family....they don't think he's going to make it. Can someone come?"

A shrill scream came from the other end of the telephone.

"My baby! My baby!" She was screaming.

"Mrs. Prescott! Mrs. Prescott!" I was screaming.

"Who the hell is this?" The gruff voice returned. "Look here...this Roosevelt Prescott and I want to know who this is calling my wife upsetting her like this?!!"

"Mr. Prescott. I'm McClain Summers. A friend of Jack. He's been in a terrible accident. He's in a coma. The doctors are doubtful that he'll make it. They told me to call his family... I…"

"Jack ain't got no damn family! Look, we don't know nothin bout what Jack doin down there in Texas. If he hurt, you say he in the hospital didn't ya? That's the best place for him. Ain't nothin we can do from New York."

"But Mr. Prescott...he may die. The doctors said..."

"I don't give a damn about what the doctors said. He disowned this family when he decided to be a sissy. We disown him too. Let his faggoty friend down there see about him."

"But he's still your son. Don't you…"

"Look! I don't need you to tellin me who he is or who I am! Now leave us alone and don't call my damn house no mo!" BAM! The phone went dead.

Jack never talked about his father. This was a stunning revelation. He spoke about his mother and sisters, and I assumed that he grew up without a male influence in his life. Like me. Secretly, I believed it was the reason he lived this lifestyle. He never spoke about Roosevelt Prescott. But after my conversation with him, I understood why. What friend would take care of him? His father implied someone in Dallas would care for Jack. Did he mean me?

Back in Jack's room, a small cot sat in the corner with a faded blue blanket resting atop starchy white sheets. I quickly

Tricked

made up the bed and walked over to Jack. I talked about Ian. The date. Plane. Coat. Boat. Helicopter. Jewels. Mansion. Man.

A nurse came into the room, checking Jack's machines. As she looked at every hose, IV, button and bag, I described the restaurant and how much I liked Ian. The date. Exhausted, I put my backpack under the pillow and slid between the sheets. I watched Jack for a long time. He never moved. Before I knew it, I was asleep too.

CHAPTER FIFTEEN

Dammit! I knew something like this might happen. Why didn't Jack listen to me? He knew he had to be careful. These people were deadly. I begged him to just ask her where the information was. She would've told him, especially if he told her that his life depended on it. After all, he knew more about McClain than anyone. Hell, he practically lived with her.

I wondered if they found it. I wondered if I'd be next. I wondered if Jack is dead. What I should do? Jack was certain the disks were in the condo. Pellman stopped by last night. He had the information. He gave it to McClain. Where was it?

Our cleverly crafted façade took three years to perfect. We worked diligently cultivating their relationship. He turned that place into a palace. "It's fit for a queen," he gushed. No expense was spared and our connections got him the write-up in Dallas Magazine.

Always bragging about how talented he is. How wonderful he is. How much she loves him. After Jack decorated her condo, she threw a huge party to benefit her favorite charity and showcase Jack's work. It made the social pages, and everybody who was anybody in Dallas was there. She praised him all night, introducing him to politicians. Athletes. Entertainers. Corporate types. Jack lapped the attention up like a starving dog. "Jack captured my essence." I planned to cut her throat.

Jack ignited my passions beyond my imagination. I love him to the point of insanity. I was his first. He integrated himself into my lifestyle completely, leaving everything and everyone behind. He loved me and proved over and over that his love was real. His perspicuity toward us was undiminished. But lately, living this double life was taking a malevolent toll on me.

When we first pledged ourselves to each other, Jack had no idea what my real work was. I couldn't risk telling him. There was too much at stake. After I explained things, he became frightened of me. He didn't want me anymore. I couldn't let him go. So I forced him to become involved in my activities. He had no choice.

My frustrations resulted in my smacking him around a little. Surrogating his pain for mine, I felt justified beating him. Hurting him. Attacking him. No one saw the bruises. I never broke any bones. We doctored his battered body together.

Horrible is insufficient to describe how I felt after each attack. It wasn't my fault. Jack pushed my buttons. I promised never to hurt him every time. A promise I never kept. Why did he push? Why did he always have to push? You must understand. Jack had to be controlled. Talking seldom worked and he provoked me. He knew I loved him. That's why he stayed. That and knowing I'd kill him if he ever tried to leave me. That's what I do. I kill people.

Men found it difficult not to be drawn into McClain's web. Alluring. Lovable. Smart. Charming. Wicked. She made me sick. She ruthlessly played the corporate game and rolled Joshua Pellman around in the palm of her hand. He taught her to win, and winning was everything. Too smart for her own good. Ambitious. Shrewd. I resented these traits in her. Traits reserved for men. Reserved for me. I hate her.

If only they'd let me kill her years ago. I had ample opportunities. Once Jack told me a story about a night she stayed at his place. They got drunk and almost had sex. Nothing happened, but I beat him anyway. He needed medical attention. We told the emergency room doctor that he fell off a ladder. That was the first time hitting him frightened me. Not because he was hurt, but because I enjoyed hurting him. I've become an animal.

But he was mine and she had no claims on him. She was a job. Nothing else. Jack did all of his jobs well. We'd been lovers seven years. He left his family. Life. Business. Surroundings. Wife. For me.

This strange woman was dangerously sweet. Her sugary innocence oozed from every pore. Jack thought she was wonderful. "She'll do anything for you," he'd say. "Do you know how many kids she sends to college? She recruits kids from all over the world into the RJP training classes. She's makes millionaires like other people make pancakes." She even helped him get approved by the home owners association board to move into her building. With them living in the same building, our meetings became nearly impossible. If he'd successfully finished the job last night, we could have left Dallas forever. That's what he wanted. That's what I wanted. I could change. I wanted to change. This is her fault.

Ways to kill her filled my head as I streaked down the highway concocting a million reasons for coming to the hospital. A thousand excuses were ready if a policeman stopped me. Ways of disposing of her body consumed my thoughts. She'd be dead before any dirt hit Jack.

What happened? I had to know. How would I contain my emotions, while providing her a shoulder to cry on? When Jack called last night, he said, "I can't find it. I've looked everywhere!" He was desperate. Frantic. "Tear the place apart! It has to be there! Pellman gave it to her. We're dead men if you don't." When did I become a prophet?

The Bennett group hired Jack and I to keep an eye on McClain. Somehow she stumbled onto information that correctly led her to believe there were undocumented international chemical securities being sold to unidentifiable investors. I work for them. Her spare time was spent cross-referencing resource data with confidential information maintained in the RJP's database.

Not much about her research interested anyone, except us. Our inside people explained away her questions as part of her endless curiosity and creative drive. "You have a criminal mind McClain."

After Jack installed a device on her computer that simultaneously reprinted everything she did into our employer's database, misinformation was easier to create. So we fashioned response data so skillfully that anyone she convinced to listen, dismissed her theories as lacking the slightest hint of believability. Behind her back, everyone had a good chuckle at her expense.

Even Pellman told her to stop, but she was stubborn and compelled. The impossibility of her hypothesis didn't cloud the genius of her determination. Impossible seemed safe we thought. Until she stumbled on St. Lisa's.

Our efforts had been successful until she bought that lap top. She began using it instead of her office PC or her PC at home. Jack was certain she was storing the data we wanted in USB files. He hadn't been able to find the disks or access the hard drive. He needed more time. But time had run out.

When Jack casually asked about her research project, she'd tell Jack, "It's sizzling." She had to find a few more pieces before she took her final theory and proof to Pellman.

An elusive parking space opened in back of the hospital. That's where I'd take McClain and strangle her. Buttermilk donuts and pineapple juice would throw her off. If only I had some arsenic to sprinkle in it. The elevator was full as I headed straight for the ICU. Jack had to be alive. He had to be alive. A nurse stopped me.

"Excuse me sir......May I help you?" she asked.

"Yes"...out of breath. "I'm looking for Jack Prescott... I'm his brother."

"Oh yes...Mr. Prescott is in recovery. You can go to the ICU surgical waiting room if you'd like. You'll find the waiting..."

"Where's McClain?"

"McClain?"

"I'm sorry... the young lady...."

"Oh yes. She spent the night with Mr. Prescott. She's in the chapel. She went in just a moment ago," she said pointing.

"Go right at the corner and it's to your left."

"Thank you." I walked down the hallway following the nurse's instructions. Out of control. I had to pull myself together so I stopped in the men's room to calm myself. My heart was beating so hard it was impossible to breathe. I was shaking. Sweating. She couldn't see me like this. I took deep breaths and splashed cold water on my face. I left the restroom and pushed the door open to the chapel. It was empty except for her.

There she was, kneeling at the alter trying to get a prayer through. She was asking God to help Jack. Save Jack. Make Jack better. She'd better throw a prayer in for herself. These were the last moments of her life. Just as I reached her, two whimpering people burst in. McClain spun around and grabbed her chest. "You scared me! What are you doing here?" she asked.

"I came to be with you. I heard about Jack. I know how much he means to you and I didn't want you to be alone. I came by early this morning. I wanted to surprise you. That's when they told me what happened. I brought you some of those donuts you like and some pineapple juice," I smiled shoving the wrinkled white bag in her direction.

"That's so sweet of you," she said taking the bag and juice bottle. "I'm sorry. It's just that with everything's that's happened, I'm a little jumpy. Did I thank you? I didn't did I? Thank you. You're so considerate. We should go out into the hallway. Do you know what time it is? I'm babbling aren't I?" She rubbed her face, grabbing her things as we went out.

We found a bench. Sadness shrunk her. Her head hung to the left as if it weighed too much. I wanted at the same time to comfort and to kill her. "Are you alright?" I whispered, pretending to care.

"I'm so worried about Jack. He's so weak. He died on the operating table, but the doctors were able to revive him. They really don't have much hope. I just asked God to let him live. You ask too. You believe don't you. Pray for Jack. Promise," she pled.

"I will. I will."

"I made a lot promises that I probably won't keep," she smiled. "I'll try though. I really will. I prayed that he'd make it through surgery and he did, but the next few hours will be critical. They told me he's in grave condition. Have you ever heard of that?

Tricked

Grave condition? But I'm going to stay positive. You stay positive too. Promise you'll stay positive with me."

"I will."

"Jack's strong. He's a fighter. A survivor. He wants to live and when he gets out of here I'm going to insist that he move in with me. I'll take care of him."

She blew her nose and looked down the hallway toward the recovery room. "I just can't figure out what happened. He was so happy. I'm sure he didn't jump off that balcony. I told the police, but I don't think they believed me. I'm going to sell the condo and buy a nice house with a pool and lot of trees. Flowers. Jack loves pools. He can't swim." She laughed though her tears. "He just likes the way they look. Don't you think that's a good idea? I think it's a good idea. I'm gonna make everything wonderful for Jack. I'll take care of him. He'll have everything…. Anything he wants. He'll like that. He's funny like that. I'm…I'm…"

She collapsed in tears. Mine burned my eye sockets straining for release. I held her close as she wept freely into my freshly starched denim shirt. My heart shriveled. My soul screamed. The voices in my head instructed me to kill. Kill. My hand moved slowly toward her neck. I could break it with one move. I didn't care. I had nothing to lose. I had nothing without Jack. No one.

Life in prison didn't faze me. Death by injection would be a comfort. I couldn't survive without him. Just as I'd convinced myself to permanently end her suffering, a nurse handed her tissues and she stopped. I'd never seen her cry and I'd never heard Jack mention ever having seen one tear fall from those beautiful eyes. "I'm sorry," she said sweetly. "I wet up your shirt. Tears won't help. They're useless. They never solve anything. Never. Never."

"It's OK if you cry. I know how much he means to you."

"No. Jack wants me to fight. I'm going to fight. No tears."

We sat quietly holding each other's hand. Loving the same man for different reasons. This was the moment I dreaded. What have I done? What have I become?

CHAPTER SIXTEEN

"Did you have a nice evening sir?" Stinson snatched back the heavy drapes revealing a brilliant sky. The brightness of the sun and the drinks from last night penetrated my eyes, causing me to place both arms over my face.

"Close those bloody drapes Stinson. Get me an aspirin." Ignoring my requests Stinson walked to the other set of velvet drapes and snatched them open as well, allowing the sun to beam through.

"I trust that everything went well last evening sir? If I may say sir, she's quite the beauty." I turned over, burying my face in the pillow. Stinson walked around the bed retrieving the clothes, piddling about marriage and settling down.

"You know sir, it's really time for you to consider finding an appropriate mate. You haven't been in a serious relationship in quite some time. And if you want my opinion..."

"I don't!"

"You need a young lady who can tolerate your vast eccentricities. God help you with that. If you ever find her, you must do everything in your power to make the relationship work. After all sir you are no spring chicken and Ms. Summers seems like a lovely person and she's no tart like the women you usually squire. You're smitten and she's not the type you'll impress with lucre or position. You'll have to open your heart to win that one."

Tricked

Never shocked at Stinson's familiarity, I opened one eye and said, "You've been on retainer how many years now Stinson old chap?"

"All of your life, sir."

"Far too long, I fear."

"I beg your pardon sir?"

"You're like one of those old mother hens clucking about deciding when I should marry. Whom I should marry? What I should wear. When I should get up. What I should eat..."

"Well someone must tend to you and fortunately for you and unfortunately for me the job is mine. If left to your own...let us say dubious devices... I dread what would have ever become of you. After all, I promised Lord Bennett...."

"Not again..."

"I promised Lord Bennett that I'd see to your proper upbringing and take care of you and your brother. I have maintained that promise for all these years and I've no intention of stopping now."

"That makes you what? 70-75 by now?" I knew Stinson was sensitive about his age.

"I'm 68 years old Ian Lawford, and I can still go round with you," he said incredulously. "You're fat and out of shape. A disgrace. Now be up with you! I've already prepared a bath and Cook will prepare a proper low fat breakfast. It will be served on the terrace in exactly 25 minutes." With his last remarks, Stinson stormed from the room. "Works every time."

Mother died in childbirth. Father died in a riding accident when I was eight and my only brother was no longer with us. Stinson was the head of household for my uncle Lord Ian Bennett. He's taken care of me since my father's death. I should have fired him years ago, but he was the only semblance of family I had left...I loved him.

I rolled out of bed and looked at myself in the mirrors surrounding the bathroom. The cold marble made me tip about. There was no fat. I eased myself into the tub and reached for the telephone. McClain's fragrance still clung to the back of my hand. She lit up my life last night and I so desperately want to pursue her, but will she ever accept my world? My life? Me?

Such unmatched longing lay beneath her steadiness. She needs to be kissed. Passionately. Seriously. Often. I want to kiss her hurts away. She needs to be touched. Sincerely. Lovingly. Deeply. I want to touch her soul. She needs to be spoiled. Thoroughly. Pricelessly. Recklessly. I want to spoil her. So spoiled that gifts are expected daily and received without question. She needs to be protected. I want to protect her from everything and everyone who would do her harm in any capacity. I want to always see the look in her eyes that I saw last night when I promised her Manhattan. She doesn't know it, but I plan to give her the world.

Perhaps I'll buy her an island for a wedding present. We'll spend our days exploring the beauty of nature and spend our night exploring each other. The party on the other end picked up.

"Do we have it?" I asked. "I see. Has it been properly disposed of? I want the trash disposed of today! Do you understand me!? For your sake I hope you do. I don't want her touched. I repeat, under no circumstances is she to be harmed. I hung up the telephone and closed my eyes.

Mangled thoughts raced through my mind as the electric razor raced over my morning growth. "Prepare a course for Washington D.C. I don't want the flight traced. Call me when we're ready to depart," I ordered my pilot. Then I bellowed for Stinson.

"Yes sir," Stinson huffed as he hastily entered the closet, picking the towel from the floor.

"Pack my bag. I have to take a trip."

"Your blue bag sir?"

"Yes Stinson, my blue bag. Prepare the guest room. I plan to have guests."

"Ian, think very carefully. You know what happened the last time...."

Tricked

"Pack the bloody bag Stinson!" I shouted, tucking a fresh white shirt into a navy suit. Stinson walked out of the closet following my directions. He met me at the door.

"Your bag sir," he said, shoving the bag in my direction.

"Remember, the guest room." I took the bag and headed out of the bedroom. "Yes sir. I'll take care of it. Be careful Ian." "I will."

Those parasites she works for were partially responsible for this tragedy. I'd take particular pleasure in having them eliminated. They made a mistake. Mistakes are unforgivable. Unacceptable. Deadly.

CHAPTER SEVENTEEN

Are we all here?" The agent in charge addressed a group of elite government agents. Some of you know me. Most of you don't. I've read your reports and I'm impressed with the thoroughness of your work. If you're wondering, Rob Kleven the former agent in charge was reassigned. Kevin Jeter convinced Mike Cunningham to transfer me to this detail personally. It is a great honor to work with you on this very important task. As you already know, this operation is a matter of national security and interest.

Secrecy surrounding this mission remains high, primarily for your protection and the civilians involved. I'd like you to meet Jonas Colby from the Service." Colby waived his hand. "Those directly involved with tactical aspect should go with him into the other room." Five agents left the room. "Joe get the lights."

The room went black. "Those of you who've been working on the encryption codes, allow me to introduce you to McClain Summers." Her face filled the screen. "As you see from the information before you, Ms. Summers is the newly appointed Vice President of International Markets for RJP in Dallas, Texas. The encrypted messages on page eight were created by private operations technology of the world's largest and most deadly international securities cartel. They specialize in chemical and biological stocks, research and development. SEC officials along with the FBI and our agency have made every attempt to identify the cartel's members. Transactions. Locations. Accounts. We have all failed.

Tricked

Somehow Ms. Summers found a wormhole into their secret society. If stocks are being bought and sold internationally outside the ordinary and customary means for monitoring them, the impact on the global economy and the safety of the United States may be in dire jeopardy. We don't know why they've concentrated on chemical and biological securities but we believe Ms. Summers may. The information she's compiled will quite possibly expose the identities of the actors, who are desperate to keep their identities unknown.

Agency operatives have been watching her closely over the past several days. We've monitored certain discussions she's had with Dr. Jonas Stovall. He's a retired economics instructor from the Wharton Business School. He was her instructor and has been helping her put together scenarios that match her theory. He's in Switzerland and under our protection.

Now allow me to introduce Ian Lawford. We photographed him outside this lower Manhattan restaurant last night. It's the most recent photograph we have. He's a renowned recluse and his fascination with Ms. Summers has brought him out of self imposed isolation. We need to know why. He's dangerous and calculating in everything he does. His interest in her is not romantic."

His face replaced hers. "Lawford's ancestral tree includes Lord Ross Bennett who left him one of the world's wealthiest men. Over the past five years his chemical company holdings have tripled, making him the largest individual owner of pharmaceutical and chemical research stock in the world. This powerful and potentially dangerous man wants something. It will be one of our challenges to find out what that is. Page twenty of your report identifies the plants he currently owns, as well as those he's trying to attain.

A shadow group has waged and attempt to buy out Lawford's interests in Ross Chemicals. Last year a poison pill attempt was made, but failed. Lawford hired RJP International to protect his interests. They did. Uncharacteristically however, Ms. Summers was kept in the dark about the transaction. We want to know why and who made the call to exclude her. He's made multiple uncharacteristic trips to Dallas and has likewise made a number of flights to Los Angeles.

We've determined that the trips to L.A. were for the purpose of finding his younger brother, Trevor. For years it was believed that Trevor Lawford was dead. However, we have confirmed through DNA analysis that Trevor Lawford is very alive. His identity was changed and he took on the name of his most infamous relative. Trevor changed his name to Ross Bennett ten years ago."

Ross' face flashed. "He's maintained a professional friendship with Ms. Summers, who helped broker the deal for him to purchase RossCorp. After the purchase, RossCorp immediately announced their plans for global expansion. A vital component of RossCorp is Ross Pharmaceuticals. Fifteen years ago RossCorp received government contracts to produce antidotes for lethal biological and chemical pathogens being developed for the military. Ross Pharmaceuticals developed the strains and maintained control of their use, formation and distribution. The government snatched the contract about 5 years ago after a whistle blower came forward, providing evidence that someone at RossCorp was flipping the antidotes and selling individual biological strains, capable of producing weapons grade chemicals to unregulated foreign entities.

The whistle blower drowned in his home swimming pool after making accusations that were never substantiated. Our inspectors cleared RossCorp of having illegally maintained or distributed classified research samples and Ross Pharmaceuticals was never investigated.

Inspector Nigel Clifford leads our international team and will brief us on those efforts. Nigel." "Thank you very much. Let's get right to it. The Bennett family has long standing historic, financial and societal roots in Europe. Purveyors of war, the family gained vast fortunes from the sell and distribution of weapons, illegal and otherwise. Their products tended to wind up in the hands of mad men hungry for power. Influence. Authority. They married into royal families and became lords and ladies in many courts. This effort legitimized their family name and secured their position with the aristocracy.

Lawford will be knighted next spring. He is well read. Devious. Charming. Amoral. Trevor on the other hand was unruly and scandalous. The facts surrounding his death were quite mysterious. Rumors circulated that he and several friends conspired to hunt and kill a young lady for sport. Those rumors were never proved, but his friends were suddenly shipped away to different boarding schools after spending a holiday with Trevor in Africa. There, he is alleged to have died in a motor car accident.

The facts surrounding his demise were never publicly announced and his body was cremated and placed in the family's crypt near London. Thereafter, Ian became the sole heir to Lord Bennett's vast fortune and estate.

Information regarding Trevor's name change and reappearance here in the States is alarming to those of us who know his past. Any association he may have with chemical plants and pharmaceutical companies raises great concern.

Having come to America with millions of dollars at his disposal, he attended Stanford University and created the Bennett musical system, making millions more. Trevor is a genius by all accounts. Brilliant. Charming. Patient. Treacherous. Unscrupulous. Unfeeling. Dangerous. Thorough. Calculating. A sociopath.

Our intelligence suggests that Ross may be involved with the principals at RossCorp. I direct your attention to page eighteen. Bennett met Ms. Summers about five years ago in New York City. They were candidates for the RJP award. She won. They've kept in touch through the years and he knows she's discovered St. Lisa's. She told him."

I remembered St. Lisa's. It was a small convent hospital in Pittsburgh. I'd seen photos of it. The quaint stone buildings on the edge of town were reminiscent of old world architecture. I heard that it burned down years ago.

"Rex Tartania has been seen in Dallas." Several agents looked at each other. His face appeared in black and white. He's expensive. The best. He specializes in making death look like accidents. He never fails to deliver on a contract. We fear he's hunting Ms. Summers. We don't know who hired him, but she's in mortal danger unless we find her first.

One of Bennett's men, Jack Prescott fell from a balcony last night. He befriended Ms. Summers and we believe when she left last night to meet Lawford, he burglarized her condominium. He'll be dead within the hour."

Someone turned on the lights. "Thanks Nigel. Turn to page 30. Joshua Pellman came to Kleven three years ago. He still believes he's dealing with Kleven. We didn't want to spook him with me as his new contact. They've never met face to face. And their communication has been primarily by secured telephone.

Somehow RJP learned of the mysterious investment fund. Without knowing the principal, they were able to strike a deal with the secret group for the purpose of washing their ill gotten profits. They stashed millions in Ross Industries, by convincing crooked bankers, politicians and others to either turn their heads or participate for large sums of money.

Pellman began tracing large capital transfers by certain politicians. Those politicians were his only link to finding how their once meager investments ballooned into huge capital. Acting as though he was part of the scheme, he invited one of the governor's involved to a Cowboy's game. Sitting in the box at Texas stadium, we have him on tape explaining the entire scheme.

We planted the story about Pellman's death. He's alive and we have him. His wife doesn't know and neither does his best friend, President-elect Sims. For everyone's protection, let's keep it that way. You people are the best in the business. The best in the world. You have your assignments. Good luck and be careful. There's a plane leaving for Dallas in thirty minutes. Those of you assigned to Texas, get out of here."

Everyone filed out of the conference room. "Oh...Agent Richards... Nigel, please stay." I walked to the end of the table and sat, while the other agents left the room. "Close the door." Nigel stood next to the table. Peterson sat on the table, looking down in a fatherly manner.

Tricked

"Richards, there's some information we didn't share with the group." I listened intently. "If I recall, you attended the University of Pennsylvania didn't you?"

"Yes sir."

"You're one of our best operatives. You should have told us about your involvement with Ms. Summers at Penn. Ordinarily, I'd pull you off this detail but I think it may work to our benefit."

"She might not be that thrilled to see me sir."

"Then that just makes your job harder. If I keep you on this one, you'll have to assure me that you can maintain your objectivity. Make her trust you. That's an order."

"I'll do my best sir."

"Go to Dallas. Speak with the agents. Grab her and bring her in as fast as you possibly can."

"Yes sir."

Sweat formed on my forehead as I ran to my office grabbing a bag and jogging down the corridor to catch the flight. Ten other agents squirmed in their seats while the flight crew went through their protocol.

Rattled about the impending storm of danger ahead, I leaned back and opened the report. The plane's engines hummed as we taxied down the runway.

Jerry Seabrooks flopped into the seat next to me. We'd been on lots of missions together. He was good, but he talked too much. "You almost missed this one didn't you buddy?"

"Almost."

"I forgot my pen with the disappearing ink. My kids gave it to me just before I came in this morning. You want to see?"

"No thanks Jer, I've seen them," I smiled pulling glasses from my jacket.

"When did you start wearing those? Look guys the pretty boy can't see," he howled. "Have you guys seen this McClain Summers? She's hot! Gorgeous! I see why Lawford wants to bag her. I'd give up a year's salary just to....."

"Put your mind on protecting her Jerry."

"Yeah Jerry. We might need to protect you from Kelly if she ever finds out about you," Steve Cole pitched in from the seat behind us.

"Alright...alright. I just think the girl is gorgeous. Did you see those eyes? But you wouldn't notice anything like that would you? Ya know what guys? After this is over I think we ought to drop this guy off in Tibet. Isn't that where the monks live? He hasn't been the same since he got that doctorate. You used to like women. They used to like you. Now all you want to do is work. You'd fit right in at the temple. Baking bread. Making wine. Cheese. Chaste. No interest in women. Sex.

Ignoring Jerry, it had fallen to me to save her. Nothing would keep me from it. Nothing.

HIGHLY CLASSIFIED
SUMMARY SHEET: IAN LAWFORD

Ian Lawford sits at the head of the largest financial chemical and scientific cartel in the world. His personal assets are reportedly in access of 75 billion dollars. Over the last twenty years he has established a legitimate empire buying and selling companies and corporations throughout the world. Those companies have all been linked to banking, real estate, gold, biotech research, diamonds, and currency. His financial wizardry has garnered him respect from industry titans, international heads of State and drug barons. He rules his vast financial empire with an iron fist and is considered ruthless and venal. He is currently attempting to buy controlling interest in Chemtech, a biological genome research and development company, but cannot put together an attractive package.

His family has profited from the distribution of drugs, military secrets and illegal arms. Since Lawford took over the family holdings, he is built a net around the Lawford empire that has been impermeable. He hires the best minds in the world to protect him, including RJP International. He's paid millions for their silence, and has made them partners in his more lucrative enterprises. To ward off governmental investigations, he over pays taxes and has become a generous philanthropist and political contributor in every country his companies operate.

In the past five years he has divested the family's interest from all its unscrupulous enterprises and the most important thing to remember is.......

What had McClain has been doing for the last five years? What was she trying to find? Who was after her? Why hadn't Pellman told her anything? Why was Ian after her? Was Ross Bennett involved? Where was he? How did she meet this man? What was she thinking? Worry saddled me for the ride of my life. At stake. My assignment. My cover. My love.

I prayed the dangers described in the report were exaggerated. Experience convinced me that they weren't. Hope shoved my detachment toward anxiety. Love stung like a thousand bees and dread covered my soul. When I opened my eyes, I was completely distracted. Desperate. Sick.

CHAPTER EIGHTEEN

Jack died at 2:15 p.m. The nurse was kind and generous. Her concern and condolences did nothing to ease the sting of this inevitability. Doctors said they'd done everything that was medically possible to save him. I acknowledged their valiant efforts and thanked them for their work. A long time passed before I spoke again. That is, until I looked over and saw how disturbed he was about Jack's death. They allowed us to go into Jack's room.

I felt faint, having never seen a dead person before. The nurse supported me as my knees buckled. Jack would be pissed if I fell apart, so I struggled to pull myself together. He'd want me to make sure the flowers were fierce and he looked fabulous. "Jack, I hope I see you again in a better place. Stop telling God how to decorate heaven. He's done a pretty good job here and you could probably learn something from him about color. You know I love you dearly. I always will," and that was it. I left the room and Jack forever.

Surprisingly, he remained behind. I wandered past other critical patients with concerned families pacing and praying. It was surreal, like watching a movie except I was in it. I took off the bracelet and called Jack's parents... again. It was 2:45.

"Hello," a girl's voice.

"May I speak with Mrs. Prescott...please?"

"Just a minute. Momma...telephone!"

"Um...hello?"

"Hello, Mrs. Prescott. Jack is dead."

"What you say? Jack...Jack dead?"

"He died 30 minutes ago. I'm very sorry."

Tricked

"Look... talk to my brother...Bill!...Bill!....Jack dead!.....Oh Sweet Jesus.... Jack dead!" she cried.

Chills ran over me as the shrieks of morbid surprise and gut wrenching mourning pierced their Saturday afternoon. "Hello...this Bill Stickland...what happened? Jack dead? Who is this?"

"Yes sir. I'm McClain Summers. Jack's friend."

"Where is he?"

"Dallas Hospital in Texas."

"They go keep him there or what's the procedure?"

"I'm not sure about the procedure. I assume they'll keep him in the morgue until a family member claims his...his body," I choked.

"OK, how can we reach the hospital?"

"I can give them this number or you can call."

"OK…OK and how do we contact you?"

"Call me on my cell phone or page me." I gave them both numbers.

"Thank you McClain."

"Yep."

My life was again without form. Color. Texture. This sudden catastrophic reality did not factor into my plans. My neck lost its ability to support my head. So I put my head on my hands and reached out for comfort.

"Hi mother."

"Hey McClain. How you doin? I was just about to get groceries. At this hour, the store will be packed, but I have to go. Can I call you back? Are you OK?"

"Jack just died."

"Jack died? How? Was he sick? What happened?"

"He fell off his balcony."

"Fell off the balcony??!! McClain...what do you mean, he fell off the balcony? What was he doing on the balcony? How can you fall off a balcony? Didn't he live on the 4th floor?"

Her barrage of questions fell on deaf ears. I couldn't answer. I wanted the warmth and safety of her voice to surround me. Support me. I wanted her to pull me from the deep. She didn't. She never had.

"I don't know."

"What do you mean, you don't know?"

"I wasn't home when it happened."

"Well where are you now?"

"At the hospital. Dallas Hospital."

"Is that the hospital where they took Kennedy? No that was another hospital. That's not important. Let me get off this phone and come down there so I can find out what's going on."

"You don't have to do that... I just wanted to tell you..."

"You suppose to tell me McClain. Why do you always do that?" I didn't answer.

"Look... call me if you need me. I love you."

What did she just say? She said it again. "I love you McClain very much." She'd never said that before. She said she was proud, but never that I was worthy of her love. Her love was like a secret. Unsure of how to acknowledge this sudden emotion, I said, "I'll call you later."

"OK....Bye."

I was about to call Iris when he came back. "Where have you been?" I asked, pathetically.

"I thought that you might want a few minutes alone," he said. His eyes were red. He was choked up.

"Maybe I should ask if you're alright." It moved me that Jack's death affected him like this."

"It's always sad when a person dies too young. Plus, he was your friend. I know how much he meant to you. It touches me how brave you're trying to be. It breaks my heart."

"You never acted particularly fond of Jack."

"I liked Jack. He must have been good people. He was funny. He lived life to the fullest and he loved you." We hugged.

"You shouldn't have stayed this long. Have you forgotten about tonight?"

"I did forget! I was supposed to let the decorators in 10 minutes ago! Can I use your phone? I left mine in the car."

"No cell phones on this floor. Here's some change, use the pay phone over there."

"Hi Vince...yeah...Look I'm sorry man, but I'm at the hospital. A friend died today and I forgot all about you guys. No....No stay there...I'll be there in 25 minutes. Thanks man. McClain, let me drop you off. I need to leave and let these people in."

"No. I'll be alright. I'm glad you were here. I don't think I'll make it tonight, but I want it to be great for you," I kissed his cheek.

"Look baby, you've been here all night. There's nothing else you can do for Jack. Come with me and I'll take you home. Or you can come with me. Come on, let's get out of here."

He led me to the elevators. I wanted to leave, but something in me needed me to stay. When the doors opened, he grabbed my arm.

"You know what? I'm not ready to leave. I need to stay a little longer," I whispered. The elevator left.

"No you need to come with me. You shouldn't stay around here. It's creepy. Sad."

She was not buying my concerned act. I had to get her out of there. I had to kill her. The light above the elevator illuminated. Just as I planned to snatch her inside, a nurse called her.

"Ms. Summers. Will you sign a few papers for us?"

"Of course. I'll call you later."

"Promise," I hissed.

"Yeah...I promise. Go. Let the decorators in."

I kissed his cheek and watched as he boarded the elevator. After signing the papers, I sat staring into space. Suddenly, my cell phone rang. "Hello. I can't speak to you on this phone. I'll need to call you back." I caught the elevator down and went outside. It was Jack's parents' number.

"Yes... this is Geneva Strickland. You spoke with my husband Bill earlier."

"I did."

"Did Jack have life insurance?"

"Life insurance?"

"His mother thinks he had a safe deposit box. Did he?"

"I don't know."

"We plan to go to our lawyer here in New York to find out what we need to do. Did Jack have a Will? Do you know what bank his money's in? Will you look and see how much money he had on him when he went into the hospital. Credit cards. Those folks in the hospital *will* steal." They had to be kidding.

"I don't think I should be the one to do that. Is anyone coming here to claim Jack? Does anyone even want to know what happened to him?"

"Of course, but first things first. My husband is Yjean's brother. His mother and I will be leaving this evening for Dallas. We're flying. Jack sent his mother some first class tickets earlier this year. We go see if we can trade them in for two regular seats. Yjean has directions Can we call you if we get lost?"

"Yes. The nurses mentioned there's a place in Dallas that prepares bodies for flights. They'll pick Jack up and fly him to New York upon your request. You need to call them. I have the number."

"OK. We need to take care of as much of Jack's business as we can before he gets back here for the funeral."

"Of course."

"McClain?"

"Yes?"

"You've been a good friend to Jack. My prejudices and those of my family separated me from my only nephew. You see we're Christians. We don't condone that kind of behavior. But, it's still hard to describe the regret I feel. A huge part of me has died today. I'm ashamed of myself. I'm glad Jack had you. Do you know if he's still involved with that man Ricardo?"

"Ricardo?"

"Yeah. Ricardo is the young man he left New York to come to Dallas for."

"I'm not sure I understand."

Tricked

"Yjean, what was that boy's name Jack left here to live with in Dallas? She shouted. "Yeah, that's what I thought. His name is Ricardo....Ricardo....Collins. Jack called him Rick sometimes. Yeah, they called him Rick. Hello....McClain are you still there? McClain!"

"Yes......yes.......I'm here."

"We'll see you when we get to town. Thank you baby for everything you've done."

"You're welcome…did you say Rick Collins?"

"Yes baby. Tall. Good looking. Jack was crazy about him. Tore up his relationship with his daddy though."

"Did Jack have a lover who died of AIDS?"

"YJean...Jack didn't have no boyfriend who died of the AIDS did he? His momma said no. Said Ricardo was the only relationship Jack ever had with a man that she knows of. Jack left his wife for him."

"His wife?!"

"Yeah....He didn't tell you? Yes, Jack had a wife. He was married to a beautiful girl. Name Desi Hudson. They were in the church and everything. Had a big beautiful wedding. A beautiful place downtown. Both of them had real good jobs. Jack was decorating. Honey, they came to church every Sunday and sang in the choir. That girl had the voice of an angel. Then all of a sudden Jack met this Ricardo somewhere in Harlem. That man just snatched Jack from that woman. Chile, it was a messy mess. Jack divorced the girl. Cleaned out the house and the bank account. Near bout drove that poor girl crazy. After he took all they money, he moved to Dallas. It was scandalous. His daddy ain't never forgave him."

"It's been a long night Mrs. Strickland," certain that one more revelation would push me over the edge.

"Call me Geneva baby. Get some rest? We go have Jack's funeral here in Brooklyn. I hope you can come. Bye now."

"Bye."

Rick and Jack? Jack and Rick? There had to be another Rick Collins in Dallas. I went back to Jack's room. I paused a moment at the nurses station. "Excuse me. Did any of you see the young man who left Mr. Prescott's room a while ago?"

"Oh yes," said one of the nurses. "He was completely broken up. They must have been very close. One of the other nurses said he was Mr. Prescott's brother."

"His brother?"

"Yes, that's what he told us when he first got here. He just got on the elevator a minute ago. He seems so caring."

"Seems so. Mr. Prescott's family will be flying him to New York. They've called a local funeral home."

"OK we'll wait for the call."

I walked slowly down the hall. "Miss?"

"Yes," I said as I turned to address the nurse.

"Get some rest."

"I will."

CHAPTER NINETEEN

Rick ? Jack? Jack and Rick? Noooooo. This couldn't be true. Could it. Rick crashed Jack's huge Juneteenth pool party not long after our brief encounter at the carwash. I was surprised, but thought he came there for me. Jack said he didn't know him. " He probably crashed the party like most of these wannabees. But he sure is was fine. I wonder if he likes men?" He even suggested that I get to know Rick. "Girl go over there and do reconnaissance while I cuss out this caterer. How you go serve greens without cornbread?"

The telephone at Rick's parents home rang. His mother answered. "Hello, this is McClain may I speak to Ricardo?"

"Ricardo?...McClain is that you? You've got to be kidding me," his mother laughed. "I haven't heard anyone call Rick that since we went to visit him in New York. All his friends up there called him that. They said he looked like a black Puerto Rican," she giggled.

"Rick never told me he lived in New York."

"He didn't? He lived there almost two years. I'm still not sure what he was doing up there, but we sure were glad when he decided to come home. You coming to the party tonight aren't you? You're so special to Rick...I'm not minding my business am I? I don't care. Rick is very fond of you. We're fond of you too. Rick's daddy and I have always wanted him to have someone special in his life. He's always been shy with girls. Can you imagine that? Girls never had a problem finding him irresistible, but until you came along, the other women he talked about never stuck around long. Daddy and I think you make a beautiful couple. I apologize for not having been particularly friendly towards you, but I'd like to start over. Do you think we can do that? I think Rick has big plans for you," she teased. "You bring out the best in him and we…I look forward to seeing you later," she smiled.

"Have you heard from him today? " I asked.

"As a matter of fact he called a little while ago. He was *so* upset. I've never heard that tone in his voice before. You know nerves and everything. His daddy just left a minute ago, over to the building to see what all the fuss is about. He sounded like he was falling apart"

"Really?"

"I've never heard my child so upset. He could barely speak. I honestly thought someone had died when he called. He was crying and everything. He's probably upset about tonight. There's a lot at stake. I told him to calm down. Everything's going to be alright. He's always been a perfectionist. Weren't y'all supposed to go fishing this morning?"

"Something came up."

"Oh."

"Mrs. Collins, did you ever hear Rick mention Jack Prescott?"

"Jack...Prescott?...no...doesn't sound familiar to me...wait a minute …is he some kind of interior decorator?"

"Yes."

"Yeah. Rick showed me an article in a magazine about him and he hired him to decorate his cabin in Colorado. He did a fantastic job. He also did Rick's house. You've seen the cabin haven't you?"

"It's lovely."

"I'm thinking about having him do something here, but I don't think we can afford him. Well we'll see you tonight darlin. Take care."

"Good bye Mrs. Collins."

Tricked

***

"Move Edward. I can't see a damned thing. I knew she was trouble when Pellman hired her. But no….she's so bright. Ambitious. Attractive. You and Pellman walking around complaining. "Its was time for us to integrate RJP upper management. We need a more diversified workplace," you said.

"RJP needs to reflect society at large. It will make us look good to potential clients, especially athletes and entertainers," you said. "We have to join the rest of the country in hiring minorities in premier positions. Bullshit! My understanding was that the person we hired would have to be the best and the brightest we could find.

We established all kinds of requirements and restrictions regarding the person's credentials and qualifications were clearly defined. And I'll be damned if Pellman didn't go out and find one.

Those Cretans in training bragging that she was the brightest they've ever taught. You and Pellman bragging to clients about her and acting so pissy because Shoemaker wanted to fuck her. Hell we all wanted to fuck her."

"She is all of those things and I never wanted to fuck her."

"So what? You and those God damned liberals make me sick with that equal opportunity shit. Why did I agree to those promotions? We should have left her black ass right where she was. Pellman threatening to quit and take our richest client's with him. He was bluffing. The arrogant son of a bitch! Don't we have enough lawyers and human resource people to justify firing her? I'd rather pay the EEOC complaint than have to spend a Saturday afternoon crawling around my *own* office looking for information that belongs to me. Like a god damn thief!!!"

"I know it's frustrating Eddie, just shut up and keep looking. We could be facing enough indictments to keep those crooks at Conley & Mason busy for the rest of our lives. There are very important people who'd rather see us dead than themselves exposed. Ruthless people. Dangerous people.

For God's sake we put those deals together. We sexed up the values of those stocks. I may have been a fool for agreeing to hire her, but you're the one who gave her unlimited access to our most discreet files. You're the one who insisted on inviting your hooded pals into our firm. You just forgot that you're not suppose to put such incriminating information out where people like McClain and that piss ant Pellman could get their hands on it. You putz!"

"OK....OK....there's enough blame to go around for everyone. Let's stop pointing fingers. What's this?"

"Edward, do I need to remind you that the President -Elect is involved in this? If the information gets into the wrong hands, they'll kill us for sure."

"That's not it. I know. I know. Pellman had no idea what we were doing, until that bitch starting snooping. When Pellman decided to promote her to V.P. of International Finance, Sims daddy called me personally. He almost had a coronary. Me too. A black. African American. Negro or whatever the hell they call themselves these days, an officer at RJP? How did that happen?

When you two put her in charge of the Analyst program, I can't tell you how many complaints I received complaining about her bias."

"Bias Smias. We both know those complaints were groundless. Bigots like you, who only want to see other Arians in positions of power, were angry that she was right. By the way, everyone who successfully finished the class became significantly more productive. Hell, I even took the course."

"Arians! How dare you!"

"How dare I what? You've always been a racist. I love you Eddie, but you're a racist. You and your best friend Newt Sims."

"I am not a racist!"

"Yes you are. If she had blue eyes and blonde hair you would have offered her full partnership a year ago."

"Yeah...but I'd have fucked her first and I haven't seen your life time membership to the N-A-A-C-P."

"And you won't. But I know talent when I see it, and she has talent. Pellman was right about that."

"Too talented. She's got us spinning on a stick. We can't even un-promote her. I'm just sorry Pellman died before we could kill the bastard."

"We've got to get our PR machine in gear. We can't afford to loose any clients if this shit hits the fan. Call that maniac in D.C. and start manufacturing stories that point directly at her. He's got a dog in this fight too. He'll annihilate her."

"Damn the clients, we can't loose our money. I like being rich. I'm used to it."

"Forget the clients and the money. We can't lose our lives."

"With Pellman out of the way, we don't have to explain anything to anyone. We just need to make her ineffectual. Blame her for everything. Fire her black ass and wait out the storm."

"Not right away. Not before the inauguration. Not before Pellman's device makes us richer. We need her to get the department on track and we need to find out what she knows or if Pellman told her anything."

"He wouldn't."

"You don't know that."

"I wonder if she'll ask for a raise. With Pellman gone, she'll want more money."

"The bitch is almost as rich as us."

"Maybe we should put someone in there to subvert her."

"Who?"

"Douglas."

"Douglas wouldn't know a balance sheet from a bee hive. He's your sister's kid and stupid as a stone. It'll have to be somebody with no scruples. We need a ringer. Somebody who no one would question or suspect, at least not out loud."

"How about Sandy?"

"Nope."

"Turner needs to send one of his henchmen down here. Now move over....let me see what's in this file. It appears to be some kind of mathematical stuff. Do you recognize this?"

"No. They already saw that. That's not it. I told you that she's too smart to leave it in the office. We have a meeting tonight with you know who. He expects us to have a report. I don't want to die, especially when I have a $5000.00 piece of ass meeting me at a hotel later this evening."

"You're a pig Eddie."

"I'm a rich pig."

"I hope you keep that sense of humor when we're washing socks in the penitentiary."

"I bet this is it."

"If she doesn't know what it is, she wouldn't have any reason to take it home or hide it. Let's get this to Newman. She'll be able to have this thing cracked by our meeting tonight or she'll be punching a computer in Katmandu tomorrow." Charles and Edward left McClain's office and gently closed the door.

"Good afternoon Mr. Jacobs. Mr. Reynolds."

The men spun around. Gerald was standing behind them. "Who the hell are you!?" Edward snapped.

"That's Gerald. He's our office mail clerk," Charles explained.

"Good afternoon Gerald. It is Gerald? How are you?"

"I'm just fine sir. Thank you sir. You gentlemen have a good afternoon." Gerald rolled his cart in the opposite direction.

"Do you think he saw us coming out of there?"

"So what if he did. This is still our office. That's what I mean Charles. They never caused trouble when they worked their traditional jobs."

"Edward!"

"Well...It's true!"

CHAPTER TWENTY

Like a professional second story man, I crept into Jack's condo after first looking both ways down the empty hallway. The security alarm blared its 20 second delay as the door closed behind me. My access code didn't work. Jack removed it. He was serious about alarms. He had them everywhere. House. Car. Business. Closets. He kept them activated at all times and they always went off. Thinking I'd entered the wrong number, I unsuccessfully tried again. He changed codes like some people play the lottery. Daily. What would Jack use? He'd just finished a beautiful home in University Park. He took me there. What was that address?

I entered 1008, but prepared to run. The little green light flickered and the system was disarmed. I entered the "Stay" code just in case someone else decided to make an unscheduled visit.

Jack was a mystery now. I didn't know him at all. Why would he trick me? What was he doing? What caused his death? Did Rick kill him? Was he going to kill me? Who was Jack Prescott?

Once familiar ground seemed bleak. Desolate. Stark. Each piece of furniture loomed like gargoyles hovering weightlessly and menacingly. Poking and peeking from dark places. Paranoia welcomed fear, but curiosity and anger pushed them back, filling my emotional gaps with determination. Anger. Resolve. What did Jack want from me? Why had they created this rouse? Why me?

One consistent characteristic attributable to Jack's quirky personality, was his neurotic documentation of everything. He was obsessive. Compulsive. Relentless. He kept lists. Drew maps. Chronicling his daily life was a vapid attempt to record history.

Jack filled daily journals and diaries with this babble. The answers were here. I had to find them.

Sneaking glances over my shoulder as though someone else was in the room, I was determined to find answers. I quickly opened and closed cabinets. Drawers. Boxes. Brief cases. Files. Bags. Luggage. Books. I looked under mattresses. Tables. Chairs. I rummaged through pockets. Socks. Shoes. Jack's office and bedroom were trashed. His computer was gone. I looked behind pictures, up the fireplace. Everywhere. Nothing.

The living room was Jack's favorite part of the house. His cherished antique secretary beckoned me. He kept papers there. I found his bankbook. Insurance information. Address books. Jack was doing better financially than I thought. Dead end. Where were his journals?

I remembered the night we spent together when we first met, and ran to his bathroom. I looked under the sink and saw the giant douche bag. I gritted my teeth and grabbed it. There was nothing inside. Nothing. After quickly washing my hands, I continued searching.

Jack might have been clever enough to trick me with Rick, but I was internationally known for my deductive and analytical skills. Every ounce of that talent had to help me now. Then like a flash, I remembered something else Jack said.

A wealthy Addison businessman made a scandalous pass. Jack said, "Girl...you better think about it, before you forget about it! At least he was straight up with you. These rich bastards try to sucker pretty young women on the cheap. White women, both smart and dumb, been doing it for years. People don't care. Look at that girl who's with that developer. He left his wife and kids to marry her and now the slut's the poster child for mistresses and scanks all over the world. Baby take that sucker's money, put it in an empty Popsicle box and live that thang!" We laughed about it.

Cold air rushed into the kitchen as I ripped the freezer door open. Two boxes of Juice Bars lay inside. One Strawberry. One Lemon. Holding my breath, I pulled them onto the counter, dropping my backpack. A lipstick fell out and rolled across the floor. I scrambled to catch it. Reaching beneath the island, I touched something. To get a better look, I lay on the floor. There I saw a small envelope taped beneath the island. Only a small hand could reach it. How did Jack put that there? Just as I grabbed the envelope the telephone rang.

I stayed glued to the floor as if the phone triggered some explosive device. The answering machine picked up. "Hello. Jack! Jack are you there?!....Jack, please pick up the phone...Romeo he ain't picking up the phone...come here...he ain't answering. I told you...I told you. My friend at the police department was right......sniff...I don't want to believe this Jack please...oh Lord...sniff."

"Hey Jack. This is Romeo. We heard you might have had an accident last night. We can't get any information. We called McClain, but she's not home. Probably still out on that date. Call me. We're all worried about you...Jack. I'm worried you....We love you...Cliff's here."

"Hi Jack. If you can't call, please tell someone to get in touch with us. I'll be at the shop all day. You have my number at home. If someone else is taking Jack's messages, please call Romeo Cartwright at 234-4269, or Cliff Smith at 770-2089. Thanks." When Romeo hung up. I stood up.

Nothing was in the Lemon Popsicle box. I tore into the Strawberry. Nothing. I opened the envelope. There was a small key and a note. Just as I was about to read it...KNOCK! KNOCK! KNOCK! exploded across the front door. I froze.

This wasn't a police knock. It wasn't friendly. Neighborly. My heart beat so hard I was afraid the person on the other side of the door would hear it beating. I rubbed my moist hands on the sides of my jeans and tipped toward the door. The knob turned. I jumped back looking at the alarm system. It was still armed. I had to find a weapon. A large African statue sat on a nearby pedestal. It would brain anyone trying to get in. Back at the door, I looked through the peephole to see the raucous visitor. A stranger. I didn't recognize him. He looked foreign. Dark. Brooding.

Cynthia A. Minor

Having found no sensible entry, he turned and walked in the direction of the elevators. Certain that he'd left, I replaced the statue, went into the kitchen, got a knife, disarmed the system, and ducked into the back hallway. No one was there.

The service elevator took an eternity. I had to go home and shower. I needed to read Jack's note. Clear my head. What did this key open?

When the elevator arrived, the same man who'd just knocked on Jack's door was standing inside. Horrified, I pretended that something was in my eye. He couldn't see my face. "Going up?" he asked in a thick unidentifiable accent. I shook my head 'no'. As soon as the door closed, I ran toward the stairs and raced down four flights into the parking garage.

Drenched with sweat and barely breathing, I locked the doors to the car. Before speeding off, I remembered Pellman's information was still in my hiding place. I got the package and sped out of the garage nearly hitting the president of the homeowners association. He waved frantically for me to slow down.

Cool air helped quench the stifling heat of fear and terror. Instinctively, I drove toward the office. My refuge. My tower. Not many people were usually around on Saturday afternoons, so I pulled in front of the building instead of the parking garage.

My once flawless instincts couldn't be trusted. I couldn't trust anything. Anyone. Uncomfortable with this new reality, I pulled from the curb and headed north on Central Expressway. Traffic was horrible, so I took the Southwest Boulevard exit and turned on the radio to get the latest traffic report.

While waiting for the light to change, the news reporter said, "Today the world of finance has been rocked by the sudden unexpected and tragic death of Joshua Pellman, Dallas' own Nobel Laureate. He was a generous contributor to countless charities around the country and here in the Metroplex. He was apparently killed in a white water rafting accident in Colorado. As Clay Sims' key economic advisor, the President-Elect is quoted as saying, "Joshua Pellman's death is a great loss for the nation and a great personal loss for me. He was a good friend who will be sorely missed." Instrumental in making RJP International a major money machine, he leaves his wife, countless friends and associates to mourn his loss."

Blood thumped in my ears drowning out the blaring horns of the traffic behind me. This was too much….too much. "Oh my God! Oh God!" I reached for the tissues inside the glove compartment knowing tears would certainly come. Not one fell. I was amazingly calm. Was this shock? Was this true? Had I lost my mind?

Someone tapped my window, shaking me back to reality. A police officer asked, "Are you alright Miss?" "What?" "Miss, are you alright?"

"Excuse me?" I asked.

"Are you OK?" He asked again.

"I...I...I just heard some disturbing news on the radio, my boss died today…I just heard the news on the radio."

"I'm sorry, but you can't stay in the middle of the street little darling." I turned around looking at the string of cars trying to get around me. "It's the turning lane and you're blocking traffic," he said pointing at the cars.

"Oh, I'm sorry. I'm sorry. I'll move." I was shaking.

"Do you need someone to come get you? I'll call someone," he offered.

"No…I'll be alright, thank you. I'm sorry for the traffic."

"No problem."

The officer went to the back to his cruiser. I turned onto Greenville Ave. I had to go somewhere. Think. Process. Plan. Pellman gave me two disks, a notebook for his speech and an envelop marked confidential. This was not time for grief. Sorrow. Pity. This was a time for action.

Something inexplicable was happening. Somehow I was in the middle of it. A stall near the front door of a computer and printing store became available. I sprayed myself with a small amount of perfume. I put on sunglasses, tinted lip gloss and dotted my shell shocked face with powder. Vanity never takes a vacation.

A linty breath mint was in the console. The place was packed with people. A computer wouldn't be free for at least thirty minutes.

While I waited, I scanned Pellman's note pads. It was all about Clay Sims. Every piece of dirt about him and his cronies was detailed. He was a mess. Pellman gave dates. Deeds. Times. Names. People. Proof. Many notations referred me to 'the tape." There was no tape. By the time the computer center coordinator called me, I was reading the entries of the last ten years.

Apparently Pellman and Sims shared deep dark secrets. Nothing like Jack and Rick, but just as devastating if the public got wind of it. Pellman wasn't the type to hold grudges. He kept records. His philosophy veered toward forgiveness no matter how egregious the offense. His capacity to operate on this level was a marvel to me. He said, "It's easy to forgive since I always win. Keep your focus and concentrate on what you want. Never allow anything or anyone to get in the way of your life. Your future. Your happiness. More importantly, never stand in the path of a man bent on his own destruction."

I read for two hours. Pellman's direction for RJP and his speech were lain out with unabashed clarity. The security system was brilliant. Seamless. Flawless. I committed every detail to memory. Every word. Flaws contained in my essay were answered with unabashed clarity. It reminded me of the paper I swiped so many years ago. I'd lost Pellman too. I'd lost him. Forever.

CHAPTER TWENTY-ONE

Jack's envelop lay crumpled in my backpack. An address and series of other numbers were on the note. Knowing that Jack had to tell or write everything, I was certain his missing history would be there. I found a map. The address was in Denton. I drove north out of Dallas, ending my search at the bus station.

The key unlocked a locker filled with a treasure trove of Jack's information. He was true to form. It was all there. Seven years of notes. After finding a fast food place where I felt safe, I began with the events of the last three days.

Friday

McClain got a big promotion. Lunch at Cheyenne's. She has dinner plans with Ian Lawford. Rich. Pellman stopped by. Last day to locate primary information. Rick's party tomorrow night. Will leave town during the party. I'll sneak out. Fly to Paris. Change planes. Go to Nigeria. Friends will be waiting. Write McClain. Explain everything. Buy a gift. Send her flowers. Leave her my Art Deco Champagne flutes. She'll laugh and know I love her. I love her. Daddy's birthday. My last chance. Its over. It's all over.

McClain left at 7. I don't know where she went. I can't find it. I hate this. I hate him. He'll hurt me. He won't stop. He can't stop. I'm afraid of him. Buy roses, toilet tissue and contact lens solution. Go back to her condo and find the disk.

Called Romeo. Still can't get the information from McClain's computer. Things too hot. Take McClain's code out of my alarm system. I'll leave alone.

Thursday
Tried to explain to Rick that McClain got new laptop. Keeps it with her. No disks. No hard drive. Looked everywhere. He's still mad. He slapped me. Won't talk to me because he heard Romeo's message. Spent the night with Romeo. Nothing happened. I'm falling in love with him. Told me to leave Rick. Told Rick I didn't want to see him anymore. Rick told me get the disk or he would kill me. I'm so afraid. God help me. I've got to get her to tell me what she knows. Find the disk. Dinner with Cliff and Buster. Get haircut.

I was too emotional to keep reading. Driving around North Dallas feeling sick and confused, I didn't know what to make of any of this. What disk did Rick and Jack want? What information was I supposed to have? Why was Jack so frightened?

Somehow I found myself in front of Matthew's house. I always seemed to find myself seeking him when my world was falling apart. He left for Florida this morning, so I decided to go inside to think. Plan. Rest. Read more. I parked around the corner and walked to the back of the house. He kept an extra key beneath a flowerpot on his deck. He didn't have an alarm system. He didn't like them.

I sat on the kitchen barstool allowing the events of the last 24 hours organize themselves. Clearly I was in danger. Jack's entries over the past six months certified this. From whom? From what? There were no answers. At 6:20 p.m. I'd summoned up enough courage to face whatever dangers lay before me. I called the office.

"Where have you been? Have you heard? We've all been waiting for you. I've called your cell and home at least a hundred times. We even sent someone to find you," Sandy said tearfully.

"I'll be there in about forty-five minutes. Call the European staff and have them ready for a telephonic conference. Find everyone. Bring them in. Where are Mr.'s Jacobs and Reynolds?"

"They're here. Do you want to speak to them?"

"No. I'll see them when I get there."

"It's all so terrible," she sobbed.

"Pull yourself together Sandy. We have work to do. There will be no tears. Do you understand?"

"Yes."

"Good. I'll see you soon."

I didn't want to risk Matthew's safety by staying any longer than absolutely necessary. Just in case someone was following me. Jack hadn't mentioned him in his notes, but that didn't mean Rick didn't know about him. I stashed the notebooks, disks and Jack's information. I'd retrieve them later. When necessary.

The lobby of the Rest Inn near Fair Park was filled with members of a boisterous wedding party. Groomsmen and other guests were yelling and laughing at such a frantic pitch that the manager ordered them to quickly go into their rented ballroom. They ignored his requests and became louder. I paid cash for a room, telling the clerk I needed the day rate. I only wanted to shower and leave.

I always kept a bag ready for travel in my car. The clerk said that I needed to show him my license. I put another $100 bill on the counter. "We have a nice quiet room in the back of the hotel. You might enjoy that room better. Less noise." I declined, telling him that I liked noise. He gave me the key and I pushed through the crowd. With the door barricaded, I showered. I left the shower curtain and the bathroom door open. Visions of Hitchcock films and paranoia prompted my behavior.

Racing toward the office, I called home to collect my messages. "McClain! Where are you? I've been calling all morning. I just heard about Jack." It was Rick. He left six messages.

"McClain.....This is your mother. You need to call me. I know you don't want me to come to Dallas, but I'm coming anyway. My plane arrives at 9:47 on American. I'll see you then....Bye."

"McClain.....are you home? We just heard that Jack was in some kind of horrible accident. We're all waiting at the shop for information...She's not there....OK....Call us when you get in. Bye Girl." Romeo.

"McClain...darling. I merely wanted to thank you again for a charming evening. I was wondering darling, if you'd like to join me for breakfast tomorrow? I planned to go to Paris, but I have a slight diversion to the west coast. I can easily slip into Dallas and we can have breakfast at the Ritz. Ring me up on my private number and I'll send my plane to fetch you. Call me soon." Ian.

"McClain. Keith. I hope you don't have plans for Sunday afternoon. I know this is short notice, but I have tickets to Jazz with the Dallas Symphony. Call me."

"Hey baby...It's me. Where are you? Me and Pitiful are on our way over to teach you how to fry chicken. I know I decided not to see you anymore. I forgive you. You're just crazy, but you're so cute. I love you no matter what. See you in a minute. Oh yeah, I decided not to go home this weekend. I want to see you instead." Matthew.

Four hang-ups. Sandy, five calls. "McClain, Pellman is dead! Everybody's looking for you. Where are you? I paged you. I've called you on your cell. Where are you? Call as soon as you get this message. Should I get the team together? Reynolds and Jacobs are yelling for you."

"Hello McClain? This is Darla Pellman. I need to speak with you before Joshua's memorial. Will you meet me? It's vital that you meet with me. Call me. Please call. Good bye."

Mrs. Pellman? I looked at my watch. It was 8:15. "Hello this is McClain Summers. May I speak with Mrs. Pellman? I'm returning her call." A man answered the telephone.

"Hello McClain, have you heard about Joshua?" She was crying.

"Yes...I'm so sorry."

"I'm sorry too. It's really our loss isn't it? I can't talk right now, but we need to speak. There's something I must tell you," she whispered. "Can we meet tomorrow?"

"Just tell me where and when."

"I'll call you. Joshua's legacy is safe with you. "

"I hope I can only do half as well."

"You will. I know you will. I have to go. I'll be in touch."

"If there's anything I can do...anything at all, let me know."

"I will. Thank you McClain. Goodbye."

RJP's staff was dispatched with pointed assignments and crucial information for maintaining our status. At the partners meeting, plans for tomorrow's memorial service and the division of Pellman's duties were initiated. Randall Sperling would oversee projections. I would take care of all other duties. Completion of the Evans merger was key and had to proceed as planned.

"We must demonstrate continuity and maintain the same level of professionalism and respect our departments gained under Mr. Pellman's guidance. Our client's confidence in our ability to provide prudent and sound fiscal information is what Mr. Pellman expected of us. So do I. We will not fail.

Continued confidence in our proficiencies and command of the market has been the RJP niche. Protecting their investment dollars is our guarantee. Mr. Pellman's legacy must live through our determination and devotion to excellence. The best eulogy to his towering strength is our ability to make everything he left better. I will depend on you for your expertise, leadership, counsel and dedication during this sad and difficult time," I choked.

"Above all else, Joshua Pellman was excellent. Let us be excellent. It does not happen by accident. It happens by practice. Thank you."

My unequivocally supportive staff vowed their allegiance to Pellman's memory and my leadership. Pats on the back and multiple hugs from the partnership let me know our mission was greater than the man we mourned. We prepared ourselves for tomorrow's memorial service and dispersed into the night to remember. Grieve. Mourn.

CHAPTER TWENTY-TWO

About fifteen minutes before mother's plane arrived, something told me to ditch my car. Everyone looked suspicious. I'm sure I did too. "Ma! Over here!" I yelled. She rushed toward me, waiving.

"Did you bring any other bags?" I asked taking the carry on she held in her hand.

"I just brought that bag. Tell me what's going on. What happened to Jack?"

"I don't know. Are you hungry?"

"Yeah. I haven't had a thing to eat since I spoke with you earlier. They used to give you something to eat on planes. Now all you get is a coke and a bag of peanuts."

We walked out of the airport and jumped into a cab. "Where's your car?"

"In the shop. What do you want to eat?"

"It doesn't matter. You don't look good McClain."

"No kidding? How do you expect me to look? My friend just died. I've been at the hospital all night and half of today. I haven't had more than an hour's sleep in the past 36 hours. Now Pellman's dead too. Let's just say that it hasn't been a great day."

"I'm sorry McClain. I see you still wearing that ponytail. You don't wear your hair like that to work do you? I have told you so many times, that…"

My mother has fought me about my looks for the greater part of my life. "Wear your hair down. Don't hold your face like that. You look just like your father. At least you put on some lipstick."

Tricked

There I was. Confused. Perplexed. Betrayed. Hurt. Jack's dead. Pellman's dead. A boyfriend who wasn't. My department may collapse. Home burglarized. Giant shoes to fill. A billionaire wants me. Killers may be after me and my mother wants to know why my hair isn't curled. Some things never change.

"Did you say Pellman died today?" she asked catching her breath.

"Yes," I whispered.

"What!? Joshua!? Dead!?" She spoke in a tone you'd expect from someone close to the man.

"He died in a rafting accident this morning."

"What will we do now?" she asked.

What will we do now? What was she talking about? "What do you mean momma?"

"Oh, I just mean he always looked out for you. Protected you. Who will protect you now?"

"Why do I need protection?"

Something snapped her back. "You know Mr. Pellman saw you as kind of a daughter. He told me that once. I was always thankful for the interest he took in you. You told me that he was your mentor and any good mentor protects the one he mentors. That's what I mean. I'm sad that he's dead and I know you must be devastated," she said, tears coming to her eyes.

"Yeah. He's highly respected all over the world."

"You're highly respected too baby. He left things in good hands. I'm sure your company has confidence in your ability to keep Pellman's legacy alive."

"I hope so. Is Burger Barn OK?"

"Burger Barn?"

"It's a restaurant."

"What kind of food do they have?"

"Burgers ma."

"Is it good?"

"They're burgers. All kinds. Chicken. Turkey. Fish. Whatever you want." The taxi pulled into the drive -through.

"You don't have anorexia or something do you?" my mother asked, feeling my arm through my jacket.

"What?"

"Do you eat? Jack wrote. He said you're too skinny. I can see the bones in your neck. How much do you weigh? I'm making you get on the scale as soon as we get to your house."

"Momma, I eat and I'm not skinny. I'm slim. I've always been slim. You know that. I eat. I just don't gain a lot of weight. Anorexics don't see bones. They see fat. I see bones, but I see muscles too. I'm just right for me and I don't have scales."

"Well you need one and you need to gain 5 or 10 more pounds. You're just hair. Boobs and butt. Shaped like a Q-Tip. If you ever get sick you won't have nothing to fight it with." I rolled my eyes.

Mother rambled on about folks at home. Her job. Some man who was trying to get her to go out with him. A new church she'd just started attending. Something troubled her. She always rambled when she couldn't deal with reality.

"The money you send every month really helps, but you really don't need to support me. I have money. Your father has never stopped sending those support checks. I've told him a number of times to stop. He just won't." Any reference to my father was proof that something else was disturbing her.

"I'm thinking of selling the house and buying a townhouse. The neighborhood is changing. I want something new."

I wasn't listening and I wasn't eating either. She touched my hand. Her perfectly beautiful face glowed. "McClain...baby...I know that you're hurting about Jack and... Joshua. If Jack jumped, fell, or was thrown from the balcony, it doesn't make one bit of difference. He loved you and you certainly loved him. I liked seeing you together. He called me every Sunday. Did you know that? Let the police find out what happened. There's absolutely nothing anyone can do to bring him back. We have to be happy that he came into our lives. I'm here for you. Jack and Pellman weren't the only people who loved you. I know that's what you're thinking. I haven't told you as much as I should or as much as you

Tricked

probably needed to hear it over the years, but I do love you, very much."

We passed Jack's favorite florist. Cleaners. Bakery. Candle shop. "You'll get through this McClain. I've learned that you can get through just about anything," she smiled holding my hand.

"Mommy, I'm thinking of taking some time off. I haven't taken a vacation since I came to Dallas. Maybe you could get some time off too. Maybe we could go somewhere together. Get to know each other better? We've never really been anywhere…together."

I paid the taxi and we walked into the building through the garage entrance. "Baby I'd love to go somewhere with you, but I already made plans for my vacation this year. Tee Tee and me are going on a cruise. Remember? You paid for it."

"Oh yeah, I forgot."

"Why don't you come with us?"

"You and Aunt Tee? No."

We boarded the elevator and I pushed twenty. I was glad she came. I didn't want to be alone. When we got to my floor, Mr. Greene was standing in the hallway. "Mr. Greene. Why are you standing out here? Are you locked out again?" I smiled.

"No. I'm wearing the chain you gave me. See? I just got off the elevator over there and I heard something in your condo. I stopped to see if I could hear it again."

"Mr. Greene, this my mother Vicky Summers. Mother, my neighbor, Abraham Greene. What exactly did you hear?"

"My pleasure Ms. Summers and may I add that it is evident where McClain inherited her considerable charm and beauty." He kissed her hand.

"Thank you," she smiled.

"I heard something break."

"Something broke?"

"Yes."

We turned and moved toward my home crowded one behind the other. I was first. Mother was next and Mr. Greene was last. "Stop pushing," I insisted. "OK," she whispered. We must have looked like three stooges creeping toward the door. I

181

unlocked them and entered my code. I felt the wind and turned on the lights.

A vase had fallen because the terrace doors were open. We breathed a collective sigh of relief given the circumstances of last night.

Mr. Greene smiled and pulled a handkerchief from his pocket. He mopped his forehead and stared at my mother. I smiled because I could tell his glaring made her uncomfortable.

"Who cleaned up? Housekeeping?" I broke the silence.

"I beg your pardon." He never stopped looking at my mother.

"Mr. Greene...who cleaned up?"

He stopped looking at my mother for a moment. "The young man you see did it."

"What young man?" I asked.

"The one with the ugly dog. He came by this afternoon. I was just leaving as he got off the elevator. I told him everything. He was so concerned about you. Such a nice boy. So handsome. He called a maid service and he stayed here the whole time. He contacted the security desk downstairs and told them before he left. Didn't they tell you downstairs? How is Mr. Prescott?"

"He died. I came up through the parking garage."

"Oh no. It's terrible. Poor Mr. Prescott. I liked him very much. He was very charming and a good dresser. I know good clothes when I see them. High quality. If there's anything I can do, just let me know."

"Thanks Mr. Greene."

"No problem. We embraced.

"Mrs. Summers, you are a *very* striking woman. I'd love you to visit me. Would you like to see my Monet?" Mother was horrified.

"No thank you. I'm sure it's very beautiful."

"It's hanging over my bed. Maybe next time. You ladies have a nice evening."

"Thank you for looking out Mr. Greene."

"It's a pleasure. Nice meeting you Mrs. Summers."

Tricked

"Thank you."

"Good night," Mr. Greene winked.

We walked inside. I bolted the double doors. "What's his story?"

"He's just a harmless rich old man."

I changed all the codes and walked to the kitchen for paper towels to clean up the water. My mother walked around inspecting the clean up job.

"He sounds like a pervert. Who's the nice young man with the ugly dog?"

"A friend. I have some work to do, so make yourself at home. I'll put your things in the guest room. Towels are under the sink. Soap is in the right drawer. The sheets are clean. If you need more blankets, I hope they put them back in the closet. When are you leaving?"

"I booked a flight back early tomorrow. I didn't want to get back in the dark. I have to be at work early Monday. I'm supervising a divisional audit."

"You know you can retire. I'll provide for you."

"How many times do I have to tell you I don't want you to support me. I like working. It keeps my mind active. Go to bed now. Try to get some rest. Good night." She kissed my cheek and walked into the guest room.

Jack and Rick were some kind of corporate spies. Spying on me. Jack kept tabs on me. Rick kept tabs on Jack. Their boss thought I was key to secrets that would rock the political landscape. Research I'd been doing was making them very uncomfortable. Apparently Jack was supposed to give them whatever I discovered.

Pellman was suspected of being a mole because he'd recently given the feds bogus information, planted to reveal the identity of the informant. After the government acted on the fake data, the operatives had their evidence that Pellman was their man. Rick was ordered to execute Pellman after Sims' inauguration. Obviously Pellman died before Rick could kill him.

Rick was a killer for hire. He'd been a contract assassin for years. After Rick killed Pellman, he was supposed to take care of Jacobs. Reynolds. Me. My murder was to take place the instant the secret was exposed. What secret?

According the Jack's notes, no one had been able to locate or identify the St. Lisa connection, until I decoded it. Jack wrote something Rick said. "She has no knowledge regarding its impact. Her discovery is fatal to our mission. When the deal is made, I'll eliminate her."

MISSION PRESCOTT:

Locate Summers. Befriend. Observe. Duplicate all records. Destroy all evidence.

MISSION COLLINS: Eliminate all problems.

"McClain?!" I jumped. It was my mother.

"Somebody's on the telephone. I think its Jack's people."

It was after 2:30 a.m. I hadn't even heard it ring. "Hello?"

"Hi McClain. This is Mrs. Strickland, Jack's aunt. I spoke with you this afternoon."

"Yes…yes."

"We're here. We're in the lobby. Security said they can't let us up because we're not on Jack's guest list. They won't give us a key under any circumstances. Would you please speak to them?"

"I will. Come to the 4th floor, unless you'd like me to come to the lobby."

"No...we'll meet you there. It's 402, right?"

"Right. Please put security on the line."

My mother was trying to go back to sleep. "Mommy, I have to go downstairs to let Jack's family at his condo."

"Do you want me to go with you?"

"No. I just wanted you to know where I was."

"I'm going. Let me put on something right quick."

Three people stood at Jack's door. His aunt was the first to speak. "You must be McClain. I'm Geneva. This is my husband

Tricked

Billy and this is my sister in law, Yjean," she said hugging me. I shook her husband's hand. Jack's mother hugged me weeping freely.

"I wish I could have met you under more pleasant circumstances. This is my mother, Vicky Summers. Shall we go in?"

For the second time since Jack death, I opened his door. The alarm paused began. I entered the new code, flipping on the light switch revealing the magnificent space. Jack's relatives stood speechless as they marveled at the sight of his home. Mother and I walked pass the trio, ushering them through the foyer containing Jack's newly acquired Chinese porcelain collection, and into the living room.

"Can I get anyone coffee?" No one answered. Mother went into the kitchen and looked for the coffee pot. She returned to the living room and stood next to me.

"Is all this Jack's stuff?" his mother asked looking around in sheer amazement.

"Yes."

"You mean my Jack was living like this? Like a millionaire? This looks like a magazine. This don't look like nothing I ever saw before. Nothing Jack would be living in anyway. Jack said he made lots of money down here decorating peoples houses and offices and things. He said he was good at it...I didn't know he was good enough to be living like this."

"He was very talented," I added.

"Do you know where Jack kept his important papers," Aunt Geneva interrupted.

"No."

"Jack didn't tell us nothing about this," his mother continued. "I wish I'd known. If I had, I would have come down here and visited before now. This is beautiful...ain't it Bill?" she cried, dabbing her eyes and nose.

"Well it sho don't look like no homo's place. Ain't no purple curtains, pink couches, or none of that kind of stuff. Do his friend live here? Where is he? I bet he go want some of this stuff.

This place looks like where one of them big time dope dealers live. Maybe even a rapper."

"Have you made funeral arrangements?" my mother chimed in.

"We think we go have it on Thursday. I wish that boy would come round here acting like he suppose have something." Aunt Geneva snarled, while looking through Jack's telephone book.

"Thursday afternoon in Brooklyn," his mother confirmed, speaking loudly to cover her brother-in-law's verbal clutter. "That way we can have all of this stuff moved and put this place up for sale. The lawyer in New York told us to do that. Jack has so much. We just didn't know. McClain is there a little something you'd like? We know Jack would want you to have something. Will you come to the funeral?"

"I gave Jack that picture on the piano. He also has my art deco champagne flutes." I lied, but I knew Jack wanted me to have them. I bought many of the items these ghouls were caressing. They meant nothing to me now and I loathe them offering me 'some little thing.'

"Is it valuable?" Aunt Geneva asked. Uncle Bill walked to the piano. "The picture ain't worth shit, but the frame look expensive."

"By all means you may have it McClain," Jack's mother said graciously, as she took it from her brother's hand.

"Where the champagne things she talkin about?" Uncle Bill asked.

"Jack keeps champagne in the refrigerator. The flutes are in a white box in the dining room side board. I'll get them. I retrieved the glasses. Everyone was anxious to see them, but I refused to open the box and handed the picture frame to my mother.

Although Jack betrayed our friendship, I was furious with his relatives. Buzzards. Vultures. Scavengers. His mother walked around like a zombie oohing and awing over her death rewards. She had never used the tickets Jack sent for holidays. Never came to an opening. Never sent birthday cards. Rarely returned

Tricked

telephone calls. Never even asked what happened to Jack. Never wondered aloud how did my son die? Didn't care how hard Jack worked to get the things she ogled. The glow in her eyes failed to match the fiery rage in mine.

Big aunt Geneva sprawled her 400-pound frame across the antique piano bench Jack bought in Paris, calculating the value of everything.

Large and in charge Uncle Bill had the audacity to compliment Jack's taste while despising his lifestyle. He looked beneath pottery, art and crystal checking and confirming their authenticity. As if he had a clue. Enough!

"Yes...well...if there's nothing else I can do for you people, I'll leave you to your inventory. I'm sure you'll find everything you want. Good night."

I never looked back at the circling buzzards. I didn't hug. Kiss. Console or understand. I don't know if they said anything else after I turned toward the door. Mother lingered a moment and almost had to run to keep up with me. "McClain, you were down right rude."

"How was I rude?"

"Inventory. That was awful. I can't believe you said that. I know I didn't raise you to speak to people that way, especially people mourning the death of a loved one."

"Did they sound like they were mourning Jack's death to you? Let's just go to bed and we'll talk in the morning."

"McClain...."

"Not tonight ma...OK?"

"OK."

We rode upstairs in silence. I double bolted the doors and got a large knife from the kitchen. I put it on the pillow next to me and lay across the bed, falling asleep with the television, radio and every light in the house on.

CHAPTER TWENTY-THREE

A telephone woke me. My private line. After the twelfth ring, I picked it up. "Hello McClain? Is that you? It's me...Matt."

"Matt?"

"Yes baby. Did I wake you up? I'm sorry sweetie. I've been so worried about you. I was up all night. When I stopped by yesterday, the doorman told me what happened. I came straight up. A man was there who said he was with the police. He was trying to get in. He got nervous and left when I asked him some questions. Mr. Greene said Jack jumped off a balcony or something. Is that true? Is he alright? Are you alright? Then this morning, I went out to get the paper and the headline says Pellman is presumed dead in Colorado. Baby are you there?"

"What?"

"OK. Did you hear me?"

"Who let you up?"

"I let myself up. I have a key remember?" I did remember.

"I'm sorry Matt. I wasn't thinking. I can't think. My head hurts. It's all been so terrible. Strange. I didn't mean to..."

"Look...look...It's OK baby. Are you really OK? Do you need anything?"

"I need you," I whispered, choking back tears.

"I'll be right there."

"No....(sniff) no, my mother's here. (sniff) She's still asleep. She came last night. She's leaving this morning (sniff)."

"Doesn't matter."

"(sniff) I want to come over there."

"Then come. Get up and come right now. You can come to me anytime you want. You know that."

"I'm too tired to drive and we broke up."

"Do you want me to come and get you? Stay with you? Hold you? Love you? Just tell me what you want. Do I meet your mother today? I'd love to meet her," he whispered.

"Why do you want to meet my mother?"

"That's a stupid question."

"Answer it anyway."

"It would be nice to meet your mother. The goose who laid the golden egg. Plus I'd count it a blessing."

"My mother isn't a bird and you always have to go there don't you?"

"With you I do."

"What time is it?"

"Hmm, 6:00."

"OK. But you'd better not say that goose stuff when you get here. She'll smack your teeth out. She'll want to cook breakfast. It's a ritual. Why don't you stop by around 8:00?"

"I'd better come at 7:00."

"Why?"

"You know you don't have any food. I don't even know why you keep your refrigerator on, wasting all of that electricity." His laughter was like good news.

"You're right."

"I know I'm right."

"Matt I....." Grief returning. A break down eminent.

"I know baby. Be strong."

"Bye."

The antique sterling silver tray with matching mirror, comb and brush set Jack gave me for my last birthday gleamed in the light. I rolled out of bed and walked into the bathroom.

The picture Jack and I took while on vacation in San Antonio last summer was on the shelf. We wore authentic Mexican dancing attire and large sombreros. Ridiculous. It always made me laugh. We loved good Mexican food and although the River Walk had a cavalcade of choices, we always ate where the Mexicans ate. Tears formed. "Be strong."

The picture Jack's mother let me take last night sat on the counter. We were celebrating the opening of his new store. Somebody caught us eating like pigs. He saw it in my briefcase and asked if he could have it and then had the scary thing framed. I thought he was kidding. I was proud of him that day. "Be strong."

The makeup brushes Jack used on my face for the date with Ian last night were neatly placed back into their containers. I'd get them back to Kevin. "Be strong."

Jack's strange combination of cologne lingered in the room. "Be strong." I wasn't crying for Jack. I was crying for me. Crying for Pellman. Crying because it was the only thing I could do.

Burying my face in a towel to muffle the wails pouring from my soul, I sank to the floor. Waves of grief consumed me. Maybe a shower would cleanse this pain. Scalding hot water made my skin ached. I scrubbed my hair until my scalp was sore. I wanted to…had to scrub the pain away. But it clung to me. I was wedged in a purgatory between what I knew of Jack and what he really was.

The shower left me raw and red from my destructive assault. I needed air. Yellow police tape waved in the brisk morning wind below. White sand covered Jack's bloodstains. A brilliant sun peeked through the sky scrapers as I stood barefoot looking at the perfect Dallas sky. It didn't seem as beautiful to me anymore.

Tears mixed with water dripping from my hair and rolled freely down my cheeks. It trickled down my back and formed puddles where I stood. Now I'm completely alone. Despite what Jack did, I still loved him. I didn't care what he'd done. I didn't care that he hadn't told me the real story about his life. Wife. Rick. My heart was crumbling and I couldn't make it stop. I couldn't make it stop.

Jack made me feel good about living. Good about me. His gifts were acceptance. Fun. Advice. Life. Love. Joy. Friendship. Betrayal. Deception. Treachery. If only he'd told me what he

Tricked

wanted, I would have given it to him. I would have helped him. Saved him.

Bo's words rang true today. "Damaged." I rejected his assessment then, but today the pain has left me breathless. Strong. Rejected by my father. Strong. Emotionally abandoned by my mother. Strong. An entire company expecting me to pick up where Pellman left off. Strong.

Strength abandoned me. It wasn't there. What was I going to do? My place in the universe was suddenly small and twisted. A silent force convinced me no one really loved me. There was something unacceptable about me. Something wrong with me. I had that thought many times when I was young. I placed both hands on the rail. Who would miss me? Who would care if I just went away?

"McClain! What you doing? It's too cold for you to be out here in a towel with wet hair and bare feet. Come on in here! Come on. How long you been out there? Lord, you go catch pneumonia." I didn't move. I couldn't.

"McClain!....McClain! Do you hear me? You scaring me. I know you hurt baby. You've been hurting your whole life. God help me. I needed you to hurt, because I was in such pain." She was crying. "Many times I thought I couldn't face another day. But I had to because of you. Because I love you. I just couldn't let myself show you. I didn't know how.

The pain I felt consumed both of us. I wasn't a good mother. I was dried up inside. All I ever gave you was a place to live, eat and sleep. You deserved so much more. You still do. You were so good. Sweet. Smart. You did everything right. Always drawing little pictures and making gifts out of paper. You did everything you could, including standing on your head to make me love you. But I was too mean. Too selfish. Too into my own sadness. I knew I was hurting you. I knew it was wrong, but I couldn't stop. I didn't know how. I didn't know how.

I'm sorry for what I did to you. How I treated you. The way it must have made you feel about yourself. I'm so sorry for making

191

you feel unworthy of love. Look at me baby. Please look at me McClain!"

I looked at the city I'd come to love. I couldn't look at her. This wasn't about her. I didn't want her. I wanted Jack. I wanted Pellman. I wanted Bo. I didn't remember ever feeling her love and I didn't miss it now. I'd grown accustomed to her indifference. Why should today be different?

"I'm sorry for using you as an excuse for my misery. Making you responsible for it. Punishing you for what your father did to me. Taking out my revenge against him on you. It took me these many years to realize what I'd done to you. Even when I realized what I'd done, I didn't have the courage to tell you. If I could have changed it, I would. I swear I would.

Jack wasn't the only person who loved you. He wasn't. Pellman wasn't the only one who thought you were very special. I've always known how special you are. How special you would become to others. Me.

I love you. I loved you before you were born. You're my little girl. If you could forgive me...find it in your heart to give me another chance...I'll show you. If it takes the rest of my life. I will. McClain...I forgot how to love. I was jealous. Jealous of you, because your life was new. Untarnished. Unstained. Unblemished. Uncorrupted. I didn't want you to be happy. It was a choice I made...but I've changed. Thank God. I've changed.

I'm so proud of you baby. You've succeeded in spite of me. I didn't contribute in any distinguishable way. You've already overcome so much. Survived so much. You'll survive this too. I'm believing God right now that he will loosen all the strength he gave you just for this moment. I rebuke defeat. Spirit of rejection, the blood of Jesus is against you. If you could find it in your heart to give me another chance I'll show you that you're not alone. You're not alone anymore. Tell me it's not too late. Please tell me we can start again. I love you. I need you. I want your love. Please forgive me. I can't loose you too," she sobbed.

I'd never heard her speak like this. She was weeping. I'd never seen her cry. I'd merely heard her through locked doors.

Tricked

Something about her tone was authentic. She was different. It shook me and I slowly stepped back from the rail. I wasn't going to jump. But I'd never let her know it had never entered my mind. I was just having a drama queen moment. Hearing her confession was good for my soul. She needed to believe she saved me and I let her.

Her tears ran their course. I wiped her face with my towel. She walked me into the living room and sat me on the couch. She ran into the bedroom, closed the doors and grabbed the comforter. "You're freezing!" She wrapped it around me and put another towel around my hair. She rubbed my head and tucked the comforter beneath my feet. I heard the teakettle on the stove and she rushed to the kitchen. Tears and snot flowed in steady streams. She caressed my face and rubbed my arms. She sat down and pulled me close. Her arms were gentle and she smelled good. She hummed a familiar tune I remembered from my childhood. I closed my eyes and inhaled.

A new pain seized me as I realized this was the first time in my life she'd ever held me or shown me any unsolicited affection. Real affection. Genuine. My father was the one who rocked me to sleep at night humming that song I can't remember. He laughed at my childish antics and let me jump on his back for countless piggyback rides. Then he was gone. No good bye. No more light. No more love.

More than affection, I felt acceptance. This was the first time she ever made me feel that she loved me just because I was her daughter. Unconditionally. This was the love I craved. Stronger. Purer. Safer.

If either of us said one word, our combined emotions would have made the room explode. I couldn't talk. Think. Move. All I could do was absorb this woman who had finally...today... became my mother. "Hello mom. I loved you Jack.....Good bye."

CHAPTER TWENTY-FOUR

"Do you know where she is?"

"She's home."

"Is she safe?"

"Yeah. I've got two men watching all exits and entrances. I've got people on the roof of the building across the street. Her phone is tapped and our man in the lobby is security."

"Good. Has Lawford contacted her?"

"Not today. Here's the record of her calls. The only call today was from Matthew Pierce. Sounds like he's the boyfriend. Her mother is up there with her. Jerry says that she was out on the balcony this morning wearing just a towel and dripping all over the place. Her mother brought her back inside. Prescott's mother, aunt and uncle came in around 4:25 a.m. They're at his place. They haven't left the building. Pierce contacted a maid service and they came over and straightened things up. A neighbor, Abraham Greene spoke with Mr. Pierce and also went with Ms. Summers and her mother into the condo last night. Tartarian made a visit too. I've got two men on him. He's at the Nickel Inn near Skillman off LBJ. He won't be able to make a move without our people. No one else has come or gone."

"What happened on the terrace?"

"I'm not sure. You'll have to speak to Jerry about that sir. But she's in."

"Good. Has anyone heard anything about Rick Collins?"

"Not yet. He spent the night at his parent's house in Oak Cliff. His car is still in the driveway. We put a tail on him when he left the hospital yesterday."

"I don't want anything to happen to her. Is that clear?"

"Yes sir."

Our man inside RJP showed up around 6:30. He relieved Callahan who went outside for a smoke. He introduced himself.

"Hello Agent Richards, I'm Gerald North."

"North. You're work has been impressive. Do you know about Prescott?"

"Yes sir."

"What do you think the next move at RJP will be?"

"Yesterday, I saw Mr. Edwards and Mr. Jacobs leaving Ms. Summers office. I planted a disk. They took it to Cher Newman. She's the resident computer genius. It's complicated and should take her at least 48 hours to decode the encryptions. It's the U.S. Criminal Conspiracy Code backwards," he smiled.

"Good work."

"Thank you sir. Joshua Pellman's memorial service is at noon. The President-Elect will be there and our men are advancing the grounds of University Baptist Church as we speak."

"Go look through everything in Sandy Trent's desk. Pull her file. Pull everything RJP has on her."

"I already have sir," Gerald said, handing Bo the file.

"You *are* sharp. But did you know that she's an operative for RossCorp? Just came over the wire two days ago. She's originally from Bulgaria. Her family moved to Algeria. She was recruited and planted in RJP five years ago to watch Pellman and ultimately McClain. Also find out everything you can on Barry Simms, the lawyer and Matthew Pierce, his paralegal."

"It's done sir. You'll find information of Pierce under tabs 5 through 9, and Simms 10 through 15 sir." Gerald walked toward the door. "Sir?"

"Yes North?"

"I know I'm out of line...but Matthew Pierce is a good man and he's as straight as an arrow. I checked him out when he first starting seeing Ms. Summers. If I may add sir...I think he really loves her."

"And why do you think that North?"

"I just see what I see sir." Gerald continued toward the door.

"North....since you see so much...and you seem to have first hand knowledge about their relationship, does she love him too?"

"I don't know sir."

"Check him out again."

"Yes sir." Gerald left. I looked up at the ceiling.

* * *

Matthew knocked on the door and mother got up to answer it. "Who is it?" she asked in her best ghetto voice. I smiled because I knew Matthew never expected anything like that coming from my place.

"Matthew. Matthew Pierce. I'm McClain's friend. She invited me to breakfast and I brought it with me," he said in that buttery voice.

He had a key and enough respect not to use it. She probably would have stabbed him if he had. Before opening the door, my mother walked back to me. I gave a slight nod. She disarmed the security system and opened the door. She deactivated the security system? I turned around in time to see the red light turn green. Why hadn't the alarm sounded when I opened the terrace doors this morning? I removed all known codes. Why was hers still activated? I vividly remember Jack telling me, "Girl keep your alarms on. You don't ever know, Spider Man, Super Man, Dracula or any of those flying white folks might try to come in here." This realization coupled with the fact that my code didn't work on Jack's system yesterday let me know that the strange visitor was after me. I had to get to out of here fast.

I plotted my escape as Matthew and my mother whispered. "Good morning Mrs. Summers. I've looked forward to meeting you for a long time. Unfortunately these are the circumstances of our first meeting, but I'm still happy for this opportunity." He was carrying three loaded bags of groceries and fresh flowers. He always brought me flowers.

"I picked up a few things from the grocery store. I knew McClain didn't have time to go shopping. She's busy most of the time." He placed the bags on the counter. He was defending me.

"You don't have to cover for McClain. I know she don't keep no food around here. I'm glad you bought something though and I'm likewise glad to meet you. You're very handsome. I already know you're nice. Thank you for having the place cleaned up. How much do we owe you?" She took the flowers and found a vase.

"I wouldn't hear of it. But I'll make a deal with you. If you cook the breakfast and keep McClain away from the stove, we'll call it even." he chuckled.

"Deal."

They shared a laugh about my cooking. It was the only thing in my life that I hadn't mastered. "Would you see if you can do anything for her? She's kinda pitiful. She was on the terrace earlier. Well...I'll let her tell you about that. Go on. See if you can cheer her up."

"Is Jack really dead?" he asked her.

"He died yesterday afternoon. That's why I'm here. I'm supposed to leave today, but I think I should stay. I don't...I can't leave her like this. Jack meant so much to her. She had an ugly scene with his family this morning. I've never seen McClain be so rude. Pellman dead too. His funeral is at 12. I don't understand how they can have a funeral so fast. He just died yesterday," mother said, placing items into the refrigerator.

"Maybe he died before yesterday. Maybe they just announced his death to the world yesterday," Matthew concluded.

"Maybe you're right. Anyway it's too much. I'm gonna put this food away and cook some breakfast. How do you like your eggs?"

"Scrambled."

"Good."

Matthew walked into the living room and knelt behind the couch. He put his head close to mine, kissing my cheek. He rubbed my shoulders and kissed the back of my neck. He took the towel from my head and gently rubbed my head.

"I like that." I kept my eyes closed.

"I know," he whispered.

My mother peeked from the kitchen but returned to her cooking. He came around to the front of the couch and lifted me onto his lap. I put my head on his shoulder and played with his fingers. A tear dribbled from the corner of my eye. I was glad to see him. He kissed my forehead and wrapped his strong arms around me. I was safe. Finally.

"You OK?" he whispered, leaning his cheek against my forehead.

"Nope."

"I brought you something."

"What?"

Matthew reached into his pocket and pulled out a package of Juicy Fruit gum. I smiled and kissed his cheek. "You remembered."

"I remember everything you say. You're easy to please."

"No I'm not."

"Hard to understand, but easy to please."

"That's because you don't really know me."

"I know you. You don't know yourself, but I'm trying..."

"Why?"

"Because I love you."

"Is that the only reason?"

"Nope."

"Tell me."

"My dog loves you too," he smiled, kissing my cheek.

"I thought we broke up?"

"We did."

I kissed Matthew again and told him that I needed to put on some clothes and do something about my hair. "Yeah baby," he teased, "Please...do something to your hair. You scared me when I came in here. I didn't want say anything. I know you're stricken with grief...but please...gone in there and get your little afro together," he purred. I tossed a couch pillow at him and walked toward the bedroom.

"What's that?"

"What's what?"

"That song?"

"What song?"

"The one my mother's humming."

Matthew tilted his head toward the kitchen and furrowed his brow. He looked back at me. "Mockingbird."

"Mockingbird?"

"Yeah...You know," he sang, "Momma's gonna buy you a Mockingbird...."

"Oh."

I listened for a moment trying to remember the song and feeling positively driven. I knew what I had to do. When my hair was dry, I put in hot rollers. By the time I returned to the living room, Matthew was setting the dining room table and the smell of turkey sausage and coffee filled the air.

"Sit down baby. You look much better. Why you got those rollers in your head with that pretty man in the house?" she whispered, nudging me as she walked by placing homemade biscuits on the table. "I fixed your favorite things. Matthew brought everything. It's like he knew exactly what you like to eat in the morning." Matthew raised his eyebrows and smiled.

Mother rushed back into the kitchen yelling orders back at us. "Matthew...come in here baby and get these grits and the meat. McClain, make sure that Matthew put the utensils on the table right. Why don't you have any paper napkins? I need to find some big spoons. Here they are. What do you drink Matthew? I bet a big boy like you drinks milk. McClain, you want some pineapple juice? Where'd I put that jelly? I just had it in my hand."

It was a Vicky Summers breakfast production. She cooked grits. Eggs. Bacon. Sausage. Potatoes and onions. Homemade biscuits and jelly. When she sat down at the table she was exhausted. "Whew!"

"Why did you cook all of this food?" I asked.

"You didn't eat anything last night when we went out to dinner. I wanted to make sure that you ate something this morning. Matthew, can you get her to eat? She never eats. Don't you think she's too thin?"

"I love the way she looks. McClain never denies herself anything she really likes." He cooed innocently, kicking me under the table.

"Matthew say the blessing and let's eat before this food gets cold."

We bowed our heads. "Lord, thank you for this food. Thank you for the blessing of yet another day. We've lost loved ones today. Dear friends. Give us the strength to overcome our grief and replace our loss with love. Bless the cook whose hands so lovingly prepared this breakfast. Thank you for the food you so graciously provided. Let us be sincerely thankful for your bounty and your enduring mercy. Lord, bless McClain. Let her know that she's loved and although she doesn't know you, you love her too. Bless this mother as she travels back to Milwaukee. Keep her safe. Bless me as I try to love this beautiful woman. And Lord draw her to you. Give her peace and power. Strength and wisdom. Open her heart to you the way you've opened her mind to numbers. Shine your light into every dark place. Show her your ways. Bless her and bless us individually in a manner consistent with your will. Bless the families of those who mourn and give them comfort. Forgive us all dear Lord for our shortcomings. Have mercy on us and through your mercy show us how to be merciful. Thank you for the opportunity to say thank you once more. We ask it all in your blessed son Jesus name. Amen."

"Amen." My mother wiped tears with my new linen napkins.

"Amen," I whispered.

Mother acted like she forgot something in the kitchen and

stood. Matthew stood up too, respectfully, and offered to go retrieve whatever she'd forgotten.

"No baby. I'll get it. Y'all start. I'll be right back."

I looked at Matthew inquisitively passing him the grits.

"What?!" he asked, raking a large helping onto his plate.

"I don't know whether to shout, eat or take up a collection."

"Just shut up and eat. Pass the butter."

CHAPTER TWENTY-FIVE

"Ben.... go in there and see if Ricky's OK. I'm worried about him. He wasn't himself last night at the party or all day yesterday. Don't you think he was acting a little funny?"

"I don't know. Funny like what? He was nervous. Who wouldn't be? Let's leave the boy alone this morning and let him have some peace. He didn't get in until after three this morning. He had a great turn out and the place looked real good. Expensive. Plush. Some man offered him one of those exercise shows or videos. I'm not sure what he said. I'll ask him when he wakes up. Those exercise videos make a lot of money. I can see it now. Maybe, he'll put Fannie and you in some of those skin tight outfits in a thong and y'all can work out behind him," he laughed, slapping his thigh. "I'd tune in for that. He's big time now baby. He's the first of our children to own his own business. That's a lot of pressure and responsibility. I understand him not being himself. He's got a lot on him. He ain't punching no clock. He's his own boss twenty four seven. I admire that. I told him too.

Rick put all of his money and some of ours into that place. I meant to tell you, but I gave him a little loan. Just enough to let him know that we support him. Not every generation should have to struggle. My father told me that. He gave me what little he had. It helped us get this house.

He'll be alright. Stop fussing around him. He hasn't stayed here at the house all night for years. Not since he got his house built. It feels good to have three of our kids here this morning. If Terri and Kerri were here, it would seem just like Christmas. I hate they moved."

Tricked

"I guess you're right honey. I worry about all the kids. I hate they moved too. It almost broke my heart. I guess it wouldn't be right to keep them here while their husbands lived somewhere else."

"I haven't forgiven those boys yet for taking my girls. I hate they gone too, but I'm glad they got married together. Twins to the end. Five years and two grandkids later, I'm still paying for that wedding. I'm thinking of doing some part-time delivery for the Post Office so that I can pay off the credit union. You know I don't like owing nobody, but they looked beautiful didn't they?"

"They did. Still do. You looked pretty good too. They got some good husbands. Ben, why don't you just go look and see if Ricky's OK."

"He's sleep Betty. I'm not go wake that boy up. Now you worry too much. We have great kids. Nice. Successful. Smart. Two girls married. My youngest son is in law school. My daughter is in medical school, and Rick is a successful businessman. How many folks these days can say that 'bout their children? We raised five. It wasn't easy either. We didn't have to go to court with none of them. The penitentiary. The cemetery. They didn't get nobody pregnant. Didn't get pregnant. The all finished college. We have something to be thankful for Bets. We did something right."

"Yeah we have good kids. But I've always worried about Ricky. Call it mother's intuition. Ricky was different from the rest of the kids. He always had big dreams."

"I taught all our kids to dream big! What were they suppose to have? Small dreams? If you go have a dream, dream a big one. You had that same intuition about him when we visited him in up there in New York. Remember what you said when we were up there? You said that you thought Rick was acting funny, like a sissy. Rick ain't never been no sissy. He was always the most athletic. Loved sports. Fishing. Hunting. Watching women."

"Are you talking about you or him?"

"Him! He liked those things just like a man's supposed to."

"There's another side of Ricky honey. It's a side he never let us into. You know he wasn't the best student. It took him five years to finish UT. You were hard on him during that period."

"I was hard on all of them. Still am. But they know I love them. Rick knows that too. He turned out good didn't he? He's got a beautiful business. A gym over there in North Dallas. Didn't you see all those rich folks last night? He's got a beautiful home and that cabin in the woods up there in Colorado is fantastic. He's got money in the bank and a beautiful girlfriend. I'm proud of him."

"I wonder why McClain wasn't at the party last night? I just knew she would be there. He was disappointed about that, but he didn't say one word when I mentioned it. Probably thought she was too wonderful. I talked to her yesterday."

"There you go, messing in that boy's business. If you knew he was disappointed about the girl not coming, why did you bring it up?"

"When she called, she asked for Ricardo. Remember that's what some of his friends up there in New York called him. She said that she never knew Ricky lived in New York. Don't you think it's strange that he never told her that he lived in New York? And now that I think about it, she sounded funny too."

"Everybody sounds funny to you Betty. We'd been married seventeen years before I told you I lived in Wink, Texas. What does that make me?" Mr. Collins laughed.

"Be quiet. I know what I heard and she sounded funny, and now Ricky's acting funny. Something ain't right....Hummmm"

"Maybe they had a fight. Couples do that ya know."

"Nope...that's not it."

"How you know? They had a fight. McClain didn't show. Rick was upset. Ruined his evening. Maybe they broke up. That would explain his behavior yesterday afternoon. Anybody could tell he loves her. They probably broke up. He was upset and hurt. He had the club opening and it was just too much drama on the same day. That's why he probably wanted to spend the night here last night. He couldn't spend the night with his girlfriend. And he didn't want to be alone, so he stayed with his family."

"You think so?"

"Yeah...so why don't you come over here and show me how much you love me."

"Ben....quit."

"Come on Bets...the kids are all sleep."

"Stop Ben....I'm going to cook breakfast. Get up and let the dog out."

"You used to be fun Betty Jean Collins. What happened to you?"

"I married you."

Betty and Ben Collins got out of bed and began their morning routine. They wouldn't take their morning walk. Last night left them tired. A good tired. They'd spend a quiet day with their family. Betty called their daughter in New Jersey for their weekly telephone conversation. Terri was excited about the opening. Because she is 8 ½ months pregnant, she couldn't join the rest of the family for the celebration. She sent Rick a wonderful antique brass cash register for decoration.

After finishing her conversation she walked into the kitchen to prepare breakfast. The telephone rang. Kerri. She couldn't come either. It was her son's third birthday yesterday. Her husband's parents flew to Chicago from Sacramento to help them celebrate, along with her husband's promotion to Chief of Obstetrics at Grant Hospital. She shared her mother's concern for Rick, but agreed with their father. She and her husband bought Rick's office furniture and were excited about Rick's gym. They planned to come to Dallas the following weekend to see it.

Meanwhile Ben walked into the family room, looking at the menagerie of photographs, certificates and trophies his children accumulated over the years. There wasn't much wall space left in the converted carport for anything else. Little league. Girl Scouts. Boy Scouts. Band. Football. Track. Baseball. Proms. Graduations. Weddings. Grandchildren. Life. He took particular pleasure in framing his children's achievements and displaying the historical litter to his bid whist buddies.

Ben's children and wife were his trophies. He'd sacrificed his dream of becoming a major league baseball player when he and Betty got pregnant during her senior year in high school. He was two years older and playing for a farm team in Oklahoma when he found out. Respectable and responsible, he forsook his dream and married the only girl he ever loved.

He smiled proudly at Rick's high school graduation picture. He remembered the day Rick was voted 'Most Attractive' in his senior class, and how he'd rushed home to make the report at their required family dinner. He remembered how disappointed Rick looked when his first comments were, "Who won Most Athletic? Most Likely To Succeed? Valedictorian." He was eager to remedy that parental indiscretion at breakfast. "Come on dog," he said, opening the sliding glass doors to the back yard.

A piercing scream disturbed Mr. Collins' mental blueprint of this year's vegetable garden. He rushed into the house and ran toward the source of the frightening wail. Upstairs. Betty Collins was on her knees while his other children clutched each other behind her.

"What's going on!!" he yelled, reaching the top of the stairs. His son turned and faced his father. Mr. Collins pushed past his children and grabbed his wife from the floor. She was limp. Then he turned. His oldest son hung from the basketball hoop they'd installed when Rick was ten years old. It took them all day to fasten the hoop to a stud in the wall. They wanted it to be secure, so Rick could practice his hanging slam-dunks. He almost dropped his wife at the sight of lifelessness in his son's open eyes.

Samantha switched into automatic. "Daddy come here and help me! Michael call 9-1-1! Now! Hurry up! Hurry up! Cut the sheets daddy while I hold him up.....Oh Lord.....Rick?......Hurry up daddy!

Michael raced to the phone. Mr. Collins lifted his unresponsive son while his daughter took the sheet from his neck. All sound left the room as Rick slumped into his sister's arms.

She immediately checked his neck for a pulse. Nothing. She ran to her room grabbing the stethoscope from her bag. Nothing.

"Is he dead Sam?" her brother whispered. She didn't answer and quickly began CPR. She breathed for him. Believed for him. Pumped his chest. Alternated back and forth until sweat poured from her. She never stopped. Nothing triggered or stimulated her brother's empty heart. She looked at her parents, closed her eyes and continued her vain attempt to resuscitate him.

Mr. Collins slumped against the bed. Mrs. Collin wails could be heard throughout the neighborhood. Neighbors poured into the house.

Police and paramedics arrived quick. Samantha was soaking wet by the time they rushed into the room. The paramedics looked at each other and told her to stop for a moment. They checked all of his vital signs and connected electronic leads to his chest. She read the flat line printout and closed her dripping eyes.

"I'm sorry...he's gone," one of them whispered.

"OK.....Will do...thanks," the other said into a radio.

Mr. Collins pushed his wife into the arms of Michael and his sister, ordering them to help their mother out of the bedroom and downstairs. Michael went into the kitchen to turn off the whistling teapot. "Does anyone need medical care?" A police officer offered the family.

The Collins' stood speechless as cold silence overwhelmed their once joyful house. A paramedic called the coroner's office as Mr. Collins sat dazed and motionless. The other paramedic closed Rick's eyes and Mr. Collins emitted a silent scream that rattled the soul and shook the spirit. EMTs rushed to him, taking his blood pressure and placing oxygen to his face. He was breaking down. Something. Someone had to save him. The oxygen was removed.

"Are you his father?" A uniformed officers asked softly.

"What? Yes," he answered, returning from the brink.

"Did you find him?"

"No.....My wife found him....at least I think my wife found him. I was outside with the dog when I heard her scream. I just....I don't know...I."

"What's his name sir?"

"Richard Benjamin Collins. Rick. We call him Rick."

"And you are Mr. Collins?"

"I'm his father. He's my son. My oldest son. My name is Benjamin Michael Collins." The blood pressure cuff was removed.

"I'm terribly sorry about your son Mr. Collins. This is a terrible shock to you, your entire family. Do you have any idea why he'd do this?"

"No. I was telling my wife this morning about how happy he was. How happy we were. Last night he opened a new business. A gym. It's called "Sweat." In North Dallas. I have no idea why he'd do this terrible thing to himself. Us." The paramedics packed their devices and left, rushing to another call.

"Did he leave a note or anything?"

"A note? We haven't looked for a note. Did anyone see a note?" he asked the empty room. "It just happened. My boy is dead."

"Yes sir. I'm terribly sorry. You'll need to go downstairs for a few minutes. The coroner is here. You may need you to answer more questions. A detective will be here any minute."

"I can't just leave my boy. Like this," Mr. Collins said, tears rolling down his cheeks.

"Mr. Collins you can come back before they take him away and spend as much time as you'd like with him. Your whole family can. The coroner needs to make a report. They will take Rick to their office. Please accept my sincere condolences. I'll stay right here with you through everything. Alright? Would you like me to contact your pastor sir?" the officer rubbed Mr. Collins shoulder. "OK…yes…thank you officer."

Mr. Collins pulled himself up and walked toward the door. He wiped away his tears and adjusted his housecoat. It seemed like he'd gained two hundred pounds in the last twenty minutes. He paused, causing the officer to walk into his back. "I'm sorry." Ben took one last look at his beautiful son lying dead on the floor. Downstairs, his wife and children huddled in familiar grief. Trying to retie his robe, he sat in his favorite chair near the picture window. He looked out onto the street in front of his home where he'd taught Rick to ride a bike. Throw a perfect curve ball. Tie a square knot. Preen for the camera. Drive a car. Be a man.

Concerned neighbors and friends of thirty years stood in the street, on porches and in front yards wondering and concerned about what was happening in the house where five perfect children had been raised. He closed his eyes and rubbed his head preparing himself for the unanswerable questions. Searing pain. Unrelenting anguish. Stabbing guilt. Unquenchable grief. But as head of this house, enduring whatever pain or torturous anguish that suddenly redefined his existence, he instinctively sucked it up to lend his rapidly dissipating strength to his wife. Children. The family he loved.

CHAPTER TWENTY- SIX

"Is the trash disposed of?"

"Yes sir. Both items."

"Good. What about the other problem?"

"We haven't found it yet sir, but we feel we're very close. We believe we'll be able to take care of it today."

"Just make sure that it's done quickly and correctly."

"Yes sir."

***

Mother and Matthew needed to get out of my house as soon as possible. After we finished our breakfast, Matthew amused my mother by passing out compliments. Her eyes. Tiny hands. Her skin. Her smile. He laid it on thick and she loved it. He was intrigued that she cooked so well and I...well...I'd never seen her like this. He helped with the dishes while I paced.

The telephone rang. Something clicked. Bugged, I thought. But by whom?

"Hello...McClain?" It was Keith.

"Hi Keith," said dryly.

"Did you get my message yesterday? I have tickets to the Jazz Explosion tonight at the Dallas Symphony. Are you interested "I can swing by and pick you up around 6:30. The show starts at 7. I'll even buy you dinner afterwards."

"You haven't heard have you?"

"Heard what?"

"Joshua Pellman died. His memorial service is today at noon."

"What?! You've got to be kidding?"

Tricked

"No one has called you? Don't you listen to the radio or read the paper?"

"I just got back to town last night. I haven't looked at the paper and I haven't checked my messages. Is the memorial open or by invitation? Where is it?"

"By invitation. You're on the list. The memorial will be held at University Baptist."

"Look McClain, I've got to make some calls and I'll see you over there. Hang in there baby."

"OK."

I watched Matthew and my mother go out onto the terrace through the kitchen doors. Matthews cell phone was on the couch. I snatched it and went into the bathroom, turning on the hair dryer. I peeked out of my bedroom. They were still talking. I called Barry.

"Hey Barry...McClain. I got your call yesterday. So your buddy and roommate are back in town, huh?"

"Yeah...hey McClain baby. I was just wondering how you were. I was about to call you. I heard about Pellman and Jack too. Are you going to the memorial?"

"It's a shock for all of us. I'm OK. Of course I'm going. You coming?"

"I'm going to miss the memorial baby. I have a house full of people here. If you need me for anything..."

"I know."

"Remember the last time I invited you over, you weren't available. Well he's back."

"Like a poltergeist?"

"He's a nice guy McClain. He's a surgeon. He's rich."

"You already said that."

"I think you too have got...."

"Lots in common. I know. What time?"

"You know me. I've already started. The grill will be smoking around 1:30."

"I'll let you know. If I come, should I bring anything?"

"Baby, please no! No offense Mac but I you can't cook. You fine as you want to be, but you can't cook worth a damn. Just bring yourself and have some fun with all of the little people Miss Vice President of International Finance and Markets for RJP. Why didn't you tell me?"

"I didn't have time. So much has happened since then."

"You ain't kidding. You go get Pellman's spot?"

"Everything is up in the air right now."

"I hear ya. Well you in high cotton or deep water now ain't ya?"

"You're the master of understatement. Talk to you later."

"Take care baby. Hang in there."

Strategies for survival developed quickly. Matthew gladly agreed to take my mother to the airport for her 11:45 flight. It was his chance to find out more about me. I'd go to the memorial and then to the office. Maybe then I could find out what this was all about.

I kept Mat's phone, stuffing as much as I possibly could into my backpack. Then I began telling the first of a thousand lies that would protect myself, and the people I loved. Mother and Matthew left at 9:45. She tearfully entered the elevator, imploring me to be careful. She wanted Matthew to stay. "I'll feel better with someone watching you. He used to be a policeman. He can protect you."

"Protect me from what?"

"I mean he'll make sure you get some sleep."

"I'm used to operating on little sleep mom. Matthew take her to the airport and you can check on me later."

He reluctantly agreed. When the elevator doors closed, I went to Mr. Greene's house to use his telephone.

CHAPTER TWENTY-SEVEN

A cab took me to the memorial service. Lots of people would be there. Mingling. Looking. Questioning. Never mind the short notice. The governor, both senators, politicians of every kind and ilk, along with captains of industry, students and fans came to pay their respects. Tycoons and moguls filled the churchyard. RJP's brass flew in from around the world. A who's who in international finance and business were represented. We awaited Mrs. Pellman's arrival.

Sandy saw me first. She waived for me to join my partners. Unmoved, I stood like a stone refusing to join them. My staff surrounded me like a human fortress, as though they instinctively knew danger was imminent. A flurry of Dallas PD, Sheriff's cars, and unmarked federal vehicles turn onto University Blvd.

President-Elect Simms arrived with Mrs. Pellman. She got out of the car and I walked in the opposite direction. Vincent Wheeler grabbed my arm saying, "I think Ms. Pellman is trying to get you're your attention.

Reluctantly, I went to her. She gave me a key and told me it opened something in Joshua's D. C. office. After our embrace, Clay Simms gave me a look so harsh it chilled me to the bone. Then they disappeared into the church where I made sure all the right people saw me as I found a seat near the back. In the middle of Mr. Reynolds' comments, unnoticed, I slid out.

* * *

The flight to Milwaukee was delayed an hour in Kansas City due to rain. I don't know how I slept through it. I was petrified. I'd done my best to protect McClain her entire life. But now I was powerless to help her. If I told her, she wouldn't believe me. But since I didn't tell her, she doesn't know how protect herself. Worse, she didn't know from whom she needed protection. I'll call her and tell her everything when I get home.

She didn't know about Joshua and me. Why hadn't I told her last night? I couldn't. I couldn't. As long as Pellman was alive, she was safe. I was safe. Maybe if I called him he'd leave her alone. Joshua warned me that speaking with him was far too dangerous. Joshua promised that he wouldn't let anything or anyone harm her. Death changed that. Death changed everything.

Devastated, danger lurked closer and closer. What do I do now? Who'll protect us? Her?

"Miss that will be $41.00," the cab driver turned around looking for his fare.

"Oh, OK. Here's $48.00. Keep the change. Do you mind pulling into the driveway?"

"No problem."

As the key turned in the lock, I heard someone behind me.

"Ms. Summers, you'll have to come with us."

"No," I protested, preparing to scream as I struggled against the man holding my arm. Another man said, "We don't want to hurt you. But you *will* come with us, so decide right now how you want to go."

"Please I have money. Let me go. I won't say anything. I promise. I've never said one word to anyone in all these years. Please. Please. She doesn't know. I swear. She doesn't know."

Scared and helpless the men held my arms, while one put his hand over my mouth. They snatched me into a van and drove away quickly. Refusing to tell me who they were or who sent them, I was blindfolded and restrained. Why were they taking me? Where were they taking me? Why was this happening? Although they assured me I wouldn't be harmed, I didn't believe them. I prepared myself to die.

Tricked

My travel agent picked me up from a coffee shop across the street. She brought tickets to Washington and San Francisco. "It needs to appear that I'll arrive in D.C. for just a few hours. Then book me to San Francisco." She scheduled a 5:15 flight to DCA and left me at Barry's house at precisely 12:45.

I met Clarence. Enough said. After changing clothes, I was casual and charming. He insisted I should be his partner in a board game. I watched the clock and the men sitting in the car across street from Barry's house. Who were they? We won. Barry said, "Clarence needs to leave for a seminar he's attending in Savannah tomorrow morning. Can somebody take him to the airport?"

"Clarence, what time does your plane leave?" I cooed.

He gave me those goo goo eyes some men master when their career alone makes them attractive. "At 5."

"Barry's convinced we have loads in common. Why don't I take you to the airport so we can get to know each other better? Alone," I flirted.

"Sounds good to me," he moaned, leaning in close enough for me to smell his aftershave. Not good.

"Good. I'll ask Barry if I can use his car and we can get out of here," I said with a sly smile. He winked at me. "Not even in your wildest dreams," I thought to myself.

"I'd love that," he smiled.

"Barry I'll take Clarence to the airport. You may have finally made a great match. Clarence and I want to spend a little time alone before he leaves town."

"What? My boy!! OK." Barry was a little drunk and a true romantic. He knew better." "My keys are in the bedroom on the dresser. Drive carefully baby. What am I talking about? Drive anyway you want. You rich. You can buy me another one. A better one," he laughed. He forgot to tell me about the naked woman passed out on his bed.

I left the suit I'd worn to Pellman's memorial on a chair. I got his keys, leaving a note along with the approximate location of

215

where I planned to leave his car. I also left the keys to my car and a $50.00 bill. The note read:

Barry,

Consider this $50.00 a legal retainer. You must maintain my confidence and you must help me. My life depends on it. You. I found something in the Calhoun file. I don't what it means yet, but Jack died trying to find it. I think someone wants to kill me too.

Ask this drunk woman to wear the suit I left on the chair. It's expensive. She's cheap. She'll do it. Pick up my car and take her to my condo. It's at the airport on the lower level, section 1. Take an extra person with you to help drive. Ask Duane, he looks a lot like you. You'll need him to drive your car. It's directly across from mine. In the trunk of my car is a suitcase. Guard it with your life. When you get to the condo take the service elevator and spend the night in the guestroom. You've always wanted to spend the night at my place. Tonight is your lucky night. Don't leave before 10 a.m. tomorrow morning. My keys and alarm code are in the glove box.

If you look down the street you'll see two men sitting in a car. They're watching me and you too. Your telephone is probably bugged so don't try to reach me. Don't use your cell and destroy this note when you've finished reading. Play the nut roll if anyone asks you anything. I'm sure they will.

I'll call you when I think it's safe. Thanks for being a good friend. Thanks for your help. You're the only one I can trust now. It's essential that you do exactly as I ask. Sober up. Be safe and be careful.

Love you lots
McClain

Clarence was beaming when I returned to the kitchen. He stood there smiling at his old roommates like he was about to get lucky. When he saw me, we said our goodbyes and left. Barry's car was in the garage.

Tricked

"Why don't you drive?" I insisted.

"I don't know the way."

"I'll give you directions. I enjoy watching you talk. There's something about your mouth," I flirted. "Especially a mouth as interesting as yours," I said rubbing my hand across his arms and gently licking my lips.

"Oh…OK…I'll drive…I love driving. I love talking too. I talk all the time. My friends say I talk too much (laughter) but I don't think so. I come from a talkative family. How'd you get that name anyway? McClain?"

He reached into his back pocket and placed his wallet on the center console and put on some frighteningly thick glasses.

"My mother named me after a street in Pittsburgh. Are you sure you have everything?"

"You're named after a street in Pittsburgh?" he asked with a hint of amusement in his voice.

"Yeah. How'd you get your name?"

"My grandfather."

"I see…a family name. Would you mind going back inside and getting me another one of those delicious chocolate chip cookies?" I put my hand on his thigh.

"No, I don't mind. I don't mind at all. They were good. I'll get some for both of us," he smiled, taking off the glasses and running back into the house.

His wallet was full of credit cards. They all had his full name. American Express. Visa. Master Card. Discover. Victoria Secret. Freak. On the Discover card "C. M. Whitaker" was embossed on the front. He came out of the house and I smiled at him. He handed me two chocolate chip cookies and he kept two for himself.

"Thanks Clarence."

"No problem. You like chocolate don't you?" he asked in a suggestive way.

"No. I like you," I flirted back, "You know Barry has tried to set me up with several of his friends, but I must admit that he got it right this time."

He giddily pressed the garage door opener as I ducked down. "What are you doing?"

"I lost a contact," I said feeling around on the floor. "Turn right at the end of the driveway and go straight. Make a left at the first corner. You'll see the expressway. You want to take 45 South."

I continued hunting around on the floor, trying my best to stay out of sight of anyone who was watching. "Don't you want me to stop and help?"

"No," I insisted.

He needed to keep his weak eyes on the road. I didn't want to miss my plane and I certainly didn't want him to miss his. By the time we reached 635W, I surmised if anyone was following us, they wouldn't have any reason to believe I was in Barry's car.

I acted like I found the lost lens and returned to my seat pulling on my sunglasses, while watching the passenger's side rear view mirror intensely. Clarence chit and chatted about his practice. His life. Boat. Patients. Plans. Practice. Prowess. "Please."

A parking place close to where I told Barry he could find my car was available. Clarence steered into the narrow spot and jumped from the car retrieving his bag from the backseat. He handed me the keys and smiled. There was something about him I hadn't noticed. Why do some men who make so much money fail to invest some of that cash in their mouth? Yuk.

"Did you hear that?" I walked around the car acting as though I heard air seeping from the rear tire, driver's side. Clarence walked around to look. "I don't hear anything." While he walked toward the rear of the car, I quickly placed the keys on top of the front tire.

"Really?"

"It looks just fine."

"Maybe it was just airport noise," I suggested.

"Probably."

We walked into the airport and I glanced at the board. His flight left at 5:25 from gate 7. On time. Mine left would be late, leaving at 5:35 from gate 17. Late. As Clarence approached the security check area, I told him I needed to go the restroom. "Go ahead. I'll come to your gate. I can get through security because of my VIP status through RJP. I don't even need a ticket."

The goof believed me. Ducking out of the bathroom I presented my ticket and ID at the VIP security check. Clarence watched impatiently. We exchanged business cards and made plans for a future meeting.

Clarence prattled on and on about how glad he was to meet me and how we had so much in common. 4:45. He'd call me as soon as he got back to Baltimore. "I can't wait." 4:50. The first call for my flight echoed through the terminal. "Clarence I must have eaten something that disagrees with me. I have to go back to the restroom."

"Maybe you have gastritis. I can catch a plane in the morning. I'd love to stay and take care of you."

"No. No. I'll be right back."

How was I going to get to my gate in time? Just then, a group of beautiful African women came into the restroom. As they used the facilities, I tied a scarf around my head to resemble a turban. When they moved. I moved. I peeked around the corner trying to see whether Clarence was still watching. He wasn't.

The women joined a large delegation of African tourists. I quickly jumped into the middle of them and started saying "Jumbo, Jumbo." They laughed acknowledging my greeting, welcoming me into their loud parade. We walked briskly toward my gate. I don't know where they were going, but when we got to gate 15, I broke out of the gaily dressed crowd and dashed at full sprint to the counter.

They checked my ticket as I raced down the jet way. "You just made it," the attendant smiled as I found my seat, wiping sweat from my forehead. Clarence will probably never speak to me again. He'll probably never speak to Barry either. I don't care. He was a necessary casualty. It's hard being a spy.

CHAPTER TWENTY-EIGHT

Except for a screaming baby six rows back, the flight to DC was uneventful. I must have looked like I needed a drink. "Would you like something to drink?" the flight attendant asked, showing me wines and other liquors. I did, but declined. This mission required me to be cold stone sober.

When we reached National Airport, I hurried from the deplaning area. "Hey Iris girl! It's me!"

"When you coming?"

"I'm here...at BWI," I lied.

"You where?!"

"I'm at the airport right now. Can you come and get me or should I catch a cab?"

"It's gonna take me about an hour to get there? Why didn't you fly into National?"

"This was the best flight I could get tonight. I don't mind. I'll catch a cab honey."

"No sweetheart. It's too difficult to give directions here. I want to pick you up. Can you wait? Get some dinner or something. I don't even know why I said that. You don't eat airport food."

"Don't worry. I'll do some work until you get here. Just get here. It's gonna take at least 40 minutes for you to get ready. You dress like you're going to the prom before you can take out the trash, so it'll take be at least two hours before you get here. "

"Look tramp.... it ain't nothing wrong with looking your best at all times. Try it...with your tired self. I'll pick you up on the street near Giant Airlines."

"OK. See ya Iris."

Tricked

"Bye baby.

"Take me to the Willard." I never removed the turban or sunglasses although it was pitch black outside. The cabbie thought I was somebody famous and kept challenging me to tell him who I was. "You're famous aren't you? I've seen you on T.V. I know I have. I just don't remember your name."

The Willard was abuzz with beltway types. The clerk asked me how long I'd be staying. I said that I wasn't sure, but I had important meetings for the next few days and didn't want to be disturbed. He gave me a key and I boarded the elevator. Never intent of going to the room, I needed to create the impression I was. I pushed 8. My room was on 10. The elevator stopped on two. Three distinguished looking men got on as I got off. Unwrapping the scarf, I tousled my hair and slipped into the vending area.

On the other side of the ice machine, I changed. I'd read enough thrillers to know you should change your look as often as possible. I was so scared someone would walk by and catch me that when the ice machine dropped ice into the holding bin, I almost peed on myself. I threw my shirt and shoes into the bag and boarded the elevator a new woman.

I exited the hotel from a side door. "Take me to BWI."

"No luggage?" "Short trip."

It was 10:05 when he pulled in front of the Giant terminal. In typical fashion, Iris was late. I could always count on that. Darkness shrouded me. Iris was driving a brand new Mercedes SEL. It still had dealer's tags. Iris jumped out and rushed toward me, waiving frantically.

"Get back in! Get back in! Let's go!" I instructed, running in her direction.

"Girl...why didn't you tell me you were coming tonight? I told you to fly into National. What's wrong with you?"

After a tremendous hug and kiss, it began. "I thought you said you weren't coming until Tuesday. I heard about Pellman. Jack too. Oh my God! Where's your stuff? How you holding up? You look good girl. Grief ain't got a chance against it. Do you ever gain weight? I like your hair. I'm glad you stopped wearing that ponytail. Girl I'm so tired. I've been working like a Hebrew slave. Are you dating? How's your mother? Did you get that dress I sent you? What did you say happened to your luggage?"

It was vintage Iris. Talking a mile a minute and never allowing an answer to the barrage of questions she asked. I loved the sound of her voice, always on the brink of laughter. Hopeful. Pure. She loved the sound of her voice too, so she always talked whether anyone was listening or not.

"They lost it. I'll have to buy all new stuff in the morning so I can take my meetings. I'm just glad I carried my backpack with me."

"That same thing happened to Craig and me. Did I tell you about Craig? He bought me this car for my birthday. I didn't get your birthday gift. Is it in your luggage? Anyway, we went to Montego Bay for one of those Old School Things to celebrate. I was soooo pissed, but Craig was cool. It didn't even bother him. He said, "Baby we won't need clothes." Isn't that funny? She laughed. "They brought the luggage to the villa he rented the next day, and you know what? I *didn't* need any clothes," she laughed more. "But you do. Are you going to buy something in the morning? I may have something you can wear. Maybe there's something at the store. We never wore the same size. I hate you. So skinny in the right places."

"Who's Craig?" I asked, knowing it would take at least forty-five minutes to get to Iris' house and at least an hour for her to describe him. I wrapped myself in the comfort of her voice and dozed. "He's fabulous! Wonderful! Smart! Cute! Sexy! Generous! He's the real thing McClain. We've been dating off and on for eight months, but now we're all the way on. I love it. I just love it! He introduced me to his mother about a month ago. I've never met a mother before. She thought I was a little too talkative."

"How do you know?" I asked.

"She told Craig that I was too talkative. Can you believe that? I don't talk that much. Do I? Anyway, he's a thoracic surgeon at Andrews. He's kind and he supports me and my business. I'm totally in love with him. And he loves me too! I didn't want to say anything to you about him because you always think I choose the wrong men, but I think I'm finally on the right track. I met him at a sorority function. He was actually with someone else and I...."

Iris was from Ft. Lauderdale. We attended 'FamU' on the same tuition scholarship program. Florida A&M made a special commitment to recruit and educate African American national merit scholarship finalists. The school provided a great social, cultural, educational, and spiritual environment, not to mention one of the best marching bands on earth.

The president of the university came all the way to Milwaukee to recruit me. He flew my mother and I to Tallahassee to take a look around, after mother advised him Princeton was at the top of my list. She was strident about my attending Princeton, Harvard, Brown or Yale.

They offered free rides too, but I was so impressed that the president of Florida A & M took the time to come to Milwaukee to offer me a personal invitation to attend his school, there was no other choice as attractive. It was the polite thing to do.

At freshman orientation, Iris sashayed into our room as though a legion of minions were holding the train to her gown. I had immediate and serious concerns about our compatibility, especially when she rushed to hug me as though I was some long lost relative. She kissed me right on the mouth and began moving beds and asking me, "Don't you like it better like this? It's fabulous." She darted around so fast I grew dizzy from her stampede. "We're going to be just like sisters. I always wanted a sister, but never had one. What's your name again?"

Her parents trudged in, laden with boxes. Microwave. Toaster oven. Rugs. Aquarium. Posters. Stuffed toys. Plants. Refrigerator. Luggage. Computer. Trunk. Makeup. Clothes. Stuff. When I thought their endless march was over, Iris was convinced she and I were related. "Momma, doesn't she look like daddy's people? Isn't she perfect? I love her already."

Then her brothers came in carrying other equipment and more bits and pieces while she gushed about my belongings and how pretty she thought I was. Her mother put her arms around me told me to call her Go Go. More hugs. More kisses. Her father smiled proudly, taking directions from both Iris and Go Go concerning the placement of everything. My things too. Her brothers investigated my two photographs and computer, but snapped to action at Iris' bidding.

This family was loud. Electric. Frenetic. They scared me. Just as I was ready to run for the hills, Iris announced, "I'm born to be a college student." Everyone laughed. So did I.

My mother didn't like noise. Our house was as quiet as a tomb. The verbal circus the Meeks created was fun. Amusing. Entertaining. I liked it. I liked them. They liked me.

Two days from our initial meeting, it was as though I'd known her my entire life. She's still extremely expressive and her laughter amuses everyone who hears it. If Iris laughs, everyone laughs.

She tried out for the FamU dance squad. Membership is extremely competitive and Iris became one of the only freshmen to join the honored team. It was a distinct honor on our campus and she could wiggle with the best of them. I would have never gone to a football game, had she not been on the field. Her moves and personality made her a social butterfly and very popular with upperclassmen.

It was hard to understand how she aced her classes with the amount of time she spent at rehearsals. Traveling with the squad. Attending campus parties. Becoming freshman queen. Flirting.

Iris was naturally brilliant with a fantastic memory. For me, studying was the only way I made the grades that came so effortlessly to her. "Stacked," is how the boys on campus described her. She still goes to the beauty shop every Saturday morning and is an absolute perfectionist.

After college Iris became an assistant buyer at an exclusive department store in New York. She worked hard for five years and became bridal buyer for the last two years she was there. She learned the ins and outs of the high end bridal business and used her contagious charm to befriend exciting new bridal designers, and veterans too. She dazzled them like she dazzles everyone.

Tricked

Iris was intent on opening her own shop. She called the business the "The Knot Shoppe". After almost three years, it was the place for people with big bucks. Unlimited budgets. Posh taste. High end style. Iris directed the weddings of the rich and famous. I referred several RJP clients to her. They were thrilled and the referrals took the business global.

Her forte is creating memorable and exclusive weddings that reeked of class, elegance and style. That was Iris all over. She had the personality and the tenacity to pull off a royal wedding without one hair coming out of place. The exclusivity of her services maintained the prominence of her clientele, which ensured high prices.

Investors consistently approached her about franchising her shops which were now located in New York, DC and LA. I told her the franchise theory looked lucrative on paper, but might not adequately translate without jeopardizing her distinctive style and touch. She was smart enough to know that franchising would dilute the exclusivity of her posh business, so she decided against it. Instead, she put on exclusive 'invitation only' wedding seminars world-wide.

Iris believed in effective networking. Efficient delivery of services. Reasonable expectation of excellence. Extraordinary professionalism. She called them the four E's. The strategy accounted for Iris' popularity and she received numerous accolades and industry honors for her savvy.

She also received the admiration of many prominent men. Black. White. Asian and Hispanic. Her version of the rainbow coalition. "Everybody wants to find my pot of gold," she'd laugh.

"MC why don't you polish your nails. Do you know how much people pay for nails like that? Why don't you wear more makeup? You look ten years old. You still haven't gotten a perm have you? It's always the girls who have a head full of hair who don't do nothin with it. It's the bald chicks keeping these beauty shops in business," she chuckled as she drove down her street. "It took me two years to get you to shave your legs. I guess it will take me ten more to get those baby curls to go."

Cynthia A. Minor

Iris was always concerned about how drab she thought my life was. It had certainly taken a turn for the dramatic recently. While we were in school, I wasn't interested in anything but economics, math and getting into Wharton Business School and Penn Law. She begged me to go to parties. No time. No interest. She couldn't see how books, plays, Keats, the economics club, math club, finance club; technology journals and computer labs could be any fun. I had my friends. She had hers. She called mine loveable nerds. Then she flitted off into the tempestuous glow of collegiate nights.

One Saturday when I returned from the computer lab, I was shocked to find that Iris' shoulder length hair had been cut into one of those chic East Coast scalpings. It took a gorgeous face and diva attitude to pull the look off. She had both.

She also had great parents. Brothers she loved. Beautiful mother. A handsome father who called her every Tuesday, just to talk. She was brilliant. Beautiful. Popular. Her Achilles heel had always been men. It was the only area in her life where poor taste and poor judgment prevailed. I wondered about this Craig person.

She had the same excited voice about a football player she dated our entire first semester and most of the next. His name was Alex Hudson. He was from St. Louis. A junior. A flirt. He lived with another football player in an apartment off campus. He was cute with a decent GPA. Alex seemed like a nice guy at first. His parents were doctors and they expected him to carry on the family tradition. After we made the Dean's list our first semester, he bought pizza to the room in the new car his parents bought him as incentive. He called our room at all hours. He and Iris talked for hours. They giggled and played to the point of distraction.

Alex started picking Iris up late on Friday nights after spring registration. I wouldn't see her again until late Sunday night when he'd drop her off in front of the dorm. It bothered me that he stopped walking her up to the room. She literally floated into the room after one of their torrid weekends. When I asked her why he stopped taking her to movies or anywhere else during day light hours and creeping around late at night, she made serial excuses, convinced he loved her. "I didn't really want to go to the dance and he'll pick me up as soon as it was over." Iris not want to go to a party? "Yeah right!"

Their wedding and unnamed children were planned. She bought him gifts and made other elaborate plans. I never saw a Valentine's gift. Birthday gift. Nothing. He didn't even invite her to the Athlete's Banquet. "It won't be fun anyway," he told her. I saw straight through his game and I never understood why Iris couldn't see she was being played.

I had enough and refused to leave the room for them anymore. Not one of his telephone messages was delivered and I treated him like the jerk he was.

One afternoon he came to our room while Iris was in class. I told him to wait for her in the lobby. He convinced me that Iris insisted that he wait in our room. Reluctantly, I agreed. I returned to my desk and concerned myself with a paper. He sat on Iris' bed staring at me. I turned my back and fixed my gaze on my computer.

When Alex began talking, I put on my headphones. He got up and came over to my desk and grabbed them. I jumped. He said that several of the football players, as well as his frat brothers, wanted to meet me. He asked me, "Are you dating anyone or have you considered running for Miss. FamU next year? You'd make a great queen. My frat and the team would love to sponsor you."

I didn't respond and continued ignoring him. He looked at the pictures of my friends from home and asked me, " Do you have a boyfriend in Milwaukee?"

I turned the computer off and began packing my things. I'd leave him to wait for Iris alone. Suddenly Alex's' hand was on my shoulder. "Boy! What are you doing?!" I shrieked, jumping from the chair.

"Relax McClain...chill baby...I just wanted to rub your shoulders. You always seem so tense." He whispered, looking directly into my eyes.

"Take your hands off of me!" I screamed, trying to get around him. He widened his stance.

Before I could find something with which to hit him, he pinned me against the desk trying to kiss me. I fought like mad, but his strength overpowered my struggle. He held both my hands with one of his, grabbing me around the waist with the other. He pulled at my shirt and tried to touch me. I screamed and pushed to no avail. He kept saying "I always preferred you to Iris and if you'd just give me a chance I'd drop her in a New York minute. I saw you first. We all did. You're gorgeous. Hot. You *are* hot aren't you McClain?" his breath seared my ear. "Iris said you're not gay, so I think you're playing hard to get. That ends today. I've been using Iris to get to you and I know you feel me. I've seen how you look at me. You want me too. Don't you?" he asked, kissing my neck and ripping at my jeans.

"I hate you! Leave me alone!" My futile fight and loud screams had not effect.

"Go ahead. Scream. I like it when they scream. This is a dorm. No one will come. Don't fight me. You're so pretty. Fresh. I bet you're a virgin too. I'll make you feel real good McClain. Real good," he whispered, kissing my ear.

I couldn't give up, continuing my useless struggling. Panicking. Pushing. "You're hurting me." He loosened his grip slightly, but never stopped his assault. That gave me enough room to knee him in the groin, but he was too close and I was too off balance to hit my mark. He laughed. "That only works in the movies."

A scream was erupting from my throat, but instead I gathered all of my strength and gave a final push. He stumbled backwards just as Iris stepped into the room. I turned toward the window, fixing my shirt and face.

Alex immediately went into his routine acting as though nothing happened. He kissed Iris, complimenting her hair. Outfit. Smile. He told her that he came by to take her to lunch. "I love you baby. You look great. You smell good too." Iris had no idea he was coming that day and knew something was wrong. Something happened.

"Are you alright?" she asked me.

Tricked

"Yeah," I said sitting in the chair, never looking in her direction.

"Are you sure?"

I nodded yes and she grabbed her sweater. "See you in a little while sweetheart."

"OK," I managed. After a brief debate with myself, I decided never to tell Iris or anyone about what Alex had done. They broke up two days later. I never asked why. Nothing more was ever said about him.

Everybody said how glad they were that it was over. "He's a dog." "I heard he's tried to rape a girl from New Jersey last year. His parents paid her off and she transferred." "You're too good for him." "You know he's messing with Jessie." He left Iris a souvenir. She was pregnant.

We lied to our parents to get fast cash. We needed $500.00. Between the two of us we had $215.00. My mother sent $100.00. Her parents sent the rest. Iris wanted to go to Atlanta to have the procedure. Too many big mouth girls from our campus worked at the local clinic. We ditched class and drove to Atlanta on a Wednesday night. She had the procedure on Thursday morning. We were back in Tallahassee by dinner time.

Iris was still Miss Popularity and decided we needed to pledge. I declined. She became active in her sorority and ran for office. Alex married Jessie Jefferson, the homecoming queen. His parents made him marry her because she was pregnant too. They both dropped out of school and moved back to St. Louis. I was glad to see them go. It made it easier for her to get over him.

Her choices hadn't been much better since then. Married men. Who forgot that they were. Obsessive men. Who wouldn't let her breathe. Users. Who saw her as her as their ticket to the good life. Abusers. Who wanted to control or destroy her. If he was completely socially neurotic, Iris tried to save him. At least I had enough sense to give up on love after Bo.

Iris pulled the big car into the garage. Once inside, we talked about Jack. His parents. His death. Iris was shocked. She gave me a wonderful gown for the night. "Keep it. I get them from designers all of the time. This is one of the most beautiful they've sent. It'll look fabulous with your coloring. Put it on baby. How are things with your mother?" she asked puffing up the pillows on my bed.

"I think we've decided to try to get to know each other better. She's different…in a good way."

I got into bed while Iris sat in a chair with her feet on the bed. We talked until 12. She talked until 1. I could still hear her as I drifted to sleep.

CHAPTER TWENTY-NINE

The doorbell chimed twice. Where was I? "Come in. Hurry up baby. It's cold out there. Did you forget your key?" It was Iris' voice. I relaxed, looking at the green glow of the clock. 3:30 a.m.

"McClain is here. Yeah...I told you...my college room mate...Are you hungry baby?"

"I thought you said she was coming Tuesday. I got something at work." A man's voice.

"She came early. (long pause) She's asleep. Her boss and best friend died tragically. She came here directly from the memorial. She's so tired. It's awful. I don't know how she does it, but she's hanging in there. She's tough. Always has been. Did everything go well tonight? I missed you. (another long pause) I'm going to get more tickets to that thing on the hill tonight? Do you have a friend you can invite? I can't wait for you to meet."

"What does she look like?" he asked.

"What difference does it make? Call one of those men you run around with. She needs an acceptable escort."

"OK baby...but come here first." (Longer pause)

"Wait a minute Craig. Let's go into the bedroom."

They walked pass my room. But it was difficult to go back to sleep. Their moans and howls made me think of Matthew. What was he doing? I knew he'd worry? If Barry had done as I asked, it would give me more time. I stared at the ceiling and drifted back to sleep.

Iris knocked on the door at 6:15 a.m. She was fully dressed. "Good morning sweet pea! I have to take Craig to the hospital. I have two meetings after that. I should get back no later than 1:15. Will that give you enough time to wakeup and get yourself together? I can take you to the mall and downtown."

"I'll catch a cab to the train station and then I'll catch the train downtown. No problem. You don't have to worry about me. I'm self sufficient and I have some other things to do."

"I know you're self-sufficient sweetheart, but I don't want you spending all that money on cabs and stuff. Why don't you just drive my car over to the mall? I can take Craig to work and we can work out all other logistics as necessary. As you know, there's a Neimans at Tyson's Corners. Ask for Veronica, she's a personal shopper. She'll get you set. Then come back here and get dressed. Leave my car at the train station and we'll pick it up later."

"Are you sure?"

"Absolutely."

"That'll work. Is Craig out there?"

"He's still in the bathroom. He'll be out in a minute. Would you like to meet him now?"

"Of course I want to meet the man who had you howling like a wolf last night. Let me wash my face and brush my teeth first," I laughed.

"Did you hear us?" she laughed, with only a hint of embarrassment in her voice. "We thought we were being quiet because you were in the house."

"Scared me. I almost called 911."

"Shut up! You so crazy McClain."

Iris wrote out directions and instructions while I busied myself in the bathroom. "How long will you be downtown?"

"Until around 4:30," I yelled, with toothpaste dripping from my mouth.

"Look, why don't we meet downtown? I have somewhere I want to take you this evening. Craig has this big evening planned. He's so romantic McClain, so don't bat those inch long eyelashes of yours at him. He's mine. I put the address is on the same paper with all of the other directions. Try to get there by 5? That way we won't have to come all the way back out here."

"OK, how's this?" I said popping from the bathroom.

"Ain't this nothing? You're the only woman I know who can look that good this early in the morning without makeup."

She hugged and kissed me ripping the barrette from my hair. "Ouch!" I shook my head. She laughed and put her arm around me. Craig was still in her room.

"Craig! Craig!...I want you to meet McClain," she yelled.

A very short light skinned brother stepped out of Iris' bedroom and walked toward us. He looked up at me, extending his hand. I almost laughed. Not because he was short. But because with all of the noises they made, I visualized a bigger man. Maybe he was, I giggled to myself.

"So you're McClain. I've heard so much about you. Iris forgot to tell me that you look like an angel. You're beautiful."

"Thank you Craig. Now I understand why Iris adores you." He was a charming little man and quite handsome.

"Craig, I told you she was fantastic."

"She is."

"Iris has said some pretty remarkable things about you too. I look forward to spending some time getting to know you. But don't let me make either of you late for work. When we get together this evening, we can trade Iris stories," I smiled.

"I look forward to it. It'll be one of those rare nights where I get to spend down time with my baby girl. Not to mention her college bud," he said hugging Iris. She was eating this stuff with a spoon. Beaming.

"I'll see you later girl. I left everything you need on the dresser. If you need anything else, just look in my room. Look in kitchen. You know where to look. My keys are on that hanger thing in the back hallway. The alarm code is my birthday. If you want something to eat, look in the fridge. I've already made a pot of coffee and luckily I have a bottle of that pineapple juice you like. Don't forget 5 o'clock. Don't be late," she said rushing around collecting her entrepreneurial weapons. Trench coat.

233

Briefcase. Appointment book. Binder. Cell phone. Umbrella and other assorted things.

"I won't. It was a pleasure meeting you Craig."

"No....it was my pleasure."

He helped Iris with her coat and opened the door for her. She kissed me and they drove out of the garage.

Jack's disks were still in my backpack. Jack had stolen my disks and replaced them without me even knowing. He put a device on my computer that automatically printed everything I entered. After the first year, Jack was afraid that he'd gotten attached to me. He told Rick that he'd lost his objectivity and he cared about me too much to continue the farce. He wanted to leave Dallas and start over somewhere else. Rick told Jack they were in too deep and convinced Jack they would be murdered if they pulled out before the job was done.

Jack couldn't convince Rick they needed to get out. Rick liked the money and the lifestyle. He didn't care about the danger. He craved it.

Jack said as long as they were merely stealing inside information and discrete forecasts, he didn't mind the work. When they ordered him to plant fake information implicating my complicity in a scheme to hide the identity and owners of the very stocks I was researching, he was out.

Turner was to make me the fall guy. Millions were placed in international bank accounts bearing my name. Jack outlined the account numbers and bank locations. There was the laundry list of their dirty deals that included government officials, captains of industry of other noteworthy citizens. With me as the puppet master, Reynolds and Jacobs would feign ignorance, though they had been bought off by the cartel with instructions that included my immediate death if I discovered the identities or the existence of the accounts.

Rick was abusing Jack. He tried in vain to escape Rick's destructive ways several times. Romeo drove him to San Antonio. He planned to fly to Mexico from there. Romeo came back to Dallas and called Jack, leaving a voice mail saying that he'd left his gloves in Jack's condo. Rick intercepted the message and flew to San Antonio. He found Jack, brought him back to Dallas and beat him unmercifully. It was the week he said he was shopping in Paris.

Jack was trapped. He couldn't trust anyone. He knew I wouldn't believe him. He knew I was in danger, but he didn't know from whom. The plan (what ever it was) was going to be carried out today. That was the last entry.

At 8:35 I turned on the radio. Tom Joyner was still cracking jokes. I planned to curse him out when I got back to Dallas. He didn't come to my last party. Didn't call either. We were friends from long before he became the sky jock. We had mutual acquaintances in Indiana and I remembered when he came back to Dallas driving that white Seville. I smiled and went into the bathroom to shower.

Veronica found two wonderful suits. I couldn't decide which I wanted, so I bought both. Two pairs of shoes. A coat. Three pairs of pantyhose. Underwear. A suitcase and accessories. The saleswoman almost passed out because of the high commission she was about to make.

She directed me to the beauty salon. I needed a new look. The only brother in the place said that he could take me. He suggested a very mild relaxer. Reluctantly, I agreed. He permed. Rubbed. Blew. Clipped. Patted. Curled and pulled on my head for about an hour and a half. When I finally looked in the mirror. I was pleased.

"You have great hair Ms. Whittaker. I loved working with it," he said, urging me to buy a myriad of products.

He gave me his card and explained how to maintain the look. The products wouldn't be useful if I weren't alive. "You'll need a touch up in about six to eight weeks." I walked out of the salon to the admiration and compliments of patrons. Hair stylists. Customers. Strangers. Clarence would need a doctor when he saw his credit card bill.

Back to Iris' place, I reviewed the train schedules and decided to catch the 12:50. It would get me downtown by 1:35. All of my moves had to be more strategic from this point forward. More lives might be at stake.

From Union Station I caught a cab back to the Willard. When I arrived I used a pay phone to call the office. Any lobby employee could identify me, which was necessary.

"Hi Sandy. McClain. What's going on?"

"McClain! Everybody's looking for you! We missed you after the memorial."

"Everybody like whom?"

"Well.....me for one. Where are you?"

"I need you to get the Evans merger information to me."

"Is everything OK?"

"Yes."

"Well...the markets....uh....are the markets...."

"The markets are covered. Hannah is handling them until I get back...is she not there?"

"Yes....uh.....she's here...but you didn't tell me."

"I didn't tell you what?" I said as indignantly as possible.

"I mean I didn't know. Did you look at your calendar? You were supposed to cover the meeting with Mr. Yashimoto tomorrow."

"It's taken care of."

I was intentionally mean. Jack's casual reference to her on one of the disks let me know she might be with the enemy. Her interrogation confirmed my suspicions. "Will you be staying at the Willard when you go to Washington?"

"I always do. Cancel my appointments for the rest of the week. I'll speak with you later."

"Where can we find you if we need you?"

"I'll call."

"You can't..." I hung up the telephone and left by the same exit I'd used last night. I told the taxi driver to take me to the Washington offices of RJP International.

The driver chattered about having driven in the capital for 32 years and how disappointed he was about the outcome of the last election. He was retiring today and I was his last fare. He said that he was going to write a book about his experiences. He'd seen everything. Kennedy. King. Viet Nam. Watergate. Iran-Contra. Politicians. Pimps. Hookers. Thieves. "The only difference between dignitaries and prostitutes is where they sleep. They all want the same thing. Money. Power. Influence. People would pay for the dirt I know. I know things about RJP too.

"What do you know about them?" I asked.

"You going over there for an interview aren't you? I could tell. You so dressed up and everything. So young. Pretty. Did you go to Howard?"

"No, Florida A&M."

"That's a good school too. The Rattlers. I'm glad to see they finally started recruiting at the black schools. I heard they started hiring black kids into their training programs a few years ago. It's about time. Racist dogs. Well I know they're doing some top secret stuff over there...probably illegal. Ain't nobody supposed to know about it."

"Like what?"

"Well...if you get that job just remember that *those* white folks make their money the old fashion way....They steal it."

"What do you mean?" I memorized his name and shield number.

"They got dirty money in there."

"Why do you think that?"

"A couple of months ago, three of them big shots from over there got into my cab up on the Hill. They tell me to take them to a place in China Town. The whole time they rattling on about illegal stock trades in some kind of chemicals. I'm talking a mile a minute you know? Then they begin arguing so loud that I shut up and start listening."

"What were they arguing about?"

"They said that somebody found out something that would blast that sleaze Clay Sims right out of office."

"Did they say what it was?"

"No, but it was bad enough that if it hits the streets, his ass would go to jail. Excuse my French. But, that Clay Sims is a bigot.

You know that don't you? He comes from a long line of bigots. His granddaddy was a Kluxer. His daddy Newt too. Newt was in the senate for years and fought against every piece of civil rights legislation that came down the pike. When he retired, Clay got his spot. Them racists go be whistling Dixie come January. Fiery summons will be sent directly from the Oval office. Watch what I say. Dirty dogs."

"That's not new news. His dad changed his philosophy and became a champion of civil rights. He became a highly respected senior statesman."

"Champion my ass. Excuse my French. If you believe that I got a bridge in Brooklyn you might be interested in too," he laughed. "Bigots change their strategy to increase their power. They don't change their minds, just their methods.

Old man Sims came to Washington right around the time I started driving. I've seen and heard a lot of stuff. Believe me he still got them sheets. Them Sims got secrets so hot that those folks over at RJP are rattled. I can't wait to hear it on the news. I can't wait to see them brought out in hand cuffs, then the real shit go hit the fan. Pardon my French again. They said that if this information got into the wrong hands, billions would be lost. They said they had to find out how much the person knew and then they have to handle it."

"They could have been talking about anything."

"Baby I know what I heard, and I know what they meant. They plan to take somebody out. I read in the paper yesterday that one of them partners at RJP drowned in Colorado or one of those states out west. An accident, they say. I think Sims did something and that guy about it, and they killed him. But I don't think he's the one they're after. Somebody else knows something and they go get killed too, to keep it quiet. They need a scapegoat and they go find one. Watch, I know a hustler when I see one."

"What are they after?"

"I don't know. But rumor has it that Sims had some roommates in college that got into something. Old man Sims got them out of it. About four of them ran together. I don't remember

238

where I heard it or how I know it, but Sims' daddy got all of them important positions with the government. All of them but the dead guy. I'm go write a book."

He didn't know, but a whole chapter was riding in his backseat. His last passenger might be the one who'll bring them all down. Hard. Pellman *was* murdered. I knew it. Jack too. It was hard to believe the men about whom the cab driver spoke felt so free to discuss this stuff in front of perfect stranger. Arrogance knows no discretion. I sat back listening to his friendly banter and gave him a $50 dollar tip. "Happy retirement Mr. Hill."

"Thank you Miss," he said, then he turned and said sincerely, "You look like a nice young girl. I can tell you smart too. May I say something sweetheart?"

"Yes."

"Be careful with them people up there. Thugs wear thousand dollar suits too. If you take that job, learn what you can and run like hell. Watch your back and don't take no shit."

"Thanks Mr. Hill. I won't."

The towering glass and chrome building loomed before me. I took a deep breath and walked toward the answers I hoped would explain this murderous puzzle.

CHAPTER THIRTY

"Dammit Armstrong! Where is she?" Bo yelled into the telephone, leaping from the couch, where he'd briefly fallen asleep.

"When we got there, she was gone."

"Did her plane arrive? Was she on it? Did she get home? Has anyone spoken with the neighbors?"

"Jerry spoke to one of the neighbors. They took her. She left with two men right before our men got there."

"How do you know?"

"The paperboy saw them. She dropped her keys in the grass."

"Search the place. See if you can find some clues. Let me speak to Jerry."

"Yes sir."

"Hey Bo. We just got here. I'm on it. You need to call Washington. I'll call you when I find something. I *will* find something. Just take care of that pretty lady and I'll call you later. Stay safe."

"Thanks Jerry. You too."

I called Peterson. He already knew. "Bo, didn't I tell you that I'd pull you off this case if you lost your objectivity?"

"Yes sir. I haven't."

"Then where's Ms. Summers?"

"Upstairs."

"Wrong! You idiot!"

"Sir?"

"She's in Washington."

"Washington!?"

"Explain to me how she's in Washington and you're not."

"I don't know. I thought she was upstairs. Our people saw her come in last night."

"Evidently, she left the party at the lawyer's house in the company of a Dr. Clarence Whittaker. He drove. She must have been hiding. We didn't see her in the car. Whittaker took a flight at 5:25 p.m. to Savannah. Barry and a young lady you thought was McClain came to her house about midnight. They haven't left. We believe she got on a plane to D.C. around 5:30 headed to National Airport. We're verifying that right now. That's where we lost her until this morning. I suggest that you get somebody up there and find out who's sleeping in her bed! She lifted Whittaker's credit card and used it this morning in Alexandria, Virginia to buy clothes at Tyson Corner's Mall. She called her secretary from downtown D.C. about 30 minutes ago. That's how we found her. Our people are questioning the GM and reviewing security video. No calls have come in or out of her room. Hold on. Hotel security is at the door. Open it. There's no one is in the room. Someone saw her in the hotel this morning. Do you have any theory regarding where she might have been last night?"

"No sir I don't."

"That's just great! Just great! An economist is out thinking my best agents. Says a lot about our training," Peterson screamed.

"She's very smart sir."

"Smart enough to sidestep you and the rest of those Keystone Cops down there with you!!!!! I told you that we didn't have the luxury of mistakes. I will hold you personally responsible for this. Are we clear!?"

"Crystal."

"Then bring your behind back to Washington and clean up this mess."

"Yes sir. I have a strong hunch that if she's in town, she'll head over to RJP."

"I have men headed there right now. I'll deal with you later."

"Yes sir." Bo sighed, grabbing his attaché case. He ran down the hall toward the elevator speaking into his phone. "I'll be at the airport in exactly 12 minutes. Be ready to roll when I get there. I need to get to Washington fast." Bo jumped into the passenger seat of a waiting car and sped toward Love Field.

She's too smart to go to another hotel. She must be with someone she trusts. I have to find that person. I ran crosschecks on every girlfriend, boyfriend, or relative within a 50 mile radius of the Willard Hotel. She won't stop until she knows. That can't happen. "Start in the Alexandria area. She used a Dr. Clarence Whittaker's credit card at Neiman Marcus in Alexandria. I have a man there now. Maybe we can get a make on a car. I'll be right back."

Peterson assigned the task of finding McClain to three agents. They input background information and crosschecked telephone records of people in Virginia. Maryland and the District.

Meanwhile, Peterson contacted the management team to let them know that McClain had arrived in Washington. Everyone went into high alert, as Peterson returned to the computer room impatiently hovering over the communication agents. Everybody worked nervously.

Peterson was one of the best in the world at what he did. Everybody knew it. They respected his courage. Valor. Efficiency. But they deplored his insensitivity. Cruelty. Pettiness. "I have it!" One of the agents yelled. Everyone gathered at his terminal. "Her name is Iris Evans. She was Ms. Summer's roommate in college. The telephone records show they've maintained constant contact. There was a call made to Ms. Evans home last night from National Airport."

"Good work!" Peterson snapped, chewing his unlit cigar as if it was a piece of gum. "I want a home address. I want a work address. I want to know every purchase she's made in the last 12 months. I want to know where she is right now. I want to know everything about her. Get on it! Now!" he yelled, pulling the computer print out from the printer and rushing out of the room.

Tricked

Agents frantically networked and compiled information about the friends. Peterson called the jet. "Richards...Peterson. Ms. Summers is staying in Virginia with a college girlfriend, Iris Evans. Did she ever tell you anything about Ms. Evans while you two were together?"

"No. I can't remember her talking about an Iris Evans. Wait a minute....yes...yes she did. Roommate in college. From Florida. Fort Lauderdale. A buyer in New York."

"Is there anything else?"

Just then one of the communications officers ran into the room with the rest of the data. "Ms. Evans owns some kind of exclusive wedding place in Alexandria. Called....let's see...The Knot Shoppe.....She..."

"I know the place... I know her boyfriend. Iris is dating one of my frat brothers, Dr. Craig Thomison. He's a thoracic man over at Andrews. I didn't realize she was the same Iris."

"Ms. Evans purchased two tickets for a concert at one of those theaters on the Hill tonight. Something tells me she'll want her college girlfriend to join her. I think you need to call your frat brother and see what his plans are for the evening. I want you at that concert."

"I'm there sir.

"By the way...North reported Rick Collins hung himself at his parent's home this morning. He left a note for McClain. Nobody's opened it. His parents have been trying to contact her."

"Took the coward's way out. I'll contact you when I have McClain."

"Let's end this successfully. Good luck Bo."

"Thank you sir."

Peterson grimaced and hung up. Bo dialed Craig's sky pager. He watched the telephone, willing it to ring. "Hello, Dr. Thomison speaking."

"Hey Craig. What's happening man? Bo. Do you want to do some midnight fishing this weekend?"

"Hey Bo! What's up man? I'm glad you called. You're just the man I need."

"Whats up?"

"I've mentioned my lady Iris to you haven't I? Yeah I know I have. Anyway, she's got a girlfriend who's in town on business. Iris bought tickets to a concert at Peaches tonight as a birthday gift for me. We plan to do the dinner thing first and then stick around for the show. I was wondering...if you don't have any other plans...if you could hang for a minute. I know about blind dates man, but she's gorgeous. Lives in Dallas. An economist. A money wizard or something like that. I've been in surgery all morning and I haven't had time to call anybody else. Iris will kill me if I don't have someone there for her best friend. Please say you'll join us."

"I don't know Craig... Blind dates man?"

"Man....I assure you it's worth your time. I saw her for the first time myself this morning. She has the face of an angel and a body to match, and the most beautiful eyes I've ever seen, except for Iris of course. You'll hate yourself missing this one...plus I'll owe ya."

"Can I have your spinner?"

"We can talk about it," he laughed.

"OK man. Where is it?"

"Peaches on the Hill. You ever been there?"

"Yeah. I know where it is. What time?"

"I'm supposed to meet Iris at 5. Dinner starts at 6. The concert starts at 7:30. So between 5 and 5:30 would be cool."

"Wait a minute, I don't have a ticket. I heard it's sold out?"

"Iris already worked it. She promised the owner a discount on his future daughter in law's wedding, so he arranged for us to have the best seats in the house. Look man I gotta go, so are you in?"

"I'm in."

"Great. I'll see you around 5:30. Later."

"Later."

Tricked

I stopped at security, where the guard checked my badge. The elevator emptied directly into the RJP lobby. They remodeled since my last visit. Everything looked liked money. Chairs. Carpet. Antiques. The receptionist was wearing the lipstick red wool suit I saw on a mannequin at Neiman's this morning. I'm glad I didn't buy it. She said, "I recognize you from company pictures. You're McClain Summers aren't you? You're much prettier in person." Never taking my eyes from her or the elevator doors, I sat on one the money green suede sofas, watching her every move. The key Mrs. Pellman gave me at Joshua's memorial service was in my hand. "You'll find the answer in time." That's what she said. What did it mean? What did it open?

"Miss Summers?" A middle-aged woman in a gray tweed suit stood before me. "I'm Carole Landry, Mr. Turner's executive assistant. We weren't expecting you today. If you'll follow me."

I stood and walked pass familiar offices holding unfamiliar people. "Where's the old gang?" I asked.

"We've had quite a bit of turn over. It's hard to keep good people. Our best and brightest are the first go. I'm surprised someone hasn't snatched you away." She smiled with the teeth of a jackal. "Mr. Turner asked me to show you to his office. He moved too. Right this way. Would you like water or coffee? By the way, congratulations on the promotion. You must have mixed emotions. Losing Mr. Pellman at the same time. It's terrible news. A lot of our staff is still in Dallas. I'm sure we'll have tons of work next week. Have a seat. When he's off the telephone, I'll show you in." She went behind her desk and began shuffling papers.

My last trip to D.C. was two months ago. There couldn't have been that much turnover without my knowledge. I watched the hallway intently. I didn't work in public relations, but I kept up with office politics. No one mentioned this. Pellman would've said something. Wouldn't he? "You can go in now Ms. Summers." Carole rose from her desk and ushered me into Turner's office.

Fred Turner is an imperialistic moron. Mean. Spiteful. Vindictive. He was a partner and earned a reputation as one of the best spin doctors in D.C. A solid RJP man. He slung mud better than anyone in the business. Turner cleverly used his cruelty creating negative TV campaigns that helped Sims win the presidency. His ability to lace lies with just enough truth to drown reasonable interpretations of either, was both hailed and assailed for their effectiveness. He was a dangerous man.

Around RJP it was universally believed he'd become Sims' press secretary. He met me at the door. "Hello there McClain. Come in. Come in." He extended his hand while patting me on the back. He grabbed my coat instructing Carole to hang it somewhere.

"No I'll keep it. I'm fine...thanks. How are you?"

"Great. Just great. Just great. Sit. Sit. Congratulations on the new position. You deserve it. You've made us tons of money. Welcome to the partnership. It's wonderful. Terrific. I wasn't able to come to the announcement meeting. Forgive me for that. It was unavoidable. I hope you received the flowers I sent. You've certainly become one of RJP's shining stars haven't you? That reminds me, before you leave I'd like you to speak with Terry Clements. He's one of our new media guys. I'd like a story featuring you in the next issue of the company paper and in the applicable trades. With Pellman's death, you'll take over some of his media commitments. TV. Speaking engagements. I saw you from a distance at the memorial, but didn't have an opportunity say hello. We missed you at the partner's luncheon afterwards and the President-Elect asked about you."

He looked for a reaction. I gave none. "You've got be reeling from the news about Pellman. Awful. Now what can I do for you today? We weren't expecting you until...let me see ...Wednesday."

"I'm here for information I need from Joshua's office. We can't find the raw data in Dallas and I remembered he told me it was here in D.C. I decided to come early to put together a comprehensive package for the Evans merger. I didn't want to be rude and just go crashing in there, so I....."

Tricked

"That's impossible McClain," he said leaning back in his large leather chair twiddling his fingers.

"Impossible?" I asked.

"Yes...I can't just let you go ferreting through Josh's stuff. I don't even know if it's legal. Nothing's left in there anyway. Everyone knows you were his number one person...but even so...It can't be allowed. Tell Carole what you're looking for and she'll find it and send it to you, by courier if necessary. Where are you staying?"

A pissing contest. I fired the first shot. "Look ...perhaps I wasn't clear or maybe I didn't adequately impress upon you the necessity of my gaining access to Mr. Pellman's office. I'm not asking you if I can go into his office. I'm telling you that I'm going in office and you're going to unlock the doors or I'm going kick them in." He freaked.

I stood, pointing my finger in his face. "Look, while you guys are up here in PR glad handling people, the rest of us are making money. You need to open the damn door or be ready to explain to Jacobs and Reynolds and about 100 key investors why we dropped the ball on a 127 million dollar deal you pompous jerk." I sat daring him to make the next move.

"Now you just wait one minute. You don't come in here talking to me like that. You don't tell me what I'd better do. I don't care what you're the vice president of. That uppity stuff might work for you down there in Dallas, but I run this office and...."

"Uppity...Is that what you said? Uppity? As in uppity nigger kind of uppity?" I stood again.

"Wait a minute McClain... I didn't say that...I just meant that your tone is abrasive. I have the highest respect for your contribution to the firm, but I still can't let you into that office or let you think that you can talk to me like that....noooo..." he said shaking his head.

"My contribution to the firm?" I chuckled, reaching across his desk and dialing a number. "Who are you calling?" he asked.

"Our international traders."

"Why?"

"I'm going to tell them to pack it up and go home because Fred Turner is ego trippin about how I spoke to him. How he won't let me get the statistical data we need to make the proper projections this week and how much money our clients are going to lose. And how much in commissions they'll loose too. You're going to be very popular, you moron. Then I'm going to call Hendrickson in San Francisco and tell him to tell the folks at Ross Pharmaceuticals to pull the plug on the Evans merger because Fred Turner doesn't like the way this uppity nigger from Dallas is speaking to him. I wonder how they'll take that? Hello let me speak to Vance Hendrickson. McClain Summers...I'll hold."

"You wouldn't dare," he scowled.

"Watch me. Hey Vance…McClain...you know that info you asked me about, well I sorry I can't get it. You're gonna have to pull..." Turner disconnected the call. He bought my bluff.

"I'll let you in."

Turner lit a cigarette. He was off guard. "I still need to call Dallas. Protocol." He knew I was lying. "Call them." I sat, crossing my legs and folding my arms. My blood pressure was increased with each movement.

"You'd better call somebody," I said defiantly, praying the Dallas staff would back up me up. They knew the Evans merger. Joshua and I worked long and hard on this kind of deal. There could be a file in the D.C. office. Could they take the risk? Turner never made the call. He put out the cigarette.

Turner marched toward the door. I followed him, quickly grabbing my coat and backpack from the sofa. We walked toward Carole. Turner stopped and had a brief conversation with her. He never said another word to me. He re-entered his office as the door slammed behind him.

Carole quietly escorted me to Pellman's office. She wasn't as friendly this time. "I'll help you locate the file," she insisted.

"I prefer to do this alone." Another line in the sand.

"I don't mind."

"Go away!" I demanded.

Tricked

I didn't have time to play with Turner's glorified secretary. She angrily walked away as I closed the doors. The key left an imprint in my moist palm. Looking around the room for cameras or anything that might be watching me, I looked on the shelves. Empty. File cabinets. Empty. I sat behind the desk and pulled out his drawers. Empty. Where was it? What was it? I walked over to the sitting area. What a perfect view of the Potomac. Glancing at my watch. It was already 4:30. Whoever was hunting me knew by now that I was at RJP Washington. I had to get out of there fast.

Paranoid feelings I had in Jack's condo returned. So did Carole. "Have you found what you needed Ms. Summers?" I jumped.

"Where are Mr. Pellman's things are?"

"Everything was cleared out four days ago. They left a box in there," she said, walking toward a wall. She pushed a panel and it popped opened revealing a large closet. "You won't find the file in there. It's basically fishing stuff."

She left again. I locked the doors behind her and returned to the closet. Carole said the office was cleared out on four days ago. Mr. Pellman was alive four days ago. Why would his office be cleaned out? I called Carole's extension.

"Hello Carole? Has Margo been reassigned? Is she here?" I asked.

"You need to speak with Mr. Turner regarding that."

"Does that mean you don't know or you won't say?"

"I'll connect you with Mr. Turner."

"No thank you."

I raced back to the closet and turned on the light. There was no time to waste. The closet was empty except for a big taped box in the corner. I found a letter opener and cracked the tape. The longer I looked, the more nervous I became. Near the bottom among a lot of fishing gear was a rosewood clock. The hands of the clock looked like the front and back of rainbow trout. It was old and fragile. Darla Pellman's words echoed in my ears, "Find the answer in time." I turned the clock over. There was no place for a key. It was one of those wind up deals so I tried to remove the clock face. It didn't budge. Sweat formed under my arms. Why did I believe Darla? She was always a little flaky.

The clock meant nothing. I shook it. I pulled it. Nothing happened. The doors of the office opened slowly. I was petrified. I thought I'd locked them. I pulled harder. Something popped. There was a tiny keyhole in the space beneath the winder. My hands were shaking as I placed the key into the lock and twisted. I worked as quickly as I could, hearing footsteps approaching. There was a small cassette hidden in the tiny space along with a ring. I put the winder back in place and dropped the clock beneath the fishing paraphernalia. The cassette and ring went into my pocket along with the key. Just as the doors to the closet moved, I noticed a folder near the bottom of the box and I grabbed it.

Turner said, "I called Dallas and they told me to tell you anything you find should be cleared through me before you take it out of here. Did you find anything?"

"Fred you shouldn't sneak up on people like that. You could get hurt. Here's the file," I said, briskly walking toward my bag and coat. Then I rushed out the door with Turner on my heels.

"Look McClain...give me that! I can't let you out of here with anything. As a matter of fact, come back to my office and speak with Mr. Reynolds. He's on the telephone."

I was running. So was he. People were waiting at the elevators. "Bye Fred. Thanks," I shouted, running down the hall. He was out of shape and couldn't keep up with me. I hit the elevator forcing the doors to reopen. "Call security!" was the last thing I heard Fred yell as the elevator doors closed.

People wiggled around to make room for me. I kept my eyes forward. My hands were shaking. Nothing I did quieted my nerves. That lump that forms in your throat right before crying edged its way past my courage. I swallowed. Hard. What if Turner had the cops and security guards waiting in the lobby for me? What if the killer's are there? What if RJP and the killers are the same people? What if they were waiting to kill me as soon as the doors open? What if someone cut the elevator cables? We reached the lobby. The elevator doors slid open and the busy occupants pushed me out. I looked around hiding among the fast paced crowd.

When I got outside, I ran at full clip across the promenade, looking for a cab. I jumped into the backseat of a taxi with a startled young executive. Looking back, Turner, two security guards and two other men ran from the building. They looked around for me. The young man whose cab I'd invaded was looking at me too. It was obvious he thought I was a mad woman. "I'm late and I can't wait for another cab. I'll pay your fare if you let me keep the cab. Deal?"

"Deal."

"Take me to the Hyatt...Fast. There's an extra 20 in it for you. I handed the young man a $50.00." A cold wind filled the cab as I sank into the 'Winter Green' air freshened East African music playing, window down at 45 degrees outside vehicle. I didn't care. Historical monuments, buildings and people raced by. The cab took every back road he could find to reach the hotel and get the tip. He got me there in record time, particularly for this time of day.

Making sure lots of people were around, I found the concierge. She'd located old Dictaphone which I took into the ladies room. Four women went in with me. My heart beat rapidly as I listened to the tape. An attendant was outside the stall. I peeked through the opening in the door making sure I wasn't alone. Pellman's voice.

"McClain, by now you've found St. Lisa. It is a hospital in Pittsburgh, PA. May 5. J.P. C.S. M.P.K.T."

Was that it? Was this is a clue? A clue to what? May 5 was my birthday. St. Lisa was the name I found in my research. A hospital? How were these things connected? How was I connected to it? I ran through the whole tape twice. "Remember. Remember everything." Ms. Pellman said that at the funeral. I pulled the ring from my pocket. Harvard. Class of 1965. Frustrated, I called my mother. No answer. Where was she?

CHAPTER THIRTY-ONE

"Are you alright?" I jumped. It was the attendant. "Yes, I'll be right out." This information meant nothing. Dr. Stovall called yesterday. Maybe he could help me. "Hello Dr. Stovall. This is McClain. Did I wake you? I'm in trouble here. I need your help."

"McClain. Are you on a secured phone?"

"I'm on a payphone. I don't think anyone knows I'm here. Not yet."

"They know you're there….you…you go first. What do know?"

"Dr. Stovall. Have you ever heard of a hospital called St. Lisa's in Pittsburgh?"

"Yes."

"Do you have any idea why Mr. Pellman would think I should have this information?"

"Yes."

"Can you tell me what's going on?"

"You were born at St. Lisa's. It was a hospital for black people. It burned the year you were born. The hospital was deliberately destroyed."

"What does that have to do with me?"

"I have a theory. Someone didn't want the events of your birth traceable."

"Who?"

"McClain. Listen carefully. Here in Europe your hypothesis regarding nefarious manipulation of chemical and scientific securities through veiled purchases is in full swing. Distribution and disbursement of development and research information is being played out here." I almost fainted. "After noticing certain patterns and trends reflecting the precise objectives your paper discussed, I began thinking who had the power to implement these actions. Certain investigators hired me as a consultant to review the data. I compared it with your outlines and to my sheer amazement, they matched. You also need to know that..." The telephone went dead.

"Dr. Stovall? Dr. Stovall?!" I was yelling. People were watching. I called the operator. She told me that the call had been disconnected on his end.

"Are you alright?" A bellman standing nearby asked.

"I'm fine. I'm fine," I lied.

Why hadn't my mother told me this? What was she hiding? I arrived at Peaches at 6:15.

* * *

"Good evening Mrs. Summers. I do trust that your trip was uneventful. Please forgive me for the way we gathered you, but I had no choice. Please allow me to introduce myself. I'm Ian Lawford."

"Where am I?"

"This is my home. I believed your safety was at stake, so I had you brought here for your own protection."

"My protection? You snatched me from my home and transported me to God knows where for my protection? Who are you? Who do you work for?"

"I'm terribly sorry to have intruded on your privacy Mrs. Summers. That was extraordinarily rude of me, but I'm confident that it had to be done. You're here because my feelings for your daughter are extremely deep and very strong. I care for her sincerely. She's wonderful and someday I hope she'll return my admiration. I couldn't bear the grief she'd suffer were an injury to befall you. You're safe here and my people are on their way to collect McClain as well. My entire staff is at your complete disposal. If there's anything at all that you require, you need only ask."

"What do you want Mr. Lawford?"

"McClain."

"You can't have her," she cried.

"I will have her Mrs. Summers."

"She doesn't know… does she?"

"She doesn't know what Mrs. Summers?"

"Mr. Lawford, my daughter's life is in great danger."

"Not as long as I'm alive. My plan will keep her alive if you're willing to do exactly what I ask."

"Anything. I'll do anything to keep my baby alive."

"Please follow this gentleman upstairs? The green room Stinson."

"Am I a prisoner?'

"Absolutely not. I hope you'll take advantage of my hospitality. My men cleared your home of all mementos of your life prior to McClain's birth. That should buy us some time."

"You know Mr. Lawford? Don't you?"

"I do."

"Thank you.'"

"I'm at your service madam."

* * *

Well dressed people stood in a long line in front of Peaches. Important people in expensive suits walked to the front of the line, where a man in a camel coat waived them in. I couldn't tell whether this was a nightclub or a restaurant. Realizing Iris would never stand in a line for anything, and because I was late, I went to the front too. "Good evening sir, I'm a member of Iris Evans' party. I'm late. Has she arrived?" He gave me a long approving look, smiled and opened the door.

"Yes, Iris is here," he grinned. He summoned a waiter and instructed him to take me to "Ms. Evans table. Her drinks are on the house tonight." He winked. Too frantic to flirt back, I smiled.

Tricked

"Have a good evening baby. Maybe I can have a drink with you before you leave," he said.

"Thank you Mr.?"

"They call me Frenchie."

"Mr. Frenchie."

A convention of Who's Who in Black D.C. swirled around me. I wondered why you never see these kinds of black folks on T.V. They always seem to show the extremes. Extremely poor. Extremely rich. Extremely controversial. Extremely ignorant. Extremely dumb. Extremely confused. Extremely extreme. Iris stood near the bar with another woman. They were laughing. She changed clothes. Upon seeing me, she waived.

"You're late! Where were you? We hugged, then walked through the crowd toward the table. "What did you do to your hair? It looks fabulous! I love it! Craig's over there with your date for the evening. He is *too* fine. He works for the government like most of these folks in here. Gimme that suit! Who did you say did your hair?! I just love it! Did your meetings go well? Are you hungry? Look at your nails! Did they do your eyebrows too? Did they have that coat in my size? Why didn't you buy a nice handbag? I get so tired of you and your obsession with backpacks. Do you want a drink? Did you buy me something? What did you get me? Did you leave it at the house? Let me tell you about that hag over there. She's a local newscaster. Thinks she's all of that. Her husband's been hittin on me for the last year."

Iris waived and blew a kiss in the direction of the woman who was being seated next to an extremely handsome man. He was making serious eye contact while his wife reciprocated Iris' kissing motion. I smiled, shaking my head. "I can't wait for you to see this pretty man Craig found. I wonder why I've never seen him around. I can't believe these cannibals haven't snatched him yet. He's really good looking and he has the sexiest voice I've ever heard. Anyway, he and Craig go fishin all the time. They're frat brothers. He has a townhouse in Georgetown. A big boat docked on the Potomac. Drives a Range Rover. Brand new. Loves antique cars.

Cynthia A. Minor

Has two. A Harley. Like's big band music, poetry and art. No ex-wife. No kids. Not gay. Well read. Well traveled. Not boring.... "

"Did you ask for his social security number and blood type?" I edged in. Iris was on fast forward. She was in pure "talk zone," going a mile a minute. She blew kisses and waived at other people as we walked past the noisy tables.

She continued identifying the impressive looking people, but my mind was on what Professor Stovall said, St. Lisa's, Pellman and how it all applied to me.

Iris waived at Craig who waived back. I noticed the man who was to be my date was walking away from the table. He was tall. I was relieved. Craig tiptoed and pecked Iris' cheek. We all sat. "Look Craig. McClain got her hair done. Doesn't it look fabulous?"

"You look stunning McClain. I really like your hair, but I liked it this morning too."

"McClain looks like an adult now. She looks like the new Vice President at RJP instead of a ten year old. You too tough for me McClain! I love that color on you too. I wish my skin was like yours. You always had perfectly flawless skin. Don't you think her skin is perfect Craig? You're a doctor. You should know. Doesn't she have perfect skin?" Iris crooned.

"McClain is a beautiful woman. There's no doubt about that, but I love your skin and from a completely medical perspective, everything about you is perfect baby," he hummed into her blushing ear.

"Did your friend see me and decide to bolt?" I asked smiling.

"Oh...no....no.....no. He had an important call. He went to the men's room so that he could hear. He'll be right back," Craig smiled back.

"McClain.... he's too cute. Craig where you been hiding him? I still don't know how the man eating women in D.C. missed him. But anyway, I have another surprise for you. Who's your favorite singer?"

"Carmen McCrae."

256

Tricked

"Alive?"

"Kathleen Battle."

"Non operatic."

"Michael Franks."

"Black"

"ZZ Hill. Nope...he's dead. Uhhh.....Phoebe Snow."

"OK McClain...listen...your favorite black, female, alive singer....." Craig began chuckling. I rolled my eyes toward the ceiling. Iris continued, "She was real popular in the mid 80's."

"Hell Iris," Craig interrupted, amused. "Just tell her who it is."

"Wait a minute; let me ask one more question. Who was your favorite singer our last month on campus?"

Before I could answer Iris yelled, "Avis Leslie! Avis Leslie is performing here tonight. She's your favorite singer? Remember? We used to try to sing her songs all of the time. Remember my mother gave us that tape of her greatest hits and we played it all of the time. I bought Craig tickets for his birthday because he just loves her too. Don't you baby?"

"I never heard of her baby, but I love you," he chimed in.

I couldn't help laughing. This was classic Iris. Some things never change. Craig clearly cared for Iris giving her the constant attention she craved. Being a surgeon didn't hurt. He could afford her. "The way this place works is that you eat first and then after dessert has been served, she comes on. Because you were late, I ordered for you. No red meat. No pork. No Garlic. No cilantro.

The people in line come in just for drinks and sit up there. It's a bar," she said pointing. "Frenchie got us the best table. He flirted with you didn't he? I know he did. Girl...he's too married. Flirts with all the pretty ladies. I'm doing his daughter's wedding for cost. One of the bridesmaids is engaged to that basketball player who has the highest salary in the NBA. I plan to make up for it with her wedding," Iris smiled.

"Thanks Iris. I forgot Avis Leslie was my favorite singer," I said, smiling at Craig. He smiled back. "I want to thank both of you for letting me crash your party tonight. Obviously this was supposed to be a very special evening for you. Thanks for going to the additional trouble of finding a blind date. You didn't have to do that. He probably feels like a victim," I chuckled. "I hate when my friends call me to go on blind dates with their college roommates. I haven't had any success. And yes Iris, I do like Avis. She hasn't done anything for a while and I'd love to hear her sing some of that old stuff."

Iris and Craig looked up. Someone was standing behind me. When I turned I saw Bo Richards. My vocal chords seized. Craig stood and walked over to his friend. Iris beamed, nudging me under the table. She mouthed the words, "He's cute. I told you." Craig made the introductions, "McClain Summers. Bo Richards." Bo extended his hand. I looked at it. Reflexes took over and I shook it. Funny how feelings you believe completely dead spring instantly to life when confronted with water from the irresolution of your past.

The time machine of my mind drove me directly into shocked. It was yesterday, six years ago. The memory of that night smacked me around. The pain. Just as fresh. The rejection. Just as biting. The love. Just as real. The need. Just as consuming. The desire. Just as intense. The anger. Just as fresh.

I knew I'd see him again one day, just not tonight. Not now. I was unprepared. Unrehearsed. Ill-equipped. This meeting wouldn't occur until I was happily involved with a fabulous man who only lived to please me. I'd be elegant and nonchalant toward him. He'd be sorry and beg me to come back. He'd confess I was the best thing that ever happened to him and then he'd say, "Those things I said to you, I never meant. I made the biggest mistake of my life. If it's not too late for us, I'd do anything to get you back."

Then with great pleasure I'd inflict the same vengeful pain on him, he so skillfully inflicted on me. "The clarity of time has proven you right. Ours was merely an immature college romance and nothing more. Isn't it funny how we think college loves last. We can always be friends," I'd chuckle.

Tonight dashed those fantasies. In this dreadful moment, I realized the substitutes, stand-ins, understudies, pretenders and contender were nothing more than that. Melting in the light of his smile, I was still his after all these years. I hated myself. I hated him.

My emotions twisted against my intellect in guerrilla warfare. My heart and mind locked in battle, ordering me to cry. Don't cry! Scream! Don't scream! Leave! Don't leave. Fall into his arms! Punch him in the face! Don't let him know how happy you are to see him! Tell him how much you've missed him! How much you still love him. Tell him to step! Beg him to stay! Smack him. Kiss him! Tell him how much you want him! No! Tell him you can barely remember him!

"McClain. How've you been?" His hot buttered voice turning the heads of every female within earshot. Waves of electricity passed through me, as he kissed my cheek. He was still beautiful. He searched my eyes for a trace of anything we once shared. I made sure they didn't betray me. I swallowed. "Fine. Thank you?"

"You're just as beautiful as I remember," his voice melting my heart but stirring my anger.

"Do you two know each other?" Craig asked in a confused voice. "It's a small world. I had no idea you two knew each other. They know each other. Iris did you know they already knew each other?" Iris shook her head. "I had no idea," sensing this was an unwelcomed blast from my past. She began chirping on and on about something she'd read in the Post. Her diatribe gave me time to recover from this ambush.

Whenever I spoke to Iris about Bo, I referred to him as 'Boyfriend.' That's our private code for men in our lives. They never had a name until they've proven themselves worthy. He hadn't.

Dinner was a blur. They engaged in lively conversation. All I managed was to smile at the appropriate moments. Out of the corner of my eye, Bo hadn't stopped looking at me. He knew I was shaken. Why didn't he do the decent thing and leave? He could have excused himself long enough to allow me to get myself together, but that would be too easy. Such a thought on his part, probably lacked definition. I was furious. I wanted to hit him. Kill him. Instead there he sits, emitting those same vibrations that drew me into the fire that ignited my heart and ultimately consumed my soul.

He seemed to enjoy watching me squirm. So when he was distracted, I knocked my water onto his lap. He jumped as Craig and Iris patted the table. The waiter rushed over to assist. I moved so the water wouldn't get on me.

"I'm sorry. I can't believe I'm so clumsy," I lied.

He knew I knocked the glass over intentionally and smiled saying, "No harm done." Just as they finished their frantic patting and wiping, the lights dimmed and the MC stepped to the microphone. He announced Ms. Leslie, and the room went black. A single spot lit the stage, and appearing in her traditional beaded, sequined, gardenia adorned beauty, she stepped into the light. A roar rose from the crowd.

Her sensuous torch songs ignited the air. I'm sure most of the people in the room played her songs as appropriate background music for nights of passion and thoughts of love. One of her songs provided the background music for the first time I danced with Bo. An explosion of sadness engulfed me. A glass of water wasn't enough to quench these feelings. I had to get out of there, but I couldn't ruin Iris and Craig's evening with this unexpected blast from my unrequited past.

The more Avis sang, the sicker I became. My emotions couldn't take it anymore as her songs laid out the first and final days our relationship. I abruptly excused myself from the table and disappeared through the crowd. Iris stood to follow. Bo said, "I'll make sure she's OK. Sit. Sit."

"Where's the bathroom?" I asked the waitress, who pointed over my shoulder.

"Do you think I should go?" Iris asked Craig.

"Whatever it is, it's between them. Bo will take care of her and I'll take care of you," he cuddled.

Tricked

"But something's wrong. I know McClain and I've never seen her act like that. Who is Bo Richards and how does he know her?"

"Bo's a great guy. He works for the government. Obviously something deep happened between them. I had no idea Bo knew her. We need to let them resolve it."

"But you don't know McClain, she's….."

"She's grown baby. Let them work it out Iris. It's their business."

"You sure?"

"I'm sure."

Bo was following me. I barged through the ladies room doors with him on my heels. Women yelled and screamed for him to get out while tears rolled down my cheeks.

"Get out of here Bo!" I shouted.

"I have to talk to you McClain. Five minutes. Just give me five minutes. I know that this was a shock to you. I'm sorry, but….."

"Get away from me! Leave me alone! I don't want to talk to you! Not now! Not ever! I don't want to have anything to do with you!" I was screaming. That's when a large man rushed into the bathroom and grabbed Bo's arm.

"Is he bothering you Miss?" he asked. Before I could say anything, Bo said, "McClain, Joshua sent me." I turned and looked at him with tears still streaming down my cheeks.

"What? What did you say?"

"Joshua sent me. I have to talk to you. It's vital. Please."

"Miss do you want me to throw him out?" The large man asked again.

Stunned that he mentioned Pellman's name, "No….no….I don't know. Joshua sent you? What are talking about?" I asked.

"Miss?" the bouncer needed an answer.

"I'll talk to him." The man released Bo's arm and took a step back.

"Y'all go have to take all that screaming and stuff outside. Is everything cool now?" he asked sternly.

"Yes...I'm sorry...It a misunderstanding. It won't happen again," I whispered.

"OK then. You go have to get out of the ladies' bathroom chief," he said to Bo, who nodded and extended his hand to me. I didn't take it and I walked out of the bathroom in front of him.

"Can we go outside? I really need to talk to you," he said.

"I'm not going anywhere with you. If you want to talk to me, talk right here. What about Joshua? How do you know Joshua?"

Bo led me around to an area near the stock rooms trying to explain his connection to Joshua and my work. "We don't have much time, so I'll have to make this fast." He showed me his credentials and explained that my life was in danger. "Tell me something I don't know," I replied sarcastically.

He told me that there was an international price on my head. He'd just received the call. That's what the telephone call was about when Iris and I saw him leave the table. The lives of everyone I knew me might be in jeopardy.

He said I couldn't remain at Iris' home and that my mother had been taken. "What do you mean my mother has been taken? Taken by whom?!" I panicked.

"We don't know yet. Our men went to her home and found her keys in the yard. The cab driver claimed he dropped her off in her driveway. The paper boy said he saw two men pull her into a van. We think she's being held for ransom."

"Oh my God! Oh my God! Ransom? Has anyone called the Milwaukee police or the FBI?" I was rattled, falling apart quickly.

"All appropriate agencies have been notified. For your mother's sake, you can't fall apart now baby. You have something the kidnappers want McClain. The information has something to do with national defense."

"What?"

"Baby I don't know what you have, but whatever it is, people are dying because of it."

"Where's my mother? Is she..."

"If you want to keep everybody safe, try to remember what you know that can help us find your mother. This is a dangerous crowd. They already killed Jack," he said. "These people are ruthless. Insidious. Deadly. I don't want them to kill you too.

"Me either. How do I know that you haven't come here to kill me? Why should I trust you?"

"I'm all you've got."

"What about Iris and Craig? I can't just leave without an explanation. I trusted you once Bo. You trashed that trust. I..."

"Grow up McClain! I know I hurt you back at Wharton but this has nothing to do with that. I made a terrible mistake. A mistake I've paid for every day since. But what about you? I called you a thousand times. I came by. I left notes. Gifts. Flowers. I wanted to tell you...I needed to tell you that I loved you, that I still love you. I wanted to explain how stupid I was. Terrified. Afraid. Afraid of what I felt for you. Afraid of what it meant. Afraid to loose control. Afraid it wouldn't last. Afraid of you. I was in Milwaukee that Christmas. Your mother told me you didn't want to talk to me. Didn't she tell you I was there? When you never called back, I came home determined to work things out. So I stalked you, but you always managed to out maneuver me. Why didn't you give me a chance to apologize? Why didn't you return one call? There's a dent in my heart I still can't get out. I never married. No serious relationships. Other women tried, but they weren't you. I'm sorry for the pain I caused you. Caused myself. I understand you not trusting me, but McClain we don't have time to bathe your hurt feelings or my stupidity and your stubbornness. If you've ever believed anything I said to you, believe me now. I'm here to protect you and we're running out of time. McClain baby..."

"Don't call me baby! I saw you kissing that girl spring semester" I snapped.

"Kissing a girl? That girl is my niece. She was there with a group of high school kids from Syracuse for a campus visit," he smiled.

"I don't believe you," I whimpered.

"They don't think I can maintain my objectivity. After seeing you tonight I realize I can't. I can't maintain anything, not when it comes to you. I love you more now than I ever have or ever could. I never stopped. I don't know how." Tears clouded his eyes. "I still can't eat chocolate chip cookies without thinking of you. I can't enjoy autumn leaves. I can't dance or take a bath without thinking of you. I'd rather die than let anything ever happened to you baby, I mean McClain. I'm not saying this to get you to believe me. I'm saying this because its true and I may never get another chance to say it if you don't leave with me right now."

Each word was a wonderful bite of reconciliatory candy. "Bo don't say these things if you don't mean them. I'm tired. Scared. Confused. I know I'm in danger. I don't trust you. I want to believe you more than anything, but you said I was damaged. You said you know Jack and Mr. Pellman. How do you know them? I..." Bo grabbed me into the comfort of his arms. He took my face in his hands and looked deeply into my eyes.

"That was cruel and untrue. You're not damaged at all. You were wonderful then and you're wonderful now. I was a fool. Selfish. Mean. I never wanted those words to mark you. I knew how much you loved me and how much that must have hurt. That's why I spent so many weeks trying to tell you how wrong I was. But McClain we need to leave right now." His heart was racing and I felt a sudden urge to protect him. Soothe him. Love him.

"Let me tell Iris and get my things."

"We'll tell Iris that you don't feel well and that I'm taking you to my place. Fix your face. We have to hurry."

"OK." Someone was watching.

* * *

"She's at Peaches on the Hill. It's a joint upscale blacks go for dinner and shows. She's here with her girlfriend, a doctor and Special Agent Bo Richards."

"Ahh, Bo Richards. Our old friend."

"Where's she been today?"

"She went to a mall and RJP. She left Turner's office about 45 minutes ago. Turner said she got something out of Pellman's office."

"Has anyone checked her room?"

"Yes sir. Nothing."

"How about the girlfriend's house?"

"Nothing."

"Whatever she has its still on her. I don't care how you get it. Just do it. Am I clear?"

"Yes sir." The men nodded to another, then loaded their guns placing silencers on the barrels. They fit another device into a camera and headed to the front of Peaches. After putting two $100.00 bills into Frenchie's fist, they wandered inside and stood near the bar.

One man surveyed to room looking for McClain while the other stood in the darkness planning her assassination. He raised the camera when Bo and McClain returned to the table. The cross hairs were on the back of McClain's head as he fired. At that instant McClain bent over to pick up her backpack from the floor. When she moved, the bullet hit Iris.

Cynthia A. Minor

CHAPTER THIRTY- TWO

Blood oozed across the front of Iris' mint green silk suit. Our eyes met in combined horror. Everything played in slow motion. The room was without sound. Only the haunting beat of blood pounding in my ears filled the once radiant room. Bo knocked me to the floor covering me with his body, pulling a gun from somewhere. He looked in the direction he thought the shot must have come and snatched me behind a table. He couldn't see anything because of the spotlights. Craig grabbed Iris ripping her jacket open and yelling into his cell phone. Avis stopped singing and rushed from the stage. Sound returned.

People were running, screaming, knocking over tables. Chairs. Each other. Bo literally carried me through the crowd, pushing and shoving people out of our path. I was screaming. He rushed me into a cab and ordered the cabbie to go. Fast. I fought against leaving. Bo held me firm. He held me in the seat and I buried my head against his heart. "Not Iris. Please not Iris too. Please God. Not again."

Bo looked in all directions as he told the cab driver to step on it. He noticed Bo's gun as we sped down the small streets of Washington onto the Belt Way. A car raced behind us. He quickly showed his credentials to the cabdriver and said, "The people in the car behind are trying to kill us. If you don't lose them, they'll kill you too." The cabbie shouted, "Hang On!" pulling his cap lower on his head and chewing the unlit cigar. The car sped at a frightening clip.

Bo pushed me to the floor. "Stay down!" Suddenly the rear window shattered. I heard "Oh Shit!" from the front seat as we

266

swerved onto another street. The car behind kept pace with us as another bullet hit the cab. Bo fired back. He hit the side of the car and it swerved across traffic barely missing a bus.

Bo gave the cab driver directions, reloading his gun and yelling location directions into a cell phone. A bullet hit the headrest above me. Bo shoved me further down as the driver ducked and made a quick left onto another street. Bo continued firing his weapon and yelling instructions to the driver who obeyed every direction. He was driving like a maniac, barely dodging cars and people. Apparently this wasn't the first time he'd done this kind of driving. Police in unmarked cars, appeared and began firing too. Then a totally inappropriate response emanated from me. Laugher. It was like being in the middle of one of those bad made for TV movies.

I was delirious. Crying and laughing at the same time. My senses had been pushed beyond reasonable limits. It was the only emotional response that hadn't been completely overwhelmed. I was hysterical. I couldn't believe myself. The more I tried to stop, the harder I laughed. It was ridiculous, like laughing at a funeral. You know you're not supposed to, but you can't help it. My sides hurt. I lost my breath. Tears flowed.

"Why are you laughing?!" Bo shouted, dodging another bullet.

"I don't know. (laughter) I believe (laughter) I'm loosing (laughter) my mind. (laughter) I just can't believe I'm in the middle (laughter) of a gunfight with a man who dumped me (laughter) because I was too ambitious (laughter) over information people he thinks I have (laughter) which was supposed to be stolen by my best friend (laughter) who was a spy (laughter) who jumped or was thrown from his balcony last night (laughter) who was sleeping with my boyfriend (laughter) who may be responsible indirectly for the death of my other best friend from college tonight (laughter) who's in love with a horny little dwarf (laughter) who was shot a minute ago because I leaned over to pick up my (laughter) bag."

The driver zigged and zagged, weaving in and out of traffic while avoiding bullets. Suddenly the chase car veered off onto a side street with police sirens, government cars and helicopter in hot pursuit. Bo pulled me onto the seat and instructed the driver to drive directly to a secret government compound just outside Washington. The driver nervously lit the cigar and seemed to relax. Bo sat back and closed his eyes. I continuously interrupted the sudden peace with more childish giggling. Bo pulled his cell from his coat and spoke another series of numbers into it.

"I have her. We're on our way in. Yellow Cab. You'll know us. We're the one that looks like Swiss cheese. Yes sir. Can I get a condition status on Iris Evans? Yes sir...Dr. Thomison? Yes sir...no she's fine...I think."

"Who are you people?" the driver asked. "Somebody's gonna have to pay for that window!"

Bo didn't answer. He reached for me and I snatched away.

"Don't touch me!" I barked. "They were trying to kill me, weren't they?"

"The important thing is they didn't. You're safe now. Iris is in surgery. Do you want my coat? It's freezing in here."

"No." My teeth chattered. The car pulled to a gate where an armed man approached us shining a bright light into the car. Bo showed his ID and the man waived for someone to open the gate.

We walked through a series of plain corridors where cameras and airport security devices were everywhere. Finally, Bo clipped a badge onto his belt and placed his gun on a tray. Another man patted down the cab driver and took my backpack. Bo retrieved his gun and left the cabbie and me sitting in a vacant hallway.

"I'm Ron," the cab driver said.

"What?"

"Ron. Ron Jackson."

"Oh...I'm McClain, you're quite the driver."

"Thanks. What kind of place is this?"

"I don't know."

"Who's the gun?"

"Somebody I used to know."

"It's like that huh?"

"Yeah."

Bo returned with visitor's badges and told us to wear them at all times while in the building. The driver was taken to one room. I was taken to another. Bo left me in the room for about 20 minutes. I was still giggling when he returned with another man.

"My name is Peterson and you're the young lady we've been looking for. I'm sure Agent Richards has explained things to you. I hope you understand the gravity of the circumstances and the quickness with which we need to act. Whatever you've discovered Ms. Summers, we need to know right now."

"Who are you again?"

"Agent Peterson. I'm in charge of this operation. I'll do everything I can to protect you, but it's vital to national security that you give us what you have."

"I have nothing. I asked Bo. Now I'm asking you. What is it that you think I have? How is Joshua connected to any of this?" The men looked at each other.

"He's not dead."

I almost fell off the chair. "He came to us because he believed his life and his wife's life was in danger. Mrs. Pellman is in a safe house near Austin. She was taken there after the memorial service. He's convinced he can't complete his work without the information you have. He told us you were the only person in the world who could help him."

That was a lie. Pellman was the smartest economist of our day. I couldn't make any significant contribution to his analysis. Conclusions. This was a message. My head spun. Doubt means stop, so I did. "The memorial service was...." I interrupted him giggling and shaking my head.

"Staged," finishing his sentence.

"When did you say he came to you?"

"He's been working with us for the past 3 years and we picked him two days ago."

"The day of my promotion..." Five days after he found out he'd be making the biggest presentation of his lifetime. Two weeks after his best friend won the office of President of United States. The day I met Ian. The day Jack was killed. "Does he know I'm here?"

"Not yet. We haven't told him."

"Does he know you were trying to find me?"

"That's not important. What's important is that you tell us what you know."

"I have no idea what you're talking about and does anyone know where my mother is?"

"We're still looking for her. I'll make a call just as soon as we finish in here," Bo assured. "Make a call now!" I ordered.

"Look McClain, we don't have time for this. Where are Pellman's disks? What did you get from his office this afternoon?" Peterson huffed impatiently.

How did he know I got something? How did he know Pellman gave me a disk? Josh was explicit about no one knowing about the information or that he gave it to me. He wouldn't tell anyone, so I won't either. "You've seen what lengths these people will go to get what they want. We're trying to protect you! And your mother," he snapped. He glared at me as though his stare would loosen my tongue or the contents of my bag.

"Let me talk to her," Bo intervened, sensing my obstinacy. Peterson stood near the door, annoyed. Suddenly his pager blared and he left the room. Bo sat on the table in front of me. "McClain, you must tell us what you've been working on. You may not even know what it is. But if Pellman gave you some disks or if you know where they are, please tell them. Tell me. We'll try to figure out the rest." Sensing something. "What is it?" he asked.

I hugged him tightly, whispering softly in his ears, "Can they hear us?"

"What?"

"Can they hear us?" I whispered, exasperated.

"No. This room is completely secured."

"Are you sure? Look around. Do one of those sweeps or whatever it is you people do."

"McClain, don't be ridiculous."

"Just do it Bo…please" I released him.

Fashioning an argument that meant nothing and led nowhere, I ranted and raved about the events of the evening. Bo walked around the room looking for listening devices. He dropped his pen looking under the chair where I sat. He motioned for me to continue speaking as he reached beneath, indicating something was there. He disabled the device and scanned the room for cameras. I babbled about our past and why I didn't trust him. He saw a small hole through which he was certain someone was watching. Positioning himself in direct view of the camera, he mouthed the words, "Don't say another word."

Bo knocked on the door and told the agents outside that I needed to go to the restroom. He'd escort me. We walked briskly down the gray corridor. "Tell me what do you know about Agent Peterson?" Me.

"What do you mean?" Bo.

"Where did he go to college?" Me.

"I don't know?" Bo.

"What's his first name?" Me.

"Martin." Bo.

"Do you know anything about him? Where he's traveled in the last 6 months? His holdings? Anything? Have you investigated him at all?" Me.

"No. He's on special assignment. Why should we investigate him?" Bo.

"Keep your voice down. Did he go to Harvard? Does he know Pellman or Clay Sims?" Me.

"I'm not sure, but I think he attended Harvard." Bo.

"Can you check?" Me.

"Why?" Bo.

"Just do it…Please. I'm not saying anything until I know. Is there someone above Peterson? Who does he report to?" Me.

"The head of NSA. This was a special assignment for him."

"Who's that?" At the same time we said, "Kevin Jeter." Clay Sims first campaign manager from 20 years ago. He attended Harvard too.

"What does it mean McClain?"

"It's all connected, but I don't know what I have to do with any of it. I don't know them. I researched some data and I have lots of dots, but they don't form a picture."

"Somebody thinks you have the picture, so you'd better think as hard as you can and fast too."

"How long did you say Pellman has been working with you?"

"For the last three years. He's given us vital and pertinent information regarding insider trading. Investment scandals. International securities fraud. As part of our investigation, we retrieved information of illegal activity on your PC. All the dirty deeds have your fingerprints all over them. Pellman assured us you're not involved. Millions are in an account in your name in Switzerland. Did you know? Girl, y'all represent and work for some crooked folks and they plan for you to take the fall when everything hits the fan. Pellman helped us identify Sims' holdings which are massive in biotech and chemical hedge funds."

"So…?"

"It's my understanding that The Bennett Group is trying to become the largest biochemical and pharmaceutical company in the world. It only needs one more major purchase before it does. Evans Chemical. One man blocks the path."

"Who?"

"Ian Lawford. He holds controlling interests in the company."

"Ian? I didn't know that. His name was not on anything related to Evans. I did the research myself. How could I have missed that?" I was surprised, but didn't let Bo know.

"But you said someone is trying to buy his stocks. Do you know who?"

"His brother."

"His brother died years go."

"He's not dead either. We don't know his identity. Pellman says you do." I stopped in my tracks. "I do?"

"Come on. Let's go this way."

How could Pellman tell anyone that I knew the identity of Ian's brother? Ian's brother was dead as far as I knew. There were pictures of him in Ian's library, but the photographs were of children. Why had Pellman told this lie?

"Pellman gave us some fascinating information regarding Lawford's holdings. We can't use anything against him because although the family has a history involving international criminal activity, he has taken major steps to legitimize their holdings by assisting us with monitoring systems keyed into federal watchdog agencies that have overseen his securities for 15 years. He's helping us watch him. He's brilliant. Strange, but clean. Are you attracted to him?" he asked, looking for my reaction. I was too distracted by Pellman's allegation that I knew Ian's brother to respond. "Pellman has proven himself reputable. Decent. Indispensable. Credible. He's the best witness we've ever had regarding this kind of activity. He's cooperated with everything we've asked of him. He's as clean as a whistle. He's never even had a parking ticket."

Bo slid his badge across a security device, unlocking a door. We went inside and he pushed numbers indicating that no one could come into the room unless he unlocked the door from the inside. "This is my office," Bo offered, picking up his telephone and speaking to someone. I looked around and saw a small laminated card I made when he taught me to dance. It was in a frame behind his desk. The message said, "I love to dance, M." It was the first gift I'd ever given him. "Yes sir." Bo turned around saying, "I'm taking you to Pellman."

"You said Pellman has had unlimited access to the same information I have, right?"

"Everything but the Calhoun file."

"The Calhoun file?"

"Yes."

"How did he know I had access to the Calhoun file? And how do you know about it?"

"He told us your research would lead you there."

"Where is he?"

"Down the hall."

"Does your computer network to any other computers in the building?"

"Of course not."

"Are you sure?"

"I'm positive."

We looked at each other as Bo grabbed the laptop from his briefcase while I emptied the contents of my backpack onto the desk. Everything clanked and pinged hitting the table, rolling and falling in different directions. I found the Light Days box. Bo looked embarrassed. In this assortment of stuff, were Jack's disks, but I had no intention of revealing anything Pellman had given me until I spoke with Pellman directly.

"I'll be!" he smiled shaking his head, sitting on the edge of the desk, still watching a monitor showing the corridor outside. Peterson called. Bo didn't answer.

"What's that?" I asked.

"It's an audio scrambler. Just in case." He smiled.

"Is it possible Joshua Pellman has been lying to us?" he asked.

"Anything's possible. Not only does he know what's going on, he's probably manipulating it. That's his style. He wants me to lead you in circles so he'd have time to implement the plan."

"What plan? Wait a minute. I want Nigel to hear this. I've worked with him before. I trust him." Bo called Nigel. About three minutes later, a tall slender man with a British accent walked into the room. "McClain, meet Inspector Clifford Nigel. He's with Interpol and coordinator of the European response to this matter."

"My pleasure Ms. Summers," he said and bowed slightly.

"Hi, as I was saying, Pellman's been playing all of us. That's his forte. He'll spend days, weeks, months, sometimes even years setting up the perfect deal. Patience is his strong suit. He likes to create situations where competitors scramble for the crumbs he sprinkles around. He makes the crumbs so appealing, that no one ever looks for the pie. So while they're scratching and fighting over bits and pieces, he swoops in and takes the whole enchilada. Our clients get fat. RJP gets rich. Pellman gets praised."

"Yeah…but what's the prize?" Bo asked.

"Me."

"You?"

I put in a disk Jack had marked JP. Alphabets and numbers filled the screen. I knew this encryption. Pellman showed me how to unscramble it once. I worked frantically. Bo's hand was on my shoulder. "Slow down baby. You can do it. Take your time." Nigel bristled at Bo's familiarity.

On the outside chance that it might work, I put in three digits I added to Pellman's original quotations. The men looked over my shoulders. "In one of my business school textbooks, Pellman wrote one sentence where he described a theory of disproportionate gain. You never loose under his theory." The computer was doing a numbers dance before our eyes. When it finished, I entered the alphabetical sequence. The computer printed 5-5-64, Pittsburgh, Pennsylvania, St. Lisa's Hospital.

"What does it mean?" the men asked as I kept entering information.

"Pellman's wife gave me a key that unlocked a clock in Pellman's office here. The clue led me to these initials, J.P, K.J., C.S and M.P."

"Whose initials are they?" the Inspector asked.

"That's what Pellman wants me to know. I'm not completely sure, but I think I've identified three of them. He needs me to identify them all. So far I've been able to determine that they all went to Harvard and that they were roommates with Pellman. The chemical trades are real but phantoms created to divert me and everyone else from the actual secret. Josh created a smoke screen to hide information he believes has the potential to rock the nation. The world. He needs me to discover it on my own. I don't know why." I never stopped typing as I spoke. "Now…let me hit this key...input this...one, two, three...merge.... Makes you goose pimply doesn't it?"

"McClain, we don't know what that is?" Nigel said impatiently.

"It a confession. Jack swiped it and kept it. He never turned it over to whoever hired him. Pellman encrypted it and here it is." We read it together.

My Dearest McClain:

If you are reading this, I am dead. I fear my death will affect you more than anyone. My life's work has included protecting you. Your mother. Your distributive loss theory. It's not been easy and lately you've made it extremely difficult. I've no time to waste and this information may shock you.

Clay Sims is your biological father. You were born at St. Lisa's hospital in Pittsburgh, Pennsylvania May 5, 1964. St. Lisa's was intentionally destroyed to hide any facts associated with your birth. Unfortunately, my death guarantees yours unless you use what I left effectively.

For historical perspectives, I first met your mother in the fall of 1963 where she a student at Pitt. I was in Pittsburgh for a huge football game. Your fascination with numbers is clearly hereditary. She was an accounting major, intent on becoming a CPA.

She also worked as a waitress at a hangout just off campus called the Chili Bowl Bar & Grill. Clay noticed her first. She was stunning, like you. She still is. Clay bribed the bartender who sent her to our table. "I've never seen a more beautiful colored girl," Clay told her, which surprised us because he wore bigotry like a badge of honor. Both his father and grandfather were notorious for their racist politics and devotion to discrimination. Segregation.

Tricked

Clay flirted and promised her a huge tip at the end of the night. She told him he had "amazing eyes." Clay kept her bringing drinks and food all night. She couldn't serve any other table because we monopolized her time completely. Your mother was friendly with a spectacular smile. There was a haunting innocence about her. She told us that both of her parents were dead and that she didn't have many relatives. This job was helping pay her way through school.

We'd had far too many drinks. Drunk, we decided to head back to school. Clay saw her walking toward the university. He pulled the car along side and offered her a ride. She kindly declined telling us she couldn't fraternize with customers. Rejected, Clay followed her yelling racist vulgarities. I was shocked given his flirty behavior earlier at the bar.

His aggressive behavior frightened her and she ran. Just as I told Clay to leave her alone, Kevin jumped from the car and chased her. After he caught her, he stuffed her into the back seat with his hand covering her mouth, muffling her petrified screams. I pled with them to let her go before I passed out in the front seat.

Loud voices and screams woke me. We were somewhere outside Pittsburgh on a deserted dirt road. The only lights were those from the car and the full moon.

Unsuccessfully shaking the alcohol's affect from my head, I noticed no one was in the car with me. Stumbling from the car and trying to keep my balance, I looked for everyone. Then I saw them.

Jeter held her, while Martin and Clay ripped at her clothes. She was screaming and begging them to stop. Clay hit her so hard that she fell backwards, motionless. Blood splattered across her tortured face. "Shut up or I'll kill you. I've always wondered if Negroes were brown all over," he hissed.

277

His determination was contagious. They were gleeful, but this wasn't fun. We weren't rapists. But they laughed and continued undressing her. "Don't do this Clay," I begged. "We'll be in so much trouble."

He ignored me, pushing past me as he went to the car where he reached into the trunk and pulled out a rifle and a blanket. I threw up at the prospect of what was about to happen. What was happening. I pled for everyone to stop. Think. Leave.

Martin pulled her to her knees while Clay held the rifle to her head. He cocked it and she closed her eyes. I closed mine too, shaking. Crying. Both frozen at the cold cruelty of the moment. Clay laughed and said, "You're all animals anyway. Scream again and I'll kill ya," he mocked, unbuckling his pants.

Brilliant boys, I once thought good and intelligent crowded around the spectacle, pointing and cheering Clay's horrendous assault. I turned away. Walked away. A coward. Helpless. Horrified. Guilty. They took turns. Humiliating her. Destroying her. I've never been able to get the sounds she made out of my mind.

Hours passed before they left her bleeding. Bruised. Battered. They climbed back into the car leaving her on the blanket. "You just can't leave her there like that," I protested, sobbing. "We need to take her somewhere."

I rushed to her, trying to help her from the ground. But she fought me screaming and crying out to God. Hysterical. Naked. Pathetic. She fought the air whimpering, "Please no…please stop," over and over again.

No matter how I tried to let her know I wasn't going to hurt her, she was out of control. Lost. Stranded. Vanquished.

"Come on Josh! Let's get out of here," Clay yelled, pulling the car close to us. I got into the car and we sped toward Cambridge. Clay laughed and bragged about what happened the

whole way. I looked at the rest of my friends. The sobering reality of what they'd done suddenly struck them silent for the remainder of the trip.

About 3 months later, I went back to Pittsburgh to find her and apologize. The bartender told me that he fired her when she didn't report for work for about a week after the incident, but that "A Negro place on the other side of town called for a reference. She might be there." When I found her, she recognized me instantly. She raced toward the kitchen and I went after her. "Please…please leave me alone. I won't tell. I won't tell," she begged, horrified.

"I'm not here to hurt you. I tried to help you that night, remember? I'm so ashamed of what happened. I didn't know how to stop it. Stop them. Stop Clay." I explained. "You must never say one word about that night. Clay's family was very rich. Influential. Dangerous. His father will have you killed if you ever tell anyone."

She assured me that she wouldn't and that she wanted to forget everything about it too, but she didn't know how because, "I'm pregnant."

Clay was the only one who assaulted her in a manner consistent with impregnation. She was eight weeks pregnant when she married her new husband. Losing him would be impossible to bear, so she never told him about that awful night.

They tried to build a life together. She hoped the truth would never come out. But he left her. You. Realizing you weren't his. Her worst fear occurred and I fear she's never recovered.

Over the years, how much she loved him and how clearly that night devastated and changed her life was unquestionable. Horrible. Tragic. I promised no matter who'd fathered you, whatever she needed she'd have. I felt somehow responsible, and as you know I take my responsibilities seriously.

After a year she reluctantly contacted me. She was alone. Scared. Broke. Broken. I bought her a home in Milwaukee and a good friend gave her a job. She finished school at Marquette and became a CPA. I sent checks every month, a small penance for my cowardice. Yet a bright spot emerged from our mutual darkness. The unparalleled pleasure of you.

I read every letter. Cherished each report card and prized twelve years of school day photographs. I looked forward to the certificates of achievement and father's day cards. You'll never know how much they meant to me. How much you mean to me.

I was there when you graduated from high school. College. Grad School. I had nothing to do with your winning the RJP award, but I can tell you it was one of the proudest moments of my life. It was all I could do not to cry.

Dr. Stovall knows about the horror of that evening. When we got back to Harvard, I confessed every detail and explained that I had to go to the police. He cautioned me against the dangers I'd faced if I told anyone. He's kept my secret all of these years. But I made him promise to tell you everything upon the occurrence of my death.

When Clay's father found out about that night, he forced us to sign an agreement that would pay us substantially for our silence. The alternative was jail or worse, death. He'd end our careers. Ruin our futures. Humiliate our families. Scandalize our names.

I accept my conspiratorial penalty in this hellish drama. But I'll not allow them to destroy you. I invested every dime of my portion in mutual bonds. They're in your mother's name. It's a small fortune that will lavishly take care of her for the rest of her life. They've done well and she's now an extremely wealthy woman.

You have a copy of the original agreement and all certificates. They're in the envelope marked 'CONFIDENTIAL' I brought to you the day I left. You have my permission to look.

Sims read your paper in the Wharton Business Review. He had a hunch and asked me about it. I told him it was hypothetically impossible. He tried it any way in Europe. It worked. The trades you tracked were evidence of its use. It motivated me to work tirelessly on the security system to protect the market from this criminal behavior. By the way, I did notice the similarities in our papers. Your careful corrections were bold and gave me inventive notions to guard against them.

Unbeknownst to Jacobs and Reynolds, patents for the device bear your name exclusively. You'll also receive a sizeable inheritance from my estate.

I apologize for not telling you sooner. Somehow it wasn't my place then, yet somehow it is now. I named the system PROTÉGÉ, after you.

Finally, your mother's purse was left in the car that horrible night. I kept it all these years. Each of our fingerprints is on it. I mailed it to you along with the signed and filmed confessions of my roommates, including that of President- Elect Clay Sims. The package will arrive at your friend Matthew's home on the 18th. Use the information judiciously. Survive this. You must.

Please allow me to leave you with these last thoughts. You are admirable in every conceivable way. Ethics. Instincts. Courage. Tenacity. Potential. Beauty. You're a genius and your thoughtful theories will one day garner international consideration and acclaim. Numbers never lie. They never disappoint. They never leave. But they never love nor share a life.

Never allow bitterness to spoil the sweetness of your inspired spirit. Learn to love ferociously. Laugh easily. Live fiercely. Thrill them, as you have thrilled me.

Who can you trust you're asking? Yourself. You always have. I've helped you as much as I can. If you've followed my directions, the last piece of the puzzle is in your pocket. Your dots are connected and the picture is clear. My boldness prompts me to ask one last thing of you, forgive me. Your mother. Darla. Dr. Stovall. What we did was purely out of love. For you. Please know that you are loved. No father has loved a child more than I loved you. Never blame your mother for any of this. Love her generously. She needs it. Her courage, love and devotion toward you have never wavered, even under the most trying conditions. You are forever my darling,

Your father…almost,

Joshua K. Pellman

* * *

"Wow!" Nigel's hand touched my shoulder. "Today is the 18th." "Are you alright baby?" Bo whispered.

"There's more. I'm sure of it."

Before Sims went to the Senate, he was CEO of Sims Chemical which overvalued its stocks when purchased by Ross Chemical. With RJP as the broker, Ross paid the inflated price, making Sims' family tremendous personal profits. Calhoun noticed the difference between inflated valuations and the actual profits derived. No real profits showed up on his audits for stockholders. He wrote internal memos tracing the undeclared profits offshore. Calhoun worked for Sims. He reported his discovery to internal regulators and upper management, as Sims and The Bennett Group began moving lethal stockpiles and selling additional stocks into an international fund.

He pursued the matter through a series of whistleblower reports that led to an investigation by the SEC. They found nothing. Investigative reporters with national correspondents sought clarification on the movement of these stocks, since Calhoun's report came to light just as Sims formed his first exploratory committee for his failed presidential race.

This time around, RJP's PR machine coupled with Sims' power and Bennett's ruthlessness, stifled the old stories and inquiries." Tears dripped onto the keypad.

"You're doing famously Ms. Summers. Stay focused," Nigel whispered. "That's where the Bennett Group came in. It played enforcer, diverting the SEC and IRS away from transactions. These are the transfers I've been documenting. I missed it. I was looking for something bigger. Something more complicated.

Sims kept a silent interest and secretive position. I bet he hasn't reported one dime of income on the profits he made, and neither have the others. Who were?" I kept decoding. "The other men in the car who raped my mother." I turned and looked at the men.

"That corroborates what Pellman said." Bo moved toward the door, looking both ways and returning to our position. "They're greed and fortunes grew as quickly as Sims ambitions. He bought their silence with untaxed, untraceable millions. And as a key member of the Senate defense oversight committee, his political maneuvering guaranteed RossCorp lucrative government contracts and no oversight.

The Bennett Group convinced Sims that Pellman was giving information about their illegal transactions to the Feds. They created bogus documents and Pellman gave them to you, triggering Clay to theorize that Pellman might give up my identity along with the facts surrounding my mother's rape, which would destroy him. His presidency. His life.

Trevor Lawford controls The Bennett Group. He is the

deceased brother of Ian Lawford." More tears fell. "Trevor was presumed dead years ago. He wasn't. His actual identity is… Ross Bennett. My friend." Bo and Nigel looked at each other.

"Pellman's cryptic confession will send the stock market and the country into a cataclysmic economic tailspin, devastating the economy.

International markets will fall and with the Lawford's wealth, Trevor will swoop in and buy major companies at bargain basement prices. He craves dominance. Power. Control.

Sims will be inaugurated in two months, and I'm a liability he's no longer willing to risk. If Pellman dies, all the secrets must die too. My mother. Me."

"We'll do everything we can to protect you Ms. Summers. You can rely on that," Nigel said, trying to convince me. Himself.

"What do we do with this?" Bo asked.

"Kevin Jeter is the head of the National Security Agency. He's K.J. There's no help there. We know about Sims. C.S. Pellman was in the car. J.P. But who's M.P.?" Nigel asked.

"I don't know. Until we do, I'm still in trouble right?"

"Why don't we ask Pellman?" Bo offered.

We hurried toward Pellman. When we arrived, the guards were gone. Bo stopped us. Nigel held me behind him, pulling a weapon from his shoulder holster. "What's wrong?" I stammered. Nigel nodded. Just as Bo placed his hand on the door, it swung open. Peterson filled the entrance, out of breath and sweating.

"What happened?" Bo yelled, pushing by. "Call a medic to the sector 4 right now," he shouted into his telephone. "We have three, maybe four men down." He came back to Peterson, checking him for injuries. "Are you alright?"

"Yeah…yeah, I'm fine…Thornton was a plant. He shot Pellman and the guards. He tried to kill me too, but I was able to get off a lucky round," Peterson panted, wiping sweat from his face.

"Are you sure you're alright?" Nigel asked, watching Peterson sternly. He shook his head and breathlessly asked, "Did Ms. Summers give you any helpful information?"

284

"Nothing we can use." He lied.

"Oh."

Paramedics and other agents rushed down the hallway, piling Peterson onto a gurney and rushing him away. More medics hovered over the men bleeding on the floor. While Nigel made a series of calls, I tipped toward the door with hope and dread. Pellman lay in a pool of blood. His eyes were open. "Is he dead?" I whimpered. No one answered.

"This is a crime scene. Let's go," Bo interrupted, jerking me from the room.

"I have to go to him," I pleaded.

"I'm sorry McClain. But we must leave right now." Nigel took my other arm as he and Bo whisked me from the building out into a van. "Where're you taking me?"

"RossCorp is purchasing Ross Pharmaceuticals tomorrow."

"That's impossible. They'll never get SEC approval." Both men looked at me.

"We need to get to Dallas. Fast."

CHAPTER THIRTY-THREE

My staff traced her to Washington, but she's nowhere to be found. I wasn't leaving until I knew precisely where she was. Her mother was safe and I was determined she'd be safe too. I hadn't felt concern of this sort for anyone, except Trevor. My parents.

I'd forgiven myself long ago for his walk on the dark side. The guilt of those days still lingers near the corners of my happiness. If only I'd been there. If only I'd spent more time with him. If only I'd listened more. Maybe I could have helped him. Realizing his ultimate choices weren't my fault, I still wondered whether I could have helped him. Stopped him. Stopped this.

Our parent's death affected Trevor immensely. He never recovered. No one does thoroughly. The family tried to get him the counseling he so desperately needed. He rebelled against it.

His rage and mental instability became apparent after the daughter of an African diplomat was found dead. He and friends from university were in Kenya on holiday. Various questionable stories concerning the young woman's death implicated Trevor. Family retainers paid off the authorities and all inquisitions stopped.

Trevor returned to England with his killing nature with tow. Some say he was involved in the death of a local girl from London's West End. She bore a striking resemblance to the girl killed in Africa. After that, he was immediately shipped to America where his identity was changed. The case was never pursued and remains unsolved.

Trevor took the name Ross Bennett. Finding success with his music inventions, the family believed him finally on the right course. He wasn't. Trevor was amazingly bright, yet compelled to walk with evil. He liked it.

It wasn't long before he compromised his part of the family fortune. I'm not certain regarding the specifics, but about five years ago, a character named Calhoun emerged. He made allegations against Trevor's chemical holdings, alleging RossCorp was peddling potentially deadly biological pathogens on the international market to the highest bidder.

Calhoun couldn't identify purchasers or sellers of stocks or the merchandise. Our investigators researched the matter fully. It sounded like something Trevor would do, but they found nothing. Still unconvinced, I contacted Trevor directly. He vociferously denied knowledge or participation. Later, Mr. Calhoun was found dead which strengthened my determination to legitimize our holdings and disassociate the family from Trevor's shady deals altogether.

I sold off companies and businesses, taking vast financial losses. My quest was to assure our family's holding were clear. Clean. Honest. Transparent.

Ian looked out of the penthouse window. The Washington monument sparkled in the distance. "I'll build you a monument that will make this pointy little rock look like a lawn ornament McClain. I promise," he whispered, raising a glass of brandy and waiting for the call.

***

Bo, Nigel and I arrived in Dallas. A car met us at the airport. Bo gave his fellow agents diversionary information while I gave the driver directions to Matthew's house.

"Hello there! I know the way."

"What are you doing here? Are you one of them? Of course you are." I flopped into the backseat next to Nigel.

"I've been working with Bo for about 7 years now. My specialty is infiltration and surveillance. I do a few other things too, but I've been keeping an eye on you. For your own protection of course. I'm primary backup for Agent Richards and Inspector Nigel tonight," Gerald laughed. "Is anyone who they appear to be? Is Matthew? Or is he some kind of plant too?" I asked.

"Except for some student loan problems several years ago and the ugliest dog I've ever seen, he's clean. A great guy." Gerald smiled, obviously happy to see me.

Bo winced debating with Nigel whether to contact local agents to provide backup. "Let's go," he ordered with urgency in his voice. Gerald sped down Central expressway and around Matthew's house twice, parking one block over. Nigel and Bo made calls and compared notes. Bo noticed a car driving slowly past Matt's house with the lights off. He told us to get down as the car turned onto the street where we sat.

"No tags," Gerald reported.

"Put on the scrambler. Call DPD and get some back up out here now," Nigel ordered. "They're the only ones to be trusted. Agreed?"

"Agreed," Bo replied.

"Who's that?" I whispered as though the people in the other car could here me. No one responded.

"Drive down Swiss," Bo ordered.

We were on the street behind Matthew's home. The lights were on. Pitiful was barking. "Is that the house?" Bo asked.

"Something's wrong. I don't see anyone," Gerald whispered, checking his gun. Two agents were supposed to be here. Do you see anyone?"

Bo looked around and agreed that he didn't see anyone either. Before he could say anything else, panicked, I jumped from the car and ran toward the house. Bo and Nigel took off after me.

When I got close, I saw people moving around inside. I ran through the garden, jumping over the low fence Matthew put up to keep out rabbits. Pitiful ran to me. He stopped barking and started jumping and licking me.

"Stop boy...stop," I whispered, throwing one of his chew toys toward the other side of the backyard. He scampered after and played happily.

Tricked

Bo reached me just as I got to the window. Nigel grabbed my shoulder, putting his hand over my mouth. "Don't you ever do that again McClain!" he whispered sternly. "Don't say one word and don't move. Do you understand? Not one word."

I nodded but I didn't understand. "What's going on in there? I can't see," I mouthed to him. It wasn't Matt's voice. Just as I raised my head, a body sat in the ledge above us. Bo, Nigel and I cowered. I heard Matt's voice.

"I told you I don't know what you're talking about." Smack! "I don't know where she is!" Smack! "I don't know anything about a disk or a package." Smack! Smack! "What information?"

"Are you in love with her Matthew?"

"Why?!" Smack!

"Who do you like better Matt? Me or her?"

"What happened between us was a long time ago. Months before I even met McClain."

"Did you tell her about us?"

"There was nothing to tell. One night stands don't count." Smack!

"This is the only place she'd come. We know she's back in Dallas. Make it easy on yourself and just tell me, or he's going to kill you slowly, and your little dog too," the female voice cackled.

"That's Sandy!" I whispered and nudged Bo. "That's Sandy, my secretary." He put his fingers to his lips telling me to be quiet. He pointed in the direction of the garage and we crawled toward the door. Bo began picking the lock. "It's always unlocked," I interrupted. "He doesn't like locks."

"Oh." Bo opened the door enough for us to slip inside. I crept behind Nigel. Bo pulled me back.

"Do not move from this spot," he ordered. "Promise me that you won't move. Promise," he said shaking my shoulders.

"I promise. I promise, but give me a gun or something. I'm not staying in here by myself without a weapon."

"Do you know how to use a gun?" Nigel asked.

"Nope. Just take the safety thing off. I'll figure it out if necessary."

Bo took out a small 9 mm pistol from his leg and handed it to me. "Do not shoot unless absolutely necessary. Aim for the chest not the head. If you aim it, shoot it. Shoot to kill. I won't lose you again...I can't lose you again."

"How many bullets do I have?" Bo kissed me gently. "I love you. Remember that no matter what," he whispered, lightly touching my cheek. Then the two men crept inside.

An eternity passed as I kept my eyes on the garage doors. Windows. The dark garage cast scary shadows that created images heightening my anxiety. Where was the back up? Where was Pitiful? Where were they? I squatted near Matt's riding mower. The smell of grass mingling with gas made me dizzy.

Five shots exploded my bubble of silence. I jumped, dropping the gun and waiting for the killers or Bo to find me. Bo never came. Neither did Nigel. Where was Gerald? No one called out and no one came into the garage. I was shaking. Sweating. Horrified. Petrified. I grabbed the gun from the floor, putting my finger on the trigger ready to kill or be killed. The former would be preferable.

Bo was explicit about my staying in the garage so I looked at my watch. Two minutes. I couldn't stand it. Three minutes. No one. I opened the door, keeping myself near the floor, trembling. The bullets in the gun's clip rattled with me. This was terror. My back was against the wall as I turned corners toward Matthew's living room. I could hear sirens in the distance. Help was on the way.

Matthew was lying on the floor in the dining room with his hands tied behind his back. Bo was crumpled near the couch. No Nigel. No Gerald.

I checked the rest of the house before running back into the room where the two most important men in my life lay bleeding on the floor. Who do I help first? Bo or Matt? Matt or Bo? Matt's eyes reached for me. His lips formed my name.

Tricked

Bo was breathing, but not moving at all. Blood was all over his shirt. I rushed to him. I couldn't help myself. I cradled his head on my lap as he looked at me and tried to smile. He wasn't dead. Thank God. Thank God. Tears plopped onto his forehead and he closed his eyes. "They're coming Bo. Please don't die," I cried.

Guns fired outside. I covered him with my body Gerald shot Sandy and another man as they tried to escape. Nigel was hit in the arm. Local officers rushed in from the garage, grabbing the loaded gun from my hand and pushing me to the floor. Gerald ran inside and quickly interceded, answering a flurry of questions and jerking the officer from my back.

Blood dripped down Nigel's hand as other important looking people arrived. He did all of he talking. Paramedics checked his wounds and readied the men for transport. Nigel gave me a stern look. It was a sign. Gerald went with me into Matthew's bedroom. He closed the door. Inside the bathroom, I lifted the lid on the toilet tank and grabbed the envelope Pellman had given me. Gerald stood at the door watching my every move.

"Are you alright in there" a new voice sounded.

"We're fine," Gerald yelled back.

"I need a towel to dry this off." Gerald tossed a towel and I dried the envelop, tossing it into my backpack. When we came out, I saw a package from Pellman's favorite men's stores sitting on Matt's kitchen counter. It hadn't been opened. Matthew never shopped there. If the handbag was anywhere, it was there. I grabbed the package and ran to the ambulance carrying Bo. I held his hand. Kissed it. Comforted him. Soothed him. Loved him. I didn't want to lose him either. Not again.

Dallas Hospital was crawling with men asking blurry questions. Gerald tapped my shoulder and said Peterson ordered us back to Washington, "Pronto."

"I can't go. I won't go, not until I know that Bo and Matt are alright."

"Peterson gave us exactly one hour to get to the plane McClain."

"I don't work for him. You do. I'm not leaving until I know they'll be OK, and I'm not leaving without Nigel. Call him back and tell him I said go to…"

"I'll tell him something. I'll be right back."

Nigel's wounds were superficial. He joined us in the corridor where three armed men stayed at my side. Doctors performed their trauma tango around Matt and Bo as people and machines ran in and out of their rooms. I was scared to death. Gerald tried to comfort me. Assure me. He couldn't.

Matthew's doctors came out first. We stood. "Hi...are you here for Mr. Pierce?"

"Yes...is he?..." I asked.

"We're taking him up to surgery in a few minutes. He's awake, but we gave him some pretty strong medicine. He was shot in his chest but lucky for him, we don't believe any major organs were hit. He's bleeding internally though and we need to stop the bleeding. A bullet fragment is nicked his sternum. He's lost a lot of blood, but we expect a good outcome. I think he'll be as good as new in a few months. He's young. Healthy. In good shape. If you want to wait, the surgical waiting area is on the fourth floor. A nurse will show you the way."

"May I speak to him? Please?" I asked.

"For a moment, but we really need to get him to the OR. We don't have much time to lose."

Nurses were preparing to wheel Matthew to surgery. He saw me standing at the door and closed his eyes. I sensed his contempt as I kissed his face, "Matt, are you asleep? The doctor said you'll be as good as new real soon. I...I'm so glad. I was so scared." I rubbed my hand across his forehead, as we walked toward the elevators. He opened his eyes, motioning me to lean in closer. I did.

"Hi…" I whispered. Tears fell freely.

"You know what?" His voice broke. "I was beginning to think you cared about me. I even convinced myself that you might even love me."

"I do Matthew. I do."

Tricked

"I was happy yesterday because I believed this was finally going to work." The nurse pressed the elevator button.

"It was. It is. There're so many things you don't know. Let me try to explain…"

"Tonight…when I saw you go to that man…instead of me… I knew you'd never feel about me the way I feel about you. I would've given anything… anything. If you ever looked at me the way you looked at him. Even once….You've never looked at me like that McClain. Ever."

"Matt…please…I…"

"You're right." Tears rolled across his cheeks. "I don't know and I'll never understand. When I come out of surgery, please don't be here. I don't want to do this anymore. I can't. I don't want you anymore," he whispered.

"Matthew…don't' say that. Please don't say that," I wiped his tears and kissed his cheek.

"Please leave me alone." The elevator arrived. He turned his head away from me. "Please McClain. Don't make me hate you."

His comments stiffened me as I left my heart on the gurney with him. Before they wheeled him away, I reached into my backpack and gave his locket to the nurse. "Please give this to him, for luck." I turned away, trying to maintain the last bit of sanity I had left.

"Wait! What do you want me to tell him?" she asked as the doors slowly closed.

"Will you tell him he's my dream come true?" The nurse took the locket and gave me the most understanding look anyone ever had as the doors slid close.

"If he really loves you, he'll forgive you. If you really love him, *show* him," Gerald whispered.

"How?"

CHAPTER THIRTY-FOUR

Peterson was pacing when we entered the room. He looked at the box I was holding as he sat behind his desk. "You're a Harvard man aren't you Peterson?" Nigel asked, pulling me into the seat next to him. Gerald stood with two uniformed agents near the door.

"What?"

"You *did* graduate from Harvard didn't you?"

"The important thing is what Ms. Summers discovered?"

"Quite, but important factors have been neglected Agent Peterson. How's Pellman?"

"He didn't make it." I closed my eyes.

"Pity. Isn't it interesting that he was already dead to the world before you killed him? That was your plan wasn't it?" I stared at Nigel amazed at what he just said.

"What the hell are you talking about Nigel? I told you what happened in that room, and yes it *was* my idea that we faked his death."

"Indeed, but the videotape suggests a different report than the one you gave."

"What video tape?"

"The one I had installed. I must admit however that you played this whole thing to your advantage. I didn't put it together until we found Pellman's confession."

"What confession?"

"Pellman explained everything. The rape. The cover-up. The stocks. The conspiracy. You *were* in the car that night weren't you." My eyes were the size of saucers. My temples throbbed.

"You're crazy! He's crazy. Nigel this is ridiculous. Preposterous. I don't know what you're talking about," Peterson shouted, watching Gerald and looking at the agents.

"It's all right here Peterson," Nigel said indicating that I should pull the handbag out. "You see I didn't put it together until I remembered that Pellman said there were four of you in the car that night. Sims, Jeter, Pellman and you Martin." Nigel said confidently, crossing his legs and lighting a pipe. My heart pounded. I hoped he knew what he was doing. I reached into my pocket and gave Nigel the Harvard class ring. The initials were M.P. Peterson was M.P. That's why Pellman needed me to come here. He knew I'd never believe who this man was.

Peterson laughed as he slowly pulled a gun from his desk. "You think you're pretty smart don't you? Don't move." Peterson pointed the gun at me. Nigel never flinched, saying, "North, take his weapon." Peterson fired the gun directly at me. The gun clicked. When I opened my eyes, to my delight I was still alive. "I had the gun unloaded when you were in the infirmary," Nigel explained. "Arrest him."

As two agents approached, he grabbed me from the chair placing a knife to my neck." Nigel pointed his gun at Peterson's head. "I told Clay to kill you and your mother years ago. He couldn't have a little black bastard running around ruining everything we believed in. Pellman was weak. I'm glad I killed him. Nigel, I'm taking her out of this building and I'm going to kill her. All secrets die tonight. By the way, your mother's already dead."

"You bastard," Nigel hissed.

"Little Ms. Summers here is the only legal bastard in this room. A freak. Misfit. Mutt. Think of it as euthanasia. I'm going to put her out of her misery, but I'll have a little fun with her first," he said, running the blade across my cheek. "The same way we did with her mother. Let's go," he ordered, backing us out of the room.

Agents surrounded us with weapons drawn. "Stand down Mr. Peterson. There's no way out. Even if you kill her, we'll have her DNA and we have Pellman's confession. You've lost. Sims has lost. You've all lost everything," Nigel bargained.

"That confession Pellman gave you is nothing. A college prank."

"He has you on film."

They argued. I had to do something fast, so I fainted. Peterson pushed me toward Nigel and the agents. Bullets whizzed above me, killing Peterson instantly. Gerald scooped me from the floor. "Are you OK? Somebody get a medic!" He yelled.

"Is she hurt?" Nigel asked.

"She doesn't seem to be." I opened my eyes.

"Are you OK?" Gerald asked.

"Is it over?"

"You fainted."

"No I didn't. I saw that on Oprah."

"Get up." Gerald took a deep breath, pulling me from the floor.

"Are you sure you're alright?" Nigel asked, grabbing my hand.

"No. I'm a wreck."

"Stay with us McClain. The worst of it is over. You've handled yourself like a professional. If you were to consider leaving the money game, you'd make an exceptional agent. You have fantastic instincts," Nigel smiled. "But it's not over. There's still work to do." Nigel walked away, speaking into his telephone.

"Gerald why didn't you tell me? That's dumb. You couldn't, could you?"

"I'm sorry. I couldn't."

"I knew you were too smart to be a mail clerk. Is anybody who they seemed to be? Has everyone tricked me?"

"No," he laughed. "I have a philosophy. Whoever you really are inside will eventually show up, no matter how hard you try to suppress it. But don't lose your faith in people. Yourself. Others. We're all flawed McClain. But the best of us try to do a little better every day."

"Is it that simple?"

"Yeah, for those of us who are honest with ourselves and believe God. We do the best we can. That's all he expects. There's something else."

"What?" I braced myself.

"Rick hung himself. He's dead. He left you a letter." Gerald pushed the letter toward me.

"Are you going to take it?"

"How's the dog?"

"What dog?"

"Pitiful? How's Pitiful?"

"The dog's fine. We've arranged a kennel in Dallas to care for him until Matthew is back in commission."

"You'll need to contact his mom. She's…"

"On her way to Dallas as we speak. We sent a plane for her and she'll be there soon." I nodded. "He'll be alright McClain."

"I know," never taking my eyes from the analysts, who busied themselves researching and crosschecking Pellman's disks with my information.

A blizzard of arrest and search warrants were being prepared and media people were being called for press conferences later that morning.

Skillfully constructed evidence needed to convict a number of important businessmen including Edward Jacobs and Charles Reynolds lay on the table with assorted other incriminating documents. There was sufficient information to vindicate innocent businessmen. Ambassadors. Senators. Pellman. Ian. Me. We did not participate in the illegal trades or money laundering.

Skilled analysts scoured Jack and Pellman's notes recovering foreign documents. Bank accounts. Bonds. Securities. Holding companies. Hedge funds. Everything.

The President was briefed. He called an emergency meeting of his Cabinet. Congressional and Senate attorneys were rounded up and hauled to the White House. The Attorney General was on his way. Congressional leadership along with Sims' handlers and attorneys, father, were rounded up and brought to FBI headquarters.

Kevin Jeter ignored the calls swamping his office. He took a drink and blew his brains out all over the new leather chair his kids gave him. He didn't leave a confession or explanation.

The SEC's Congressional oversight committee raced to the Hill as federal judges and foreign magistrates reviewed probable cause affidavits, issuing search and arrest warrants.

Worldwide law enforcement formed a ring around the inner circle of conspirators. Morning talk show producers and twenty-four hour news stations caught wind that something big was happening. They prepared to pounce. Turner shredded documents at RJP Washington. He prepared press statements. Plotted a response on behalf of the conglomerate. Put his lie machine on full and woke Clay Sims with rumblings of a big story filling the air.

His informants were clueless. They believed Peterson and Jeter had taken care of me. He sought information tirelessly from government insiders. No information came. Not one leak. This was a matter of national security.

Just before sunrise, U.S. Marshals, the FBI with state and local law enforcement descended like locusts. They seized property. Homes. Businesses. Bank accounts. Records. Cars. Boats. Planes. Computers. Everything. They raided the homes and offices of prominent business people. Congressmen. Three governors. Ten senators. Six mayors. Three televangelists and one President-Elect of the United States of America.

Television cameras arrived. The SEC suspended all RJP's public and private trading privileges. The NASDAQ, Chicago Board of Trade and New York Stock Exchanges along with all foreign exchanges were enjoined from allowing one stock RJP handled from being traded. RJP's bank accounts and the accounts of all its partners were seized nationally and internationally.

My eyes burned as I turned to Nigel. "Is my mother really dead?" "No dear. She's quite alive and on her way here to be with you. Mr. Lawford collected her yesterday. She's signing affidavits. Her sworn statement will help establish sufficient evidence to prove conspiracy to commit murder supporting the arrest and indictment of Clay Sims and others." It was finally time to cry.

CHAPTER THIRTY-FIVE

"McClain, you need to change." Instinctively feeling my worry, "He'll be fine. They'll all be fine. Ms. Evans is out of recovery and in a private room. She'll make a full recovery. She was shot in the shoulder and the bullet went straight through. She may have a small scar." Gerald smiled sympathetically acknowledging the enormity of my pain.

"You should be very proud of what you've done. You're a great woman and I'm grateful to have known you. I heard somewhere that the path of your destiny is determined by the greatness of your call, and the sincerity of your sacrifice. It is neither bought nor sold, but captured in fleeting moments of extraordinary strength."

"Who said that?"

"You did, when you spoke to the young investor's group at Greenly High School this spring. During the past several hours you've achieved the greatness you defined so skillfully. You've paid a great price for it. Your sincerity is unquestionable. I hope you know how valuable you are. You're a national treasure and you belong to the people.

Your life may never be the same because you've saved us all from evil men whose greed and contempt almost landed them in the most powerful office in the free world. On behalf of the agency and myself, I offer you my most sincere gratitude.

I'm sure others will show their appreciation on a grander scale. But for the courage you demonstrated last night and what you'll face in the weeks and months to come, I have tremendous respect and admiration for you."

"Thanks Gerald." We hugged and I knew we'd be very good friends forever. Nigel joined us. He led me to another room.

"Get a little rest and change. We're expected at the White House."

"The White House?" I asked.

"The President wants to meet you."

The clothes I left at Iris' house and at the Willard were there. Hearing that Bo, Matt, Iris and my mother were OK filled me with sudden excitement. "I'm going to the White House to meet the President, I sung, running into the shower. I didn't like him, but I was happy for the chance to meet him.

Checking my new hairdo. Perfume. Outfit. Makeup. I was ready. Someone knocked at the door while I was putting on my shoes. "Come in," I yelled.

Gerald opened the door. "It's time." When I looked up Gerald was standing there with two other agents and my mother.

"Good morning baby." I grabbed her and held her tightly. No words were needed. She was safe. She was here. "Are you ready?" she cried. "Why didn't you tell me?" I cried too.

"I couldn't. I wanted you to stay alive. I was lost. Hurt. Unhappy. Alone."

"You weren't alone. Never alone. You had me. Thank you for keeping me," I cried.

She cried too. "I never thought for a moment about not keeping you. I loved you, no matter who your father was. Wipe your face. We'll have plenty of time for tears later, but right now we have work to do. Now go in there and put on some powder and lipstick and let's go."

I ran to the bed to retrieve my backpack. We walked into the hallway and down the corridor together, holdings hands. She kept me when she could have easily destroyed me. No one would have blamed her if she had. But she loved me anyway, when loving me killed the only relationship she valued. She loved me. The evidence of her greatest pain, knowing that the most powerful man in the world could have had us both killed at any time. She loved me enough to let me believe all these years that I had a father who loved me. That took real courage. Audacity. Guts.

A huge black car idled in the driveway. Nigel was inside. "Hi there. You look marvelous. How do you feel?" Gerald closed the door and we headed down the long drive toward the White House.

Television cameras clicked, buzzed and whined as the President was joined by many of his Secretaries and Intel agency directors on the small stage. Network newsmen and white house correspondents were breathless. He began. "My fellow Americans, our country has been saved from certain and catastrophic terror from within. Bombs. Bullets. Devices of destruction typically associated with terrorism were not the methods of the proposed destruction. Our financial markets and our way of life were the direct targets.

A small group of unknown investors own 75% of all chemical and biological stocks. Without government approval or oversight, the companies bought and sold strains of lethal weapon grade pathogens. Crucial research and development data regarding antidotes to these drugs were altered, then given to our military for production. The proper data was to be sold on the international black market to the highest bidders. We have successfully intercepted and thwarted those efforts.

Last night, our country's best agents broke the codes that kept the identities of the purchasers and sellers of the stocks virtually undetectable. The group managed to purchase controlling shares of the world's largest chemical and pharmaceutical companies, earning billions of undeclared income over the last 28 years.

All of those involved will be brought to justice and vigorously prosecuted. Arrest warrants are being served all over the world as I speak. I'd like to thank Justice. Defense. Treasury. State. FBI. CIA. SEC. They will take your questions later. Our friends at Interpol and other international intelligence agencies were vital to this operation's success. This coordinated effort has saved our economy and the diverse economies and markets of the entire world. This fiendish plan had the potential not only to disrupt our economy, but the world's economic integrity was at stake. Thank you for your hard work and prompt action.

It shocks and saddens me to report that certain high ranking and prominent members of this government, along with highly respected members of the business community were involved in this vast conspiracy. Profiteering from this illegal enterprise.

Most notably, the largest most influential and respected brokerage house in the world, RJP International was directly involved, laundering if you will, billions in stock and securities diverted. Today, the SEC and its international counterparts have suspended all RJP's trading rights. Their assets have been seized and their doors are locked.

The U.S. Marshal Service, FBI and I.R.S. are in the process of seizing the personal assets of RJP's principals and their international offices. Banks have been ordered to dishonor any attempts by RJP, its officers or employees to negotiate funds or instruments. Any legitimate RJP investors will be protected. Secretary Kelly will explain that process.

It further saddens me to announce that Kevin Jeter, the director of the National Security Agency committed suicide early this morning. The facts surrounding his death are incomplete, but it appears he was associated with the conspirators.

I am also profoundly dismayed to advise you that Clay Sims has been arrested for his alleged role in this matter. Federal agents arrested him at his home in Georgetown this morning." An audible gasp rushed around the room.

"I can assure you that the democratic process will prevail. Congressional leaders, constitutional scholars and lawyers from both sides of the aisle are caucusing to determine the proper formalities. The Electoral College has not met to cast their official votes. Until that is done he is not formally the President, although we suspect he will be so named at that time. Until then, I would caution you that Mr. Sims should be considered innocent until he is proven otherwise in a court of law.

Tricked

There will be no constitutional crises. The country will remain vibrant. We will persevere.

Yet a hero rises from the midst of this historic calamity. I met her briefly this morning and take great pleasure in presenting to the American people McClain Summers, a partner at RJP-Dallas. She helped uncover the scheme and with great risk to her own life and the safety of others, helped our federal agencies by providing the identities, means and methods of this deadly cabal.

International as well as national trade of chemical, nuclear and biological technology and securities will never be traded as it has in the past. I will issue an Executive Order today directing that the SEC implement the security device Ms. Summers created for our market watchers. I have spoken with my international counterparts who are eager to learn about this brilliant safeguard and use it in their countries as well.

On behalf of the American people thank you for your courage. Tenacity. Intellect. Brilliance and patriotism. Some say patriotism is dead in America. They believe greed is everything. Some say that everyone has a price. Today McClain Summers is living proof that there is no price on patriotism. Ethics. Courage. She risked her life and because of that risk, we as a country…the world breathes a sigh of economic relief. God bless you Ms. Summers and thank you for your service to our nation."

All eyes were on me as I nodded from the side of the room. The President motioned for me to come forward. His staff pushed me toward the stage and up the stairs. Reporters leapt from their seats. Flash bulbs and lights blinded me. Camera shutters drowned out the hammering beat of my heart. Large network camera's zoomed in. Their unquenchable thirst and curiosity marveled at the mirage that was me.

"Miss Summers! Miss Summers! How did you discover the plot? Comment Ms. Summers! This way Ms. Summers! Over here Ms. Summers! Ms. Summers do you know the perpetrators? Ms. Summers what was your source? Ms. Summers when did you discover the plot? How did you discover the plot Ms. Summers?

How long have you worked for RJP? Was Joshua Pellman involved? What does Clay Sims have to do with this?"

I cleared my throat and the room grew silent. "Thank you Mr. President, for your kind words and generous offer. I credit my small contribution in this matter to the greatest and most influential man in my life, Joshua Pellman. I thank him for teaching me about greatness. Grace over greed. Generosity over avarice." I was about to lose it, but I couldn't. "He was the greatest economist of our time. A national treasure." I had to stop. One tear rolled down my cheek. "He was vital in the development of the security system the President spoke of and he lost his life protecting the financial markets he so desperately loved. Joshua Pellman, recruited, hired and mentored me. I will never forget him and I will be eternally grateful for what he has meant in my life and the life of my family." I looked at my mother who was wiping tears from beautifully proud eyes.

"I'd also like to thank my mother for her courage and commitment. She is my hero. Inspector Clifford Nigel, Agents Bo Richards and Gerald North saved my life last night. Thank you. Thank you from the bottom of my heart," I nodded in their direction. "Mr. President, thank you again for your steadfastness and prompt call to action. Thank you very much sir."

With that the President shook my hand and escorted me from the podium and the room. Reporters were tripping over each other. Pushing. Shoving Heaving Shouting. Leaping. Jumping. Running.

The President's press secretary took the podium and continued the raucous press conference. "All of the fundamental information regarding indictments and arrests are in the packets being handed out to you now. Address your questions to the agency heads, starting with Justice. Mr. Attorney General.

The reporters asked important questions, but the big story was me. They sent runners with telephones. "Find everything you can on McClain Summers."

Tricked

* * *

Two months and three weeks following the press conference, my life was still frantic. I was briefed. Debriefed. Interviewed. Deposed. Challenged and embraced. At least one hundred people, including foreign prosecutors, lawyers and SEC inspectors crammed themselves into my life daily. They needed statements to prosecute or defend their clients.

Congressional and Senate oversight committees subpoenaed my input. Internationally renowned economists and financial experts quizzed my theories and drew their own conclusions about my discoveries and solutions. T.V. news, talk shows and grocery store tabloids hounded me. My friends. Colleagues. Co-workers. They wanted dirt, lots of it. When the taped confession of the rape surfaced, I took shelter at Heaven's Gate with my mother.

Clay Sims declared his innocence to the end. He died of a heart attack the day after the Electoral College cast its votes. Howard Gleason, the Vice President resigned prior to the inauguration in an effort to save his party and the integrity of the office. Leonard Wilson, Speaker of the House became President. The newly inaugurated President planned a White House dinner in my honor later that year.

Headhunters went berserk. Publishing companies made insane offers. The patent office reviewed Pellman's security device and approved Protégé, giving it pending status paving the way for the manufacture and sell of the system.

Letters from lawyers, agents, managers and public relations firms wanting to represent me flooded Barry's office. He quit Conley & Mason and started his own firm. I was his first client. I turned down the opportunity to address the World Economic Symposium in London. Darla Pellman gave Joshua's speech. Brilliantly. We became good friends.

Iris was released from the hospital after about five days. It was a huge production. Her parents and brothers carted away cards. Letters. Flowers. Telegrams. Balloons and other assorted gifts she received. "I'm going to be on Entertainment This Evening and all the morning talk shows," she chirped. "I'm the best friend who was shot. I've been all over television. Have you seen me? How did I look? I was fabulous. There's no way I could pay for this publicity."

"I saw you. You looked wonderful. The perpetual prom queen."

"Do you think I should wear pink or yellow? I think yellow. Mommy don't you think yellow? McClain, is this my best side or this?"

"Yellow is your signature color," her mother giggled as they took off into a diatribe of laughter and conversation that would last all day.

Craig pushed the wheel chair while Iris chatted about how amazing she looked. "Iris, are you angry at me?" I asked.

"Angry? Girl no. Are you nuts? This free publicity will earn me millions in new business. That national morning show news lady wants me to do her wedding. In Florence. If I knew being shot would lead to all of this, I would have gotten shot long ago," She reached up, kissing me directly on the mouth and laughing to the delight of everyone. Again.

Photographers met us at the door. Iris preened and smiled for the paparazzi, as I rushed into the limo patiently waiting for the diva to step inside.

Craig proposed to her later that evening, presenting her with a 4 Karat perfect diamond. It was all very romantic. Naturally she accepted. They'll marry New Year's Eve. I'll be the Maid of Honor.

Three weeks ago, Bo was back in Washington. I hadn't spoken with him directly but Nigel gave me regular updates on his condition. He asked to be transferred to the European office.

"My job here is finished. I have to go home. When you come to London, ring me up. I'll take you out for tea," Nigel offered.

"It's a date," I hugged and thanked him for saving my life again. "After all my dear, it's what I do. You are very welcomed."

Tricked

Spotlights illuminated the skies the night I attended the White House dinner given in my honor. Iris. Craig. Ian. Barry. Mother and her new boyfriend came. Darla Pellman and Dr. Stovall came too.

Dignitaries from all over the world celebrated me. Iris flitted around charming everyone, especially the first lady. They had two daughters. Keith was so happy, he couldn't believe where he was. Everyone treated me like a celebrity or a head of state. Nigel surprised me, joining us for the evening. We danced.

The President of Florida A & M and his wife were my special guests. Preparations for presenting me an honorary doctorate were on his desk. He didn't know, but a multimillion dollar endowment to the school was on mine.

Rick's letter sat unread. I sent his parents a note after it became public Rick was a paid assassin.

Jack's family sold everything for the money. They even sold his cherished antique secretary that took him three years to find. Ian found it and had it put in my dressing area. Vultures.

Keith called so often that whenever the telephone rang I answered, "Hi Keith." His father wanted me to speak to his men's group. His mother wanted me to speak to her women's group. Keith wanted to speak for me. I tempted him. "Keith would you consider running my company? I need someone in charge I can trust. You'll be President and CEO. I'm Chairman of the Board." He was thrilled, but realized the offer spelled doom to the relationship he thought we'd have. Success. I sent Keith roses every Monday.

Matthew still wouldn't take my calls. His mother moved from Florida and decided to stay in Dallas, relocating permanently. He was attending law school fulltime and refused to be interviewed by anyone. Barry kept me up to date with his progress and found a realtor to put my condo on the market. "I was clueless about the scheme, but you know what? The file clerk was in on it. That's how they knew you'd seen the Calhoun file," he confessed.

Mother built a fabulous new home, filled with color and

friends. She joined the Saint's Home Church and is now saved, sanctified and filled with the Holy Spirit. She teaches in the church economic program and declares herself, "A new creature." Indeed she was. The best kind. Her dedication to her beliefs healed her heart and her spirit. She was luminous. Glowing. Free. To love. Be loved. Love me.

Whenever I was in town I attended church with her. Their joy moved me. There was wonder. Mystery. Destiny. Purpose. Forgiveness. Redemption. Hope. Slowly I began to believe. I wasn't where she was, but I guess I was right where God needed to be in order to show me the wonder of his glory. I prayed every night for Matthew to forgive me.

Bo and I met at the Heathrow. He looked fitter and finer than he ever had. He wore a crisp pale yellow shirt and khaki pants. He was rested. Fresh. Beautiful. We discussed our breakup intelligently, confessing our mutual pain and considerable blunders. The experience crippled both our ability to express love again. My mother called it a 'soul tie.' One I was determined to unknot. People thought we were honeymooners, feeling free to comment on how wonderful we looked together. We had no future. It was over.

Paris became a playground our last few days together. He created wonderfully sweet memories, where we walked down ancient Parisian streets. Watched the city pass by from crowded cafes. We engaged in French bread fights much to the chagrin of native Parisians and Bo had a street artist do a caricature of us. He kept it. Finally, we danced at the foot of Eiffel Tower saying our goodbyes without regret and finally closing that chapter in our lives forever. I'll always love Bo. The way you always love your first love.

Ian sent daily bouquets of exotic and vibrant flowers to my room. His confessions were resolute with devotion. We spent hours on the telephone between interviews. Airports. Meetings. Fatigue. Ian apologized for missing my birthday with a surprise trip to Dubai and a scandalously beautiful necklace. He spoiled me.

Tricked

The private jet Ian provided was suppose to take me home to Ian from Paris. Instead he surprised me, flying to the City of Lights so we could return to the States together in his new custom 747. I introduced him to Bo. "Thank you for taking such wonderful care of her Mr. Richards. She is after all the most important person in my life. I plan to marry her as soon as all of this dies down, that is if she'll have me of course." Bo was jealous. I was glad.

CHAPTER THIRTY-SIX

Without Pellman's camaraderie, Jack's friendship or Matthew's love, there was nothing left for me in Dallas. I bought a fabulous brownstone in Manhattan. Ian thought I should move into his penthouse. "I can protect you there." But I treasured my independence and had to make a new life. Alone. For a while. I promised to live at the penthouse until renovations were complete.

Reconstruction progressed slowly but beautifully. While I was in California on company business, Ian's decorators swarmed my place. He surprised me with a stunningly restored four story brownstone upon my return. He replicated my taste with the same ease as Jack had.

I liked Ian. I liked being near him. He made me feel safe. Appreciated. Adored. Everything he said he'd do, he did. More. And he drenched me in light with each look. Gaze. Stare. Everyone should know that feeling.

The condo sold for 4.7 million dollars. Thousands more than my asking price on the contingency that I turn over possession day of closing. I agreed, and a closing date was set.

At dinner the night before I planned to go to Dallas, Ian suddenly insisted that I join him for a business trip he had in Italy. He scheduled us to leave early the next morning. "Darling, my people will take care of all moving details in Dallas and we'll fly to Florence for a few days. Surely Barry with your power of attorney in hand can proceed with the closing expeditiously. You don't have to be there darling. Come with me and my attorney will draw up the documents directly."

Tricked

Ian refused to understand why I needed to close on my home myself. There were memories there. Having not returned since everything happened, I needed to say goodbye.

An argument ensued. Ian was adamant about my going to Florence with him. "Ian it's not that I need to go. I want to go. I have to go." In the middle of our great debate, Ian said, "McClain you're being completely unreasonable darling. Will you marry me?"

Caught off guard and before I could answer, Ian was on his knees pushing a ring in my direction. "Don't give me an answer until I return from Europe. It's obvious that you're determined to go to Dallas and finish your business there. I concede defeat for now, but I expect your answer." We spent the night at the estate.

Although Ian drifted happily to sleep. I couldn't. Sleep had become difficult since Pellman's death. "McClain...What are you doing?" he asked yawning. "Can't you sleep darling?"

Standing near the massive bank of windows that looked out across the perfectly manicured grounds, I didn't respond. A full moon gave everything in the room a wonderfully bluish glow. "Did you hear me sweetheart? Do you need something darling? Are you alright?" Ian whispered, getting out of bed.

"Did I wake you? Go back to sleep Ian. I'm alright," I whispered.

"But you're not. Not really are you? I reached for you and you weren't there." He lifted my face and I looked away. "Darling...you've been crying. Please tell me...whatever is the matter? I'll make it better. I promise," He held me gently.

"I can't..."

"You can't what? Tell me darling. Don't shut me out. I can't bear it. You can tell me anything. You can't what?"

"I can't marry you."

"Don't you love me at all McClain?"

"I love you very much," I assured him, embracing him forcefully.

"Then why can't you marry me sweetheart?" I shook my head negatively.

He took me into his arms and held me for a long time. He picked me up and carried me to a large chair that looked out at the gardens. I placed my head on his shoulder. "This breaks my heart," he whispered into my hair. "I love you McClain. So very much."

"I'm sorry," I cried.

"Never say you're sorry for how you truly feel. I always want you to be honest with me. It's one of your more endearing qualities. May I remain in your life? If not as your husband, perhaps as your very very good friend?"

"I want that. I want that very much. You mean so much to me Ian. I do care for you so deeply. Sincerely. Genuinely."

"I know you do. Then let this night be ours forever."

When I woke Ian was gone. He left a note and the 12 Karat pear shaped diamond engagement ring on the nightstand. The note read:

My Darling McClain,

Keep this little ring or I'll throw it into the Atlantic. I trust that the fellow who owns your heart will always fill it with love and joy. I'll always be waiting for you with open arms and an open heart. Know that I'll work tirelessly for the remainder of my life to make you mine. This falling in love is so American. It's also very contagious.

I love you more than life,
Ian

He made the arrangements for my travel to Dallas. I left a note, leaving my lip prints on it. I took the ring. That would make him smile. I hoped.

Tricked

Barry met me at the private jet terminal. "Daddy Warbucks got you sprung. Look at you," Barry smiled hugging me. "You flying strong and you look fantastic. It must be all that polluted New York City air. Living above the clouds and crowds looks good on you girl. So how's the penthouse and cocktail party set?"

"He wants to marry me. He gave me this." I showed Barry the ring.

"Daaaammmmnnnn! What you do to that white boy? I want to marry you too, but I ain't got that kind of loot. What you go do!?"

"I told him no."

"You told him what!? You told him what!? You told him what!? Why you tell him that!? Call him right now and tell him you changed your mind. Tell him yes. Y'all been together all this time. What's the matter with you? Are you crazy?! "

"I must be. He's wonderful."

"Don't be no fool McClain. The man obviously loves you baby. Let me see that thing again. You must be putting it *on him*. Damn!"

"Barry I'm not sure about anything anymore. I'm just trying to do a little better everyday."

"I understand baby. Seriously, don't marry him if you don't love. I don't care how much money he has, especially if he's not what you really want." Barry took my hand and squeezed. I was amused by his sincerity.

"Sometimes we can't have what we *really* want."

"Bullshit. I'm sorry baby I got your anti-cursing policy, but who told you that? You know better than that. You can have whatever you want if you're willing to pay the price and work for it. Look, marry Ian for a little while and let him buy us whatever we want. Then we'll file and keep a lot of stuff. What you got to lose?" Barry laughed. "Did he ask you for a pre-nup?"

"No. What do you mean us?"

"Lord have mercy. I'm sick. Wait. Stop. I'm dizzy. Whew! I need to sit down. Did you say he didn't ask you for a pre-nup? Get me a pill. I'm going to faint."

313

"He didn't mention it," I laughed.

"He didn't mention it? He didn't mention it? He…"

"Barry…"

"Look here little girl, as your lawyer and new best friend, I'm advising you to reconsider Ian's proposal and marry the man immediately."

"You're so crazy. You know I don't need his money. I've got my own."

"See that's what's wrong with you. You think it's just about money. It ain't. It's about access to power. Ian has that in spades. Or knights in his case. I saw y'all on TV with the queen. How was that?"

"Amazing."

"I know it was. Did you swipe something from the castle for me?"

Our car pulled into the familiar driveway. Mike ran to the car. "Ms. Summers!! Ms. Summers is that you?!! Have we missed you?!! You're a regular hero! We've kept up with everything. I saw you on Nightline. Today Show. Dateline. Twenty-Twenty. Everywhere. When I told my wife you lived in the building, she was so excited. I'm so sorry you're leaving us. I'll miss you very much. Will you take a picture with me before you leave? Let me help you out of there!"

"I missed you too Mike. Barry take a picture. What's the latest good gossip around here? Is there anything new? Have you been good?"

"I don't know if I've been good, but I've been consistent," he laughed. "The only news around here is you. Let's take the picture by the sculpture. That's a good spot."

The movers arrived just as Barry snapped the photo. Mike rushed toward the trucks, pointing and directing then to the loading docks out back.

"How you like being a celebrity?" Barry yawned.

"I don't."

Tricked

"Well...get used to it. When I read about Jack. Sims. Rick. Girl...I got drunk for you. I can't keep up with it. Clay Sims is your father?"

"Seems so."

"You a regular scandal."

"I know."

We rode up to the condo where the local movers had already packed most of my things in big boxes. Small items sat in the middle of the living room floor. The place reeked of Jack. He was everywhere. Fresh air would help cleanse the memories. I walked out onto the terrace and took a deep breath while the movers marched in and out pushing. Pulling. Lifting. Moving.

Barry joined me, leaning against the rails looking at the skyline. "You've always had a beautiful view from here. How you doin?"

"Fine," I wiped a tear from my eye.

"He's good McClain."

"Who?"

"You know who."

"I'm glad."

"Call him."

"I have."

"Call *him*."

"He won't. I've tried. He doesn't. You know what? I'm gonna miss you. Come here." We hugged and he kissed me on the cheek.

"I'll miss you too. We'll see each other though. Lots. With you as my number one client, I'll make enough money to keep me in potato chips and pussy for years."

"You are completely sick." We laughed.

"I appreciate you McClain. You didn't forget your friends. Thanks for shooting your business to my new firm. I like being in practice for myself, especially knowing I can count on your money. Lawford shot me some big retainers too. That was you. I know it. So I want you to be happy baby and I'm stepping way out there, but I don't think Ian makes you happy. He makes you safe.

Comfortable. Secure. He might even keep you mentally and otherwise stimulated, but Matthew made you live. He got you deep and you owe it to yourself to see if there's anything left before you leave. Y'all both so stubborn."

"He made it perfectly clear that there's nothing left. Barry, he told me to leave him alone. He said….don't make me hate you. Let's get out of here and get to that closing." We hugged again.

"He was hurt. That was anger talking. Men do that sometimes."

"Barry. I love you, but you're the last person on earth I'd take relationship advice from. You're…"

"A coward. A cad. A dog. A brother who finds himself getting older everyday. Alone. A man who dates young girls who love Barry because of what he can buy them. Give them. Provide them. I know exactly what I am McClain. Pathetic. Its what good women find out after about two or three months with me."

"You're not a dog. You're a great friend. You just…you're inconsistent. You come on strong, making them fall in love with you then you dump them for no reason. Hard. It's like you don't care about their feelings at all. It doesn't make you a dog. It makes you inconsiderate and irresponsible," I said attempting to console him.

"That makes me feel better." We laughed. "There was this girl I dated about three years ago. Lita." "Barry, I introduced you to Lita," I said sarcastically.

"Yeah you did. I loved her McClain. It was as though we were the same person sometimes. She made me laugh. I was completely at home with her. Just watching her was a gift. We didn't do anything. She made me happy. She never demanded all my free time and she was so nice. Other than you, Lita was the prettiest girl in Dallas. I really miss her. Funny huh?

My friends accused me of being whipped. You know how guys are. So I cheated. I broke her heart to prove something to them. She caught me. I'll never forget watching the light of my image melting from her eyes. I don't think I'll ever get over it. You see, I'm a victim of my own construction," he choked, "They still have planes that go to New York everyday don't they?" Barry asked, gathering himself and turning away from me.

"Everyday," I assured him, choking too, hugging him from behind. I understood.

"McClain, there's one other thing." He turned around, facing me directly.

"What's that?" I asked, looking into his moistened eyes.

"Why didn't you ever give me some?"

"Boy!" I playfully pushed him away, hitting him on the back of head. "There I was feeling sorry for you. You need Jesus."

We laughed and walked back into the near empty condominium. Just as we were about to walk out, the doorman called. "Ms. Summers I've sent some people up who say they're your friends. I think they are, and I hope you don't mind."

The doorbell rang and Barry opened the door. Romeo. Kevin and Cliff. I howled with excitement. "Hey girlfriend," Kevin gushed. "I saw you on TV. Your hair looked fabulous."

"Shut up Kevin," Romeo chimed in. "We know you're leaving today. We had to see you and say goodbye in person. We love you. Barry told us you'd be here today. Jack would have wanted us to see you off. Thanks for being our friend. Stay in touch." I hugged the men who loved Jack. We all wiped tears from our eyes and reminisced about our old friend.

"Oh yeah," Cliff sniffed. "Jack bought you this. He said you'd understand." Cliff handed me the brightly wrapped box. "He left it at my house the day he died."

Inside was the large silver vibrator. The men looked at it and looked at me, laughing until tears were everywhere. Jack was still making me laugh. The rowdy bunch walked toward the elevator.

"Wait everyone. Let me make one stop. Get the elevator Barry."

Mr. Greene came to the door. Silent goodbyes filled the hallway. Tears sprang from his eyes as he kissed my hand. "You're just like a daughter to me. You've lived here all this time. I looked forward to you checking on me. A confession."

317

"What is it Mr. Greene?"

"Some of those times you thought I was locked out. I wasn't. I just wanted to see you. I'll miss you. Everyday. No one…," he sniffed.

"I love you Mr. Greene. I'll call you every Thursday. Just like always," I cried too.

"My brother Abraham lives in Queens. I told him all about you. He read about you in the newspaper. He'll give you a great deal on linoleum. Tell him that I sent ya. It's coming back you know."

He promised to visit. "Don't forget to wear your chain Mr. Greene and keep your keys on it. Don't get locked out. Promise."

"You're a good girl. I hope you and the man with the ugly dog much happiness." There was no need to correct him.

Barry was already in the car when I came out. Kevin, Romeo and Cliff covered me with love, promising to visit New York soon. Kevin wanted to become my personal hair stylist and Cliff offered to dress me. I agreed. They left.

Someone is watching. Paranoia left this unexpected consequence when it touched my life. Something was across the street. As I glanced over the driver's shoulder, standing next to a brand new dark blue truck was the most beautiful sight I'd seen in months. "Matthew," I whispered.

He leaned casually against the truck as Pitiful sat in the driver's seat. He knew I saw him, but he didn't move or say anything. I was breathless. My heart pounded. His scalding stare compelled me to move toward him, but I was afraid. He twirled something on his finger.

"What's wrong McClain?" Barry asked from inside the car. "Let's go baby, we go be late."

"Girl gone over there and get that pretty man," Jack whispered from heaven. "He ain't running. You need to stop running too." I didn't move. "What's stopping you?"
"Nothing." I walked toward the truck.

Tricked

"McClain, we have to go baby. The closing is in 25 minutes and you know how traffic is. Come on! Where you going?" Barry yelled.

I never stopped watching Matthew. Was there a chance he'd speak to me? Love me? Want me? Need me? Forgive me? I wouldn't disappoint him this time. With one more chance, I'd love him passionately. Completely. Sincerely. Fiercely.

Oblivious to cars or danger, I walked into the busy street. He never moved. Cars blew their horns and cursed at the obstacle I became. Tears filled my eyes as his lips formed that perfectly familiar smile. He was twirling my locket.

"How are you? Are you alright? I didn't know...well I hoped...I mean...I." Stuttering. Nervous. Hopeful. Optimistic.

"You forgot something." I loved his voice. I missed it. Missed him.

"What?"

"My heart," He said with twinkling eyes.

"Your heart?" I didn't know what he meant.

"You can't leave without my heart."

"Matthew...I"

"All you need to say is that you love me. Nothing else matters. Do you? Do you love me?"

"I love you," I whispered. "With my whole heart," tears rolling down my cheeks.

"Good. Then this belongs to you." He closed the locket around my neck, lifting me so I would be eye level with him when he kissed me. It was like being kissed for the first time.

Barry stuck his head out of the car and looked across the street. "Dawn...Hey baby, this is Barry. Yeah I'm calling about the closing. Yeah...we're still on...we'll be there...but we'll be a few minutes late. Take those people to lunch or something. Tell them...tell them anything."

Cynthia A. Minor

POSTLOGUE

FIVE YEARS LATER

"McClain where's that crystal punch bowl?" My mother was making her famous punch. This group drinks wine or hard liquor, but she insisted punch would be great for nondrinkers and Christians. Arguing with her would be futile so I ran to the basement to retrieve it. After looking in the fifth box I found it. Next to it was a box marked "Jack."

Treasures from years ago lay inside. Jack was my best friend and I loved him. Missed him. Cliff and Romeo were coming. Kevin had the flu, but sent a glorious floral arrangement for the centerpiece.

Dr. Stovall had telephone duty, monitoring all calls. The Nobel committee was announcing its nominations tonight. My distributive loss theory was being considered. Friends came to celebrate or console depending on the outcome. Being considered for a nomination was a distinct honor. A nomination would be great. Winning, unbelievable.

"McClain the people will be here any minute. Have you found that punch bowl yet? Hurry up!" she yelled from the basement door. "I found it. I'll be right up."

I cooked all day. Old friends would be impressed that I finally learned how. I closed Jack's box for another day. Then I rubbed my fingers across the locket Matthew gave me. Rarely off my neck, I turned it over to read the inscription for the millionth time.

Tricked

He still transported me beyond ordinary passion. I felt blessed for the privilege of knowing this extraordinary man's love. He kept me balanced. Friends noisily arrived as Matthew greeted them at the door. I was thrilled to see everyone.

Soon the house overflowed with friends, old and new. Administrators and colleagues from Morehouse, where I taught world economics along with several of my more gifted students.

Matthew's friends from the Court and Bar Association came. He was appointed Judge of one of the Fulton County Superior Court two years, garnering praise from the American Bar Association and City for the success of his innovative programs helping troubled youth. His mother lived near us in Atlanta. She was very proud of her only son and pestered us unrelentingly about grandchildren.

Keith arrived with his new wife. She was well educated. Beautiful. Three degrees and totally in love with him. His parents came too. They were happily content because they were equally shallow. He ran my companies with devotion and expertise. We were extremely profitable. Ethical. Charitable. Additionally, he was banned from discussing politics in my presence, although his views softened over the years. Several of my other executives joined him.

Iris, Craig and their three children arrived the day before the party. Her parents came too. They kept the children at the hotel for the evening so Iris could help keep discussions sharp and lively. She played her role aptly, filling every conversational gap with the marvel of her gregariousness.

Mother on the other hand was a nervous wreck. She dashed in and out of the kitchen a thousand times, ordering Matthew around. His mother took his place as they cheerfully worked together, putting food and finery on the table.

Ian sent a stunning diamond pin and fabulous flowers. It became a monthly tradition that Matthew didn't seem to mind. I think Ian just liked buying jewelry and I was happy to be the recipient of his generosity. Ian invited us to stay on his private island as a honeymoon present. There were twenty servants at our disposal. It was utterly unforgettable. Self-indulgent. Decadent. I told Matt to find an island for us too.

They became great friends and Ian made large donations to Matthew's community projects. He was in London tonight, but we'd see him tomorrow for dinner.

Barry bombarded the door an hour after the party started with a hoochie and five bottles of expensive champagne. He was late as usual and went directly into the kitchen to put the bubbly on ice, leaving the young lady alone in a room filled with intellectual giants. She applied more lip gloss and tugged at her dress, knowing it was far too short and tight for the occasion.

"Barry… what's with you and that little girl? Can't you find a woman to date?" I whispered. Peeping at her from the kitchen.

"Mind your business. You know I like young. Stupid. Cute and oversexed. Now leave me alone and give me something to eat."

Barry stayed in the kitchen annoying my mother while I did everything I could to make the young girl feel comfortable. It didn't work. Barry didn't care.

The telephone rang. Quiet surrounded us. Dr. Stovall answered waving his hand ordering everyone to be still. "McClain, it's for you."

"Who is it?"

"I don't know, but get them off of this line." Noise and gaiety returned.

"Hello McClain." My blood ran cold.

"Call me on my other line," I whispered.

"Alright."

Tricked

I handed the receiver to Dr. Stovall, who looked at me intensely. "Is everything alright?"

"Yeah. I really need to take this call. I'll be in my office." My private line lit up.

"What do you want?" I asked sternly.

"I didn't think you could pull it off. I was wrong. You did it. Congratulations."

"Never call me again."

"But it's been so long since we last spoke. Don't you miss me? I wanted to be the first to congratulate you on your nomination. You're very clever. No surprise there. You are your father's daughter. You said you'd do it and you did, with just a little help from your friends."

"What do you want?"

"Nothing.

"I don't know of any reason why you'd ever call me again."

"One favor. You owe me that."

"I owe you nothing," I hissed.

"Convince Ian to call off his dogs. I don't want to be found. You don't want me found," he sniffed.

"Don't tell me what to do. Never bother me or anyone I love again, or I'll find you myself and kill you with my bare hands."

I hung up the telephone and joined my guests. "Who was that baby?" Matthew asked.

"Someone who wanted to wish me luck."

Barry hovered around the dining room table nibbling and munching things as the rest of us waited for the call. "McClain can I cut the turkey?" he yelled.

"Yeah Barry. Go ahead."

The telephone rang again. Dr. Stovall answered on the third ring. We grew silent for the second time. Matthew put his arm around me. "Thank you sir. Thank you very much."

We watched Dr. Stovall for any sign of good news. His expressionless face was blank. Unreadable. I thought the worst.

Mother grabbed my hand. Dr. Stovall took my shoulders and looked deeply into my eyes.

"My dear the Nobel Committee has reviewed your concepts thoroughly. After considerable investigation it has decided to accept your distributive loss theory for nomination for this year's Nobel Prize in economics. Congratulations. I am very proud." He leaned over and kissed my cheek. An explosion of applause and cheers rang out.

"Are you serious?"

"Very serious."

"Dr. Stovall."

"I apologize for my comments at Wharton. You were right. I was wrong. You've proven yourself knowledgeable and formidable. In eastern cultures, success is measured by a student's ability to defeat the teacher. You are now the teacher."

"We settled that long ago. Your apology is not accepted. You challenged an untested, illogical, impractical hypothetical notion. Neither of us could have known then that it would work in any practical political environment. You will always be my teacher and I always love you. I know Joshua's smiling from heaven tonight." I looked at Mrs. Pellman, who wiped her eyes. "He's smiling tonight at all of us."

Applause filled the house. Matthew swung me around. He almost burst with pride and excitement. This was the anticipated end of long range planning. Everyone was excited and congratulations fell like rain. "Lets eat!" Mother ordered as we headed toward the dining room. "McClain cooked everything," she bragged. "Doesn't it look and smell wonderful? She's become a very good cook."

"Well who cooked the turkey?" Barry asked dryly, chewing a piece of meat and looking at the bird inquisitively.

"McClain did." My mother answered as though she was going to smack him. "Well…ain't you supposed to take that neck bag thing out before you cook it?"

Laugher rolled through the house like a metal tire. Everyone stared at the newly nominated Nobel laureate, trembling with silent laughter. Iris yelled, "Let's order pizza. Who likes anchovies?"

Cynthia A. Minor

Closure is a word used indiscriminately by those who needn't any. There's no closure to issues of lost love. Missing family. Sudden loss. Unexpected mystery. Betrayal. We merely learn to live with pain. Sorrow. Grief. Questions. Loss. Death. They sit on the ledges of our hearts ready to sing the chorus of their sad refrain, when past memories overtake current blessings. Closure is the cruel phantom of our desires and a reflection of how we felt before the choir of our discontent tuned up...

McClain